Praise for Black Artemis

Picture Me Rollin'

"Black Artemis has penned yet another piece of hip-hop fiction that'll have you at the edge of your seat 'til the very last page." —*Black Beat*

"Black Artemis does an excellent job with this story, providing a picturesque view of street life. The characters are fresh, intense, and provide a hauntingly close reality of an environment all too familiar to some. With constant references to Tupac Shakur, a lyrical genius, *Picture Me Rollin'* is filled with poetry that parallels life. A deep, thought-provoking novel, this story is sure to keep you wanting more." —Rawsistaz.com

Explicit Content

"Fans of Sister Souljah's *The Coldest Winter Ever* will find this debut novel just as tantalizing. Full of suspense and twists, this is a page-turner of an urban story about friendship and the importance of being patient and doing things the right—not quick—way." —*Booklist*

"Love. Drama. Honor. Death. Heart. Black Artemis in her debut drop, *Explicit Content,* delivers the goods. A classic story fueled by hip-hop sensibilities about strivers . . . about what it takes to make it, and that some prices are too high no matter how many ducats are dangled."
—Gary Phillips, author of *bangers*

"And the Sun Gods sent down a powerful ray of light toward earth and named her Black Artemis. The streets, yearning for a serving of realness and truth, in a language that speaks to all of us, celebrate the arrival of *Explicit Content,* eating up the pages as if it were the Last Supper."
—Toni Blackman, hip-hop artist and author of *Inner-Course*

"Cutting-edge hip-hop noir—a sista-centered, cipher-crushing thriller that can be so real it hurts."
—Jeff Chang, author of *Can't Stop Won't Stop: A History of the Hip-Hop Generation*

Black Artemis

New American Library
Published by New American Library, a division of
Penguin Group (USA) Inc., 375 Hudson Street,
New York, New York 10014, USA
Penguin Group (Canada), 90 Eglinton Avenue East, Suite 700, Toronto,
Ontario M4P 2Y3, Canada (a division of Pearson Penguin Canada Inc.)
Penguin Books Ltd., 80 Strand, London WC2R 0RL, England
Penguin Ireland, 25 St. Stephen's Green, Dublin 2,
Ireland (a division of Penguin Books Ltd.)
Penguin Group (Australia), 250 Camberwell Road, Camberwell, Victoria 3124,
Australia (a division of Pearson Australia Group Pty. Ltd.)
Penguin Books India Pvt. Ltd., 11 Community Centre, Panchsheel Park,
New Delhi - 110 017, India
Penguin Group (NZ), cnr Airborne and Rosedale Roads, Albany,
Auckland 1310, New Zealand (a division of Pearson New Zealand Ltd.)
Penguin Books (South Africa) (Pty.) Ltd., 24 Sturdee Avenue,
Rosebank, Johannesburg 2196, South Africa

Penguin Books Ltd., Registered Offices:
80 Strand, London WC2R 0RL, England

First published by New American Library,
a division of Penguin Group (USA) Inc.

First Printing, August 2006
10 9 8 7 6 5 4 3 2 1

REGISTERED TRADEMARK—MARCA REGISTRADA

LIBRARY OF CONGRESS CATALOGING-IN-PUBLICATION DATA:

Black Artemis.
Burn / Black Artemis.
p. cm.
ISBN 0-451-21857-4
1. Bail bond agents—Fiction. 2. Puerto Rican women—Fiction. 3. Bronx (New York, N.Y.)—Fiction. 4. Artists—Fiction. 5. Graffiti—Fiction. 6. Brothers and sisters—Fiction. I. Title.
PS3602.L24B87 2006
813'.6—dc22 2006002280

Set in Horley Old Style
Designed by Spring Hoteling

Printed in the United States of America

For all those who live in the shadows
yet still refuse to remain invisible.

one

Jasmine had been sitting in that waiting area for over two hours just to interview one freakin' inmate. He had better be worth it, or Diana was as good as fired. With Lorraine appearing in court today on behalf of another client, Diana should have come to Rikers Island herself, instead of Jasmine, to screen this Malcolm Booker. But ever since she gave birth to her daughter, Zoë, Diana had treated her job like an annoying inconvenience, although she had never shown that much interest in it in the first place.

Jasmine almost never came to Rikers Island, and she preferred it that way. Inmates were not the only ones for whom the place got old real quick, and this particular facility held ugly memories for her. Named after a corrections officer shot to death by an escaping inmate, the George Motchan Detention Center had added her brother Jason to its two thousand–plus population six years ago. He'd only lasted forty-one days. Although she had not seen him for herself, every time she crossed the mile-long bridge from Queens onto the island, Jasmine pictured Jason as they must have found him: in his underwear on his knees, leaning away from the gate of his cell with one leg of his jailhouse greens tied around the bars and the other knotted around his neck. She hated this fuckin' place almost as badly as anyone who actually had to do time there. Jasmine would never understand Zachary's obsessive aspiration to work for the Department of Corrections. What difference did it make if you wore a badge or a jumpsuit? Regardless of which side of the gate you stood on, your ass was still on lockdown.

Dying for a cigarette, Jasmine pulled Booker's paperwork from her knapsack just to occupy her jittery hands. She had reviewed the information so many times, however, that her eyes leaped across the now-familiar details.

Name: *Malcolm Charles Booker*

Nicknames/Alias(es): *Macho*

Sex: *M*

Race: *Black, Hispanic*

DOB: *11/17/84*

Birthplace: *Bronx, New York*

Date of Arrest: *01/17/06*
Bail Amount: *$10,000*

Charge: *PL 160.10*
Robbery in the 2nd Degree
Offense Class: *C Felony*

Parents: *Charles Ellis Booker, whereabouts unknown; Mercedes Marie Booker (maiden name: Guignard, deceased.)*

Sibling(s): *Crystal Maria Booker, born 03/09/79, full-time secretary at Cablevision corporate headquarters in Bethpage, part-time student at Briarcliffe College, also in Bethpage.*

Notes: *Candidate is a nonviolent offender with two prior convictions for vandalism. Resides with his sister in a basement apartment at 2210 Blackrock Avenue in Castle Hill. Graduated from the Bronx HS for the Visual Arts. Unemployed.*

If Booker gave her a good vibe, Jasmine would send Zachary to visit the sister at home. Too many times during the preliminary interview, an inmate would tell Diana, "Yeah, when I get out I'ma move back in with my moms," or "I live with my girlfriend." Then Zachary would conduct the home visit, only to find out that homeboy was not welcome at Ma Dukes because he stole money from her, or "his" shorty was already playing house with his cousin. Some of them straight-out lied about having a place to go once bailed, and others truly had no clue that getting arrested had also rendered them homeless. Can never be too sure with these heads that call from inside. You have to put the question to them: *If Ma Dukes or Shorty got your back like that, why didn't she call the bail bond company when you got knocked?*

"Booker, Malcolm," the CO called. Jasmine gave the papers one last scan, stuffed them into her bag, and made a mental list of questions. Of course, she had to get a sense of how close (or not) Booker was with his sister, Crystal, and if he had peoples in other places, especially outside of New York City. Jasmine guessed that with a maiden name like Guignard, his mother's people were Haitian. However unlikely it might be for Booker to skip the country, she had to determine if he had relatives on the troubled island. The preliminary screening form indicated that Booker was also Hispanic, so Jasmine made a note to learn what other tropical climates he might run to if he decided to jump bail. And she definitely had to know the story behind the two vandalism convictions to be sure they were not evidence of violent tendencies.

Every other item on the five-page questionnaire, she would skip. Jasmine had only created it to guide her staff, since they usually conducted these interviews. For all her clinical prowess, Lorraine could not spot a hustler if he gave her a lap dance, while Zachary saw a perp around every freakin' corner, from the guy delivering his mail to the chick asking him what kind of sauce he wanted with his chicken nuggets. But unlike them, Jasmine had sharp instincts cultivated on the streets and refined from five years in the business. With just a few key questions, she would know whether this Malcolm Booker had any business being put back on the street.

Jasmine felt eyes on her. She looked up to catch the corrections officer squinting at her. "Do I know you?" he asked.

"No." But he probably did. As rarely as she visited Rikers, Jasmine had a reputation among law enforcement personnel that she wore both like a scarlet letter and a badge of honor. When the resentment of the assistant district attorneys, judges, cops, corrections officers, and even other bail bond agents did not get in Jasmine's way, she shook it off like water off a duck's back. But sometimes these he-men wanted to trip her up and watch her fall on her face simply for being a woman gaining yards on their field. "You don't know me," Jasmine said.

"Are you sure?" asked the CO. "You seem familiar." Perhaps he had worked at Rikers long enough to recognize her as the twin sister of that suicide on Quad 4 six years ago. When Jason hanged himself it had shocked even the most hardened of the corrections officers.

Or maybe he was just flirting with her, which would be the most pathetic explanation of all. These law enforcement types worked her nerves. If they weren't trying to fuck her one way, they were trying to fuck her another. Jasmine's past had become an urban legend among them, and those who had heard but were unable to confirm the rumors sometimes pressed up, trying to acquire "intelligence" firsthand.

"No, I'm not."

"Okay!"

"You couldn't possibly," she said with a much softer tone. "I don't come here much." Not smart to antagonize a CO just because she managed to steer clear of this place. Diana, Lorraine, and Zachary still had to come to Rikers on a regular basis, and these guards had no problem lengthening the two-hour wait just to fuck with them because they worked for Reyes Bonds.

"Don't come around here much, huh?" the CO scoffed. "Wish I could say that." He led Jasmine to a concrete cubicle with two plain wooden chairs and a matching table. "I'll be back with the inmate."

She took a seat and waited. Jasmine had started the bail bond agency with the money Jason had left her, and doing so had pitted her against the Bronx criminal justice system from the jump. This was still Giuliani's New York, where rehabilitation as a crime prevention strategy got called out and shut down as a failed experiment of the liberal imagination. A foolish demonstration of the irrational belief in the innate goodness of human nature. A fuckin' joke. Despite New York being held up as a bastion of liberalism to the rest of the nation, however, criminal justice had become big business in the Empire State a good decade before the towers crumbled. Alternative-to-incarceration programs became an endangered species once America's mayor came to power, with an approach to public safety that ultimately redefined the phrase "Crime pays." The new millennium brought with it plenty of opportunities for intrepid cynics, whether they had the resources to build their own prisons and sell inmate labor to the highest bidder or just enough of a nest egg to go into the bail business to take advantage of the spike in bondable arrests. But Jasmine could not just hang her shingle, post bond for whoever could raise the collateral, and occasionally hire a pseudo-thug with mercenary fantasies to pursue bail jumpers. She had to go and get altruistic, bailing out a charity case with no money down on the strength of a "release agreement" that would split the side of any judge who happened to read it.

Jasmine heard shuffling across the floor and looked up. Malcolm Booker stood before her in jailhouse greens, which took her by surprise. From what she recalled, only sentenced inmates had to wear the jumpsuits, while the detainees waiting to make bail or going to trial were allowed to wear their own clothes. She had learned this when Jason killed himself, because his public defender had told her that it was unusual for him to have had jail-issued pants, since he had yet to be convicted and sentenced. "They only make detainees wear uniforms if they're rearrested," he'd said. Jason's PD wanted Jasmine to make noise—ask questions, write letters, even contact the media—but Jasmine let it go. Even if an inmate or CO forced him to put on the greens to intimidate or humiliate him, it did not change the fact that Jason wanted to die. Jasmine knew that the last time she visited him by the way his ordinarily downy skin wrinkled with anguish as he begged her to make his bail. Forty-one days on Rikers Island had quartered Jason's span, and it did not matter if he had been ordered to wear the jailhouse greens or allowed to keep his rust fleet pants. The clock started ticking the second the bars clanged shut behind him.

Jasmine eyed Booker as he made his way toward their table. He was a wiry five-nine, and she might not have noticed him had she not been expecting him. Malcolm's eyes were brown and fuzzy like coconuts, and he wore tightly wound cornrows that curled slightly toward his collarbone. His skin reminded Jasmine of honey mustard in both color and texture, except for the long dimple that slashed his left cheek.

"What're you smiling about?" Jasmine asked. These inmates saw a woman and got stupid. Nothing about being in jail should make a sensible human being smile except the news that he was getting the fuck out.

But he seemed unfazed by her attitude. "I'm smiling at you," Booker said. "You don't like it when people smile at you?"

"Honestly?" Jasmine motioned for him to have a seat. As Booker complied, the CO hovered behind him. She dismissed him with a shooing motion. The officer glared at her but eventually stepped away to give them a semblance of privacy. Jasmine turned back to Booker and said, "I don't give a shit one way or the other."

Booker shrugged as he pulled a black hardcover notebook from under his arm and placed it on the table. "Then why'd you ask?"

He said it as if he genuinely wanted an answer. Jasmine had shed herself of life's excesses, right down to rhetorical questions. She said what she meant and meant what she said, no more, no less. Then she would meet the rare person like Jason who would pose a question too sincere to dismiss.

"Because I know you have an agenda," said Jasmine, "and I wanted you to know that and not to waste my time."

"Ah, see, you really do care why I'm smiling after all." Booker's smile broadened. "C'mon, my agenda's obvious. To get the hell out of here. And you're the woman who can make that happen, right?" He clasped his hands on top of his book. "But like you said, you know all that already. Me, I got nothing but time in here, and God knows I can use the company."

Jasmine smirked at him and leaned back in her seat. "Your sister doesn't visit you much?"

"Crystal comes every chance she gets, but it's hard for her. Working all the way out in Long Island and going to school at night out there, too, and . . ." He started to say more about her, but instead switched topics. "Hey, no one told me to go and get locked up. Especially since Crystal can't pay the rent by herself, and I sure as hell can't make any money up in here."

"So your sister can't keep that place unless you live there and split the expenses."

"No."

"Maybe she hasn't visited you because she's out shopping for a roommate."

Malcolm's eyes fluttered. "Yeah, but I doubt it. Don't get me wrong. My sister's really pissed at me for the boneheaded thing I did." He laughed and added, "Even if she had the money to bail me out, Crystal totally would've let me sit here for a few days to think about what I had done. But, nah, my sister wants me to come home, and not just 'cause she needs me to make ends meet, but because we're all we've got, you know what I'm sayin'?"

Jasmine knew exactly what he was saying, but she could not let that influence her decision. She leaned toward the table and said, "Let's talk about that boneheaded thing you did. You went from vandalism to armed robbery. What's up with that?"

Now Malcolm pulled back and threw his arms up in the air. "I'ma tell you, but you're not gonna believe me."

"Probably not, but I'm here, so try me."

"The cops didn't believe me, the DA doesn't believe me. Hell, my PD thinks I'm on some shit, but it's the God's honest truth."

"Leave God out of it, and tell me the damn story already."

Malcolm exhaled. "There is no story. I walked into the bodega for a can of soda and some cigarettes. I saw it behind the counter, and I had to have it."

"Saw what?" Jasmine presumed it was not money, but it had to be something of value. A piece of jewelry. An expensive appliance. Maybe even a leather jacket.

"The Krylon."

Jasmine had not heard that word in years. "Krylon?"

Malcolm nodded, smiling apologetically for her incredulity.

"You robbed a bodega at gunpoint for a can of spray paint?"

"That's the thing, though, Miss Reyes," he said. "It wasn't just any ol' can of spray paint. Not even any ol' color of Krylon. This shit was Jungle Green." Malcolm's eyes darted desperately. "Look, I don't expect you to get it. Just believe me when I say that I know I fucked up, Miss Reyes. That's something really stupid that I did, but it's not who I am, you feel me?"

But she did get it. Perhaps she got it too well. Jasmine checked herself by asking him, "Your sister? She's all you got?"

Malcolm nodded, confused at the sudden return to that topic.

"You told her that you robbed the bodega for a can of spray paint?"

"Hey, I offered the dude money for it first, but it's like once he realized how much I wanted it, he just wanted to fuck with me. I could've offered him a thousand dollars, and the bastard wouldn't have sold it to me."

"Malcolm, focus. Answer what I'm asking you. Did Crystal believe you when you told her why you robbed the bodega?"

"Yeah, she believed me!" Malcolm said. "My sister knows me. She knows what I do. Crystal always said writing was going to get me into some shit, and I guess she was right." He pondered for a few seconds as he nervously tapped the notebook beneath his fingertips. "It was a stupid impulse, Miss Reyes, I swear. I borrowed the gat from a friend, and it was never loaded."

Jasmine reached over and placed her palm on the top of his book. "Is this your piecebook?"

Booker grinned. "What you know about this?" He opened the book and flipped through the pages.

"Enough." Jason had been a "writer," too. People outside of yet sympathetic to the subculture referred to them as graffiti artists. The cops and politicians called them vandals, if not something much worse.

Booker stopped turning pages, coming to rest on a sketch that spanned two pages in colored pencil. He spun the book around on its spine so Jasmine could read it. In bloodred block letters, Malcolm had drawn SUÁREZ CHC. The letters hovered over a sea of faces of different ages and colors. Underneath his characterization of community residents, in white, angular letters, was *Don't Talk About It . . . Be About It.*

"What does CHC mean?"

"Community Health Center." Booker flipped to the back cover and pulled out a sheet of newsprint. He unfolded and handed it to Jasmine. He had torn a full-page advertisement from a recent issue of the *Bronx Beat*. Apparently, Dr. Adriano Suárez, Jr., the founder and executive director of a new health clinic in the Mott Haven section of the South Bronx, was sponsoring an art competition in search of an artist to paint a mural on the building for the clinic's grand opening on Valentine's Day. Malcolm said, "I sketched it out in my book first, you know, and then transferred it to paper. Then Crystal filled out the entry form and submitted everything for me."

Jasmine scanned the announcement, then asked, "Prize money?"

Booker probably saw in the competition an opportunity to raise bail. She wondered if he noticed the irony of exploiting the same obsession that had landed him behind bars to set himself free.

"No, I just thought it'd be a cool thing to do. I mean, if I gotta be in here. . . . See, this is my vision of what the mural should look like, given what the doctor says he wants." Booker darted his agile finger between Suárez's criteria and the elements of his sketch that corresponded to them. "Community, diversity . . . and the slogan's mine, too, 'cause he said he wanted something culturally relevant. So when my sister explained to me what that meant, I came up with this. *Don't talk about it . . . Be about it.*" Word by word, Booker's finger underscored the slogan.

"I don't get it," said Jasmine.

"The way Crystal explained it to me was that he wanted a slogan that folks around the way could relate to. Like you wouldn't say *¿Cómo estás?* to a Korean woman and expect her to understand you. *¿Cómo estás?* ain't culturally relevant to her 'cause she ain't Hispanic."

Jasmine shrugged. "Don't be so sure. Let's say this Korean woman owns one of those nail salons on Westchester Avenue. You might ask her *¿Cómo estás?* and she just might tell you *Estoy jodía.*"

Booker burst out in snickers that reminded Jasmine of Diwali claps, and for a second she swore she saw Jason sitting across from her. "True, true," he said. "But that still proves my point. Because the Korean lady got her business in a Hispanic 'hood, she went and learned her some Spanish, which makes *her* culturally relevant, and that's why all the 'Spanic folks be giving her their business."

Jasmine laughed in spite of herself. "So *Don't Talk About It . . . Be About It.* How'd you come up with that?"

"'Cause the clinic's in the 'hood, and that's what heads in the 'hood always say. And if you think about it, what does everybody do when it comes to their health? They say *I need my eyes checked* or *I gotta get my teeth cleaned*, but do they go and do it?"

"No." She herself had not visited a doctor of any sort in ages. The only times Jasmine even entered a clinic, she walked into the reception area, grabbed a handful of free condoms from the bowl near the magazine rack, and headed out to work.

"And that includes folks who got, like, benefits, insurance or whatever. But you don't even need any of that at this clinic. All the services are free. If you can pay Suárez, you do, but if you can't, you don't." Booker's voice grew higher and faster, impressed as much with the doctor's social vision as with his own artistic interpretation of that vision. "So if you don't have to come out of pocket, you ain't got no excuses to not take care of yourself. Come and get your checkups. Bring your whole family. Tell your friends. Don't talk about it, be about it." He pounded his fist once on his open book, signaling the end of his pitch.

"Relax, Booker," the CO warned.

"It's okay," said Jasmine.

"I'm the one who determines what's okay and what isn't."

Jasmine ignored the CO and gave Booker a look that advised him to do the same. "So there's no prize money."

"Well, Suárez is gonna hire the winner of the competition to paint the mural, and he's going to pay 'im two and a half gs, including supplies."

"Would that include Jungle Green Krylon?"

"Nah, if I could get my hands on that or a can of Icy Grape . . ." Booker let out that hauntingly familiar chuckle. "Shit, I'd have to save that for something mad special." Then he stopped and said, "But if I win, and I'm still in here . . ."

Jasmine pushed her chair away from the table and rose to her feet. "Next week my assistant, Diana, will come visit you again. She'll have an agreement, stipulating a few conditions for your release. Like you'll find a job or go back to school, stuff like that." If and when this point in the interview finally arrived, the inmate either started nodding like a bobble-head doll or protesting the conditions, but Malcolm frowned respectfully, like a child accepting a reprimand he knew he deserved. "Just read it. Ask Diana any questions, make sure you understand it. When you sign it, I'll post your bail."

Malcolm stood up and offered his hand to Jasmine. As they shook, he said, "Thank you, Miss Reyes."

She almost told him he could call her Jasmine. Instead she pulled her hand away, taking one last glance at Malcolm's open piecebook and feeling her chest burn with regret. "Just hang in there, Jason, I'm going to get you out of here."

"Malcolm."

"What?"

"You called me Jason. My name's Malcolm. But everybody calls me Macho. That's the nickname my mother gave me. She was part Dominican and part Haitian, and she always used to call me her little *macho* because I was her only son. You Dominican?"

"Puerto Rican." Then she gave in. "I'm Jasmine, and I'm going to get you out of here so you can paint that mural when you win that contest."

Having no doubts that Booker would sign any release agreement she might draft, Jasmine went from Rikers Island to her bank. There she acquired a teller's check in the full amount of his bail. Then she returned to the office to fill out the bond and write his agreement. While consulting all the notes accumulated in his file, Jasmine sat in front of her computer and modified the template. She entered the Castle Hill address as Booker's mandatory place of residence and kept the ten p.m. curfew. A kid with a jones for bombing had to be relegated to the house at night. If Booker gave them no trouble during his first month or so back on the street, Jasmine would consider pushing back the curfew or eliminating it altogether.

She also decided to strike the drug testing clause in the standard agreement. In his preliminary interview with Diana, Booker copped to smoking weed and downing forties once or twice every week. Even though Zachary had scored a wholesale deal that brought the cost down to eight dollars per test, Jasmine could not justify spending sixteen bucks every week just to "catch" Booker messing with that trivial shit.

Thinking of Zachary, Jasmine dialed his cell phone number, even though she knew he had an afternoon class at John Jay College of Criminal Justice, where he was majoring in correctional studies. "Hey, Zach, when you get out of class, make this home visit," she said. "You're going to see a Crystal Booker at 2210 Blackrock Avenue, basement apartment. She's the sister of Malcolm Booker. You know the drill." Jasmine realized that she had never made a decision to post bail before the home visit. If Zachary found out, he would surely have a fit. In the interest of her own sanity, Jasmine would not allow Diana to deliver the teller's check until Zachary submitted his report.

She returned to modifying the agreement, giving Booker thirty days to find employment or enroll in an educational program. Then she saved the agreement, printed five copies, and signed each one. Jasmine brought the teller's check, signed agreements, and bond forms to the reception area.

Through the storefront's window, she spotted Diana on the sidewalk imposing pictures of her newborn onto a stenographer Jasmine occasionally saw at the courthouse across the street. The poor chick bounced in place and rubbed her arms, failing to warm herself against the numbing January air. Jasmine almost banged on the window and barked for Diana to come back inside but decided against it. Just because the stenographer did not have the sense to wear pants in the winter or blow off Diana didn't give Jasmine a reason to mind her business.

Then again, it was Jasmine's business. If Diana caught the slightest sniffle, she would use that as an excuse to call in sick the next day. Jasmine threw open the front door and an icy gust cracked her face. "For Christ's sake, Diana, it's freezing out here."

Diana looked up from the miniature photo album in her gloved hands. "I got a few more minutes left on my lunch break."

"Lunch break? It's almost four o'clock."

"And I didn't take lunch until three because of all those calls you had me make."

Jasmine did not bother to ask Diana if she had actually completed the calls. She already knew the answer. Nor would Diana finish making them before rushing off to pick up Zoë from the babysitter's house. Jasmine let the door go and went back to her task. The both of them could freeze.

After placing the teller's check in a security envelope and locking it in the petty cash box that Diana stowed away in her bottom drawer, Jasmine placed the signed agreements in her inbox on her desk. After Booker signed them, Diana would give him a copy to keep, mail one to his public defender (who probably would toss it in the trash), place one each in Zachary and Lorraine's mailboxes, and stash the last one in the new file she would create for him.

Feeling good about her decision, Jasmine headed to Ramon's and waited for Calvin. On her third vodka tonic, he entered the bar with a few other cops just finishing their shifts at the borough command down the street. As always, they caught eye and pretended not to. Jasmine finished her drink, tossed a few bills on the bar, and headed toward the door. By the time she climbed into her black Escalade, she saw Calvin strolling toward it through her side-view mirror. Jasmine rolled down the window.

"Hi."

"Hey."

"Nice ride." Cal took a step back to admire the SUV.

"Thanks. Courtesy of Tommy Crespo," Even to Jasmine, it sounded like bragging. Calvin thought it unladylike, but she could not help herself.

"So I heard."

"What else did you hear?" Since Jasmine had difficulty keeping much of her business dealings from Calvin, at least she had to ensure he heard everything right. Sometimes cops were no better than a fuckin' knitting circle.

"That you smashed a bottle of Colt .45 over Crespo's head while he was getting a lap dance at the Crazy Horse."

Jasmine glared at him. Did Calvin really get half the story or was he testing her? "Your sources got it twisted, Cal. The second I walked into the Moroccan Lounge, Angel stopped dancing, as she should have. But Crespo ignored me and put his hands on her, and I did what I had to do to bring him in."

"To Rikers or Calvary? The guy needed fifty-six stitches from here to here," Calvin said, dragging his finger from the back of his head to the end of his eyebrow.

Since when did a cop acknowledge there was such a thing as excessive force? Jasmine placed her key into the ignition and turned it. "If Crespo had time to make a date to see Angel, he damn sure had the time to keep his date with Judge Brathwaite." She left it at that. The law gave her as a bail bond agent extensive leeway to apprehend someone who had skipped court. Jasmine nestled into the heated seat. "You gonna arrest me for assaulting some mope?"

Calvin ignored her sarcastic question by posing one of his own. "Adopt any strays today?" He always referred to her pro bono clients as strays. After they had just met and she described her "community supervision program," he first referred to them as orphans, and Jasmine ripped him a new one. It took Calvin three weeks of begging her to forgive him and plying her with a half gallon of rum and Coke to get the personal history behind her rage. Even then Jasmine only offered him a chip off the wall, letting him know that she herself had been orphaned by the age of thirteen and had a brother who committed suicide while detained on Rikers Island.

Since then Jasmine had not told him more than that, but still, she had not been able to shake him. They sought each other despite themselves. Calvin suffered from an annoying savior complex, but she kept him around because he had his uses.

"Yup."

"What's his name?"

"Booker, Malcolm." To facilitate his inevitable search through the NYPD's arrest database, Jasmine rattled off Booker's New York State identification number as listed on his rap sheet. She hid her distaste behind a façade of nonchalance to preserve her ability to ask Calvin for the occasional favor that only a man with a badge could grant. "One sixty ten," she added.

"Robbery in the second?"

Beating him to his next question, Jasmine volunteered, "Used a thirty-eight to hold up a bodega owner for a can of spray paint. Krylon's Jungle Green. Apparently, it's discontinued and highly coveted by writers."

"Writers?"

"Graffiti."

"That's what they're calling themselves now?"

"That's what they've always called themselves."

"Apparently, this Booker character can call himself a licker, too. And a gangbanger, for all you know."

"Get the hell out of here."

"Seriously, Jasmine, didn't you know that some graffiti is gang-related? They tag up to mark their territories and send death threats to rivals." A burst of rowdy laughter interrupted his rant. Up the block several off-duty cops were leaving Ramon's and drifting toward their cars. Calvin backed away from the Escalade as if he were loitering alone on the street.

One of his colleagues spotted him. "What you doing over there, Quinones? Need a lift home?"

"No, I'm parked around the corner, but thanks."

His fellow cop waited for Calvin to explain further, but he offered nothing more than a self-conscious wave. Jasmine resisted the urge to rev up and drive off. She would have given into the impulse if her leaving at that moment might have revealed to Calvin's peers exactly what he wanted desperately to hide. "I'm out," she warned him.

"No, wait," he insisted without looking her in the eye. Eventually, Calvin's fellow officers drove away, and he again stationed himself at her window. "Did you post bail yet? I can have the Vandals Task Force run his name through their database for you."

"The NYPD keeps a database of graffiti writers?" Jasmine laughed in disbelief. "So, like, instead of a mug shot, they take a photograph of some kid's tag." She found the idea ridiculous, considering that the daily paper always carried dozens of stories about men stalking and shooting their ex-wives, politicians using taxpayer money to visit Caribbean resorts, and children with no history of trouble disappearing on their way to the store, among other gory tales. There had to be better law enforcement initiatives to pour taxpayer monies into.

Calvin scowled. "That's exactly what they do. Every precinct has a digital camera and a list of the top hundred offenders." His voice took on an evangelical tone. "And with Graffitistat, we can update and analyze arrests and complaints data on a regular basis and crack down on these quality-of-life offenses that have a nasty habit of spiraling into more serious crimes."

Why she and Calvin did not end at the beginning, she would never know. Perhaps they were both addicted to anxiety. Jasmine already had her fix for the day, so she turned the ignition key. "What's done is done," she said.

"Christ, Jasmine. You're going to put that guy back out on the street without any collateral? When he skips, you won't have a goddamned thing to show for it."

"He's not going to skip."

"The guy's been charged with a Class C felony," said Calvin. "Any priors?"

"Just two counts of criminal mischief. In both instances, he paid a fine and restitution to the property owners."

"Jasmine, he's a predicate felon," Calvin said, pounding against the roof of the car.

"A nonviolent predicate!" She hated when Calvin spoke to her as if she had no clue what she was doing. "And don't bang my ride."

"It doesn't matter. With two felonies on his record, he's facing at least five years," said Calvin. "This isn't one of your buy-'n'-bust charity cases, Jasmine. Your man can enter the monastery while out on bail, no way is the ADA going to let him plead guilty to second-degree robbery in exchange for probation." Calvin stepped away from the Escalade and threw his hands in the air. "Of course, the kid's going to skip. What the hell were you thinking?"

"Yeah, Cal, what the hell am I ever thinking?" Since he had no intention of getting into the car, Jasmine put it in reverse. She released the brake and looked over her shoulder. "Maybe you should stick with your own kind." Then Jasmine turned the wheel, put the car in drive and tore down the block.

A balmy night in late July found Jasmine in her Escalade looking in her rearview mirror as she applied makeup the only way she knew how. With a brush she had dipped in a bottle of water, she coated her lower eyelid with deep blue eye shadow. Then she rubbed her fingertips into the charcoal-gray shadow and blotted it under the same eye. After adding touches of shiny olive shadow to the edges of her eyes, she smudged all three colors to finish her bruise.

Jasmine peeked in her side-view mirror. She had parked the SUV a few yards from the corner bodega. It had closed fifteen minutes earlier at two a.m., but she knew damned well Poncho was in there. The minute she'd met him, Jasmine had suspected the flake would skip his court date. But she posted his bail anyway, knowing that the big baby would run straight to his auntie's store.

Every once in a while Jasmine took on an obvious but simple jumper for the thrill of the chase. Once she nabbed Poncho and surrendered him to the four-four, not only would Jasmine get back the twenty-five-hundred-dollar bond she had posted on his behalf, she also would seize the Ford Escape his Titi Juana had put up as collateral. Having grown fond of the Escalade Tommy Crespo had forfeited when he decided to appear at a strip club instead of the courthouse eight months earlier, Jasmine had no need or desire for another SUV. Instead she would sell Titi Juana's Escape for twenty grand at her favorite used-car dealer in Queens.

When Zachary's informant confirmed that Poncho's aunt was harboring him in her storeroom, Jasmine told Zachary they would stake out the bodega on Friday night, with every intention of surrendering Poncho on Thursday by herself. When Zachary found out, he would be pissed, but she had no guilt or regrets. You would think he was the one who would be in a financial hole if they did not locate the principal. His eagerness to follow Jasmine through the underbelly of the borough searching for bail jumpers would get him killed if she did not check it, and Jasmine already had one body on her conscience. He had yet to accept this, but Zachary's job was to trace the skips, while it was hers to bring them back to jail.

After telling Zachary Thursday to wait for her call on Friday night, Jasmine went home to change into what Calvin liked to call her "prey clothes." Tonight she chose the denim jacket with the huge tear on the right shoulder. She unlaced her Tims and switched into flip-flops. "Why you go through all that, I'll never know," he had once complained. "You have a badge."

Jasmine never used it, and Calvin knew damned well why. "The last thing I need is to get charged with impersonating a police officer," she had said.

"But you're not. Are you?"

"No! But it's too easy to be accused of it. The surety company might drop me, and I could lose my license." Sometimes she wondered if that was exactly what Calvin wanted, even before he'd found out about her past.

Jasmine checked her reflection in the rearview mirror. The bruiser looked realistic in the dim light, but she still felt underdressed for the task at hand. Jasmine reached into the backseat for her tool box. She opened it and selected the scissors. After poking a small hole into the knee of her jeans, Jasmine dug in her fingers and ripped it wider. Then she reached back into the makeup bag for the fake blood she concocted at home with corn syrup, liquid soap, food coloring, and hot water. Jasmine spread a glob across her exposed knee, and on a whim dabbed some on her bottom lip. She returned everything to its proper place and stored the kit on the floor of her backseat.

Jasmine took a deep breath and climbed out of the Escalade. She gave herself one last look in the side-view mirror and thanked Judge Eisenberg for issuing a bench warrant for Poncho's arrest. Her constant sniffling had deteriorated into a relentless cold. Jasmine had called Nathalie Dieudonné, who she'd run into at the courthouse, and made an appointment, but when Zachary had come through with the information about the bodega, Jasmine had felt better and had blown off the appointment to track Poncho down. As she crossed the street to the closed bodega, Jasmine actually hoped he did not make apprehension too easy for her. If Zachary's informant had given them correct information, the bodega only had one entrance, so if Jasmine tricked her way into the store, she would have Poncho cornered.

Jasmine broke into a shuffling run with her flip-flops chafing the warm concrete. When she reached the glass door, she pounded on it frantically, rattling the CLOSED sign hanging in the window. "Let me in! Help me! Please!" A pudgy, middle-aged woman with a head of frazzled yellow hair and dark roots peeked around a shelf of assorted cans. Jasmine recognized her from Poncho's file as his aunt Juana. She banged on the glass again. "Let me in, please! I think he's coming after me! Hurry!" Titi Juana ambled to the door and unlocked it. Jasmine rushed inside.

"Dios mío, ¿que está pasando?" Titi Juana asked. She looked out the window and up the street for Jasmine's phantom attacker.

"Lock the door!"

Juana did as Jasmine ordered.

"He just threw me out of the car, and I think he's right behind me," she said, pretending to catch her breath. "You have to call the police!"

"Ay, nena, I sorry, *pero yo no quiero nada que 'cer con esto."*

How could the woman let her into the store and then suddenly plead see no evil? "I'm telling you, lady, I think my husband saw me come in here. He's either going to wait until I leave or he's coming in here after me. You have to call the cops now!"

Juana hesitated but then rushed behind the counter toward the phone. Now that she had secured backup, Jasmine had to get into that storeroom. "You have to hide me. If he comes by and sees me in here, I swear to God he'll break the fuckin' glass."

Juana picked up the telephone receiver and dialed 911. "Go back there," she said, pointing toward a door at the end of the last aisle. "My nephew will hide you. *¡Vete, antes que tu esposo viene y me tumba la puerta!"*

Jasmine fled down the aisle toward the back room, feeling a pang of sympathy for the old lady. She rarely had any for the relatives that harbored her FTAs, but Jasmine remembered when Juana had called the agency in hysterics upon her nephew's arrest. Diana had gone to Rikers Island that morning to interview Frank Echevarría, so Jasmine had to juggle the phones. It took her a half hour to calm down Juana to explain Poncho's case. No matter how much Jasmine pressed her to stick to the facts, she kept bursting into tears and saying things like *I promised my sister—may she rest in peace—that I would take care of her only child,* and *Ponchito's a handful, but he's the son I never had, God bless him.* Juana had offered her store as collateral, but Jasmine had refused it. Jasmine could not bring herself to ask the old woman to risk her business over a standard buy-'n'-bust, even if her nephew was skittish and likely to fail to appear. She settled for the Ford Escape as collateral, telling herself that if she were in Juana's shoes, she would do no differently.

But as Jasmine neared the storeroom and listened to Juana speak to the emergency assistance operator, she reconsidered. Juana expressed more concern over some abusive lunatic breaking her glass door than she did about him beating his wife before her eyes. As far as Jasmine was concerned, Juana could share a cell with her precious Poncho for hindering prosecution by harboring a person sought by law enforcement officials.

She inched her way down the aisle while calculating the odds in her head. When Poncho heard the pounding on the door, he probably assumed the cops had come for him and hid somewhere in the storeroom. She could not continue to play victim, running into the storeroom feigning hysteria. Jasmine made a point to limit contact with her collateral clients, preferring that they never meet her, in case she had to pursue them. Diana had handled all the steps involved in posting Poncho's bail, so she had met with Juana to collect the title to the Escape, and Jasmine thought her assistant understood the rationale behind that. But one afternoon, Poncho had come by the agency after a court appearance, curious to see the man behind Reyes Bonds. Without getting his name or screening his visit with Jasmine, Diana called Jasmine on the intercom and announced him.

When the name registered with her, Jasmine seethed, "Take me off the speaker phone now!" Before Diana complied, Jasmine heard Poncho in the background say, "That ain't Mr. Reyes, is it?"

Diana put the receiver to her ear. "What's up?"

"That's a client."

"I know."

"You told him I was here?"

"Of course."

"Jesus. . . . Tell him *Mr.* Reyes is in an important meeting and cannot be disturbed." Gambling that Poncho would not make another trip to the courthouse just to see her, Jasmine said, "Tell him to come back tomorrow."

"Okay."

But when Jasmine left the agency that night, she spotted Poncho Ferrer watching and waiting across the street. They made eye contact, and she knew that he had made her as his bondswoman. Poncho smirked at Jasmine then blew her a kiss. As she watched him head toward the train station, she suspected that he might skip his next court date.

So if Poncho Ferrer recognized Jasmine when she entered the storeroom, they would have to wrestle. Within minutes Juana would end her call and join the ruckus, making it two against one. If she had any chance of catching him, Jasmine had to corner Poncho before he spotted her. In the worst-case scenario, she had to prepare herself to get dirty, maybe even hurt, if she had to fight Poncho as he scrambled for the bodega exit.

Jasmine found the storeroom door wide open, with only the melodramatic dialogue of a Spanish *telenovela* to greet her. She crept inside and quickly scanned the room. Piles of cardboard boxes stood in every corner. In front of the television sat a small card table holding a half-eaten container of spare ribs and fried rice. Of the three mismatched chairs surrounding the table, one had fallen to the floor.

Jasmine heard a scratching sound from behind a stack of boxes. As she stole toward the box, the scratching grew louder. Jasmine gave the box a sharp kick, and a rat the size of a squirrel scurried across the room. She leaped and squealed. "Fuck!"

She regained her wits in time to catch the extra shadow on the wall.

Seconds before Poncho could slam a gallon of canned grapefruit onto Jasmine's head, she unleashed a crescent kick into his fleshy belly, and he flew back against a pile of boxes. Soup cans tumbled out of a box and rolled across the floor.

"You fuckin' bitch," Poncho yelled as he clutched his stomach.

She grabbed him by the straps of his undershirt and flung him headfirst into another stack of boxes marked Del Monte. Jasmine straddled Poncho's back, yanked his arms behind him, and slapped on the handcuffs. Then she heard the click of the handgun behind her.

"*¡Suertale!*"

Jasmine turned to find the old lady aiming a .38 at her. "I said let him go!" Jasmine had to give it to the *viejita*. She had heart.

Jasmine pulled out her own .45, grabbed Poncho by his collar, and pressed the barrel against his temple. Titi Juana gasped in horror. "Sorry, Juana," Jasmine said. "Your nephew's worth twenty-five hundred dollars to me. He's the only thing standing between paying the mortgage on my co-op and filling up the tank of my SUV. I'll be damned if I go back to a life of motels and MetroCards." She dug Shorty's barrel into Poncho's bruised temple, and he whinnied like an injured pony. "So it's up to you, Titi. It doesn't matter if I bring him in dead or alive. I still get paid."

"How much does Poncho owe you?" Juana's arms trembled as she pointed the gun. "Maybe I can pay you?"

If Juana had that kind of cash lying around, she never would have needed Jasmine to post Poncho's bail in the first place. "I'm not interested in your money," she said. "I'm only interested in your nephew."

"Who are you?"

Jasmine pinched Poncho, and he yelped. "Tell her who I am and to drop the fuckin' gun."

"Titi, it's the lady who posted my bail," said Poncho. "Now please put the gun down."

"Then let him go and keep my car," said Juana. "It's worth ten times as much." Funny how people relied on a service they failed to understand. It did not matter that after Jasmine sold the car and paid the bond, she would have money left over. In order to become a bail bond agent, she had to convince an insurance company to underwrite the bonds she wrote. If they decided she wrote too many bad bonds just to rack up premiums and convert collateral into cash, they would drop her. Out of either greed or ignorance, many new bail bond agents screwed themselves out of the business in a year or two just that way.

Jasmine had no intention of risking the one thing she had managed to build in life over a fuckup like Poncho Ferrer, who lost respect for her the moment he learned that she was not a man. "It doesn't work that way, Juana."

"I think I can get her, Ponchito." But Juana's hands quivered as she tried to pull the hammer back on the .38.

Poncho was not having it. "Goddamnit, Titi, put the gun down!" Jasmine reinforced that instinct by tightening the grip on his collar. "Put it down now, I said, before she shoots me."

Juana dropped the pistol and, before Jasmine could even ask, raised her hands in the air and stepped away from the door. Jasmine shook her head. Apparently, Juana had learned a thing or two from watching those *telenovelas.*

"Now get facedown on the floor and put your hands behind your head." Juana looked as if to say *That's right, I forgot,* and hastened to the floor. Jasmine jabbed Poncho in his side to keep him still with pain while she fetched Juana's .38 and slipped it into her waistband. She slapped her spare pair of handcuffs onto one of Juana's wrists and then latched her to the nearest metal shelf. Suddenly, a crash of shattering glass came from the front of the store.

"Keep quiet!" Jasmine ordered and went to investigate. When she heard the static of police radios, she placed both guns at her feet, pulled out her badge, raised her arms in the air, and waited for the uniformed officers to appear. Even though Jasmine was licensed to carry a gun, and it pained her to yield to the NYPD, she would be damned if she'd become the next person to be gunned down by a Bronx cop under suspicious circumstances. She had better ways to kill herself.

A uniform turned the corner. To be hired by the NYPD, a candidate had to be at least twenty-one years old, and despite having a wingspan as wide as a bus, the kid did not look a day older than that. He'd probably filed to take his written exam as soon as he'd reached his seventeenth and a half birthday, then pumped iron every day for the next thirty months. He had to be a rookie, because Jasmine recognized all the beat cops in the four of the twelve Bronx precincts where most of her clients lived. The stocky rookie eyed her garb. "Miss, are you the one who called?" he asked.

His partner turned the corner, and Jasmine immediately recognized him as a veteran named Flaherty. She couldn't fuckin' stand Flaherty. Not only was he as old school as they came, but Jasmine suspected that he had told Calvin about her past. He peered at Jasmine until recognition came over his face. "Luggio, remember the female bounty hunter I told you about?"

"Bail enforcement agent, Flaherty," said Jasmine. "And that's the last time I'm going to tell you." She hated being called a bounty hunter, especially by those who knew better. It gave people the false impression that she fancied herself some kind of superhero more capable of apprehending a fugitive than the cops were. Jasmine saw no advantage and took no honor in being perceived as the Latina answer to Domino Harvey. It made an already hard job even more difficult.

"Almost three in the morning, Reyes, and instead of cuddling up to a husband, you're in the middle of a closed bodega in one of your getups," Flaherty said. "But then again, you're not the marrying kind, are you?"

She snapped, "And you're obviously not the promoting kind if after all this time on the force you don't know the fuckin' difference between a bail bondsman and a bounty hunter." The quizzical look on Luggio's face revealed that he didn't either, but Jasmine had no interest in schooling Flaherty's protégé.

Flaherty's face flushed at her comeback. He never could beat her in a verbal joust. If she were lucky, he never would realize that because Flaherty was not beyond stooping to the gutter to one-up her. Why did the old man hate her so much? Flaherty did not know Jasmine like that, minding her business and judging her on some old dirt.

Jasmine got back to work. "I've got a bail jumper in the storeroom by the name of Poncho Ferrer. Judge Eisenberg issued the bench warrant for his arrest yesterday. I've also got his aunt Juana de la Torre cuffed back there, who should go down for hindering prosecution, possession of a firearm, and tons of other shit, I bet, if you bother to look around." Jasmine motioned at the guns at her feet. "The forty-five's mine, but that's the thirty-eight she pointed at me. How much you want to bet that isn't registered?"

Flaherty reached down to pick up Juana's gun as the rookie squinted at Jasmine. He leaned toward Flaherty and muttered, "This is the chick that puts them back on the street for free?" Throughout her life Jasmine had been told she was pretty, and despite her runny nose and phony bruises, she could tell that Luggio thought so. She never gave a shit about things like that, least of all what men thought of her, never mind cops and johns. Keeping the city's Administration for Children's Services at bay and hustling to pay the rent left no time to play with makeup and harbor crushes on schoolboys when she was a kid. And being pretty never got her anywhere that being smart had not.

"Yeah, but only if they promise to be good little boys."

"Tell him the cute little nickname you have for me."

"He already knows it."

Jasmine waited for Flaherty to repeat it, savoring it as he did. The Death Wish Bitch. Female bail bond agents were nothing new, but only a crazy bitch with a death wish would post bail for someone with no collateral and chase him herself instead of hiring a bona fide bounty hunter. If she were lucky, all she might lose was her home, because no way would a defendant who'd FTAed go back to Rikers Island without a fight to the death. The police who patrolled the neighborhoods of her clientele believed not only that Jasmine's days were numbered, but that if the worst of the rumors were true, she courted death. Long ago Jasmine accepted that she would never befriend a cop in this borough. Most days she barely considered Calvin a friend, even though they slept together every once in a while, only for him to pretend that he could barely stand Jasmine.

Jasmine picked up Shorty and returned her to her waistband. "Do what you gotta do so I can get out of here." She stepped aside to make room for Flaherty and Luggio to walk past her toward the storeroom. Jasmine continued down the aisle. "I have the paperwork in my car." She had an understanding with most of the cops she dealt with, so she did not have to stick around for surrenders or tag along on the ride back to Rikers Island. Jasmine did not want to deal with them any longer than she had to, and the feeling was mutual. She just needed proof of the defendant's rearrest to go to court and request that the judge exonerate the bail. But with Flaherty on the case, Jasmine had little choice but to stick around and subject herself to more snide remarks. She would be damned if she gave him the opportunity to screw her out of getting back her twenty-five hundred by being sloppy, if not malicious.

As Jasmine made her way back to the Escalade to retrieve Poncho Ferrer's paperwork, she made a mental date. She did not care how late it became. Once Flaherty and Luggio carted away Ferrer and de la Torre to jail, Jasmine would make time with a shot glass at Ramon's.

After that she had to go home and get some sleep. Next week Malcolm Booker would go to his last court appearance and either plead guilty and be sentenced to three and half to five years in prison or he would go to trial, and Jasmine wanted to put in a full day tomorrow to prepare. She expected that his sister, Crystal, would take the day off from work to be by Malcolm's side no matter what he chose. Jasmine intended to be there for him as well. She always assigned one of the staff to be present at the dates of disposition for all her pro bono clients. But Jasmine was the only one who should be there for Malcolm Booker.

Life only allowed Jasmine so much luck at once, so she arrived at Ramon's during a shift change at borough command. Still, she held up her head as she drifted toward the bar through the forest of musky bodies. When Slip the bartender saw Jasmine approach, he slapped a shot glass onto the bar and poured her a shot of Dewar's. Slip liked her. Said her mere presence broke the monotonous stream of cop braggadocio. Slip also said that he did not believe all the things that the regulars tried to feed him about Jasmine. And she let him believe what he wanted. So long as he allowed her to run a tab, Jasmine accepted the kindness, even if offered out of the blindness of puppy love.

Leave it to a bail jumper to introduce her to Ramon's. A few years after she had started the business, Jasmine had to trace Adam Brozi, an Albanian kid from Belmont with a penchant for pranks. He was her first legitimate FTA, since his folks gave up the deed to their house as collateral. Adam failed to appear in court for his assault case, and the presiding judge issued the bench warrant. New to skip tracing and unfamiliar with his section of the Bronx, as well as the immigrants who had moved there from Balkan refugee camps, Jasmine showed her hand to the wrong people. After a week of searching for Adam without luck, she received an anonymous call at the office. The male caller claimed to have information on Adam's whereabouts and asked her to meet him at a bar named Ramon's on Washington Avenue off the Cross Bronx Expressway.

Until she'd received the call, Jasmine had sworn his parents had shipped him back to Albania to evade prosecution, just like in the case of those Italian kids in Queens who beat that Dominican kid to death, trying to impress the local Mafia boss. At the time, her yen to catch Adam overrode her bullshit detector, something that rarely happened. But Jasmine wanted to catch the kid as much for his parents' sake as her own. The Brozis had put their home on the line to bail him out of jail, and Adam ran. The inconsiderate brat had parents who cared for him, and that was how he showed his appreciation? He deserved to rot in jail for that alone.

The second Jasmine walked into Ramon's, she realized she had been duped. Whether trying to throw her off Adam's trail or just getting an easy laugh at her expense, the bullshit artist had led Jasmine into a cop bar. She had never been in one before but knew instantaneously. Frustrated machismo clouded the air like cigar smoke. Trying to cover her embarrassment and discomfort, Jasmine marched to the bar and ordered a shot of Dewar's as if she always frequented the place.

Having completed a grueling day on the beat, including a near riot at the East Tremont shopping district, Calvin dropped himself onto the stool next to her. "You on the force, too?" he asked her.

Not believing that anyone could ever confuse her for a cop, Jasmine put up her guard. For a moment she entertained the possibility that he might have been the informant after all, testing her before revealing his true identity. She even caught herself leaning into Calvin in an attempt to match his voice to that of her faceless tipster. "Do I look like a cop to you?"

"I don't know," said Calvin. "What's a cop supposed to look like?"

"You ought to know, being one and all."

"But I've only been one for twenty-seven days. Right now you're probably a better judge than I am." Calvin put his beer mug on the bar, planted his feet on the floor, and rose to his full height of six-one. "So do I look like a cop?"

Jasmine checked him out. He was the best-looking guy she had been near in too long. The last dude she had slept with was a sweaty john with a hairy back. When Jasmine had decided to start the business, she'd kept a few regulars on hand while waiting for the agency to turn a comfortable profit. About a year before meeting Calvin, she turned her last trick and had not had sex with anyone else since.

Jasmine did not know if cops prided themselves on looking like cops or not, but she listened to what her instinct told her Calvin wanted to hear. "I'm no cop, but I'm around law enforcement all the time, and, yeah, you reek of New York's finest to me." Then she called for Slip to refill his beer and spent the next hour hearing every detail about Calvin's first month on the force and his plans to get his gold shield before he turned thirty-five. She had forgotten about Adam Brozi until Calvin finally asked her what she did. He only believed Jasmine when she downed her last shot and said she had to get back on the case. Once Calvin got over his shock, he agreed to help her. Two days later they nabbed Brozi at Kennedy Airport in front of his parents just before he boarded a plane to Albania.

Jasmine took her seat at the bar as Slip poured her whiskey. "Who underestimated you this time, Jas?" he asked.

"Just some mama's boy." Jasmine took her shot glass and raised it in the air. "To the goddess of apprehension." She downed the whiskey and slammed the glass onto the bar. Slip poured her another shot and then left to serve a cluster of off-duty cops who had just entered. Jasmine watched them as they laughed raucously at each other's jokes and slapped one another on the back. Once in a while, one of them would glance her way. If he were decent, he would pretend to not have seen her at all and turn back to his conversation. But usually he was a dickhead who glared at Jasmine as if her presence offended him. She hated to admit it, but being in Ramon's without Calvin was a bitch. He tried to convince her that no one at borough command knew that they "were spending time together," as he liked to put it. Calvin wished that were true, but it was not, and they both damned well knew it. She hoped that after all the absconders she had recovered, the cops eventually would accept her, but they just tolerated her, and only because of Calvin.

Jasmine summoned Slip to pour her one last shot. After this last drink, she would head home and go straight to sleep, because this cold was dogging her mercilessly. No sooner had Slip refilled her glass and moved onto the next customer than a red-nosed guy who smelled like stale cigar dropped his fat ass onto the stool next to her. "That seat's taken," she said.

"By who?"

"My guardian angel."

"And here I thought God had written you off."

"Fuck you very much." Jasmine downed her shot and headed toward the door.

"Off to look for Malcolm Booker?"

Jasmine stopped in her tracks and turned around to face him. "What'd you just say?"

"You didn't hear, Reyes?" the off-duty said, making his pleasure in her ignorance obvious. "Your model client failed to appear in court today, and the judge issued a bench warrant. Two uniforms went to his house in Castle Hill, his job at the health clinic. . . . No one's seen him in the last three days. Booker's on the lam."

"Tell me something I don't know," Jasmine said, and she marched to the exit.

But she had not known, and the news hit her like a rabbit punch. She threw open the door and stepped out into the thick air. Before the door shut behind her, Jasmine heard the cop laugh, bragging to his friends that Jasmine had no idea that her favorite stray had run away from home.

Jasmine took one look at the unwelcome mat in front of her apartment door and knew her luck had worsened. The perfectly straight mat revealed that in her apartment sat an uninvited guest. Twice in the five years since she founded the bail bond agency a bail jumper had found her address, then his way into Jasmine's apartment. Neither had been dangerous, at least not as far as she was concerned. They had just wanted a place to crash, something to eat, and, of course, a little mercy from their bond agent for skipping court. Both times Jasmine had allowed the guy to scour her half-empty refrigerator for something edible and to sleep on her sofa. In both instances, when the jumper awoke the next morning, he found himself handcuffed to the living room radiator while beat cops from the four-five hovered over him waiting to escort him back to Rikers Island.

After the second time a jumper made himself at home in her place, Jasmine conceived a way to determine if anyone had broken into her apartment before she entered it. Whether going to the agency for the day or only to the mini-mall for a pack of cigarettes, every time she left her apartment, Jasmine lodged the corner of her doormat—which read *Come Back With a Warrant*—into the doorway and forced the door shut over it. It was impossible to open the door without moving the mat, and tonight someone had done precisely that. The intruder had even lined the mat neatly in front of the door as it belonged to tip her off.

Could it have been Malcolm? Jasmine never thought he would run when it could only hurt his already slim chance at leniency. A conviction of robbery in the second degree typically carried a sentence of five to seven years, and for almost seven months without trial the assistant district attorney had insisted on the maximum. For every appearance, Jasmine wrote a stellar progress report that Malcolm's attorney submitted to the court, yet the prosecutor requested an adjournment for more time to build her case. At the last appearance, however, ADA Mackie had finally agreed to negotiate. She offered three and a half to five in exchange for a guilty plea. Crystal urged Malcolm to accept the ADA's offer, but he hesitated. He even considered calling her bluff and going to trial. Malcolm's PD warned him that if he went to trial and lost the case, he absolutely would do no less than five years. By the next court date, Malcolm had to make a choice: accept the ADA's latest and final offer, go to trial by jury, or request a bench trial like one out of five Bronx defendants opted to do.

Or he could run. And after months of living like a model citizen, Malcolm had done just that. He went from vandalism to robbery in the second to failure to appear. Why should he stop at breaking and entering?

Jasmine dropped her keys into her bag and pulled out her gun with one hand as she inched open the apartment door with the other. Light emanated from the living room into the hallway as Sade crooned on the stereo. Whoever was in there had made himself quite comfortable. Jasmine slowly made her way down the hallway, peeking into the wall mirror into the living room. The bastard was snoozing—face up, arm draped across his face, feet dangling over the armrest—on her crème-colored Fairmont love seat. The one damn thing in the room she had not bought at Ikea, and this animal had his hoofs all over it. She could bust a cap in him for just that.

Jasmine crept into the living room, cocked Shorty, and pressed her squarely against the prowler's big toe. He stirred beneath the crook of his elbow. Then he either saw her or felt the barrel on his foot or both, because he dove to the floor. "Jesus, Jasmine!" Calvin said. "You scared the shit out of me."

"That's what you get for putting your feet all over my sofa." Her pleasure at seeing him caught Jasmine by surprise, and not just because he was not a burglar or absconder. But she could not let Calvin know that just yet. Not after allowing six weeks to pass since she saw him last. True, he had called every once in a while to say nothing in particular, and had called just that morning, but after confronting Jasmine as he had, those calls hardly sufficed. Jasmine uncocked Shorty and put her back into her purse. "Not to mention breaking into my place."

"I did no such thing," Calvin said as he sat back down on the sofa. "I have a key, remember?"

"No, I remember asking for my keys back," she said.

Calvin gave a stretch. "I came across a spare I still had. I've been meaning to give it to you, but you're hard to catch lately."

"Spare?" Jasmine said as she kicked off her sandals and sat down on the love seat next to him. "When'd you get this spare made and for what reason?" And Jasmine had always been hard to catch. Since their falling out, Calvin had not made a genuine effort until now.

"You're supposed to be asking me why I am here."

"If you're talking about Macho Booker, I know." She leaned forward for the stereo remote on the table and halted Sade in mid-note. "I don't get it, Cal. He was doing great on release. . . ."

"You knew he was likely to get time when you bonded him." He leaned over and began kneading Jasmine's shoulders. "And he did, too."

Jasmine shrugged off Calvin, stood up, and walked across the room. "Why is the goddamn ADA insisting on coming down so hard on him?"

Jasmine went over to her wine cart and poured herself a shot of whiskey. She offered one to Calvin, but he passed.

"Should you be drinking that?"

Jasmine regretted telling him that morning about her appointment with Nathalie. But rather than tell him that and have Calvin scold her for skipping it to chase Poncho Ferrer, she much preferred the argument currently in development. "Macho's been showing up to that courtroom every six weeks for the past six months, and Mackie insists on throwing the book at him."

"Jasmine, she doesn't have much choice," Calvin said. "Three and a half is as low as the sentencing laws will let her. Unless he's acquitted in a trial, the kid's doing time." Jasmine felt the weight of his stare as she recapped the whiskey and reached for the vodka. "When'd you last see him?"

Jasmine thought about it as she fixed herself a vodka and tonic. "About two, maybe three weeks ago." The second she said it, she realized how unusual it sounded. Ever since she posted Malcolm's bail, he'd visited Jasmine at the office at least once every week. Unlike most of her other pro bono clients, his release agreement did not require these trips to the agency to receive counseling and service referrals from Lorraine or undergo drug tests under Zachary's supervision. Malcolm came anyway to visit Jasmine, which she reminded Zachary of whenever he complained about Malcolm's occasional curfew violations.

Zachary's job as Jasmine's "director of enforcement," as she referred to him in her court reports, included making unannounced visits to her pro bono principals to ensure they honored their release agreements.

At least twice every week, Zachary arrived at the approved residence at the curfew hour or later. Sometimes he subjected the principal to a spontaneous drug test, other times he either pretended to leave, only to camp out in his car across the street, or make a second visit later the same night to be sure the client did not take to the streets. At least once every month, Jasmine received a late-night call from Zachary to complain about Malcolm.

"Yo, Jas, Booker violated curfew again," he said last month. "His sister thinks he's out there bombin' with some of his boys. I'ma go pick him up."

"No, I'd rather you go check on Asad Mukherjee," said Jasmine. The forty-three-year-old Bengali immigrant owned a restaurant in Manhattan but lived in Parkchester in the same complex as Calvin. During Zachary's home visit, Asad's wife, Tazima, revealed that her husband did fine so long as he did not drink, something he began doing after their restaurant had been vandalized several times after the September 11 attacks. He tended to seek out the bottle when home alone, while Tazima worked the night shift at Jacobi Medical Center. and booze had led Asad to crack a half-empty bottle of vodka over the head of a street thug who took one look at him and threatened to send his "terrorist ass back to the Middle East," even though the middle-aged businessman hailed from Asia.

"I already checked on Mukherjee," said Zachary. "He's home where he belongs watching TV."

"Well, double back and make sure he's still there, and that he ain't drinking."

"I don't have time for that mess. I gotta find Malcolm Booker. I'm telling you, Jasmine, we should just surrender this kid. He's a pain in the ass to supervise, and it's only a matter of time before he gets himself rearrested."

"Zachary, not only are you going back to Parkchester to check in on Mukherjee again, you're going to sit down with the man and have a cup of tea with him." Jasmine's instinct had hit the target that night. Zachary returned to the Mukherjee apartment in time to catch Asad on the way back from a run to the corner liquor store. Malcolm Booker called Zachary in the middle of Asad's detailed but sober lecture on the history of Bangladesh to apologize for missing curfew. He had run an errand downtown for his boss, Dr. Suárez, decided to window shop for art supplies in SoHo, ran into some friends and lost track of time.

"Last time I spoke with Macho, he was talking about going back to school full-time for his BA," she said as she carried her vodka and tonic back to the love seat. Jasmine set her drink on the coffee table and reached for her purse. She pulled out her cigarettes and lighter.

"And then you wonder why you're coughing all the time."

Absorbed in her own thoughts, Jasmine ignored Calvin's sarcasm. "Crystal wasn't wild about him going to art school, but they were getting along fine. In fact, Macho seemed more worried about Crystal's health than his own case. He said something about how she worked too hard and had to take better care of herself." She lit a cigarette and took a drag. Calvin waved the smoke, and Jasmine looked at him, as if noting his presence for the first time. "And don't go defending fuckin' Mackie."

"I'm not defending Mackie."

"You said she had no choice, as if she would do anything differently if she did. Even if the law gave her room, she still would throw the book at Macho. She doesn't give a fuck about him." Jasmine picked up her drink and downed most of it in one shot.

"No, she doesn't," said Calvin. "And that's the risk you took bonding someone charged with rob two."

Jasmine slammed her glass down on the table. "So that's why you're here. To tell me 'I told you so.'" She jumped to her feet and stormed over to the terrace door. She threw it open, walked out onto the balcony, and tapped her ashes over the side.

Calvin followed her. "No, Jasmine, that's not why I'm here. I was already on my way over here when I found out about Booker. In fact, before I left the precinct, I checked all the jails to be sure he hadn't gotten rearrested." Had Jasmine learned about Malcolm's FTA during business hours, she would have done the same thing: check to be sure that his absence in court was not due to getting rearrested. Calvin put his hands on Jasmine's waist and pulled her toward him. "And I didn't come to fight with you either."

Jasmine pulled away. "But you still feel I was wrong to bail him out." Why was he being so touchy-feely? Not that long ago, he had treated her like a leper.

Calvin threw up his hands. "Yeah, Jasmine, you went for the long shot on this one. I know that. And so do you," he said. Jasmine tried to step around him, but Calvin blocked her. "But I understand why you did it, and I know it hurts."

Had she not been drunk, Jasmine never would have told Calvin about Jason, and now she did not know whether to be relieved or regretful to have done so. "I'm fine." But Calvin pulled her toward him again, and this time Jasmine did not resist. She felt his warm breath against her neck and pressed herself against him. When she felt his fingers sliding through her hair, Jasmine stepped back and looked Calvin in the eye. "So why are you here?"

He brushed her hair off her face. "I wanted to know how your doctor's appointment went." Then Calvin pressed his lips against her forehead.

"Like I said, I'm fine," Jasmine lied. She had been on the streets for the past twelve hours, and she felt numb from the cocktail of alcohol and exhaustion. "I've just got a really stubborn summer cold."

"A stubborn cold for a stubborn gal," Calvin said before dragging his lips from her forehead to her nose and then to her lips. It dawned upon Jasmine that Calvin might have been worried that she could be pregnant. She muffled her laugh at the ridiculous idea. Jasmine had no intention of being anyone's girlfriend, let alone someone's mother. She was not wired for that shit, and she was doing everyone a favor by not even considering it. But Jasmine had had a rough night tonight, and she would allow herself to be a bit selfish and let Calvin spend the night, even if it was a mistake.

THREE

The next morning Jasmine skipped out on Calvin before breakfast. He always hated when she did that. It irked him when Jasmine threw him out of her apartment or stormed out of his, but he loathed nothing more than their making it through the night, only for Jasmine to leave for the office before the morning's afterplay. Calvin once complained that it made him feel set up. But with Malcolm Booker on the run and a quart of hard liquor in her stomach, Jasmine barely slept. Besides, she had other work to do, too. So once again Calvin would have to get over it. This time it should be easier for him. After all, Calvin's act of charity last night did not change her past or how he felt about it, so leaving before he woke up was her way of thanking him.

On the way to the agency, Jasmine stopped at Woodlawn. She parked on Jerome Avenue and walked over to the cemetery. There were much less expensive places to bury Jason, but it only seemed right to lay him to rest among the likes of Miles Davis and Duke Ellington. She knew nothing about jazz music, but she liked Miles's gigantic stone of black marble engraved with a musical scale across the bottom and a trumpet down the right side. It made Jasmine think that by burying her brother among such artistic luminaries she had done one last good thing for him. The comfort of that thought always faded, however, as soon as she stepped away from Miles's elaborate stone to Jason's modest grave.

The first thing Jasmine did with the money he had buried in the dirt in front of the wall of his mural was buy a granite headstone in charcoal gray. At forty-eight by fourteen by four, the face ran long enough for two names, so she asked the engraver to flush her brother's lettering to the extreme left.

REYES

Jason Pedro	Jasmine Aliya
1980–2000	1980–

Next to Jason's side of the headstone, Jasmine lowered herself to the grass and sat on her haunches. "Hey, Jas. Sorry it's been a minute since I last came to see you, but you know the crazy hours I keep. Anyway, you know about Macho, right?" She scoffed and stroked his engraved name. "Why do y'all keep doing me like that? Y'all never give a sister a chance. Still, I know you be looking out for me while I'm out there." Jasmine leaned forward and kissed Jason's name. Then she stood up, wiped the soil off her knees, and walked away.

As she drove to the agency, Jasmine considered the last resort. Why not just let Malcolm be? His judge had already issued the bench warrant for his arrest. Sure, the police would not make him a priority, but they eventually would find him. Shit, once the beat cops found out that he was one of her pro bono principals, they would hunt him for bragging rights and an opportunity to humiliate the Death Wish Bitch. Probably get a little action going among themselves as to who collared one of Reyes's "strays." And one of them would. Some time would pass, and Malcolm would feel safe to come out of hiding. So safe that he would trip himself up and get himself pinched. He would do something stupid like run a red light or make an illegal U-turn and get pulled over by a traffic cop. For a chance to prove something to his peers and make points with his superiors, Calvin probably put Malcolm on his own radar, and had come over last night just to find out what she knew that might be useful in his search.

If Jasmine herself did not find and surrender Malcolm within one hundred and eighty days, she would forfeit the ten-thousand-dollar bond she had posted for him. Her surety company hated underwriting clients for which she had not demanded any collateral, even though she did so rarely and judiciously. But Jasmine had such an excellent track record and a decent backup fund, it begrudgingly did so. Why shouldn't it? Only her assets were on the line when a principal absconded. The company paid the bond, and Jasmine paid the company.

But if she failed to find Malcolm, and despite her reimbursing them for the forfeited bond, the company still could decide to cancel her contract. No contract, no license, and good-bye license, good-bye business. Jasmine would no longer be able to serve anyone, whether they had collateral or not.

Even if the surety company cut her slack, she could not afford to lose ten thousand dollars. While it would take time for it to happen, her tight budget eventually would burst. When it did, her mortgage payment would be late, and her already underpaid staff would see only half a paycheck. In the worst-case scenario, Jasmine could lose her home, her staff, and her storefront because she had no collateral to plug the hole shot into her resources by Malcolm's disappearance.

But ultimately money would not drive Jasmine to find him. She understood why Malcolm absconded. Many inmates survived their bids by discovering their artistic selves while on lockdown. They picked up a pen or a brush and unlocked the bars around their souls. But what happens when a creative spirit is put behind bars? How did an inmate who already knew that kind of freedom learn to survive? Jason had never learned. Maybe Malcolm did the calculus and concluded that he would last longer on the streets than he would upstate.

But the news still took Jasmine by surprise. If he were that afraid of doing hard time, why had he not come to speak with her? Although shame had kept her from confessing everything, Jasmine had told Malcolm about Jason. Jasmine shared things with him she had never told her own staff. At the time, she convinced herself that she was revealing these things to Malcolm for his own benefit. To prove that she understood him, and that he could trust her, but a day must have come recently when Malcolm doubted it.

And now his disappearance forced Jasmine to realize that she told him about Jason for her own sake. And that was why Jasmine took Malcolm's disappearance as personally as her brother's suicide. The burning in her heart told her to take it that way. Something more than fear of prison had to have made Malcolm run. And while Jasmine could not save Jason, she could find Malcolm.

* * *

"New Life Village, how may I help you?"

"Yeah, my brother's in jail, and I heard you guys might be able to help me get him out."

"Well, let me ask you a few questions."

"OK."

"What's his name?"

"Jason."

"Jason . . . ?"

"Do I have to give you all this information before you can tell me if you can help me or not? I mean . . ."

"You don't have to tell me anything, miss, but I can't help you if you don't."

"Jason Reyes."

"OK, and you are?"

"Jasmine. Jasmine Reyes."

"And you're his sister."

"Yeah."

"Does Jason live in the Bronx?"

"Yeah. He lives with me. I heard you bail people out of jail."

"No, New Life is an alternative-to-incarceration program for drug users. This is how we work. Our clients have to meet some basic criteria. They have to be of a certain age, charged with a particular crime and things like that. Now if your brother meets the preliminary criteria, we send someone to interview him in jail. If his answers to all our questions are satisfactory then we would go to the ADA and say, 'Look, this is a good kid with a bad problem. Jason's breaking the law because he's on drugs. If you release him under our supervision, we'll treat him. ROR him . . ."

"ROR?"

"Release him on his own recognizance, and we'll keep an eye on him and give him the help he needs."

"So y'all are like some kind of boot camp?"

"No, like I told you, we're an outpatient drug treatment program. If we accept Jason into our program and negotiate his release with the ADA, then he would be required to undergo drug treatment at our facility. But he

would still get to live at home with you. We would give him an assessment and design a treatment plan for him, and that might include individual and group counseling, joining AA, getting on methadone . . ."

"Methadone!"

"Only if we think Jason needs it. We won't know that until we . . .

"He doesn't need it. My brother's not a drug addict."

"Then I don't think we can help him, Jasmine. Not that we don't want to. But if he doesn't have an alcohol or substance abuse problem, then he's not right for our program. It wouldn't be good for him, and it's not fair to give him a space over someone who genuinely needs treatment. I'm sorry."

"So do you know of any other programs that might be able to help me get him out of jail?"

"There used to be quite a few I could refer you to, but so many of them have folded because of budget cuts. Let's see who might be able to help your brother. Tell me this. Does Jason have any kind of mental illness?"

Jasmine hung up the telephone and cried until her next customer knocked on the motel door.

After Jason died, Jasmine gave up the run-down one-bedroom they shared in a tenement building on Vyse Avenue and moved into a basement apartment in Soundview. Unwilling to trust herself with an escort service, she placed an ad in a few neighborhood weeklies and limited herself to out-calls. In the meantime, Jasmine submitted her license application to the state's department of insurance, studied for the surety exam, and prayed that her single arrest would not come back to haunt her. She studied for her exam during the day and turned tricks at night. Jasmine never brought her work home, so the old lady who owned the house and rented her the apartment never had a clue. As far as the *viejita* was concerned, Jasmine was a conscientious college student and the ideal tenant.

When she passed the surety test and acquired her license, Jasmine invested in a cell phone and changed her home number. She gave her new home phone number to a select group of johns on whom she could rely for regular patronage and a safe if boring time. She tricked for a year to save enough money, build her credit, and open the backup account she needed to convince a surety company to underwrite the bonds she posted.

Once she had, Jasmine invested in a computer and created a flyer that simply read NEED BAIL NOW? CALL REYES BONDS—24 HOUR SERVICE followed by her new cell phone number. Jasmine made copies and left them everywhere within a five-block radius of the courthouse that the law allowed. Hell, most of the damn questions on the surety exam covered all the shit a bail bond agent could not do, from price shearing to handing out business cards on government property.

Those first few months were the toughest for Jasmine, as she had to juggle her dates with urgent phone calls from detainees at Rikers Island or their loved ones seeking someone to post bail. She lost one of her johns when she answered her phone in the middle of a hand job and ultimately decided to leave to meet the potential indemnitor. He did not believe Jasmine when she told him she had become a bail bond agent, and being a twenty-four-business, she had to follow up immediately with clients regardless of the hour they called. She had told him the truth, fully expecting that he would not believe her. He demanded to know who she was really going to see, what she was doing for him, and how much he was paying her for it. Jasmine gave him the option of her finishing him off or refunding his money, but she refused to stay any longer than that. The john chose neither, and because he was the least favorite of her regulars, for the first time Jasmine felt she had made a good decision by entering the bail bond industry.

Jasmine took all calls, ran background checks on her computer, and used the last booth of the McDonald's across the street from Yankee Stadium to finalize transactions. She rejected over two dozen clients in that first month or so, and half as many rejected her. After all, every other bail bond agent in the borough had hung a shingle on a storefront near the courthouse. What legitimate agent negotiated collateral in a fast-food restaurant? And desperation had no bearing on sexism, since quite a few potential clients took issue with doing business with a woman, and Jasmine secretly thanked them for removing themselves from consideration.

Jasmine played it safe with the first client she bonded without collateral—a good kid named Ross McCalla who landed himself in a bad situation. An honor student longing for street cred, he'd jumped into a stolen car with the neighborhood badasses and went on a joy ride until the cops busted them for running a stop sign. Having never been in trouble with the law before, he could have been charged with unauthorized use of a vehicle, a Class A misdemeanor charge that should have gotten Ross RORed (released on recognizance) and perhaps would have eventually been dropped. But because his so-called friends had previous arrests for auto theft, possession with intent to sell, and a hodgepodge of other crimes between them, the ADA upgraded the charge to a Class E felony and the judge set bail at fifteen hundred dollars—cash only.

His mother had called four bondsmen before coming across Jasmine's flyer. Every single one told her that because the judge set cash-only bail, they were unable to assist her. The one at Reliable Bonds had been both knowledgeable and compassionate enough to advise Miss McCalla to pressure Ross's public defender to take a writ of habeas corpus.

Because Miss McCalla's desperation made it safe for Jasmine to reveal her ignorance, she asked her, "And what's that?"

"It's like an appeal," Miss McCalla explained. "The lawyer said that it's usually improper for a judge to not set both cash bail and a bond amount as an alternative. But he said the appeal could take several days to be heard, and that the judge would just set the bond amount so high that it really wouldn't be an alternative to cash anyway."

"Meaning he would put it at, say, five thousand because he knows that the typical bondsman would ask for as much as fifteen hundred dollars in both cash and collateral anyway," said Jasmine.

"Yes."

"Well, if you understand that, why did you call me?"

The woman gazed at Jasmine with eyes made hazy from overwork and worry. She shook her head. "I don't know."

"I mean, are you going to ask me to lend you fifteen hundred dollars in cash so you can get Ross out of jail? That's where we stand, because there is no bond to post. You need cash to post your son's bail, and you don't have enough, nor do you have anything else of equal value to offer should he fail to appear in court."

Miss McCalla's eyes dropped to her cup of cold black coffee. The woman had not thought through the implications of what the other bond agents and Ross's attorney had told her. "No, I guess I can't ask you that." But in Jasmine's clarity, the woman found one last unlikely possibility. "I already have five hundred dollars, and I'll sign anything you want for the remaining thousand."

"Miss McCalla, I'm a bond agent, not a banker or a loan shark."

"And I'm a good mother, Miss Reyes. I work two jobs and sleep on a sofa bed so my son can have his own room and attend a good parochial school." She pressed her face into her palms and let out a long exhale. When Miss McCalla's shoulders started to tremble, Jasmine thought she had lost it. But then the woman dropped her hands, revealing eyes glassy with laughter and a smile of small twisted teeth. "You really have nothing to lose, Miss Reyes. I pay almost six hundred dollars every month for him to attend that Catholic school. If Ross gets himself into trouble with the law again, I'll gladly keep his butt in jail and pay you in sixty days from the money I save in tuition."

Then Miss McCalla laughed, and Jasmine understood that she meant every word. She indeed was a good mother and a proud woman. If Ross got rearrested, Miss McCalla, out of love for her only child and her own integrity, would let him sit in jail as she repaid her debt to Jasmine in an effort to teach him many lessons. And with Ross as low a risk as a principal could be, Jasmine agreed after making some quick calculations across her napkin. "I'll lend you one thousand dollars at fifteen percent interest. That's the same amount as the fee you would pay me if I were posting a bond for fifteen hundred dollars." She gave Miss McCalla the chance to do the math herself to prove she was right, and they agreed to meet the next day. Ross's mother signed an IOU, and Jasmine gave her a certified check for one thousand dollars.

For the next four months, however, Jasmine became Miss McCalla's second pair of eyes. She once shadowed Ross in a gypsy cab when instead of going to school he headed toward the movie theater with two of the same guys who were busted with him. "Hey, Ross," she yelled through the backseat window. "Where ya going?"

"To school."

"But isn't the train station that way?" Before he could answer, Jasmine told the driver to stop and swung open the back door. "Get in the cab."

"What?"

"You heard me."

"Who the fuck is that?" asked one of his bad influences.

"None of your goddamn business."

"Bitch, I know you ain't talking to me."

"Yeah, this bitch is talking to you."

The guy pushed Ross aside and bounded toward Jasmine. The second he came within arm's reach, she hauled back and punched him square on the chin. The loudmouth dropped to his knees, but unwilling to take any chances, Jasmine fired a kick into his stomach. While the third guy stood flabbergasted on the curb, she grabbed Ross and threw him into the backseat of the cab. "To the train station," Jasmine directed the cabbie.

Eventually, the ADA on Ross's case agreed to let him plead to a string of misdemeanors and offered him two years' probation. Jasmine contacted Miss McCalla to remind her that now that the court had exonerated bail, she had to repay the loan along with the agreed-upon interest. They planned to meet at the McDonald's one last time the following morning.

Jasmine arrived at the McDonald's to find Ross's mother already waiting for her. She barely made it on time. Miss McCalla had to meet at seven a.m. to make it to her first job, and Jasmine had been up until three with a wealthy and demanding john. When Ross's mother saw her, she stood up from her seat and said, "My son told me what you did." Miss McCalla slipped a folded check into Jasmine's hand and left the restaurant. Jasmine unfolded the check, which was made out to cash in the amount of seventeen hundred and fifty dollars. It took Jasmine a few minutes to calculate both the difference in what Miss McCalla owed and the reason for the "bonus." She had repaid Jasmine six hundred more dollars than the eleven hundred fifty she owed her—an additional fifteen percent for every one of the four months that Jasmine had "supervised" Ross while he was out on bail.

Jasmine had come far from those humble days. After her first two years of steady business from principals with collateral, Jasmine had found office space, had acquired a handgun and the appropriate permits, and had hired an assistant, Diana. She had scores of bonds exonerated, traced a few skips, and won the confidence of her surety company. But Jasmine never derived the same satisfaction as she had from the McCalla case. She wondered if what she did was what the alternative-to-incarceration programs meant by "pretrial supervision"? Would Ross have qualified for any of those programs if she had not accepted Miss McCalla's offer? Could Jasmine provide the same kind of services as these organizations to the Jasons they were unable to serve, offering them not only the opportunity to get out of jail but the chance to stay out?

She decided to institute her own de facto community supervision program, imagining the other Ross McCallas she could help with the right mix of services and supervision. Knowing she needed someone with more experience and passion for the work than Diana, she sent an e-mail to all the city's social work schools in search of an enterprising graduate student who could research and compile a directory of free services from GED programs to drug rehab. Only three responded to her call. The first never showed up for the interview, and the second lost interest when Jasmine told her the internship offered no pay.

And then she found Lorraine, who took so much initiative that Jasmine eventually felt guilty for not paying her. Not only did Lorraine create a comprehensive list of services and organize them into an electronic database, she asked Jasmine for permission to interview her pro bono clients and make referrals on their behalf. When Lorraine decided to pursue her doctorate in social work, Jasmine offered her a part-time job as her "Director of Social Services" and paid her as a consultant. Although she usually worked from home, Lorraine came into the agency for the weekly staff meetings and counseling sessions with clients.

After the first of her pro bono clients jumped bail, Jasmine hired Zachary. She found the jumper on her own with no problem only days later, playing hoops in the playground like a teenager who'd cut school. That added insult to injury, and if he had been alone, Jasmine would have taken him down. But he was surrounded by his boys, so instead she called the cops and let them handle the surrender. Jasmine learned from the experience and made adjustments. She realized that she had a right to put conditions on these people. Even if not legally binding in court, she would have them sign release agreements, and if they balked at the idea of keeping a curfew or submitting to drug tests, they could opt to sit in Rikers Island until their case went to trial. And Jasmine had to face the fact that she needed a man on her team. Someone who would enforce the conditions of the release agreement and help her find the next guy who decided to skip a court appearance. Jasmine could bitch and moan all she wanted, but she had to accept the fact that when it came to certain matters, men ultimately would respect another man.

This time she wrote a complete job description for a part-time "enforcement agent for a cutting-edge bail bond agency" and e-mailed it to several departments at the John Jay College of Criminal Justice. When she went to her post office box, she had a note to go to the window. The postal clerk gave her almost fifty assorted envelopes of résumés. Jasmine held interviews for the next two weeks, sometimes as many as four a day. She ruled out a dozen applicants who made it obvious in one way or another that they would have problems taking orders from a woman. Jasmine suspected that another handful—usually retired police or corrections officers—did not want to be supervised by someone much younger than they were. Although she made it clear in the posting that "Superheroes Need Not Apply," the rest of the lot came off as a bunch of wannabe bounty hunters. In virtually every interview she had to explain the difference between a bail enforcement agent and a bounty hunter. Being the least of the Neanderthals and showing some appreciation for the difference, Zachary got the job. Three weeks later Jasmine almost fired him for smacking a guy in the back of the head for giving a dirty urine sample. Zachary begged for another chance, and Jasmine conceded.

In five years, Jasmine had handled over two hundred cases—about a quarter of them pro bono—and virtually all of them were resolved successfully in one way or another. About sixty-five percent of her clients kept their noses clean until their cases were adjudicated one way or another, and the court exonerated their bail. Because Jasmine mostly stuck to sidewalk dealers peddling herb on street corners and other nonviolent offenders, the judges eventually released them on their own recognizance until the case went to trial or the ADAs offered probation for a guilty plea. The remaining thirty-five percent, Jasmine had to surrender for one reason or another, but only ten actually tried to run, all except one, a collateral client. With the occasional paid assistance of an informant or one of Zachary's classmates at John Jay, Jasmine and Zachary nabbed all but one absconder, who the cops eventually collared. So in her five-year history, Jasmine had forfeited only one bond. And even then, she never questioned her decision to post his bail until Malcolm Booker disappeared.

Jasmine pulled her SUV into the parking garage near the courthouse, then made her way to the agency. She now had a storefront office off the Grand Concourse right across the street from the criminal court building. She walked into the office and found Diana making color photocopies of an eight-by-ten of her seven-month-old infant, Zoë, who lay sleeping in her stroller beside her desk. Diana made no attempt to hide her task.

"Do you know how much those fuckin' cartridges cost?" Jasmine said.

"Of course I know. I order them. And lower your voice before you wake up Zoë."

Jasmine grabbed the photos out of the tray and shoved them toward Diana. "What the hell is she doing here anyway?"

"My babysitter's kid has a nasty stomach virus, and I don't want her to catch it."

"This is no place for a kid, Diana, and you fuckin' know it."

"Jesus, Jas, it's only for today."

Before she could respond, a loud roar came from down the hall. "Get me Malcolm Booker's file," Jasmine said before leaving the reception area to investigate the ruckus. The office used to be a pediatric clinic, and Jasmine had converted the large waiting area into a rec room for her pro bono clients. Lorraine found someone to donate a huge television set, and Jasmine sprung for cable service and an Xbox, which someone quickly stole. If a client could not or would not get a job or go to school, she preferred they hang out at the agency rather than on the street waiting for trouble to turn the corner.

Jasmine reached the rec room in time to catch the next wave of hollers. Five guys were on their feet, crowded around the television. "That's a dude!" one yelled. "See the Adam's apple right there?"

"Nah, that's just the shadow of her chin. Look at 'em legs. She's a woman."

"I'm telling you, man, that's a dude!"

Jasmine hovered behind the crowd of men, bobbing her head to catch a glimpse of the screen—another one of those ridiculous episodes of *The Maury Povich Show* where he paraded a dozen or so women in front of the audience so its members could guess which of them—usually only three—actually were born female. She held her tongue and headed to her office. At least they weren't fighting over the damned remote.

Diana appeared behind Jasmine with a green folder in hand. Jasmine took it and headed to her office. "You're welcome!" Diana yelled.

When she entered her office, Jasmine sat at her desk, lit a cigarette, and opened Malcolm's file. She went directly to the enforcement section to read Zachary's notes. According to Zachary, Malcolm had been home for his curfew check the night before his scheduled court appearance. Jasmine knew instantly that he had fled that night. Had Zachary chosen to double back, he would have returned to the basement apartment to find Malcolm gone, and then Malcolm would have had only a slight jump on them instead of thirty-six hours. But Jasmine did not fault Zachary for not double-checking. Although Malcolm sometimes missed curfew, he always called from the home telephone to check in. When he felt particularly zealous, Zachary would turn around and go back to the house just in case Malcolm decided to bounce after checking in. According to the curfew check log, Zachary found Malcolm at home each and every time. So why should he suspect anything unusual the night before a date in court?

Still, Jasmine could not shake the feeling that had she done the curfew checks, she would have sensed something. Despite all the model behavior, she would have opened herself to the possibility of trouble. She grabbed a legal pad and made a note to herself to circulate a new memo to the staff, instituting a new supervision and enforcement policy. If the staff knew or at least anticipated that a client's next court date might actually lead to a disposition of his case, they had to indicate that in the agency court book. The book was a typical red diary, with one page devoted to each day, in which they tracked court appearances for all the pro bono clients and briefly summarized what happened. For the most part, on any given date, only one client's name would be listed with a simple note—*Adjourned*—with the date of his next court appearance. At the weekly staff meeting, the court book was circulated so that each person could review and update it. In the new memo, Jasmine would write that from now on if a disposition seemed likely at the client's next court date, she herself would do the curfew check the night before.

Calvin had already saved Jasmine the trouble of finding out if Malcolm had missed court because of being rearrested, so she moved to the next step on her mental skip-trace checklist. Without needing to consult his file because she knew the number by heart, Jasmine called the court part in which Malcolm's case had been meeting. So many times a defendant seemed to FTA when he had only been late, had forgotten about the date, had gone to the wrong courtroom, or some other silly, benign reason. Although Jasmine doubted that this happened to Malcolm, she had to call the courtroom and be sure that he had not shown up later. She reached the clerk, who confirmed that he never appeared in court. Jasmine finally accepted that either Malcolm Booker was on the lam or something terrible had happened to him.

Had he been a commercial principal, Jasmine would have called his indemnitor next. She rarely ran across people like Adam Brozi's parents in the business. Chances were that being unversed in the American system of bail, when the Brozis attempted to place their wayward son on a plane to Albania, they did not understand that had Calvin and Jasmine not thwarted them, they would have lost the home they had worked themselves to the bone to afford. Unlike Adam's parents, people who put up collateral—especially in the form of cash or real estate—to bail out a friend, relative, or lover usually cooperated with her.

But Jasmine bailed out Malcolm on her own dime. Having no indemnitor to call, she moved to her next step: contacting all those he interacted with on a regular basis to see if they had any information about his whereabouts or might be complicit in his disappearance. Of course, Jasmine first called Crystal at her job at the Cablevision headquarters in Bethpage, Long Island. Jasmine expected Crystal to be cooperative. Not only did she not have any collateral at stake, she always wanted him to do the right thing no matter how hard it might be, believing that the righteous path would always keep Malcolm from any and all dangers, moral and physical alike. If Crystal Booker knew that her brother had disappeared, she would search for him herself and worry to death if she failed to find him.

"You have reached Crystal Booker at Cablevision headquarters . . ."

"Shit." Jasmine did not like this. According to Malcolm, Crystal prided herself on her attendance and punctuality at work. Jasmine knew that she was not merely away from her desk, but had not gone to work today. Still, she left a message on the off chance that her gut was wrong. "Crystal, this is Jasmine Reyes, and I suspect that you already know why I'm calling, so I need you to get back to me as soon as you get this message." She rattled off both her cell phone and direct office numbers, even though she knew Crystal kept her business card in her wallet.

She retrieved a fresh dial tone and called the clinic. "Suárez CHC, this is Lisa, how may I help you this morning?"

"I'm looking for Macho, I mean, Malcolm Booker."

"Malcolm's not in."

Jasmine waited, but Lisa offered no more information. Why had she not given her the option to leave a message or to call again later? Jasmine carefully chose her next question. "When will he be back?"

"I'm sorry, miss, I don't know."

"Well, is he in today? Is he out sick?"

"Would you please hold, ma'am? I have another call." Lisa put her on hold.

Jasmine hung up. Clearly, Lisa knew something she did not want to reveal, and Jasmine could not tell if that was a good or bad thing.

She made one last call to Zachary and left him a message telling him what she had already done, and asking him to call everyone else in Malcolm's file that might provide information. Jasmine scanned the file one last time, jotted a few notes, and took her search to the streets.

According to Malcolm's file, he still resided with Crystal in the basement apartment of a private house in Castle Hill. Jasmine parked her SUV around the corner. She wanted to call the house to determine if anyone was home without having her number appear on the Bookers' Caller ID display. Jasmine dialed for directory assistance. "Yes, ma'am, I'm trying to call a number and keep getting an 'all lines are currently busy' message."

"And what is the number?" asked the operator. Jasmine rattled off the Bookers' number and waited for the operator to dial it for her. The line rang, and the operator said, "Seems to be clear now, ma'am."

"Thank you." The operator disconnected herself, and Jasmine stayed on the line. After a few more rings, the voice mail answered the call. Satisfied that neither of the Bookers was home, Jasmine hung up, got out of the Escalade, and walked to the house.

Jasmine turned into the sloping driveway and bent down to peek through the window. The place seemed empty, so she proceeded to the door. Jasmine checked her surroundings. Because this was a working-class neighborhood of two- and three-family homes, she gambled that most of the home owners and their tenants were already at their nine-to-five jobs. She pulled open the screen door.

Jasmine avoided breaking the law to do her job, but she had no qualms doing so to locate an absconder. Not only had she assumed all the financial risk of posting bail, she hardly could rely on the police to help her locate a jumper. If sometimes she had to trespass or misrepresent herself to find a missing principal, Jasmine readily took on the risk of arrest, too.

She grasped and twisted the locked doorknob. Then Jasmine ran her hand down the door. It was made of aging wood that had been repainted multiple times, and she could easily kick it open, but she did not want to leave behind evidence of her presence in the quiet neighborhood. Because the door had been installed sloppily, she could remove it from its hinges, but that would take time and tools, which also entailed more risk than Jasmine wanted to take. She decided to pick the lock. A former client who had been charged with criminal trespass and possession of burglar's tools had once admitted to her that he sometimes bought locks at the hardware store and practiced his "trade." Without telling anyone, Jasmine had started to do the same, knowing that the skill would come in handy.

She reached into her bag for lock picking tools. Rather than buy them and leave a paper trail, Jasmine made her own, using household items that would garner no attention if her pocketbook spilled and instructions she found on the Internet. To make several picks in different shapes, she sanded the end of several sturdy safety pins until they were smooth. Then Jasmine created a tension wrench by bending the tip of a small flathead screwdriver. She selected the pick that she thought might work best and slipped it into the key hole. Then she inserted her homemade wrench beneath it. Jasmine adjusted the pick until she felt each pin in the lock raise to its opening position, applying pressure with the wrench to keep the pins in place. Within seconds, she heard that affirming click and opened the door.

The doorway led to two staircases; a long column ascending toward the ground-level residence and three wide steps that descended into a laundry room with a door on either side of the washing machine and dryer. Jasmine opened one door and found the utility closet. She tried the other door and found it locked. Knowing this door led to the Booker apartment, Jasmine also picked that lock. She patted the wall until her fingers tickled the light switch.

Like many entrepreneurial homeowners in New York City, the Bookers' landlord had converted a traditional basement for rental income by building walls, installing plumbing and adding upholstery. A once large, open room had been transformed into a small one-bedroom apartment. The living room, kitchen and dining area occupied one space with each "room" separated only by a few feet of polyester carpet and assembly-required furniture.

As Jasmine moved deeper into the apartment, she remembered how she and Jason talked about living in a place like this one day. While other kids bragged about the mansions they would own across the globe when they became rap stars and millionaire athletes, the Reyes twins never dreamed of leaving the borough, let alone being rich. They only fantasized about becoming squares with regular nine-to-fives and a clean place to live, just like this. Jason even cracked about their knowing they had arrived in "decent society" when they could afford to live in Morris Park or Van Nest or some other Bronx neighborhood where the last remaining white ethnics would be leery of the Puerto Ricans next door. He said, "Man, I'd rather we live in a neighborhood where the white people might not want us because they're afraid we're up to no good than stay here where the folks who look just like us do want us 'cause they know *we're* afraid that *they're* up to no good!" When the Reyes twins were kids, "rich" looked to them like an apartment with heat and hot water, a civil service job, a reliable if used car, enough money at the end of the month for a trip to the movies, and neighbors who minded their own business. As Jasmine looked around the Booker apartment, it still looked good to her.

She walked over to a wardrobe against the wall by the sofa and opened it. By the feminine clothes hanging in it and the array of pumps lined against the floorboards, she guessed that Crystal slept on the sofa and let Malcolm have the bedroom. She made a quick stop in the bathroom and opened the medicine cabinet. Among the expected assortment of tubes and bottles, Jasmine saw two vials of prescription medication for Crystal Booker. One vial contained a drug called meperidine, and the pharmacist directed her to use it as necessary. The other prescription was for hydroxyurea, and she had to take it regularly. Out of curiosity, Jasmine pulled her scanner pen from her pocketbook and ran it across the labels. The she refocused on her primary objective.

The large mural on the door confirmed that Malcolm had the bedroom. In blocky white letters, he had vertically painted his tag, BOUK X. Jasmine opened the door and was stung by the odor of spray paint and marker pens. With graffiti on every inch of three walls, Malcolm's room resembled a New York City subway car of the late seventies. He devoted the fourth wall to photos of graffiti from all over the globe and torn from e-zines, photocopied from art books, and printed from the Internet. Against this wall stood a rack of spray paints, and beside it a bookshelf of other graffiti supplies, markers and tips. The only bedroom furniture was a twin bed with a maple bookshelf as a headboard and a matching desk.

Jasmine sat on the bed and scanned the books on the shelf. Most were old piecebooks, with virtually every page filled. She also found magazines, books, and videos about graffiti, including the classic *Wild Style* and the documentary *Style Wars.* Malcolm also owned an extensive collection of about fifty Homie dolls, crowded along the top of the headboard like spectators at a parade. Jasmine picked up one that reminded her of Jason, with his backward baseball cap and sleepy eyes. Only when she looked closer did she realize that this Homie had a word written across his oversized T-shirt: *Painter*. A chill crept over Jasmine, and she placed the doll back so fast that she knocked over a few others. She hastily put them back in place and leaped from the bed.

Jasmine then walked to the desk and yanked on the center drawer. It was locked. She reached into her pocketbook for another pick and the tension wrench and jiggled it open. In the drawer she found an Apple iBook, and the sight of the computer gave her mixed feelings. On the one hand, it might contain information that could lead to Malcolm's whereabouts. On the other, its presence suggested that he left abruptly.

As Jasmine waited for the laptop to boot, she opened the other desk drawers and rifled through the random papers tossed into them. She came across several check stubs from the Suárez Community Health Center, where Malcolm last worked. The most recent was two weeks old.

Then Jasmine found carbon copies of registration forms from both the School of Visual Arts and nearby Baruch College, the public college in the city's university system known for its business programs. Malcolm had enrolled in two art courses at SVA, each an introduction to Photoshop and Illustrator. The course at Baruch, however, was on database management systems. The eclectic coursework struck Jasmine as odd. Malcolm never expressed an interest in computers. Maybe he wanted to learn how to use a computer to do what he ordinarily did by hand, but why would such an unapologetic artist subject himself to the technicalities of databases? The tuition for the SVA courses was paid with a credit card, while the class at Baruch was paid for with cash. Jasmine dragged her scanner pen over the pertinent data on the registration forms to give to Zachary. As the inputting figures flashed across the green screen, she tried to find logic in Malcolm's academic choices.

Soon after Jasmine had bailed him from jail, Malcolm and Crystal had stopped by the agency to thank her. They were the first pro bono clients to ever do that. In fact, like a mother bringing her troubled child to meet with the school principal, Crystal wanted to discuss her brother's release agreement. Alternating her verbal jabs between Malcolm and Jasmine, she endorsed the conditions that Malcolm find a job and pursue some kind of additional education, but she wanted him to study something practical. Crystal virtually demanded that Jasmine modify the agreement to require her brother to register for a job-training program or enroll in a trade school. "I'm all for this curfew, Miss Reyes, but if you think he's going to be home by ten o'clock every night while he's still running with those wall crawlers, you got another think coming," said Crystal. "And tell him, Miss Reyes, that he needs to get an education in something that can lead to a career."

Initially, Jasmine failed to respond. It had stunned her to hear a woman of the same age refer to her as Miss Reyes. And she had no clue what the hell Crystal was talking about. Before she could ask, Malcolm interjected, "I have a career. Writing is my career."

Crystal scoffed. "A criminal career, getting yourself arrested for stealing paint and scrawling your name over other people's property."

"Damn, Crystal, you make it sound like I be tagging up on people's houses and shit. I've never done that."

"You hear this, Miss Reyes? He's a vandal with a conscience. Please!"

"Yo, I only tag up on public property. Like handball courts, mailboxes. . . ."

"Still ain't your property. . . ."

"It's public property," argued Malcolm, chopping his hands from left to right as he made each point. "That's property owned by the public. I'm part of the public so that's my property. That's my handball court, my mailbox . . . that's why I put my name on it."

Crystal gave Jasmine an exasperated look. "You see the way he thinks? You see what I have to deal with? I've been putting up with this shit since he was fifteen." She turned back to Malcolm and said, "Public property is paid for with tax money. You don't have a job, Macho. Which means you don't pay taxes. So guess what? You don't own shit! Me, I have a job. I pay taxes. So you know what? That's *my* mailbox, and I don't want you writing your name all over it."

A mischievous grin broke out on Malcolm's face, and Jasmine clasped her hands in front of her mouth to hide her own smile. She saw much of herself in Crystal. And much like her own brother, when bombarded with such relentless logic, Malcolm could only concede or reposition or some combination of the two. "Look, let me not front—I might throw up something on the wall of a building, but it's not like I go over the windows of people's apartments. I wouldn't be feelin' it if someone tagged up on my house so I don't do that. I mean, some heads don't care about that and do it all the time, but that's not how I get down."

"Do you see what I'm saying, Miss Reyes?" Crystal pleaded. "This is why he needs to have a full-time job during the day and go to school at night, learning something that'll enable him to earn a decent and honest living." She looked at her younger brother with reservation clouding her small, dark eyes. "Don't you get it, Macho? If the cops catch you out there vandalizing, it's over!" Then Crystal turned to Jasmine and said, "Honestly, Miss Reyes, sometimes I think we should have kept him in jail. That ADA Mackie ain't playing with him. If he gets busted while out on bail, she's going to throw the book at him. My brother might have been better off staying on Rikers Island until he copped a plea or went to trial."

Jasmine no longer saw herself in Crystal and finally spoke. "No one is ever better off staying in Rikers Island, Miss Booker." She kept to herself her conflicted feelings about Crystal's request. No, she could not deny that "making graffiti," as it was referred to in New York penal law, was illegal. But Jasmine also could not deny Malcolm's desire to do it. Because of her own experience with Jason's unquenchable passion, Jasmine accepted that efforts to stop Malcolm were futile. "Do you mind if I speak to your brother alone?"

Crystal minded but conceded. After she left the room, Jasmine told

Malcolm, "If you do it, I don't want to know about it." And the release agreement between them remained as originally drawn.

In the beginning, Crystal blew up Zachary's cell phone with many false alarms. "It's ten minutes past his curfew, and he's not here," she would yell. "You people put him back out on these streets, but you're not watching him like you said you would." Usually, Malcolm walked through the door five minutes later. In the spring, Dr. Suárez increased his workload, giving him enough projects to fill a thirty-hour workweek, and when the summer came and his new classes started, Malcolm began to honor his curfew. Every time Zachary begrudgingly reported this at the weekly staff meeting, Jasmine never failed to tell him, "I told you so."

Jasmine concluded that Malcolm enrolled in the computer course at Baruch to throw his sister a bone. She mentally calculated the cost of all three courses and wondered how Macho could afford to take them all. When, where, and how did Malcolm get a credit card to pay for the courses at SVA? Jasmine shuffled the papers in her hand, looking for statements, and found none. Did he even have a bank account? With her scanner pen Jasmine captured the last four digits of the credit card then turned her attention to Malcolm's computer.

Unfamiliar with Mac computers, it took a few minutes for Jasmine to acclimate herself to the operating environment. Eventually, she figured out how to determine which applications had been installed onto the computer and how to access them. She searched for an address book or calendar but found nothing. She clicked on an icon of a giant palette labeled "BOUK X" and found several folders. She selected one named "Suárez CHC," then clicked on a random file. A software program called Adobe Photoshop launched and opened the file. A colorful logo for the center filled the computer screen with the slogan *Don't Talk About It . . . Be About It.*

After checking that file name's extension, she opened other files in the Suárez CHC folder that ended in the same letters. The artwork Malcolm did for the community health center exploded across the monitor, from health brochures to professional letterhead. Jasmine decided that she did not need copies of these and clicked each one closed.

Then a particular file named "BURN" with a different extension caught Jasmine's eye. The only file of its kind in the Suárez folder, she clicked on it. Neat columns of text burst across the computer screen. She scanned the headings of each column. *First name. Last name. Date of birth.* Jasmine presumed that she had happened upon a database of the clinic's patients until she scrolled down and saw the list only contained twenty-three names. Surely Dr. Suárez had a much larger clientele than that, especially since he had a policy of turning no one away because of their inability to pay. Either the file had to be incomplete or the patients on this particular list represented only a segment of the population served by the center. Why would Malcolm have incomplete data on his home computer, let alone patient information? Perhaps he accidentally copied the file to his own portable drive or storage disk, but the possibility rang hollow. These patients meant something to Malcolm. The twenty-three individuals on this list had something in common that set them apart from the other patients in Suárez's practice. The more she thought along these lines, the warmer Jasmine became, and when she finally gave in to the instinct to copy the database file to her flash drive, she felt like a lighted match.

She spent another half hour searching through Malcolm's laptop. Finding nothing that piqued her instinct, Jasmine eventually logged off. She unplugged her flash drive, collected her other surveillance tools, and dropped them in her pocketbook. As she stood up, she took one last look around Malcolm's bedroom. Jasmine walked over to the utility shelf and scanned the cans of spray paint for their colors. Not one of them was Jungle Green, and for some reason, that brought her down.

Jasmine turned toward the door when her eye caught a sliver of black peeking out from between Malcolm's mattress and bedspring. She crossed the room, crouched down, and extracted a black hardcover journal. Recognizing it as another one of Malcolm's sketchbooks—or piecebooks, as he preferred to call them—she opened it. Malcolm had shown her some of these sketches when they were just outlines in gray pencil. As she thumbed through the first dozen pages, they burst with color from a set of markers with felt tips and translucent ink. Jason had explained to her that writers used these designer pens in their piecebooks because they often existed in the same colors as Krylon paint.

Trying to show off, she had dropped this knowledge on Malcolm, who added, "And we also like 'em because they bleed and blend on the page just like the paint might on the wall when we're fading." Still, he grinned at Jasmine, appreciating what understanding of graffiti she did have.

Why was this particular book hidden under the mattress instead of lined along the headboard with all the others? Jasmine tucked Malcolm's piecebook into her pocketbook and headed for the door. Given where he had hidden it, no one probably would miss it. Malcolm himself did not think to take it with him to wherever the hell he went. That was, if he voluntarily left in the first place. Jasmine still believed that he did. All the evidence she had collected pointed to an abrupt departure, but nothing suggested that Malcolm had been abducted. He ran on his own volition, albeit suddenly.

Jasmine cracked open the door upstairs. She peeked and waited, assuring herself that no witnesses were around before crossing the threshold into the driveway. She closed the door and reinserted her tension wrench into the keyhole. Before leaving she had to return the lock to normal so Crystal would not realize that someone had tampered with it and perhaps call the police. Checking over her shoulder one last time, Jasmine climbed back into her SUV and drove back to the office.

While stopped at a red light, she took a closer look at Macho's piecebook. The initial pages were mostly of his tag, BOUK X, in an array of styles and letters. Then she came across the completed caricature of his sister with her name spelled CRISTAL in bubble letters like champagne. Cristal wore a power suit and ghetto jewelry exactly like her real life inspiration. Jasmine turned the page to where Malcolm had drawn another caricature of PRIESTS. The name seemed familiar, and she wondered if he might have mentioned it in passing. In Malcolm's caricature, PRIESTS' face was cloaked by a hooded sweatshirt and he carried a canvas bag of spray cans slung over his shoulder. He had to be one of Macho's writing associates, and she had read his name in the enforcement notes that Zachary wrote in Malcolm's file. Jasmine made a note to have Zachary track down PRIESTS and ask him a few questions.

Then Jasmine found the caricature of herself that she never knew existed. Malcolm had never shown it to her perhaps because it remained incomplete. In pencil, he had sketched Jasmine like a superhero, flying in the air with her fist raised above her head and hovering over a pantheon of faces that included the assistant district attorney, the judge presiding over Malcolm's case and even the mayor of New York City. He gave her a modest costume of bootleg jeans and a men's sleeveless undershirt. The only color in the piece appeared in the moniker he had given her—SUPERJAS. Malcolm outlined the letters in white and filled them in with red, slanting them so that they appeared to move in her character's wind. He drew jagged lines across the center of the vowels and curled the ends of all the letters, making the A seem like a cracked heart turned on its head.

The delivery truck driver behind her blared his horn and startled Jasmine. So absorbed in Malcolm's art, she had not noticed that the traffic light had turned green. "Calm the fuck down," she yelled out the window. To make her point, Jasmine took her time placing the book in her bag before finally giving in to the mounting dissonance behind her.

Business had been slow that week. Three days had passed, and no one had called requesting bail. Jasmine wondered if those fuckers at Liberty were price shearing again. She headed to the reception area to ask Diana to do something she absolutely hated—call them pretending to be a potential client.

As always she peeked into the rec room as she passed it. Epps and Peña were playing with the new Xbox. Sitting alone and quietly by the window, Malcolm scribbled away in his piecebook. Jasmine walked over to him, sat next to him on the sill, and peeked over the spine. To her surprise, Malcolm clutched the book to his chest. He had never done that before, so she waited for a sneaky grin to appear on his face that never did.

"I can't see?"

"It's not done."

"Never stopped you from showing me your stuff before. C'mon, let me see."

"I said no."

"Fine." Jasmine started to walk away from him. Then she stopped and turned around. "If you let me have a peek, I'll tell you a secret."

Malcolm eyed her. "Tell first."

Jasmine walked back to him and sat on the sill again. "You want to know how I know so much about graffiti? You know, for someone who's never done it."

"Yeah."

"I had a brother who was a writer."

"What was his tag?"

"Ah, that was years ago. You wouldn't remember him."

"If you don't tell me, you don't get to see what I'm doing."

"His tag was REY squared."

"Wait. Hold up. REY Two or REY Squared?"

"Like I said, REY Squared."

"Oh, shit!" Malcolm jumped to his feet.

"Wuh?" asked Peña.

Jasmine grabbed his hand and yanked down. Malcolm remembered that this was secret, although he seemed confused as to why. "Never mind." He sat down again and looked at Jasmine with eyes ablaze. "Your brother was REY Squared!" he said, as if announcing that she had just won the lottery.

"You've heard of him?"

"Hell, yeah, I've heard of him. His shit was dope." Then Malcolm became serious. "Is it true what they say?"

"What do they say?"

"That they killed him while on lockdown for beating the shit out of someone. No one's really sure why he did it, but they say that the guy was connected in some way. The kid of a congressman or senator or some shit, so they had REY Squared beat down on Rikers Island. Some say that the COs did it, and others say that they just looked away while some gangbangers took him out."

Jasmine shook her head. "I didn't even know folks realized who he was known, let alone make him the subject of urban legend."

"So it's not true."

"No. Jason committed suicide while on lockdown. He hanged himself."

"Damn, what the fuck for?"

She just shrugged. Jasmine almost joked that she wished the rumors were true. But then Malcolm would want to know how she could say a fucked-up thing like that, and she would have to explain to him that she actually was the reason Jason was dead. Even though Jasmine caught herself before saying that awful thing, she realized what a loser she was for having even thought it for a second. "Yeah, the real story's pretty bad, but nothing like what's circulating out there on the streets. But remember, Macho. You can't say anything."

"No doubt."

"So are you going to show me what you're working on now or what?"

Malcolm dropped his piecebook so Jasmine could see his work in progress—a caricature of his sister, Crystal. "This is cool! How come you didn't want to show me this? Acting like you're doing some Da Vinci Code *type shit for the Illuminati or whatever."*

Malcolm shrugged. "I guess I didn't want you to see it until I was done 'cause . . . I don't know. You remind me a lot of my sister."

"Is that good or bad?"

"Both." They laughed. "For real, y'all both work mad hard, but you don't, like, take care of yourselves."

"Working hard is a way of taking care of ourselves. We can't take care of ourselves unless we work hard."

"See! That's something Crystal would say. But all I'm saying is what's the point of working so hard if you're not going to take care of yourself so you can enjoy it?"

"Who says I'm not enjoying it?"

"Yeah, whatever."

They laughed again, and then Jasmine asked, "What makes you say that Crystal doesn't take care of herself."

Malcolm closed his piecebook. "She'd be mad if I told you."

"I'm not going to say anything to her. You know that."

"Nah, she told me not to say anything to anyone. Crystal's real proud and private and everything. I mean, you're mad cool and all, Jasmine, and I owe you a lot. But some stuff has to stay between fam."

Jasmine admired his loyalty to his sister, even though it hurt her for him to draw that line between them. She had that with Jason and understood it. Still, she had to say, "At least tell me it's not serious."

"Nah, nah, nah. It's not serious. We're gonna handle our business, and take care of each other. It's just that sometimes it's hard to know exactly what's the right way to go about it."

Damn if she did not understand that, too. Jasmine patted Malcolm's knee and stood up. "You'll show me the piece when you're done?"

"No doubt."

"Cool." As she turned her back on him to walk across the rec room, Jasmine had a weird feeling. Was the piece Malcolm showed her the one he truly had been working on when she asked to see it?

FOUR

Diana handed several messages to Jasmine as soon as she walked into the office. "Calvin called," she said as she cradled her sleeping infant in her other arm. "He sounded really pissed." Pleased to deliver this news, Diana enjoyed drama almost as much as she liked to think of herself as the keeper of Jasmine's secrets. The little information Diana had about her employer's personal life had taken over five years of constant meddling to accumulate, because Jasmine offered her nothing. She did not even know that Jasmine once had any siblings, let alone a fraternal twin brother.

"Tell me something I don't know." Jasmine sifted through the stack of messages. On Calvin's message, Diana had checked every other option that scrolled along the bottom of the slip. *Telephoned. Please Call. Will Call Again. Wants to See You.* Calvin probably intended these things, but Jasmine suspected that he had said none of them and that Diana had merely assumed. At least, he had not stopped by the agency.

"And some doctor called you. Nathalie Done Something. The message is in there somewhere." Rather than ask the doctor to spell her name, Diana had scribbled it across the slip just like that—*Dr. Nataly Done Something. Called. Please Call. To reschedule appointment.* "You didn't tell me you had a doctor's appointment, Jasmine. If you had, I would've reminded you."

"I didn't forget the appointment." Sometimes Jasmine hated Diana's occasional attempts at efficiency as much as she disliked her usual lackadaisical approach to work. "I had a lead on Poncho Ferrer and couldn't make it." Flipping through the assorted messages from public defenders, probation officers, and other criminal justice personnel, Jasmine headed to her office.

"You want me to call her back and reschedule?"

"Nah, I'll do it myself."

"You see how you are, Jasmine?" Diana yelled. "You bitch about my work ethic, but then you don't let me do shit for you."

"Quiet, you'll wake the baby." Arriving at her office, Jasmine pulled out her keys to unlock the door. "All I need from you now is to prepare for the staff meeting."

"Whatever."

Jasmine entered her office and closed the door behind her. She threw Calvin's message in the trash bin and debated whether to call back Nathalie Dieudonné. It was so bizarre for Jasmine to run into her again after all these years, and at the courthouse of all places.

Nathalie had lived in the apartment next door to Jasmine's family. At first, her parents asked the gangly Haitian teen to watch the twins several nights per week, but eventually Nathalie took to checking in on them on her own accord. She brought them *pain patate* with rum syrup or offered to take them to the playground. Then she left for college, and the Reyes twins never saw her again.

Then last week Jasmine went to the courthouse to meet with an ADA at the request of the public defender for one of her pro bono clients named Richard Lawrence. She thought the prosecutor finally would agree to offer probation for a guilty plea if she heard about the defendant's progress under pretrial supervision from Jasmine herself. During their premeeting conference call, Richie's PD, a feisty Italian kid from Brooklyn named Calapano, said, "This particular assistant district attorney doesn't trust a word of progress reports that come from the ATIs. Says that these nonprofits have a stake in writing glowing reports and making every client look like the second coming of Gandhi. That the more sentences they score that don't involve prison time, the better their chances to get funding from the state and foundations, which I think is absolute bullshit. . . ."

"Yeah, well, I'm not running a nonprofit organization here anyway," Jasmine explained. "My sole concern is that he keeps his court dates until his case is adjudicated one way or another. It makes no difference to me if Lawrence gets or avoids time." She hated meeting with ADAs, and although the opportunities to sit with them had been rare, she avoided them as much as possible.

"Oh, I didn't realize that," said Calapano. "I thought you ran one of those agencies like CASES or the Fortune Society or something." He obviously was a big fan of ATIs and unafraid to show it.

"Nope, I'm a bona fide, for-profit, bail bond businesswoman. All that matters to me is that Lawrence doesn't jump bail."

"I've never heard of a bail bond agent—male or female—who hires a social service director and writes progress reports for every court appearance. And what about that guy who does visits to Richie's home every night to enforce his curfew? A curfew! I mean, no bail bond agent takes forfeiting a bond casually, but your competitors are hardly going to the lengths you do to prevent it." Calapano saw right through Jasmine. "You care a lot more than you say, Miss Reyes, and it's not about getting the bond exonerated and your bail money back either. And that's why I want us to meet with ADA Nelson, so she can hear directly from you how well Richie's doing under your supervision, nonprofit or not."

Swayed by Calapano's passion, Jasmine agreed to the meeting. She understood that public defenders were overloaded with cases and had almost no resources to adequately argue them, which made her want to go to bat for this Calapano, since he went the extra mile for Richie Lawrence. So Jasmine went to the courthouse and convinced ADA Nelson to offer him five years' probation.

Afterward, she bounded down the courthouse steps in a spurt of contained resentment. She should have been happy, even proud, over what she had accomplished, but the meeting only reminded Jasmine of how life had cheated her. Sure, Calapano thought to reach out to her and set up the face-to-face with the ADA. Whether out of exhaustion or apathy, the typical public defender did not think outside the box, much less take any initiative on behalf of a client. Still, in making Richard Lawrence's case to the prosecutor, Jasmine did in one hour what Calapano had not been able to do in five months. She had everything it took to become a lawyer except the fuckin' chance.

And then, as if destiny wanted to rub her face in it, Nathalie Dieudonné reappeared before her. "Jasmine?"

"Yeah?"

"It's Nathalie. I used to babysit you and your brother. Oh my God, Jasmine, it's so good to see you." The lanky teenager with troubled skin and Payless sneakers had grown into a sophisticated professional with polished makeup and Stuart Weitzman pumps. Still, Nathalie had that blinding smile and those vibrant eyes, and for a moment Jasmine remembered how she had introduced them to zouk, soca, compas, and other French Caribbean music by slipping her Kassav' and Boukman Exsperyans CDs into her portable player and dancing for them in their cluttered living room, only stopping to explain the lyrics. She made it a game for Jasmine and Jason to listen for cognates and guess if the familiar word in Creole had the same meaning as the word with the same sound in Spanish. For those few seconds, it was good for Jasmine to see Nathalie, too.

But then she asked, "And how are your parents?" Her tone revealed to Jasmine that Nathalie understood just how problematic her parents had been. Until then it had never occurred to Jasmine that Pedro and Marisol's antics were public knowledge. Because no social worker or police officer ever came knocking on their door when they disappeared, she had always assumed that they had managed to keep their hustles secret. Perhaps in her youthful naïveté, Jasmine assumed that Nathalie's constant presence at their apartment reflected her ignorance of her parents' lifestyle, but now she realized that the teenager's frequent visits actually were an acknowledgment of the destructiveness that transpired next door.

"Gone." Jasmine provided no details. She did not have any to offer. Because they disappeared together, Jasmine always suspected that they were both dead, even killed by someone they had cheated. At least they were dead by now. Even if she did know exactly what had happened to her parents, Jasmine would have kept the details to herself. She never ascribed to the silly practice of divulging useless information.

"Oh, I'm sorry."

"Don't be."

"And Jason? How's he?"

Jasmine hesitated. "He's gone, too."

Nathalie did not respond, but her face said it all. *You're alone?* Yes, she was alone. So what? As were thousands of people in this godforsaken city, and some of these people who were alone were surrounded daily by friends, relatives, and colleagues.

"What brought you back here?" Jasmine asked.

"Well, after I graduated from Johns Hopkins, I came back to go to med school at Columbia, and now I'm an OBY/GYN."

"That's peace," said Jasmine, and she meant it. Nathalie deserved to be successful. Some people worked hard to acquire good fortune, and others attracted it with their unshakable goodness. Jasmine found it rare for both qualities to exist in the same person, and yet on both counts, Nathalie had earned only the best in life. "So you came back and decided to stay, huh?"

"Yes, I even opened my own practice. I have an office here in Wakefield on White Plains Road and another in Jamaica, Queens, on Hillside Avenue."

"What brings you to the courthouse?" Jasmine snickered. "You don't have a malpractice suit on your hands, do ya?"

Nathalie laughed. "No, I was actually invited by the district attorney to participate in a brown-bag luncheon with the assistant district attorneys about doctor-patient privilege, undocumented immigrants, confidentiality laws, and that kind of thing."

As much as Nathalie tried to downplay it, her status both impressed and bothered Jasmine. "Wow, you're buddies with the Bronx DA?"

"Depending on what month it is," said Nathalie, grinning. "I'm married to her son. This month I'm back in favor."

"Oh." Having had her fill of Nathalie's blessings, Jasmine walked around her and descended a few steps. "Well, I won't keep you from your luncheon, and I have to get back to work myself, so . . ." Feeling like a shit-heel, Jasmine stopped, turned, and offered Nathalie her hand. "Nice seeing you again and to know things are going well for you."

Nathalie took her hand and said, "Are you okay?"

"I'm fine. Just a bit under the weather," Jasmine replied. "I got one of those hard-to-kick summer colds because of the schizophrenic weather. You know, one day you can fry an egg on a sidewalk, and the next you have to swim through freezing rain to get to work."

Nathalie reached into her purse and pulled out a business card. "Come see me for a checkup."

Jasmine took her business card and fished into her lapel pocket for one of her own. "No, I'm okay. I just need to take a day off, drink some tea or something." She probably could kick the fuckin' thing if she got more than five hours of sleep each night, gave up her pack-a-day habit, cut down on the greasy fast food, and substituted a glass of warm milk for her bedtime whiskey. She found one of her cards and handed it to Nathalie.

"Actually, there's no such thing as a summer cold," said Nathalie. "You may actually have hay fever, and that can lead to sinusitis or asthma if you don't treat it."

Jasmine tried to laugh off her uneasiness. "Thought you said you were an OBY/GYN?"

"Well, medical school requires you to dabble in a little bit of everything before you choose a specialty." Nathalie looked down to read Jasmine's card. "Bail bond agent? You're a bounty hunter?"

"Not exactly." With all that she had to do, Jasmine had neither the time nor temperament to explain to Nathalie the difference and relationship between the two professions. "Can't explain it right now since we both have to run. . . ."

"Yes, I'm so sorry. So I tell you what. I'll call you to make a date for lunch, and you can explain it to me then." Nathalie dashed up the courthouse steps, pausing once to flash Jasmine a smile and wave good-bye.

Nathalie had called the next morning, and because Diana had another one of her damned child care emergencies, Jasmine herself answered the phone. Nathalie managed to maneuver small talk into a medical interrogation. Having been caught off guard, Jasmine confessed to not having seen a doctor in years, and Nathalie insisted that she come in for an examination. By the end of the call, Jasmine had not only scheduled an appointment for the following week, but had also capitulated to lunch after the examination. Bad enough she agreed to let the woman who used to fix her bowls of Chef Boyardee in a past lifetime poke around her privates, but after that Jasmine had to sit across a diner booth from her and act as if they were girlfriends. How was she supposed to handle Nathalie's inevitable questions about the sordid past Jasmine wanted nothing more than to forget?

Nathalie may have been only four, maybe five years older than Jasmine, but they had nothing to talk about. Nathalie went to medical school. Jasmine barely graduated junior high school. Nathalie had a husband. At best, Jasmine had a fuck buddy, who acted distant in front of his cronies, only to throw a fit when she left before they could cuddle. True, they had both gone into business for themselves, but there the similarities ended. Nathalie had founded a practice on a vocation that involved caring for those in the process of giving life, but Jasmine had built an enterprise that consisted of reinforcing the principle of innocent until proven guilty for those who more often than not *were* engaged in some kind of wrongdoing at the time of their arrest. The telephone call with the tip on Poncho Ferrer's whereabouts could not have come at a better time, and Jasmine redirected her attention to executing his surrender.

Jasmine crumpled up Nathalie's message and hurled it into the aluminum trash bin that read *Your Suggestions Please*—a Christmas present from Diana. She spent the next hour making and returning other calls. She worked a few bonds, verifying the employment of both defendants and indemnitors, negotiating collateral with potential new clients, and arranging to return collateral to existing ones for whom the bond had been exonerated. Then after consulting her appointment book, Jasmine made reminder calls to a handful of defendants who had court appearances scheduled the following week. Then she made similar calls to those principals' indemnitors. Diana generally handled this task, but once a person skipped one court date, he and the person who put up the collateral to bail him landed on Jasmine's list. Pro bono clients were in constant touch with her staff, so they received reminders all the time, whether Lorraine mentioned it during a counseling session or Zachary warned them at an unannounced curfew check.

Jasmine moved on to the paperwork. She opened and skimmed all her mail except for the envelope she knew contained the court's notice of bail forfeiture in Malcolm Booker's case. Jasmine already knew that she had one hundred and eighty days to surrender him before she actually forfeited his bail. She wrote Malcolm's name across the front of the envelope and dropped it into her outbox for Diana to file.

Then Jasmine reviewed the docket sheet Diana had retrieved from the courthouse every other week. Finally, she happened onto some good new. Two of her collateral principals were no longer her responsibility. One had been RORed, and the other had finally made a plea deal with the prosecutor. With both cases disposed, she could move to have the bail money returned. From the form sorter sitting on the corner of her desk, Jasmine selected and completed motions to have the bond exonerated in each case. She added them to her outbox for Diana to file with the respective courts.

Diana whisked into her office, holding a stack of papers in her hand. Without a word, she dropped them into her inbox and collected the papers in the outbox. Jasmine barely noticed Diana until she heard the office door click behind her when she left. She checked her watch, and realizing she had less than an hour before the weekly staff meeting, Jasmine turned her attention to the memoranda in her inbox.

She read both Lorraine and Zachary's reports on the pro bono clients and saw no flags. Then Jasmine signed bonds for several clients who had provided sufficient collateral, and finally reviewed the application for a detainee under the agency's "pro bono initiative," as Zachary referred to it with alternating tones of sarcasm and nonchalance, depending on whether those in earshot were members of law enforcement.

Name: *Felipe Miguel Rivera* Nicknames/Alias(es): *Felicidad*

Sex: *M* Race: *Hispanic (White)*

DOB: *01/24/82* Birthplace: *Bronx, New York*

Date of Arrest: *07/28/2006*
Bail Amount: *$2,000*
Charge: *PL 230.00 Prostitution*
Offense Class: *B Misdemeanor*

Parents: *Antonio Rivera, Sears delivery truck driver; Elvira Rivera, mail processing operator for Con Ed. Reside at Noble Mansion Apartments.*

Candidate is estranged from parents due to their disapproval over his sexual orientation.

Sibling(s): *Rafael Rivera, construction manager in Deltona, Florida.*

Notes: *Candidate is a nonviolent but repeat offender with transsexual tendencies. Currently resides on Manida Street in Hunts Point with two other known prostitutes and plies his trade within blocks of his residence. Possesses diploma from Christopher Columbus High School and associate degree in business technology from Monroe College and several years experience as an administrative assistant for various businesses.*

Jasmine braced herself for a contentious staff meeting over Rivera's application. By the small, rounded handwriting and detailed yet objective notes, she knew Lorraine had conducted the preliminary interview. The possibility of counseling a transsexual probably made her salivate. Jasmine expected Zachary to take issue with supervising a male repeatedly charged with prostitution, however, especially since his johns were not janes.

The meeting time came, and Jasmine opened her office door to allow in her staff. "Diana, round everyone up," she yelled down the corridor before going back to her seat. A minute later, Jasmine's staff of three—along with Diana's baby sucking on a bottle in her stroller—assembled in their usual places around her desk. Zachary insisted on the middle seat, while Diana preferred to remain close to the door. By default, Lorraine took her seat on Zachary's right, moving the chair as close to the wall as possible. Jasmine handed Diana the folder of signed bonds and said, "Okay, folks, unless anything has changed since everyone wrote your reports, we're looking at a short meeting."

Zachary said, "Yesterday Bernie Epps's urine came up dirty."

"For what?"

"Weed."

"So?" All the release agreements prohibited any kind of drug use, but Jasmine had no intention of surrendering a nonviolent offender for smoking a blunt with his boys. Maybe medical experts preferred to erase distinctions between "soft" and "hard" drugs, but she found it impractical, even foolish, to treat cannabis and hashish as if they were as potent as cocaine and heroin. "Did he cop to smoking herb during his preliminary interview?"

"Yeah, but . . ."

"C'mon, Zach, you're wasting my time with this. When coke or something else equally hard shows up in his system, then you holler at me."

"Fine," said Zachary. "When he does something stupid under the influence or goes down for possession—"

"Then we'll surrender him," interrupted Jasmine. "Otherwise, I don't want to hear about it." Jasmine reached for Rivera's file. "Now what's the story with this Felipe Rivera?"

Lorraine said, "Felicidad Rivera—"

"Rivera's a fuckin' she-male."

"Watch your mouth around my kid."

"Excuse me, Zachary, but I was talking."

"He thinks he's a chick with a dick," said Zachary. "A beat cop from the four-one busted him giving head to some trucker off the Bruckner Expressway."

"I said to watch your mouth around my kid."

"She's a freakin' baby. She doesn't understand what I'm saying."

"Both of you, knock it off," said Jasmine as she took another glance at Rivera's file. "So let me guess. The judge wouldn't ROR him because of the four previous charges."

"Right."

"With a bail of only two grand, why didn't his pimp just bail him out?"

"According to him, he doesn't have one," said Lorraine.

Zachary scoffed. "What it does have is the monster."

"He is not an *it*."

Zoë began to cry, and Diana leaped to console her. "You see what you guys did?" She lifted her daughter out of the carriage and to her shoulder.

Jasmine cringed at the baby's shrieking. "You know what, Diana? Just take the baby out of here, please. We don't need you for this part of the meeting."

"You mean I'm not gonna get a say in whether we bail out some diseased freak who might be hanging out here around my daughter?"

"No, because you don't bail out anyone. I do. And I told you that this is no place for a kid regardless of who's here or not." The baby screeched louder, as if to defend her mother. "Now take Zoë out of here."

"Fine." Without placing the baby back into her stroller, Diana grabbed it and shoved it toward the door. "I don't need this shit."

"Watch your mouth," Jasmine deadpanned. "There's a child present." She waited for Diana to slam the door shut and then went back to business. She scanned the preliminary screening form once again. "Lorraine, you don't have any mention here of any medical condition, let alone HIV."

"I just found out. Felicidad called me this morning from jail—"

"Collect," said Zachary.

"—knowing that we would be meeting today to decide whether or not her application for community supervision continues to the next step in the process."

"Did you just say *her*?"

"Zachary, please." Sometimes he acted like such a fuckin' kid, and Jasmine had to scold him as such. "Lorraine, you were saying?"

"She admitted to me that she was HIV positive and a recovering addict. She also assured me that she's been clean for the past three years."

"So give me your honest assessment of the risk here, Lorraine."

"Felicidad—"

"Christ."

"Jasmine!"

"You'll have your say in a minute, Zach, so just chill out, will you?"

"Thank you," said Lorraine. "Felicidad—that's the name he, I mean she, prefers, and that's the name I'm going to use—currently lives with a group of other women—"

"Real women. They're hoes, but at least they're real."

"—who are also prostitutes. Her roommates and the other sex workers in the area were forbidden by their pimps to pool their money to raise Felicidad's bail."

"So where's . . ." Jasmine could not bring herself to refer to this man by such a feminine name. "Where's Rivera going to live if we post bail?"

"He's going straight to the whorehouse on Manida Street, then right back to the street spreading that nasty fuckin' disease," yelled Zachary. "And don't think he won't lie to us and tell us he won't. He already lied in the preliminary interview."

"She's a target in jail, Jasmine. Any day now, someone's going to hurt Felicidad or worse if we don't get her out of there soon. Not to mention that the treatment for inmates with HIV is atrocious." Lorraine leaned forward in her seat to emphasize her last point. "And let's be honest here. If not for the gender issue and medical condition, we wouldn't be debating this. Since when do we have qualms with bonding out a nonviolent principal charged with a Class B misdemeanor?"

Jasmine finally looked to Zachary. "She's right."

"Give me a fuckin' break, Jasmine. If this cat doesn't move back in with the same hoes, he's going to be sleeping on the goddamn street. His parents threw his ass out when he was sixteen."

Jasmine guessed, "Because of the cross-dressing thing?"

"I don't think cross-dressing is the correct name for it," said Lorraine.

"The point is," Zachary said, raising his voice over hers, "is that Rivera's got no place to live. He's got a deadly medical condition. He's got mental problems. Say what you want, Lorraine, but these aren't trivial issues. Who the fuck's going to give Rivera a job swishing and swaying the way he does? Jasmine, I'm telling you, the dude is impossible to supervise. And no offense, Lorraine, I know you're good at your job and all, but you can't help him either. We need to pass on this drama magnet."

"I can speak for myself, Zachary."

Jasmine ruminated on both their arguments. She wholeheartedly agreed with Zachary; Rivera's HIV and transsexualism were not minor issues by a long stretch. Yet Jasmine had no doubts that these same things placed him at great risk on lockdown, just as Lorraine insisted. Rivera could die just as violently on Rikers Island as in the streets of Hunts Point. Jasmine did not know whether to hold his initial omission against him or cut him slack for telling the truth before they had made a decision. What motivated Rivera to come clean—his conscience or his circumstances?

Jasmine closed Rivera's paperwork and placed it in her bag above Malcolm's file. Wanting to return to that search, she said, "The only way to settle this is for me to interview Rivera myself." She knew that neither Lorraine nor Zachary was satisfied with that decision, but neither would dare to question it and antagonize her into siding with the other. "Y'all know I hate to go to fuckin' Rikers, so when I make this call, it stands. I don't want any arguments. If there's nothing else, let's end this meeting and get back to work." Lorraine and Zachary rose to their feet and exchanged smug glances. Jasmine said, "Zach, hang back a minute. I wanted to go over your enforcement notes on Malcolm Booker."

Zachary retook his seat. "Okay."

"I've looked through them, and I see you've listed the names and addresses of some of Macho's friends."

He clapped his hands with arrogance. "Once I heard Booker ran, I jumped on that. I paid a visit to all his homies, and no one even knew he was missing."

"All of them?" Jasmine scrawled the name PRIESTS on a yellow note sheet, tore it off, and handed it to him. "Does that name mean anything to you?"

Zachary read the note. "I've seen it before, but I can't remember where."

"I think it's the name of a graffiti writer. Someone Macho knew."

"Right!"

"So why is there no contact information for him in the file?"

"He probably is in Booker's file. He's just referred to by his real name. I mean, you don't think a graffiti writer is going to reveal his tag to me, do you?"

"I guess not." But she still expected Zachary to make an effort to learn these things. Then again, she remembered how secretive Jason and his writing buddies could be. They had their names everywhere, and yet no one knew who they were. Their ability to be at once visible yet anonymous always amazed and impressed Jasmine. As she made a quick list of the names of Malcolm's friends who were mentioned in his file, she wondered if she should call Calvin to run them through Graffitistat. This reminded her of the database she had downloaded.

"Is that all?"

"One more thing." Jasmine reached into her bag for her keys and removed the flash drive. "There's a database on here with twenty-some names on it. Give it to Diana, have her print out the names and contact information for you, and go check them out."

"Database of what?"

"Honestly, I'm not sure. It seems like they're patients of that clinic Macho was working for." Jasmine held out the flash drive, and Zachary took it from her. "But the clientele for that place has to be much larger than that, so see if you can find out what it is the people in that database have in common and what that's got to do with Macho."

"What makes you think they have anything to do with Booker?" asked Zachary. "Where did you get this database?"

"There's got to be a reason why these particular names were pulled from the rest of the patient list, and Macho had them on his computer," she replied, ignoring his last question. If she told Zachary that she broke the law to get her hands on that file, he would feel entitled to do the same and actually would. Zachary gave her enough of a headache with his occasional *NYPD Blue* tactics without Jasmine placing her own questionable tricks on display. "Maybe it's nothing at all, but I don't know, I've got this feeling."

Zachary took the hint and scoffed. "Yeah, we all know about you and your feelings."

"Can you handle this or what?"

"No doubt." Grateful for the meaty assignment, Zachary made for the door.

"Good, because I don't think I'm going to be able to find Macho without your help, Zach." He grinned, saluted her with the flash drive in his hand, and swept out the door. It annoyed Jasmine to have to stroke his ego like that, but the bottom line was she truly needed help with this case. Her instincts rarely led her astray, but she had to own up to the fact that her feelings might get in the way on this one.

* * *

They survived by doing odd jobs both within and beyond the law, from washing windows and bagging groceries to picking pockets and boosting knickknacks from one store to sell them to the one across the street. Then one night someone broke into the apartment and stole the rent money they barely managed to scrape together that month. Jason took to the streets on a desperate crime spree while Jasmine went to plead with the landlord for more time. Before going she had boiled hot water to bathe herself and put on her cleanest jeans and T-shirt.

"Where the hell are your parents?" he boomed at her. "I'm going to call social services."

"You can't do that!" Jasmine cried. "They'll separate us." Kids like them—not at their age, of their background, under their circumstances—did not stay together, let alone get adopted. In two more years, the law would consider them adults, and they would be freer to seek whatever legitimate help might be available to them. Until then they had to hide from the government to keep one another. As siblings, as the last in their family, as fraternal twins with that indescribable bond, they had to stay together if they were to survive. "I'll do anything you want. Just please don't call ACS, okay?"

"Get in here," he ordered. As Jasmine walked past him into the apartment, she caught the landlord unzipping his pants. Jasmine never doubted that her life would come to this. The best she could do was delay the inevitable. She even felt a little lucky to have made it to sixteen before fate kicked in.

But as Jasmine sunk to her knees, she wielded the little power she had left. "If I do this for you on a regular basis, will you let me and my brother live in the apartment rent-free?"

The landlord pondered the offer. "You have to come every week. And you have to do whatever I want."

"No! I won't. . . . You can't take me from back there. And I won't do any of your friends. They have to pay."

"If you want free rent, I have to take a cut. Like thirty percent."

"Fine. But don't get it twisted. You're not my pimp. I'm my own boss. You can refer people to me, but I'll go with who and when I want. If I do, you get your thirty percent for as long as we live here."

"And you come to me one a week," he said, locking the front door and sliding the security chain into place. "Starting now."

When she told Jason, he cried. Even when it became obvious that their parents were never coming back, Jason had suppressed his feelings. But then he cried as he should have then with deep sobs that made him convulse. Jasmine held him in her arms and tried to console him. "The good thing is that I won't be out there, walking the streets. If I have to do this, better it be this way. I mean, I'm never going to be some high-class call girl meeting rich men in fancy hotels, but at least I won't have to deal with all the ugly shit that can happen to hoes on the street." And then she heard the hiss. "Jason, you hear that?"

She tapped him on the shoulder until he finally lifted his face off her chest. "What?" He dragged his sleeve across his runny noise.

"You see that, Jason? Things are already looking up for us." Jasmine pointed to the radiator. For the first time in months, it sizzled and gave off steam. "The son of a bitch finally gave us heat."

Jasmine felt a need to prepare to interview Felipe or Felicidad or whatever. She never had to interact with one of those kinds of people. Even when she herself was turning tricks, she only took to the stroll for four critical days. Instead, she just turned a bad situation into a lucrative opportunity.

When Jasmine went home that night, she got on the Internet and did some research. Not knowing what term to use, she entered *transsexual* into the search engine. After generating scores of porn sites, she backed up to her original search and added the words *mental illness.* Jasmine scanned the results until she came upon a familiar term: *DSM-IV.* Wondering where she had seen that term before, she opened another window and entered it into the search engine. *DSM—IV—Diagnostic and Statistical Manual of Mental Disorders*—that massive book published by the American Psychiatric Association. Several years ago, Lorraine had asked Jasmine for a small supply budget for her "department." Jasmine almost nixed the idea in the interest of frugality, but instead she asked Lorraine to list the things she wanted. The ever-meticulous Lorraine composed a five-page memo describing a dozen items. Not only did she hunt for the lowest prices, she made a case for each request, and placed an asterisk next to the four she believed to be the most important. Lorraine wrote, "If you're willing to reimburse me, I can purchase some of the requested material myself using my personal credit card and student discount, which will enable the agency to save considerable money."

Impressed with—and even a bit surprised by—Lorraine's thorough professionalism, Jasmine approved the entire request, which included the latest edition of the *DSM*. For a bleeding heart, the gal had a business mind, and Jasmine respected that tremendously.

Jasmine wished she had thought to borrow Lorraine's *DSM* before leaving the office and hoped she might find relevant excerpts on the Internet. As she scanned the search results, the term *gender identity disorder* caught her eye. After several clicks, Jasmine came across a definition taken from the *DSM-IV,* and it seemed to fit the Rivera case. According to the definition, a person with gender identity disorder (or GID) exhibited two behaviors. The first was a persistent desire to be—and maybe even an insistence that she or he already is—of the opposite sex, and the second was an unrelenting discomfort with his or her actual sex. For a diagnosis of GID, both traits had to be present. Jasmine made a note on Rivera's file to ask him questions to detect the existence of "a profound disturbance of the individual's sense of identity with regard to maleness or femaleness." She could not confuse that with the simple rejection of stereotypes by sex. For that, someone might say that Jasmine herself had GID, which was fuckin' ridiculous. She had too many issues as it was, so thank God this wasn't one of them. Just because on most days Jasmine did not like being a woman, she never forgot she was one. Who in the criminal justice system would let her? Nor did she ever want to be a man.

When it came to Felipe/Felicidad/Whoever Rivera, Jasmine only cared about one thing, and that was determining whether whatever problems he had were too big for the agency to handle. Jasmine did not give a shit if Rivera wanted to wear makeup and put on a dress so long as he did not come to the office in such a getup. Hell, one bad experience with the guys in the rec room would put an end to such bizarre public displays anyway. But on her hierarchy of concerns, his penchant for cross-dressing ranked the lowest. Chances were that Rivera had been and would continue to get HIV treatment via Medicaid. In fact, Medicaid might also cover any psychiatric treatment Lorraine would find for him if she were to post his bail. Such services were never adequate, but millions of New Yorkers managed to avail themselves of them without landing in prison. Only after the interview would she be sure, but Jasmine saw nothing on paper about Rivera's medical and mental condition that made him untreatable.

She had another question to answer: Was Rivera amenable to community supervision? After all, what he did behind closed doors only concerned Jasmine in certain respects. One, whatever he did in the privacy of his own home—or on the streets, for that matter—could not be against the law. Two, his home environment should not compel him to break the law. Basically, Rivera had to find another line of work and move into another place. Jasmine would not post his bail if she sensed he had the slightest reservation about retiring from tricking or distancing himself from his roommates in the sex trade.

Then again, his hooker friends might be the only community Rivera had, which brought Jasmine to the ultimate question. Was Rivera a flight risk? With two and a half Gs on the line, those odds carried the most weight of all. It always proved to be a difficult call with principals who had no one and everyone at once. Rivera had parents and an older brother, but they shunned him. Would he decide to jump bail and run to his family for shelter, or would he stay put because of the assumption that he had no refuge in his family? During her interview, Jasmine would have to listen closely to what Rivera had to say—and not say—about his immediate kin.

Jasmine checked his file for his location on Rikers Island. He was being housed at the Anna M. Kross Center, the correctional complex's mental health facility. Jasmine would have made a telephone call to the clinical staff at AMKC, but she did not trust them to diagnose anyone appropriately. She was no expert, yet she could tell that Jason had suffered from severe depression. They could've assigned Rivera there simply because the city had shut down the "gay" dormitory at Rikers.

Just as Jasmine turned off her computer and climbed into bed, her cell phone rang. She flipped the top and saw Zachary's name and number flash across the screen. Damn it, he had better have a good reason to be calling her at this hour. Then Jasmine reversed. No, better Zachary have a stupid reason, because she really needed to dismiss him and try to get some sleep. Without it she would never kick her unyielding cold.

"What do you want, Zach?"

"I want to sit in on this interview with Rivera."

"That's not necessary, Zach. I got this."

"C'mon, Jasmine. . . ."

"How's it going to look to Lorraine if I allow you to come with me to Rikers and I don't bring her along with us?"

"So call her and tell her to be there."

"At one in the fuckin' morning? Yeah, right. Look, Zach, the answer's no."

"You're not going to bail out Rivera?" Zachary's voice sounded giddy.

"No, you're not going to Rikers with me."

"That's not fair, Jasmine. I'm the only one who hasn't spoken to this cat. Lorraine has spoken to him, you're going to see him. . . ."

"Plenty of times you've interviewed people without Lorraine or me meeting with them—"

"Yeah, but I'm the one who has to monitor—"

"Don't fuckin' interrupt me. Even if Lorraine was able and willing to sit in on a face-to-face with Rivera, I wouldn't do it. If anything's clear, this guy's been through enough without having to subject himself to a committee to make bail over a lousy misdemeanor—"

"Then he shoulda thought of that shit when—"

Jasmine cut off Zachary the same way he had just done to her. She turned off her cell phone and flung it across the night table. She had a good mind to check Zachary by posting Rivera's bail without interviewing him, but Jasmine knew she had to meet him. Whether or not she got sufficient sleep, she needed to get to Rikers first thing in the morning, make a final decision, and then get back to looking for Malcolm Booker.

"Good morning," Rivera sang as the CO led him to the seat across from Jasmine. In those few paces, he infused more swish in his hips than she ever had. A five-day growth of sandy brown hair sprouted across high cheekbones, and he wore thick, shoulder-length hair in a loose French braid. Rivera naturally possessed the plush lips, full lashes, and arched eyebrows that starlets often bought from Hollywood aestheticians. By the way his prison greens hung from his bronze arms, Jasmine guessed that he was in good shape. Before taking his seat, Rivera extended his right wrist toward Jasmine. "Good morning, I'm Felicidad Rivera."

Jasmine suppressed her urge to snicker and offered him a brisk handshake. "Jasmine Reyes, Reyes Bonds." She noticed the folded sheet of yellow paper in Rivera's other hand. "What's that?"

"This, Miss Reyes, is for you." Rivera handed her the sheet. "When my defense attorney told me that you wanted to conduct a follow-up interview before deciding to post my bail, I took the liberty of drawing up that little FAQ to facilitate our conversation." Rivera took his seat, glaring at the CO for not pulling out his chair. "Chivalry has gone the way of eight-track tapes and Polaroid cameras, don't you think?"

"I wouldn't know." Was this guy for real? Only a man would have the balls to attempt to direct the interview. Jasmine suspected that Rivera may not be half cooked after all, and actually considered that a strike against him. As she took her seat, she unfolded the paper. Handwritten in soft pencil in a girly cursive down a legal-sized sheet of lined paper was a list of questions.

> 8 MOST FREQUENTLY ASKED QUESTIONS FOR FELICIDAD RIVERA
>
> Q: What the hell am I supposed to call you?
> A: My legal name is Felipe Miguel Rivera, but kindly refer to me as Felicidad. My friends call me Feliz, which is pronounced Felice and means happy in Spanish. I will let you know if you're my friend and are permitted to call me Feliz. Until that time, Felicidad or Miss Rivera will suffice.
> Q: But you're a man, dude.
> A: No. Biologically, yes, I am a male, but in every other aspect of my being, I am a woman (hear me roar!). I may be of the male <u>sex</u>, but I belong to the female <u>gender</u>. Sadly, if my sex had matched my gender, you would not be reading this now.
> Q: So are you, like, gay?

A: No. I may have a penis, but because I'm essentially a woman who likes men, that makes me straight.
Q: Damn, I'm confused.
A: That's okay. It's not your fault. Almost everyone confuses biological sex, gender identity, and sexual orientation. Just remember: your sex is about what you have, your gender is about how you think and feel, and your sexual orientation is about who you love (or want to!).
Q: Okay, let's see if I have this right. Your sex is male. Your gender is female. Your sexual orientation is . . . heterosexual?
A: Brava!
Q: So if you were to hook up with a guy—meaning someone with a pecker—who really felt like a woman inside but still was attracted to you, y'all would be . . . a couple of lesbians?
A. More like a lesbian couple, but you've got it! Now you can call me Feliz.
Q. Cool. I like this game. Can we play again?
A. Oh, honey, this is so not a game. It's a very serious thing called my life.
Q: Yeah, but you're not suggesting that you're, like, normal, are you?
A: ANYONE who tells you that they are 100 percent NORMAL is FULL OF SHIT. I know I've got issues, but it's not because I've got the virus, and it certainly isn't because God thought it'd be a kick to give me the wrong body. That's everybody else's problem.

Jasmine's poker face dropped into a reluctant grin. "So you've got it all figured out, don't you, Felicidad?" To her surprise, she no longer felt silly calling the obvious male before her by such a feminine name, nor did derision creep into her tone when she did.

"Not by a long shot, Miss Reyes, but unlike most people out here,

I'm at least trying," said Felicidad as she crossed her legs at the knee and laced her fingers around it. "Trying to understand myself, if nothing else. It's the least a person can do, you know?"

"So why have you taken to turning tricks?"

"First, I did it to survive," Felicidad answered quickly. Then after a few seconds, she added, "Then it just became a very ugly habit, I guess. An ugly habit used to support an even uglier one."

"You think you can kick it?"

"What I wouldn't give for the chance! Miss Reyes, I'm a modest gal. All I've ever wanted was the Katharine Gibbs fantasy. You know, go to an unpretentious but reputable little training institute, get a decent, secure job as someone's executive assistant, settle down with someone . . . I never wanted the glamorous life. I'm not even looking for the white picket fence and two-point-five kids." Felicidad laughed with a slight rasp dangling from her falsetto. "I'll take the condo in Parkchester and a cute little dachshund."

"And what about your immediate family?"

Felicidad sighed then chuckled. "All I can say is my name is not Vida Boheme?"

"Vida Boheme?"

"Haven't you ever seen that movie *To Wong Foo, Thanks for Everything, Julie Newmar*?" Jasmine shook her head and Felicidad looked at her the way others probably looked at Felicidad all the time. "You know, the movie about the drag queens who drive from New York to Hollywood with John Leguizamo, Wesley Snipes—"

"Wesley Snipes played a drag queen?" If not for the occasional glimpse at the television screen as she passed the agency rec room or the thundering bass of car stereos as they rolled past her during surveillance, Jasmine lived a life devoid of pop culture. She rarely watched TV, getting her weather reports from her co-op balcony and listening to the morning news on the ride to work.

"Unfortunately, no. Funny as he was, Wesley merely played a man in a dress. Anyway, Patrick Swayze plays a queen named Vida Boheme who yearns for his stuffy parents to accept him. Well, like I said, my name's not Vida Boheme."

"You don't want your parents to accept you."

"Miss Reyes, being desperate for a relationship with my parents is how I got hooked on drugs and caught HIV in the first place."

"So it's their fault."

"Absolutely not! I take full responsibility for everything I have done in my life. And one of the worst things I ever did was expect my parents to be something they're not, in the very same way they wanted me to be something I was not. Only when I let go of the idea that I would never be happy if they didn't accept me was I able to get clean. I'm not saying that I don't fantasize about reunions and reconciliations from time to time. But no matter what happens in my life—being the wrong sex, losing my family to find myself, getting HIV—I'm only committed to one thing: being happy. And I am. Especially if you get me out of this hellhole."

Although Jasmine already knew the answer, she still asked, "And what about your brother in Florida?"

"What can I say about Ralphy?" Felicidad paused for effect, since she had said this many times in her life. "My brother is my parents' son, *el pobrecito*."

Jasmine imagined that Felicidad's humor got her through some very difficult situations. Perhaps she would not fare so poorly among the clients that monopolized the television in the agency's rec room after all. Then again, if she had a better home life and job prospects, Felicidad would never need to seek refuge at the office. "Well, I can't do anything for Ralphy. I might be able to do something for you. You know, happiness is a lot easier to come by if you have an adequate and steady income from a legitimate source."

"Amen."

"How're you going to accomplish that living with prostitutes and showing up to job interviews in a dress?" Before she could answer, Jasmine offered, "Is there any other place you can live upon your release?"

"I know a few people I can stay with." Then Felicidad dropped her gaze and shook her head. "But it wouldn't be that much different if I stayed in here."

"If we bail you out, you have to find another place to live. Lorraine might be able to help you." Felicidad nodded obediently. "And she might be able to find you work, but you have to do your part." Jasmine paused to give Felicidad the opportunity to promise to do anything and everything she asked, as the most desperate—and usually the most untrustworthy—inmates did. But she said nothing. Felicidad just folded her arms across her chest as if she were contemplating the offer. Jasmine recalled what Lorraine had said. Jail was hell for the toughest thug looking to build his street credibility, so she could not fathom what Felicidad had to endure. And yet she seriously preferred this hellhole to dealing with her parents or pulling on a pair of slacks. Jasmine asked, "If we can find you some help, will you accept it?"

"Of course!" Felicidad cried. "It's too hard to adhere to my treatment in here. I'll take whatever help your agency can give me."

"I wasn't talking about the . . ." Jasmine could not bring herself to mention the virus. "I meant your gender identity disorder."

Felicidad looked squarely in Jasmine's eye and cocked her head. "I don't even know what that means."

When Jasmine walked into the agency on Monday morning, she found Zachary in the reception area talking to a potential client on the telephone. He put his hand over the mouthpiece and whispered to her, "Would you accept a payment plan?"

"You've got to be kidding me."

Jasmine walked around him to the file cabinet next to Diana's desk as Zachary returned to the caller. "Nah, man, we can't do that." Jasmine opened the drawer and reached for a blank bond form. "Wait a minute." Again, covering the mouthpiece, Zachary turned to Jasmine and asked, "What about a credit card?"

She hit the HOLD button on the telephone. "Think, Zachary. If the guy has a credit card, why doesn't he just get a cash advance and bail his own ass out of jail?"

Zachary gave that point thought. "Maybe it's not his card. Maybe it belongs to a relative. They're the ones putting it up for collateral."

"So why don't they get the cash advance for him?"

He paused again. "Okay, maybe the cash advance limit is not enough. But maybe the credit card is worth the same amount as the bail. Or they have enough to cover the ten percent premium so—"

"Zachary, I don't accept credit cards." As far as she knew, Jasmine was the only bail bond agent who refused them. The idea of someone using a credit card to bail a defendant out of jail always struck her as bizarre, and she decided that the risk and expense involved in accepting them seemed far greater than the convenience they provided. If the City of New York did not accept credit cards for the payment of bail, why should she? She preferred that cashless indemnitors use their credit to buy jewelry or electronics and then fork over the purchase as collateral. "Send him to Reliable," she said, referring to one of her competitors on the Concourse. Jasmine used to also refer potential clients to Liberty Bails until a teenage girl told Jasmine that the bondsman across the street said he could bail out her boyfriend much cheaper. After she informed the girl that it was illegal for bail agents to set their own rates, Jasmine put a call into Calvin. After several weeks of an undercover sting operation, Liberty got hit with a multitude of fines for price shearing.

Zachary shrugged. "I don't know. If you ask me, collateral's collateral. In fact, if I were running this place, I'd take credit before I take cash." Then he noticed the form in Jasmine's hand. With his eyes fixed on the form, Zachary reached over to release the HOLD button on the telephone. "Look, dude, we can't help you. Try Reliable Bonds." He rattled off the number then hung up the telephone. "Who's that for?" Zachary said, gesturing toward the form.

"I decided to post bail for Felicidad Rivera."

"Jasmine . . ."

"I don't have time to argue with you about it. Let's find some common ground on her release agreement."

"Her?"

"And turn our attention to the Booker case, where it belongs."

"You can't be serious."

"Did you find out anything about the people listed in that database I gave you?"

"Hold up."

"No, Zachary, we're not discussing Rivera anymore. If she skips, who loses money? Me, not you. And I'm losing money right now fighting with you about how to run *my* business." Jasmine checked herself. Although she meant every word, she had to throw Zachary a bone. "Look, let's just give Rivera thirty days under community supervision. If after a month you still feel the same—"

"I will."

"Then we'll surrender her." Before Zachary could respond to Jasmine's proposition, someone knocked on the glass door of the storefront. Zachary reached under Diana's desk to buzz in the potential customer. "Where the hell is Diana?"

"Baby's sick."

"Christ." She turned around to see who had entered and came face-to-face with a petite black woman in a rayon pantsuit. "Crystal."

"I need to speak with you."

"Of course, in my office." Jasmine turned to Zachary and asked, "What's your schedule today?" With Diana out for the day, she needed someone else to head to the courthouse to post the most recent bonds she had approved. Each judge would sign and return the documents to Zachary, and he would eventually deliver them to Rikers Island, proving that bail had been posted and permitting the release of those defendants.

"I'm really not supposed to be here right now," he said. "I just came in to pick up some drug tests for tonight's curfew checks. If I don't bounce right now, I'm going to be late for my class."

"Fine. Go." Jasmine followed Malcolm's sister down the hallway. She had meant to pay her a visit to see if she might have any idea where her brother might have gone. By the burn in Jasmine's chest, she knew that Crystal's decision to come to her was a bad sign.

When they entered her office, Jasmine closed the door behind them and said, "Have a seat."

"I'll stand."

"Suit yourself." No, Crystal's appearance was not a good thing.

"Miss Reyes . . ."

"Jasmine." Malcolm had stopped calling her Miss Reyes months ago, and she extended the privilege to his sister.

"Jasmine, I assume you're looking for my brother."

"You assume correctly."

"I'm here to ask you to just please leave Macho be."

"Excuse me."

"Stop looking for my brother."

"What would be the point of that?"

"He's a good guy. A danger to no one, and you know that. Otherwise, you never would have bailed him out of jail."

"And I never would have thought he would skip out on a court date either." Jasmine still believed Malcolm had a good soul. That, more than money, credibility, or even principle, drove her to search for him.

"There has to be a good reason."

Jasmine always believed that Malcolm had a compelling reason to jump bail. She just had no idea what it could be. But whatever his reason, she now also suspected that Crystal knew it. "Like what?"

"I wouldn't know."

"Yes, you would know, Crystal. And you do, and eventually, so will I. You might as well spare us both a great deal of time and emotion by telling me now."

Crystal took a few steps toward Jasmine, her face tight and hard. "Spare *us* both time and emotion? You have no emotional stake in this." Inside, Jasmine protested angrily, but she knew better than to tip her hand just as Crystal was about to reveal her own. "This is just about money to you."

Jasmine went with that. "Ten grand, to be exact." Such a hideous lie, it almost killed her to say it, but she had to maintain her ruthless posture.

Crystal's eyes swelled with tears. "You put my brother back out on the street supposedly to help him. Well, now he's somewhere out there scared to death. The best way for you to help him now, Miss Reyes, is to just leave him the fuck alone." Crystal flung open the door and raced out of Jasmine's office.

Jasmine called after her, "No, the best thing I can do for Macho right now is to find him before the cops do, so where is he?" She started to chase Crystal, and she rushed for the front door in a flurry of tears and curses. "At least tell me why, Crystal."

Without answering her, Malcolm's sister ran outside and jumped into a gypsy cab.

Did Jasmine really need her to answer? Facing five to seven years in prison, Malcolm decided to become a fugitive with his sister's blessing and perhaps even her assistance. It probably was as simple as that. So simple that with some help and perseverance, Jasmine should find him quickly and easily. Except that she really could not convince herself of that at all.

Jasmine overslept the next day and awoke to a nasty cough. Still, she washed and dressed. She rarely took time off from work, and today would be no different. After Crystal's unexpected visit, Jasmine felt pressed to move on her search for Malcolm.

She arrived at the agency after eleven that morning to find Diana sitting at her desk sans infant daughter. "You look familiar," Jasmine said.

"Very funny, Jasmine."

"There's more where that came from. Hear this. What brings you into work on this gorgeous August morning?"

"You know me. I'm the queen of *bochinche*, and Lorraine told me that the drag queen was gonna be here today. No way was I gonna miss that."

After Crystal's visit, Jasmine proceeded to post Felicidad's bail and have Lorraine schedule her counseling orientation. She required her pro bono clients to have face-to-face meetings with both Lorraine and Zachary within twenty-four hours of their release from jail. Each staff member reiterated certain aspects of the individual's unique release agreement. Lorraine conducted a more thorough needs assessment and designed a service plan, which might include individual or group counseling sessions, while Zachary reminded them of mandatory activities, such as curfews and drug tests. Because of Felicidad's unusual "issue," Jasmine requested that her staff be more thorough and diligent. She wanted Lorraine to identify affordable yet intensive psychiatric treatment for Felicidad, if such a thing existed, and Zachary to ensure that she made earnest attempts to find more suitable living arrangements and gainful employment.

"Is she here already?" asked Jasmine.

"Yeah, Lorraine came in early today just to meet with him. Her. Whatever."

Jasmine actually meant Felicidad, but since Diana had not volunteered any outlandish comments about her appearance, she presumed that Felicidad had yet to arrive. "As soon as Zach arrives, tell him I need to speak to him ASAP."

Zachary probably called the colleges to determine if Malcolm had missed any classes. At least, he already should have, but after weighing in again on Felicidad Rivera, Zachary had left without a word about his end of the Booker search. Jasmine did not want to wait for his report. She retrieved her scanner pen, connected it to her computer, and uploaded the data she had captured from the various forms she had found in Booker's room. Using online directories, Jasmine called all three of his instructors at the two schools he attended.

"Hello, Professor Vasquez, my name is Crystal Booker, I'm Malcolm's sister," she said. "I hope you don't mind this call, but I'm just checking up on my brother. Would you please tell me how his attendance in your class has been?"

Of Malcolm's three instructors, Jasmine connected with the two at the School of Visual Arts, and she left voice mail for the third at Baruch College. The ones she reached confirmed that Malcolm had attended all class sessions except for the week he missed his court date. Before that solitary absence, he had even availed himself once or twice of his instructor's office hours to discuss possible final projects. Both teachers raved about Malcolm's talent, discipline, and charisma, and neither indicated that she was aware of anything amiss. Jasmine hung up the phone, feeling the void inside of her yawning. She snatched the receiver. Consulting Malcolm's file, she dialed a fourth number.

"Suárez Community Health, this is Lisa speaking."

"Hi, I'd like to speak to Macho. I mean, Malcolm. Please."

"Malcolm is not in today."

The void tore wider. "Do you know—" A loud clang and the roar of excited men interrupted her. Jasmine dropped the receiver and raced out of her office.

By the time Jasmine reached the rec room, Zachary and two other clients were pulling apart two red-faced men. Someone had tossed a wooden club chair across the room and overturned the matching table. In the corner farthest from the melee stood a frightened Felicidad, looking impeccably feminine in a mocha-colored wig cut in short layers and flawless makeup. She wore a floor-length denim skirt with a lavender wrap blouse and bejeweled mules of the same color.

"What the hell is going on in here?" Jasmine yelled.

"Yo, Jas," said Frankie Echeverría, who Jasmine had bailed out on a typical buy-and-bust case several months ago. He had no savings, a steady job as a mechanic, and sole custody of his seven-year-old daughter. Jasmine rarely clocked the potheads, but she ordered him to undergo outpatient rehab and to submit to urinalysis twice a week. No sense for a forty-year-old man with a decent job and a dependent child to be trolling the streets for weed like a teenage slacker. "That's a woman, right?" Frankie asked, pointing an accusatory finger over Zachary's shoulder.

"Nah, man, that's a fuckin' dude," said Antoine Watkins from behind two other clients holding him back. Just the sight of him boiled Jasmine's blood. The ADA should have disposed his case long ago. Accused of possession with intent to sell with no priors, twenty-three-year-old Antoine just needed something constructive to do with his time instead of hanging with the homies on the corner of 138th and Brook. Upon discovering his knowledge of music and love for talking shit, Lorraine helped him apply to and receive financial aid from a technical college with a program in radio production. Had Jasmine not posted his fifteen-hundred-dollar bond, the City of New York would have spent almost eighty grand to date for housing and feeding him at Rikers Island. Instead of earning his associates degree in communication arts, Antoine would have devolved from petty drug dealing to something much worse. "You're just a faggot."

Frankie lunged for Antoine, and Zachary thwarted him by pressing his forearm to his collarbone. By now Lorraine and Diana had joined the small crowd of male spectators. Lorraine hurried across the room, took Felicidad by the hand, and ushered her out.

"You," Jasmine said to Antoine. "Get the fuck out of here right now."

"What?"

"You heard me. I don't want to see your face for the rest of the day."

"Why I gotta go? He started the whole shit. Me and my boys were just sittin' here when the freak walked in. So this muthafucka says . . ."

Jasmine finally looked at Antoine's friends. Neither one of them were her clients. In fact, she was pretty sure that they were the usual troublemakers from 'Toine's 'hood he would be better off avoiding. "Antoine, any minute now your lawyer's gonna call me to say that, after all this freakin' time, the ADA's finally going to offer you probation," she said. "You don't want to test me before that happens."

Calling Jasmine all kinds of bitch, Antoine stormed out of the agency with his homeboys on his heels like two lapdogs.

Then Jasmine turned to Frankie. "What business you got here?"

Zachary said, "He's here to submit to urinalysis."

"Go handle your business right now," said Jasmine to Frankie. "When you're done, you can bounce, too." She pointed to Diana and Zachary. "When Zach's finished with Frank, you two round up Lorraine, and come into my office immediately."

Within fifteen minutes, Diana, Lorraine, and Zachary filed into Jasmine's office and took their seats like apprehensive schoolchildren. "This is how it's going to be. One, Felicidad is to be referred to as Felicidad, she, her, Miss Rivera, whatever. Not he, him, it, faggot, freak, or any shit like that."

"Jasmine—" Zachary attempted to interrupt her.

"*Two*, any client who violates this rule and harasses Felicidad in any way risks getting surrendered. And three, any staff person who does not enforce these rules or breaks them will be fired. Am I clear?" Lorraine inched her hand in the air. "What, Lorraine? Put your hand down. You're not in class."

"I want to suggest that anyone who reveals Felicidad's HIV status should be fired as well."

Zachary sucked his teeth. "Ain't no civil rights laws protecting—" He caught himself before violating one of the rules Jasmine had just established. "—people like that."

"Maybe not," said Jasmine. "But I like it. And you should, too, Zach. These rules are going to make your job easier. After what just happened, you don't need those knuckleheads to know that she's got the virus as well."

"He . . . Rivera shouldn't be here in the first place."

"Zachary, we made an agreement. Thirty days. I'm going to honor that agreement, and I expect you to do the same. Now are you a man of your word or not?"

He fell silent, and Jasmine motioned for Diana and Lorraine to leave the room. When they did, she said, "You've got to stop sweatin' me on this, Zach. I've got more important things for you to do than babysit Rivera. Have you found out anything at all for me on the Booker case?"

Zachary threw his hands up in the air. "Man, I haven't even begun to track down this priest guy with all the time I wasted on that stupid database."

"Why you say that?"

"It's full of bullshit information. I went to see five people on that list, and not one of them lives at the address given for them. The shit is useless."

His attitude infuriated Jasmine. "And that didn't make you suspicious?" Before Zachary could answer, she said, "Just give me the fuckin' disk."

"What's the big deal with this database, Jasmine?" He leaned forward to reach into his back pocket. "If the information on it is wrong, what else am I supposed to do with it?"

"Nothing, Zach. Absolutely nothing." Jasmine just sighed in frustration. Let Zachary pursue a career in corrections, because despite what his ego fed him, he had no investigatory instincts. She would not waste any more of his precious time by explaining why the imperfect data should have aroused his curiosity. "Just give me the disk."

He slapped the flash drive into Jasmine's open palm. Then Zachary stood up and said, "I'm getting sick and tired of all this disrespect. I don't know how much of it I'm going to take."

"I hired you to do certain things, Zachary, and not one of them is to question my authority." Jasmine reached for her office phone and dialed Calvin's number. "How much you want to bet that when you finally get that, all that disrespect you keep feeling miraculously disappears. Just get back to work." Zachary muttered something and marched out of her office.

Calvin answered the call after the second ring. "Officer Quinones," he said, with an irritated tone clearly intended for her. He had her numbers programmed into his phone, so he always knew she was calling before he picked up.

"Cal, it's Jas." She kicked herself for saying the obvious and falling into his game. If Calvin really did not want to speak to her, he should have ignored her call. "I need a favor."

"Of course you do. Hold on a minute." Jasmine visualized him moving out of the earshot of his partner. "I wouldn't be hearing from you otherwise, right?"

"All right, Cal. What the hell is it that you want from me?"

"I definitely want better than . . . this."

"This?" Jasmine laughed. "Is that what you call it when the boys in blue ask you what's going on between us? Oh, she and I just have *this*. Six weeks ago, you didn't even want *this*."

"You have to understand. I'm a cop. You should have told me."

"I did tell you."

"I had to ask."

"Do you really expect me to believe that you did not already know?" On the beat with his partner in listening distance, Calvin could not speak freely. But in her office behind closed doors, Jasmine could. She sprung to her feet and said, "You already knew, which is precisely why you asked. You already knew when you had asked me, Calvin, that I had been arrested for prostitution. And you already suspected that I had had sex for money before and since that single arrest." The only time Jasmine ever picked a guy off the street, and the bastard turned out to be an off-duty plainclothes cop.

"Look, we've been through all that shit before. You already painted me a picture with all the pretty details. I really don't need to hear it again."

"Did you want me to lie to you?"

For several long seconds, she heard only police radio static, passing traffic, and other background noise. Then Calvin sighed. "Why didn't you lie to me?"

What a hypocrite. He hounded her for *better*—whatever the hell that means—when he barely acknowledged that they were something besides colleagues. Did Calvin even describe her to his peers on the force as a friend? His ambition did not allow it. If he wanted to move up the ranks of the NYPD, the other boys in blue could not know that he socialized, let alone slept with, the "bitch with the death wish." Her own indifference gave an upside to the ugly situation and kept it from becoming truly messy. Calvin's hypocrisy only irked her in principle. She could not have cared less, because the last thing she wanted or needed was an emotional attachment, especially from a man who pressured her for some kind of commitment when he offered nothing in return except sex on his schedule. Her "relationship" with tricks had been more honest and egalitarian.

"Are you still there?"

"I didn't call you to discuss this, and you know it," she finally said. "I called because I need help with the Booker case, and I thought the collar might earn you points with the department."

Calvin mulled over the proposition, and Jasmine tipped her hand. "Macho had a database on his computer that I think is worth looking into."

"Database of what?"

"I'm not sure, and that's why I'm curious. He was doing some graphic design work for that clinic that just opened in Mott Haven."

"Yeah, the one founded by that guy. Sánchez, Suárez, whatever his name is. The one with political ambitions."

"I think it's Suárez. Political ambitions? I never heard that."

"C'mon, Jasmine, it's obvious. He's got this whole Robin Hood operation going on with that clinic. Why would the guy spend all that time and money going to med school to open a free health clinic if he's eventually not going to try to springboard that into a political career? Either that or he's scamming Medicaid. Double billing or inflated reimbursements or some kind of fraud like that."

The way he looked for a racket beneath any act of charity, Calvin made Zachary seem downright idealistic. She remembered how fascinated then incredulous he was when she first told him that, yes, the rumors about her were true. In the beginning, Jasmine wondered if Calvin spent time with her just waiting for her to trip and expose the true scam beneath her occasional willingness to post bail for a principal who had no collateral to offer. Instead of debating with Calvin, however, Jasmine opted to close the deal. "Anyway, I found a database with twenty-some names on it, and it got me thinking. Why would Macho take home information on any of Suárez's patients? He hired him to design brochures and the like."

Calvin thought for a moment. "Maybe they're models," he said. "You know how they take pictures of real, supposedly satisfied customers." But Calvin sounded dismissive of his own theory.

"So he has his secretary print out a contact sheet. That's no reason to filter them out of the master patient database and take it home." Jasmine jumped to her feet and began to pace behind her desk. "And even if he did do that, why are all the addresses in the database wrong?" The more she thought about it, the less she believed that Malcolm had those names and addresses with his employer's knowledge or permission.

"How do you know that?"

"Because I had Zach check them out, and he said the people on the list don't live at the addresses given for them."

"All twenty-plus?"

"Well, after five came up wrong, he quit."

"Figures." Calvin never cared for Zachary, cracking that he watched too many episodes of *Oz*.

"Which made me all the more suspicious. If the information's wrong, why keep it, let alone take it home? And with only, like, twenty-three names, no way is it a complete database of Suárez's entire clientele. My gut tells me that they have something else in common besides incorrect addresses."

"Well, we don't know that just yet."

Jasmine reeled him in. "So can you come to pick up this flash disk and look into these names for me?"

"Yeah, how long will you be at the office?"

Jasmine should have known that Calvin would attempt to leverage this favor into a chance to see her. "Not sure." But she really needed his help. "You know the crazy hours I keep."

Calvin knew her too well. "I get that, but when I get off at four, are you going to be working in the office or do you think you'll be in the field?"

With no leads to follow, Jasmine had no reason to run the streets. Perhaps she needed to stick around the office to ensure that the Felicidad situation remained under control. "Nah, I should be around." Then she remembered another database. "Oh, Calvin, one more thing."

"What?"

"Remember that database you told me you guys have for tracking graffiti artists?"

"Yeah?"

"If I gave you a writer's tag, you'd be able to get his real name for me, right?"

"If he's in the system."

"The name's PRIESTS. Like clergymen. P-R-I-E-S-T-S."

"PRIESTS. Got it. I'll see you about four thirty, five."

"All right." Jasmine hung up and flopped back in her seat. Although she appreciated having Calvin's assistance in finding Malcolm, she loathed having to wait for him to move on *her* case. No sooner had Jasmine retaken her seat than she jumped back to her feet and rushed out of her office.

She bounded around the corner and knocked on Lorraine's door. After she got no response, Jasmine opened the door and took a peek. Lorraine's small but tidy office was empty. She closed the door and went across the hall to Zachary's office and found no one there. On her way to the front, Jasmine popped her head into the rec room. A trio of clients sat around a Spanish talk show. She walked into the reception area and asked Diana, "Where the hell is everybody?"

"Zachary has class today, remember?"

"Right."

"And Lorraine and Felicidad went on a coffee run because you're too cheap to get us a machine."

"Oh, right, I forgot."

Jasmine refused to make the agency *that* hospitable. "It's not the machine, it's all the other shit you have to get with it. Coffee, sugar, cups, stirrers, and all that. In case you've been out too often to remember, you don't work for Martha fuckin' Stewart." Not only did amenities cost, they led to problems such as thefts, fights, and vagabonds looking for handouts. Bad enough clients like Antoine treated the place like a clubhouse, telling their friends to swing by and look them up. Jasmine looked around the place. She had done little to erase the clinical aura of its past life, and that made her all the more restless. It also inspired Jasmine for something to do.

She reached into her pocket for her keys. She unlatched the flash drive and handed it to Diana. "About four thirty, five, Calvin's going to swing by for this."

"He knows what to do with it?"

"Yeah, the file is called BURN. If he asks where I went, tell him I went to go see the doctor."

As per their routine, the twins left the apartment together. Jasmine went to the motel where she met her dates, and Jason took to the streets. That night he decided to take the night off from his petty offenses to go bombing, so she expected to beat him home. After putting in a night's work, Jasmine returned to the apartment, took a long, hot shower, and crawled into bed. She slept until dawn cracked and the odor of aerosol paint awakened her.

When she opened her eyes that particular morning, she found Jason sitting at the edge of her bed, almost bursting with pride and impatience. The second she saw the glint in his eye, Jasmine realized that after all those months of talking, planning, and practicing, he'd finally done it. His first burner. She never understood this obsession of his, yet she embraced his enthusiasm as much as someone could adopt the passion of a loved one that they genuinely did not share. Jasmine sat up in bed and asked him, "Where?"

"You know that wall on the triangle down the block a little from Freeman Street and Southern Boulevard." She nodded. "I killed it!" Jason grasped her arm with a paint-splattered hand. "C'mon, I'll take you to it right now."

"You need to wash up and get some sleep first," Jasmine urged him. "I mean, it's not like it won't still be there in a couple of hours."

"I'm too wired to sleep," said Jason. "And besides, the way things are now, you never know."

"What are you talking about?"

"I'm just sayin' that between the Vandal Squad and these toy haters out there who like to go over pieces just for the hell of it, you can't take shit for granted." Jasmine rolled onto her side and pulled the covers to her ears, but Jason's pacing and rambling made it impossible for her to fall back asleep. "Know what I need to do? I need to boost a camera, take some flicks, and put them in my black book. Shit, I should've gone to the twenty-four hour drugstore and done that first." Jason grasped her covered ankle and shook it like a rattle. "C'mon, Jazzy, get out of bed and put some clothes on!"

"Jason, it's five in the damned morning," she mumbled from under the sheets. "We'll go in the afternoon. If some cops spot us by it at this hour, they're gonna know we did it."

"We?" Anyone else would have become indignant, reminding Jasmine that she had done none of the work or taken any of the risk. But Jason just laughed, lay down at the foot of the bed, and dreamed awake while Jasmine slept.

seven

The last time Jasmine saw Jason's piece, he had directed her to it from his jail cell. Jason got into a tit-for-tat with a few of the neighborhood drifters, where they would steal from the Reyes twins and he would steal from them. Nothing they did protected their apartment from burglars, and word had traveled that the twin urchins in 3C always had some cash around and were easy targets. Eventually, Jason told Jasmine that their money would be more secure in the street. He boosted a cash box from a hardware store and gave her one of the keys to keep with her at all times. For Jasmine's protection, however, Jason kept the location of the box a secret until the police nabbed him for assault. "Go to my piece," he whispered to her on her last visit to Rikers Island. "I buried the box under the *Y*."

Jasmine had no faith that she would find the box, but she waited until the dead of night to do as Jason had instructed. Feeling both fear and relief to be alone at that hour, she scraped the earth beneath the *Y* until her nails grazed steel. After checking over both shoulders, she pulled the key from around her neck and unlocked the box. On sight Jasmine could tell her earnings from his. She always rolled up her cash and wrapped a rubber band around it before giving it to Jason for safekeeping. Jason's bills were tossed among the rings, chains, and watches like a salad. Jasmine scooped up everything in the lockbox and stuffed it in all the pockets she had. Afraid to go home, she waited until the public library opened, found herself a cubicle, and emptied their savings onto the desk.

Jasmine decided to sell the jewelry rather than offer it to a bail bond agent as collateral and risk raising his suspicions about the origins of the eclectic collection. Neither of the twins had ever been married, but they owned three wedding bands between them? Even though neither of them had completed high school, they possessed seven high school and college class rings of assorted sizes? Despite the fact that both their names began with *J*, they had rings and pendants that read *M*, *Junior*, *Rubia*, *G*, *Pisces*, and other letters, nicknames, and attributes that applied to neither one of them? Although entering the bail bond business was far from her mind at that time, even then Jasmine understood that an agent worth his salt would take one look at the jewelry and refuse to post bail. It took Jasmine three days to sell all the jewelry, and she netted a little over a thousand dollars. That covered the ten percent premium that the bail bond agent would charge on Jason's ten-thousand-dollar bond.

But with only fifteen hundred in cash and no other collateral to offer, Jasmine fell way short of the amount she needed to get her brother out of jail. For the next four days, after servicing her regulars at the motel, she walked the stroll like she never had. Jasmine gleaned potential spots to go to from her regulars, asking them if and where they ever picked up women on the streets and pretending that she cared how she compared. Without a pimp and uninterested in securing one for this temporary, emergency stint, Jasmine chose a different strip each day to avoid the ire of established hookers and their pimps.

She started in the Bronx on Lafayette and Tiffany near the monastery. Catching the angry buzz about the young renegade in the wifebeater and straight-legged jeans who stole clients in her tomboyish gear from veterans brazenly advertising their goods in cheap lingerie and tawdry stilettos, Jasmine headed to the Long Island City underside of the Queensborough Bridge the next night. Being a young Latina who looked of legal age and had no signs of addiction on her body, Jasmine pulled in another grand despite fierce competition from the teenage runaways, who'd been lured into the life by pimps who were barely old enough themselves to drink. She overheard one guy coaching an apprehensive girl he had just lured into the life by saying, "Do you want me to take you to Great Adventure on Saturday or do you want to go back to your stepfather in Massachusetts?" That incident killed Jasmine's intense temptation to return to Queens for a second night, despite a regular mentioning that he stopped going there because the police were getting particularly aggressive with their sting operations. The money had been so easy, and Jason had sounded so desperate when he gave her a collect call at the motel, that Jasmine would have gambled another stint under the bridge the following night had she not overheard that.

Instead she headed into Manhattan and wasted her time in Gramercy Park. She failed to compete with the hustlers in cars with New Jersey and Pennsylvania plates, who solicited work by winking at male drivers when they stopped at a red light. Jasmine barely cleared five hundred dollars, and that drove her back to Queens on the fourth night.

The next day she went to see Jason to report on her progress and lift his spirits. Of the ten thousand dollars she needed to post his bail, she only needed to raise three thousand more. Jasmine imagined the grin of relief that would overtake his sunken face when she promised to free him in three to five days. Despite being exhausted and sore from her increased workload, she hummed to herself the entire bus ride to the jail. She even considered buying a cheap used car so she could head back to Gramercy Park for the last stretch. Perhaps the additional expense would pay for itself in the time she gained by not having to take the subway to and from Manhattan. With New York plates she might outdo her competition on the strip, where out-of-state plates might attract police attention and make potential johns skittish. And being in her own car would make Jasmine feel safer. Maybe it would save her time and money to rent one.

Feeling hopeful for the first time in days, Jasmine arrived at AMKC and waited to see Jason. As she fingered the colored pencils she had bought for him, her mind made a rare turn into wishful thinking, and she thought about what they could do with the bail money once Jason beat the rap and the court returned it to her. Jasmine viewed the entire affair as a warning to buckle down and fly right. If she and Jason could survive this ordeal, surely they were smart and resilient enough to find a healthier, safer, and cleaner way to live. Then the idea of going into the bail bond business first came to her. With hundreds of people being arrested then bonded every day at a ten percent premium, the money had to be good. Would the ten thousand dollars in returned bail money be enough to start?

By the time the corrections officer called her name, Jasmine was committed to researching the idea. If she determined it was doable and conveyed that to Jason, he would cosign with nothing but enthusiasm. They trusted each other that way. Or so she thought, because the second Jasmine caught the CO's eye, she knew that the warning incident had deteriorated into the nightmare experience itself.

For the first time in six years, Jasmine made a pilgrimage to Jason's piece. She parked her SUV on Boston Road and made the short trek to the lot. As she neared the wall and caught a glimpse of its corner, her stomach dropped. The slice of red she remembered had turned black. Jasmine jogged to the lot. "Fuck!" Jason's beautiful but illegal piece had been painted over for a Nike ad featuring a nineteen-year-old point guard from Detroit who skipped college to enter the draft. Jasmine walked toward the ad like a train wreck, both loathing it and not being able to look away. She looked at the bottom of the mural to learn who was responsible—Burn Masters Syndicate.

What would Jason think of this? On the one hand, he understood the transient nature of the illegal art. He had come home one morning depressed after discovering that another writer had gone over his first throw-up. After months of hitting bus shelters, lampposts, and mailboxes with a black marker and practicing on the back wall of their bedroom, Jason finally allowed himself to graduate and apply his new skill on the streets. Jasmine would watch him as he prepared himself, filling in the black outline of REY^2 with silver paint and psyching himself up. "I can't get up on some toy shit," Jason said, speaking like a rank-and-file employee at a Fortune 500 company who finally had earned a slot in the management training program.

After weeks of practice he finally painted his throw-up on a school playground, and several months later another writer named ILL-1 painted over it. When Jasmine realized that Jason knew the identity of his rival, she said, "I'm surprised you didn't track him down and beat his ass."

To her surprise, Jason shrugged. "He didn't mean no disrespect."

"But he ragged you," she answered, using the same term she always heard him say under these circumstances.

"He went over me with a dope piece." Jason handed her a photo of ILL-1's creation. "I can't front if he's a better writer than I am."

While he used one more color than her brother had, the interlocking letters looked the same to Jasmine. If Jason had not told her his name, she would not have been able to distinguish the *I* from the *1* from the *L*s and read it for herself. "I don't see what the big deal is."

Jason laughed, attributing Jasmine's blindness to ILL-1's artistry to sibling loyalty. "Yeah, well, how am I going to sound, whining about his going over my throw-up with a burn like that?"

Looking at the Nike ad painted over Jason's burn, however, Jasmine could not imagine that he would have been so resigned to see his creation "buffed," as he would put it. And not with a superior piece by a fellow writer either, but a multinational corporation desperate to "keep it real" by doing something completely antithetical. She glared at the wall. It looked no different from any other sneaker ad in a hip-hop or sports magazine. Having photographs of Jason's piece at home offered little consolation, and Jasmine cursed herself for taking so long to visit it. She closed her eyes and envisioned the mural only to be further saddened by the late realization that although she had buried him at Woodlawn Cemetery, this vacant lot had become the resting place of his disembodied spirit. And now some apparel company with suspicious labor practices had defaced Jason's self-made tombstone to sell two-hundred dollar sneakers to kids living under the poverty line.

Jasmine spit on the mural and spun on her heel. She had to make a second overdue visit to another mural. At least, she knew this one would still be there.

As Jasmine drove to the clinic, she wondered if Malcolm would approve of the Nike mural. She once asked him why he did not pursue his art strictly legally, making a living at what he loved most and did best without any of the risk and consequences of running afoul of the law. Malcolm said, "Any true writer—even one fortunate enough to make a living doing commercial work—needs to keep getting up. There are living legends who do everything from legal walls to video games, and they're still killing the city."

"To keep their street cred," Jasmine guessed.

"No, Jasmine, it's deeper than that. There's a rush that comes from painting at night that you never truly kick. Not if you're a real writer. You crave that rush just as much as you want to be recognized for the piece itself."

At the time, Jasmine just shook her head. "Must be the fumes because y'all sound like you're in serious need of a twelve-step program. Graffiti Anonymous." Then she laughed and added, "I'll let you meet here at the agency."

Malcolm dished a rare scowl. "Nobody would fuckin' come."

"My name is Malcolm Booker, and I am a writer," Jasmine said. "It's been fifty-seven days since I last painted or referred to myself as BOUK X."

He finally conceded a short chuckle but quickly grew serious again. "You know how I'm a hip-hop head through and through, Jasmine? Because I'm not content to just go watch a video or buy an album. I don't want to sit back and observe hip-hop. I don't want to buy it. I need to create hip-hop. To live it. To be hip-hop. But I can't dance, I don't know how to spin, and the only flow I got goes like this." Malcolm mimed spraying BOUK X on an imaginary wall between himself and Jasmine. "That's my rhyme right there," he said, pointing to the invisible tag that hovered in the air. "My break beat. My cut. Write is how I do hip-hop."

She spotted Malcolm's mural from over a block away. The sketch he had shown Jasmine when she interviewed him at Rikers hardly captured the vibrancy of the final result. She parked her SUV directly across the street and made her way to it. As her eyes traveled over the rendition of community faces, the mural struck her as different in some way. Better. Fuller. More complete. But Jasmine had no idea how.

"Beautiful, isn't it?" a deep voice said behind her. Jasmine turned to face a man in his early thirties with dark, shiny hair and large eyes to match. He wore boot-leg jeans so dark they almost seemed like slacks. The mango shade of his dress shirt brought out the reddish undertone of his sun-kissed skin.

"Amazing," said Jasmine. And then she darted her gaze away from him and back to the mural. "This mural, it's . . . wow."

"You should see the van."

"The van?"

"Like a mobile clinic," said the handsome stranger. "Every few months, it tours the borough conducting free tests and giving out health information. A rendition of this mural is on the van."

"You mean a wrap?" Malcolm had explained this to her. "Like the hip-hop record labels do. When they want to promote an artist, they paint the album cover on a van and just drive it around the city."

"Oh, I see that around here all the time, but I never knew what it was called." He grinned and shrugged. "I didn't even know they had a name for it." The man moved closer to her, and he smelled of coconuts. "You know a lot about this stuff?"

"I wouldn't say a lot." Jasmine inhaled deeply, as much to calm herself as to take in more of his delicious scent. "But more than the average person who doesn't actually write or paint."

"But you instinctively know good work when you see it," he said, gesturing to the mural without ever taking his eyes off Jasmine. "You have a natural sense for art, don't you?" She dropped his gaze, finding it too intense to maintain. He continued, "I walk by this mural several times every day, and it never ceases to impress me. You're the first person I've ever seen appreciate it the way I do. You actually stopped to examine it."

Jasmine caught her breath as she thought of a response. She usually tuned out the men she encountered in the street, whether they were attractive or not. They always had something to say yet never anything she wanted to hear. But this man smiled at her with so much genuine interest, Jasmine almost feared that it had less to do with her than with Malcolm's mural. She finally said, "Maybe it's because I haven't come by it in a while, but it seems different to me." A violent scratch burst into her chest, and Jasmine began to cough.

"Are you okay?"

She sucked in a deep breath and swallowed hard to repress the cough. "I'm fine." But she was not. She felt sick and embarrassed. "I just can't seem to kick this damned cold."

The man glanced at the elegant watch on his wrist, and Jasmine wanted to kick herself. But he looked up at her again with another smile. "I have to run for an appointment, but maybe you should stop inside the clinic. I hear the guy who runs it is pretty good and won't turn you away for inability to pay. You take care now."

"Same to you," Jasmine said. She had come to acquire information on Malcolm from his unsuspecting coworkers, but she waited for the man to distance himself before proceeding into the clinic. From the corner of her eye, she admired his taut frame as he swaggered up the street and turned the corner. As she followed his path, Jasmine chastised herself for entertaining the possibility that a man like that would pay her that much attention. At least he had been polite and respectful. She did not come across many people, let alone men, who treated her that way.

Jasmine turned the corner and entered the clinic. Bathed in earth tones and soft lighting, the reception area hummed with a handful of patients. In the farthest corner, two young women with their infants in strollers chatted in Spanish. Across from them sat a guy with long hair and an eye patch, somehow napping through the loud reggaetón tune playing through his Walkman. A prematurely gray-haired man with a large paunch and a walking cane skimmed through a newspaper with an unusual alphabet.

"Good afternoon, how may I help you?" asked the naturally tan receptionist with wispy hair in a loose bun.

Teach my secretary how to greet a potential customer. "Yes, I was just driving by when I noticed your amazing mural," Jasmine said. "Can I speak to the person who can answer my questions about it?"

The receptionist sighed and said, "Well, he's really, really busy right now."

"The person who painted it is here?"

"No, miss, the person who hired the artist is here, but he's busy seeing patients."

"So maybe you can just make an appointment for me at a time that's more convenient for him." Jasmine leaned on the counter as if she planned to take root. She gestured toward the open appointment book on the receptionist's desk. "Does he have any openings for this week?"

"I have a small one right now." Jasmine looked up to follow that same, deep voice. The man she had spoken to in front of Malcolm's mural now donned a lab coat and stethoscope over his clothes. He grinned, then offered her his hand. "You are?"

Jasmine straightened up and accepted his hand. It felt warm and strong. "Jasmine."

"I'm Dr. Adriano Suárez, the founder and director of this center."

As she pulled back her hand, his fingertips grazed her palm, sending a warm current throughout Jasmine's body. "Well, from our conversation outside and the looks of it in here, I can see you're busy. I'll just make an appointment with your receptionist. Maybe we can just speak over the telephone."

Dr. Suárez reached out and placed his hand on her forearm. "Not at all. I have a few moments between patients. Come into my office." Jasmine took a last glance at his receptionist and caught her glowering at her. Although Diana often looked at Jasmine that way when she overrode her stance, Jasmine sensed that this assistant's irritation had little to do with the doctor's willingness to accommodate a walk-in after she had adamantly defended his limited availability.

Jasmine took in the paintings suspended from the bamboo-colored walls as she followed Dr. Suárez down the corridor. She recognized that they were all done by the same artist, and each painting depicted a crowd. In one a group of men of different colors seemed to trade jewels. Another crowd participated in an outdoor party with balloons and instruments. In yet another painting of a party Jasmine recognized white men in top hats and Mexican revolutionaries sporting sombreros and bandoliers. She started to wonder if some of the figures in the paintings were of real people.

"Are you a fan of Diego Rivera, too?" Dr. Suárez asked as he waited in his doorway for Jasmine to reach him.

"Of course," she said, although she had no idea who Diego Rivera was. Jasmine understood though that the doctor was such an admirer of this painter Rivera that he had requested that Malcolm emulate him when painting the center's mural. "And I see what drew you to the artist you had paint the wall outside."

As if he could read her mind, Dr. Suárez said, "Not that he copied

Rivera or that I wanted him to. On the contrary, I was very impressed with his unique style. I just introduced him to Rivera's work and asked him to interpret the themes within his own aesthetic." He stepped aside to allow Jasmine to walk past him into his office.

The doctor's eloquence made Jasmine's head spin with both respect and confusion, and Jasmine headed toward one of the two seats across from his desk. Again, as if he suspected he had overwhelmed her, Dr. Suárez reached out and touched her arm. "Please, join me here," he said, motioning toward the crème leather sofa. The doctor lowered himself onto the plush couch, and if not for his lab coat and stethoscope, he would have seemed as if he were in his living room. Jasmine sat down at the opposite end of the sofa, and the doctor inched closer to her. She fought the urge to slide away. "So you have questions about the mural."

"Has it changed since it's been painted?"

"You have such a keen eye." Dr. Suárez reached for an album sitting on the coffee table. He flipped toward the end of the album and gently laid it across Jasmine's lap. With one hand the doctor pointed to a picture of the original mural. She felt the knuckles of his other hand beneath the album pressed gently into her thigh. "This was taken in February after it was completed." After giving Jasmine an opportunity to examine it, Dr. Suárez turned the page. "And this is the mural now."

"He added faces."

The doctor grinned. "That's right. When Malcolm—the artist—and I discussed the mural, I suggested that he leave space to expand it later. This community is ever-changing, and I wanted the mural to . . ." He stopped, waiting for the perfect word to come to him.

"Live."

"Yes." Dr. Suárez gazed at Jasmine with genuine gratitude. "It needed room to breathe. So when Malcolm first painted it, he had Puerto Ricans, Dominicans, African Americans, Chinese, Koreans . . ." He pointed out the additions as he named them. "Now it also has Albanians, Ecuadorans . . ." The doctor stopped to laugh as he rested his finger on a cluster of people linked at the arms, all of different races and features, yet all wearing green shirts with red triangles with yellow trim, as if they belonged to a team. "When I told Malcolm that Guyana was known as the Land of Six Peoples, he insisted on representing all of them."

Jasmine's eye fell on Malcolm's signature, BOUK X in the lower right corner of the mural. "Seems like you should've added your name to it."

"Oh, no. Suggesting that he leave space to add new immigrants to the mural was my only contribution. The vision was all his." Dr. Suárez pulled the album off Jasmine's lap and returned it to the coffee table. "Are you a patron of the arts?"

"On my income?" She laughed. "Hardly."

"What is it that you do, Jasmine?"

He pronounced her name Jazz-meen, as if she were a foreign supermodel with a single moniker. It made her feel extraordinary, and that left her with the notion that if Suárez had any information about Malcolm's disappearance, he would not share it if she told him the truth. Jasmine already had pretended to not know who painted the mural, so she proceeded with the ruse. Remembering that Lorraine did a brief stint as a counselor at an alternative school between college and graduate school, Jasmine said, "I'm the principal at one of those new schools, and I thought I might recruit Macho to teach art."

"Elementary school?"

"K through eight."

"I can see Malcolm working very well with that age group," said Suárez, as if he had no idea that Malcolm had disappeared. Jasmine took note and just nodded. "When I decided to have a mural painted on that wall, I organized an art contest, and Malcolm won it. On the day of the unveiling, I was floored because the sheet dropped and the mural was incomplete. I had the media there, local elected officials . . . I even had the Parks Department close the street for the day so we could have a health fair. So you can imagine my embarrassment when we unveiled the mural before hundreds of community residents and VIPs, and some of the faces were blank! When I suggested he leave room for the mural to grow with the community, I never meant for Malcolm to create faceless ovals. Just as I'm about to pull Malcolm aside and give him a few choice words, he selects a few children from the crowd, teaches them how to fill in the empty spaces, and together they complete the mural. He showed me an entire new outlook on the concept of art for the people, and I hired him as a consultant to do other design work for the clinic. Brochures, newsletters, and the like," he said.

Guilt seeped into Jasmine's gut. Proud Malcolm had invited the entire office to the unveiling, from his fellow pro bono clients to the staff. He handmade the invitations and sent them to his public defender and prosecutor. Jasmine promised to go, only to spend the day with a raging hangover. The following Monday, she called him to apologize and asked how the event went. Malcolm just said, "It was cool," then rushed off the telephone. The next time he saw her, he acted as if nothing had happened, teasing her for details about the hot date that had kept her from making the clinic's opening and the mural's unveiling.

"So would you mind giving me Malcolm's contact information so that I can poach him from you?" Jasmine stood up to indicate that once Suárez gave her the information, she would be on her way.

Suárez smiled and rose to his feet. "If I lose my consultant to a steady job with full benefits, I can blame no one but myself." He walked to his desk and scrawled something along a notepad. "I'll give you Malcolm's information, but I doubt you'll be able to reach him." He tore off the page and handed it to Jasmine. The number and e-mail address were the same she'd always had on file for him.

Still, she took it, folded it, and stuffed it into her back pocket. "What makes you say that?" Now Jasmine might learn something useful from Suárez about Malcolm.

"He's disappeared."

She never expected him to be so blunt. "Disappeared?"

"Without a trace."

"What do you think happened to him?"

"I'm not sure, but as you can see, he was a graffiti artist—or a writer, as they like to call themselves—and he had a 'crew.' " Suárez squeezed imaginary quotes into the air. Occasionally, Malcolm referred to his "old crew," but she thought he spoke of assorted friends with whom he no longer associated, in an effort to stay out of trouble while on bail. Jason never had a crew, tagging along with whoever invited him to go bombing, yet never pursuing a solid affiliation. The way they lived made it impossible for them to get too close to anyone. "They call themselves the Burn Masters Syndicate, or BMS."

"Sounds harmless," Jasmine quipped.

"Hardly. These so-called writers are street kids, and when Malcolm told them that if he developed some more commercial pieces I would introduce him to several SoHo curators, they gave him the hardest time. Said he wasn't 'keepin' it real.' But if you ask me, I think they were jealous."

"Hating. That's how they put it nowadays." But Jasmine's mind dwelled on the phrase *street kid* and the judgmental tone in which Suárez had uttered it. Having been a street kid, she struggled to hide her offense. But did she have any business feeling insulted? She stole, she tricked . . . but she never hurt anyone, nor did Jason. He sold drugs for a short time. Then a junkie they knew broke into their place while Jasmine slept off the previous night's work and Jason went bombing. He returned home in time to chase the junkie out the window and decided to quit. "I see now what Pa turned people into," he said. And perhaps that rare ethos separated the Reyes twins from the typical street kids, but it failed to erase the dirt they did do to survive. Suárez did not know the first thing about her, but his implicit take on the street-kid ethos still applied to Jasmine, despite whatever boundaries she had maintained.

Suárez stepped around his desk and approached her. "What true artist doesn't want to capture a broad audience and earn a living at his work?"

"You think these Burn Masters harmed this kid?" Malcolm never mentioned to her that Suárez showed interest in directing his artistic career. Perhaps he did not take the doctor's offer seriously, and it was therefore unworthy of mention. "I can't imagine a group of artists wanting to hurt someone because he's successful. I mean, these are kids who paint."

Suárez shrugged. "But these kids who paint, as you refer to them, do so illegally. And isn't illegality par for the course in the hip-hop scene? Violence. Beefs. Isn't that what hip-hop is all about?"

Jasmine had no answer for him. Except for the occasional song she caught on the radio in her SUV or a glimpse of a rap video as she passed the rec room on her way in or out of the agency, she knew nothing about hip-hop. "Thank you anyway for his contact information, Dr. Suárez," she said as she moved for the door. "Maybe Malcolm will reappear safe and sound, and I can have my chance to steal him from you." Jasmine opened the door. "I'll let you get back to your patients."

"Jasmine?" She stopped and turned to face him. "You have a lovely voice, but I noticed outside and even now that you have some kind of nasal condition or allergy. Would you like me to examine you?" Then he flashed Jasmine a smile that made her feel warm in a way she could not afford. "At no cost, of course."

Although her cold had overstayed its welcome, Jasmine knew she had to go. "Yeah, it's an allergy," she said with her hand on the doorknob. "In fact, I'm headed to the drugstore for a decongestant right now."

Jasmine opened the door, and Suárez said, "So how about dinner?"

The idea of a date made her uneasy. Not only did Jasmine come into the clinic under false pretenses, she had experienced only one kind of dating. Still, the possibility of coaxing some information out of Suárez through a social conversation outside of the clinic proved tempting. And although he suspected nothing, Jasmine had something to prove. "How 'bout Thursday?" Even if the date yielded nothing, Jasmine could do far worse than to break bread with a handsome and successful man, even if only because he mistook her for a school principal with an eye for artistic talent. Jasmine rattled off her cell phone number and Suárez wrote it down.

Then he handed her a business card. "I can hardly wait." Suárez escorted her back to the reception area, where he greeted the middle-aged gentleman with the cane in his native tongue. Jasmine caught the Slavic edge the language possessed and presumed that the man hailed from Central Europe. Remembering the new addition to the mural and her own experience with Adam Brozi, she guessed that Suárez's patient had emigrated from Albania.

Jasmine left the clinic and rushed back to her Escalade. Once in the privacy and relative silence of her SUV, she connected to her voice mail and entered her access code. Her greeting played into her ear. *This is Jasmine Reyes of Reyes Bonds. . . .* She interrupted the playback by hitting another key. *To record a new greeting . . .* Jasmine changed her greeting, deleting the reference to the bail bond agency in the event Suárez called her. She not only knew that he would, but hoped he would.

EIGHT

"Next . . . Michael Peña," Jasmine said, reading the next name on the current list of the agency's pro bono clients. The list contained eleven names, and the staff had reported on nine over the past hour of their conference in her office. Despite the occasional missed curfew or dirty urine—typical occurrences for clients under community supervision—all seemed well.

"He tested dirty," said Zachary.

"For?"

"Marijuana."

"Noted. Next . . . Felicidad Rivera." Jasmine chuckled.

"What's so funny?" asked Zachary.

"Our first female client in, like, two years." Diana and Lorraine laughed along with her, and even Zachary offered a smirk. Out of every ten principals in Jasmine's collateral clientele, two were women who resembled their male counterparts. They were black or Hispanic women under the age of thirty-five caught in a buy-and-bust operation and charged with possession with intent to sell. Like many of the men Jasmine bailed, they often sold drugs to support their own habits. But the similarities between the men and women were superficial. Women proved to be much harder to supervise, and despite the fact that their requests for bail increased steadily each year, Jasmine rarely selected them for community supervision. Much of the spike in applications came from young women charged with violent offenses as a result of gang activity, and Jasmine rejected them as readily as she did men who called under the same circumstances. She was not trying to mess with violent offenders at all, let alone have her office become a piece of turf in some gang war.

But one afternoon Lorraine called out her bias against women after Jasmine turned down an application from a female pusher, the latest in a string of rejections. "I hate to say this, Jasmine, but it has to be said," said Lorraine, fidgeting in front of her desk like a teenager confronting a parent. "You'll bail out a drug dealer, even place him under community supervision, but you'll let his girlfriend sit at Rose M. Singer," she said, referring to the women's facility on Rikers Island. "You want to tell me what that's about?"

At first Jasmine grew defensive, but after giving it some thought, she admitted that Lorraine was right. But it was not the case that Jasmine did not want to help women or held them to a higher standard than men. Of the few surrenders she had executed to date, most had been women, and she could no longer take the risk. Jasmine explained to Lorraine, "See, I can get that guy to go into a treatment program. Why? Because he still has her bringing in money and watching his kids. But who's there to do that for her? No one. Until I can make enough money to build a day care facility in here and hire someone like you who can help these women get out of these fucked-up relationships, I'd just be setting them up." Jasmine knew it sounded like an excuse, but she meant every word. And every time she thought about it, it made her feel guilty. After all, where might she be if someone had helped her?

"So what's up with Miss Rivera?" Jasmine asked her staff, bracing herself for another one of Zachary's homophobic tirades.

Instead he announced nonchalantly, "She's still living with those hoes at that house in Hunts Point."

It irked Jasmine to hear that, but she had to check herself. "Are they operating from the house?"

"I don't know about that," replied Zachary, maintaining his calm tone. "But I do know they don't live far from the stroll." He folded his arms across his chest and eyed Jasmine, waiting for her response to Felicidad's blatant violation of her release agreement.

Although she wanted to move on to the Booker case, Jasmine had to handle the Rivera matter with caution. "That's a problem," she conceded. "Remind her that moving out of there's not an option, and then give her some time to do it."

Lorraine added, "And remember, it's hard enough to find a decent place to live without being . . ."

Jasmine acknowledged her point with a nod and then looked back at Zachary. He seemed resigned, yet satisfied to not have his report challenged, and she took the opportunity to divert his attention to the more fulfilling aspects of his job. "Zachary, what do you know about the Burn Masters Syndicate?"

"They're one of the most commercially successful graffiti crews in the entire city."

"Really?" Jasmine grinned at Zachary. "What's an ol' fogy like you doing knowing something like that?" And she wondered why she did not. Then again, she had let those interests die with Jason and only attended to them now that Malcolm had disappeared.

Zachary took the teasing in stride. "All those murals you see around for Nike, Pepsi, or whoever? All done by the Burn Masters." Then he grinned back at Jasmine. "Anyone with a life outside of the office can see that. Why you ask?"

"Turns out Macho had some kind of association with them. Maybe even a rivalry. So where do we find these Burn Masters?"

"They got a storefront on Southern Boulevard around Longwood Avenue, I think."

"Right off the Bruckner Expressway?"

"Yeah, you want me to head over there with you?"

"Thanks, Zach, but I got this." Jasmine stood up and gathered her papers to signal the end of the meeting. "But what you can do for me is have a conversation with Miss Rivera about the consequences of violating her release agreement."

"Will do, Boss Lady." Zachary bounded out the door with too much enthusiasm for his assignment. Jasmine almost regretted unleashing him on Felicidad, but she needed to get the message. Men and women alike needed to comply with the conditions Jasmine had set for their release.

"Diana, see if the Burn Masters have a Web site with their address on it. Oh, and call Officer Quinones and ask him if he's made any progress on that request I made of him."

"Yes, Boss Lady."

Felicidad's situation remained a nagging presence in the back of Jasmine's mind. "Lorraine, remind me to ask you about something at one point."

"Yes, Boss Lady."

Jasmine slammed her stack of files back onto her desk. "What the fuck with all this Boss Lady shit?"

Jasmine pulled off the Bruckner Expressway and coasted up Southern Boulevard. She found the Burn Masters' storefront between a Dominican restaurant and a Korean nail salon. She parked her SUV around the corner and out of sight and walked back to the store.

In a back corner, drawing at an easel, sat a petite black woman in her early twenties. She wore a hooded sweatshirt with the Bronx's zip codes scrolling down the sleeve of her right arm. Thin dreads with red highlights grazed her mahogany cheekbones as she crowded over the easel, as if she were attempting to create and protect her creation all at once. The young woman glanced Jasmine's way long enough for Jasmine to catch the stroke of black ink that stained her jaw. "Can I help you?"

Jasmine pointed to the woman's sleeve. "One-oh-four-nine-nine? I've lived and worked in the Bronx all my life, and I never knew it had a one-oh-four-nine-nine zip code. I always thought they only ran from four-five-one to four-seven-five."

The woman turned back to the easel to make an adjustment to her work in progress. "Ninety-nine's up north near Bronxville, Yonkers, Eastchester." Her eyes never left her canvas.

"Oh." In her line of work, Jasmine should have known that. "You know what zip code's missing from your sleeve?"

She finally had the woman's attention. "What?"

"One-one-three-seven-oh."

"One-one-three-seven-oh?" She pondered the familiar number. "That's not the Bronx. That's Queens. East Elmhurst, I think." Her gaze fell to her paint-splattered hands. "Like where Rikers is and whatnot." Not only did the woman know her city, she clearly had visited or at least written the facility enough to remember its zip code. Jasmine suspected that if she were a true writer according to Malcolm's definition, between the bombing excursions and maybe even the occasional stints in jail she collected such trivia as a by-product of her trade.

Jasmine said, "Exactly. Even though you can only get to Rikers Island through Queens, and it has a Queens address, that land is deemed part of the Bronx."

"Get out of here!"

"I kid you not. Census data for the Bronx includes the jail population."

The woman scoffed and folded her arms across her chest. "Okay, first of all, it's a freakin' island. . . ."

"So are all the other boroughs except the Bronx. Manhattan, Queens, Brooklyn, Staten Island . . . all of them are islands. Only the Bronx is attached to the mainland U.S."

The woman grew too incensed to appreciate this tidbit of information. "And what the hell they tryin' to say about us? That we're all criminals? If it has a Queens address, why not consider it a part of Queens then?" She stopped in the middle of her tirade and eyed Jasmine with suspicion. "You know a lot about Rikers Island."

"I should." Jasmine's instinct always informed her how transparent she should be, which was not very. But she had the feeling she would make more headway with the young woman if she were forthcoming but nonthreatening. "I'm trying to find Macho Booker."

The woman froze for a few seconds, then slowly put down her marker. She lowered herself from her stool and made her way toward the front of the store. "And who are you?"

Jasmine obliged, although she suspected the woman already knew. "I'm Jasmine Reyes. Macho's bondswoman." As she introduced herself, the woman eyed Jasmine in a way that made Jasmine deduce she had some kind of romantic attachment to Malcolm. He had never mentioned a girlfriend to Jasmine, and perhaps therein lay the reason for the girl's suspicious looks. "Guess he never mentioned me."

"Oh, he's mentioned you."

Jasmine burned to know what Malcolm had said about her, but the timing was wrong. In an attempt to put her at ease, she offered the young woman her hand and said, "I'm quite concerned about him. . . ."

"Yvette." She gave Jasmine a tepid handshake. "So am I."

"Bet the whole crew is. Malcolm was down with you guys, wasn't he?" Jasmine smiled at Yvette. "Or was that just wishful thinking."

Yvette sighed. "No, he was down for a minute. He hooked up with us a few months before he got knocked. We had gotten a few steady clients, you know. Schools, nonprofits . . ."

"And the clinic."

Yvette abruptly turned away from Jasmine to head back to her easel. "Well, that was something totally different. Anyway, we managed to get some corporate clients, and Macho wasn't feelin' that."

Jasmine scoffed for Yvette's benefit. "He had a problem painting for real money? I mean, he struck me as sort of a romantic, but let's get real. That starving artist shit gets tired real quick."

Yvette positioned herself in front of her easel and studied it. "No, it wasn't that. Macho was totally down with all of us being able to earn a living doing our thing. He just wanted us to set some limits."

"Limits?"

"Like Macho thought it was one thing if the guy who owns the furniture store down the block hires you to paint his name on his security gate. But it was another thing to take money from a soda company to paint its logo on a school-yard handball court. Macho had a problem with shit like that."

Jasmine wondered if Suárez might have influenced Malcolm's views, but then she had to remember that he did not meet the doctor until after he had been arrested for attempted robbery. "I guess that is a helluva lot different from the mural he did for the Suárez Community Health Center."

"Yeah, but Macho made that all about him."

"What do you mean?"

"Well, he complained a lot about the kind of clients we were taking on, but then he went and entered that contest all by himself," explained Yvette. "He never mentioned it to any of us until he won. Nor did he use the opportunity to publicize the crew."

Jasmine thought back to her interview with Malcolm at Rikers Island. Although some time had passed, she doubted he mentioned the Burn Masters at that time. In fact, he only mentioned Crystal. Jasmine wondered if Malcolm's decision to enter the contest as a solo artist might have been payback to his crew for not helping him get out of jail. "That must've really pissed all of you off."

"Don't get it twisted," Yvette snapped. "He'd been done thrown out the crew by then."

"Really?" That explained why Malcolm never mentioned the Burn Masters to her or anyone else at the agency. "Why?"

" 'Cause we're not about that shit. Once he got knocked for robbing that bodega, we were done with him. How're we supposed to land gigs with car companies and record labels if they think we're a bunch of thugs?"

But because Yvette spoke as if parroting someone else's words rather than articulating her own convictions, Jasmine said, "Not like there aren't a bunch of gangsters running up and down Wall Street."

Yvette gave a small laugh then grew somber. "I tried to have his back. I said at least Macho didn't flap, you know. The way the Vandal Squad is coming down on heads, he could've snitched to save his own ass. He told me how the cops pressed him for the names and addresses of writers they have in that anti-graffiti database."

"Graffitistat."

"They were showing him flicks of pieces, telling him they would convince the prosecutor to give him a deal if he told them who did them. Some of those writers were kids. Fifteen, sixteen, seventeen, and you can get an automatic bullet for doing graffiti now."

" 'Cause it's a felony now. Has been since eighty-eight, eighty-nine. Then Giuliani came along with Executive Order twenty-four in ninety-five," said Jasmine. Ever since she bailed out Malcolm and Calvin reprimanded her for it, she'd done her homework with some assistance from Zachary, who'd accessed John Jay's college library. In the order that inspired politicians across the country to institute zero-tolerance graffiti policies, America's favorite mayor espoused his famous broken-window theory. Giuliani likened a tag to a broken window; if left unfixed, people would be encouraged to break other windows. He even equated graffiti with drugs and gangs, overlooking the verifiable fact that the overwhelming majority of writers were kids seeking nothing more than the notoriety that came from getting up.

The more she learned about zealous anti-graffiti initiatives that virtually rendered adolescence illegal, the more amazed Jasmine became that Jason ultimately got knocked for assault, and one spawned by her own criminality. "I can't imagine locking up a kid in the jump for a whole year over graffiti. I mean, they hand down bullets to people for gun possession. You just can't compare a spray can to a gun."

"That's what I'm saying!" said Yvette. "But no matter what the cops threw at him, Macho never would've flapped. And he never would've hurt that bodega owner either."

"Because you knew him like that."

Yvette eyed Jasmine. "Yeah, I did."

"Must've been hard. You want to stand by your man, but your crew wants to distance itself from him. What'd you do?"

Yvette raised her arms to gesture at the cluttered storefront. "I'm still here, ain't I?" So when forced to choose, Yvette chose her crew over her man. That explained to Jasmine why Malcolm never mentioned her either. As far as he was concerned, everyone except his sister had abandoned him. Then Yvette shook her head as a short smile twisted onto her face. "When I first met Macho, he thought I might be a cop."

"No way."

"We met on MySpace. You know, I'm looking for other writers in my area I may not already know, and I catch the name BOUK X and instead of a photo of his real self, he has a flick of a character he drew of himself. And I recognize his tag, you know, I've seen it before on the streets. So I click on his profile, and he has *Graffiti Bridge* playing, other flicks of his pieces, some of his friends are writers I recognize, too. So I reach out to him, and invite him to check out my profile. You know what he writes me? You're really cute . . . how do I know you're not a DT on the Vandal Squad?"

Jasmine asked, "Why would he say something like that?"

"I told you the Vandal Squad's no joke. They have cops up in MySpace posing as girls wanting to hook up with writers. It took Macho three months to go out with me."

"Let me guess," said Jasmine. "Y'all went bombing on your first date." The way Yvette dropped her gaze made Jasmine wonder if in her jest she actually had guessed the truth. Yvette fixed her eyes on her canvas, and Jasmine sensed that her loyalty to the other Burn Masters did little to quell the guilt of breaking Malcolm's heart. She clearly still loved him. "Seems like Macho did well for himself after all," she said. "Supposedly that doctor he worked for was going to hook him up with some connections he had in SoHo."

Yvette hissed and leaned into her canvas. "Macho wasn't trying to have Suárez for no patron. Which really pissed off Suárez. Especially after he paid Macho's tuition for art school. That's why Macho wanted to quit working for him. He told me that as soon as he finished designing the clinic's Web site, he was out of there."

Malcolm had never expressed any discontent with Suárez. And even when suggesting that Malcolm ran with a band of criminals, Suárez displayed no ill will toward his protégé. In fact, even though he bragged about his small contribution to the mural, Suárez chose not to boast about sending Malcolm to art school. She had no ready explanation for the doctor's humility. Perhaps Malcolm kept his plans from her and the rest of the staff because being employed had been an integral part of his release agreement. Collateral and pro bono principals alike often tried to hide when they quit or lost a job out of fear of being deemed high risk and ultimately surrendered. The more honest ones sought other jobs, only confessing to their brief stints of unemployment when they found them. Perhaps Malcolm intended to do the same. But that possibility did not ring true to their relationship.

Jasmine said, "Sounds like you don't care for the doctor."

"Never met him, never wanted to." Yvette's contempt for Suárez caught Jasmine's attention. But she knew if she asked Yvette for an explanation, she would shut down.

Instead Jasmine asked her one last thing. "Damn, Yvette, do you have any idea why he would run?" It seemed like a safe question given all that Yvette had already revealed.

"No."

And just like that, Jasmine knew she was lying. Yvette had so many complicated and unresolved feelings for Malcolm, and yet seemed unbothered by his sudden disappearance. She at least knew that Malcolm was alive, if not exactly where he was hiding.

Jasmine reached into her pocket for her business card and offered it to Yvette. "If you hear from him or recall anything—no matter how small you might think it is—give me a call."

Without taking her eyes off her work, Yvette said, "Just leave it there on the desk."

Jasmine complied and walked out of the store. Mulling over her conversation with Yvette, she wished her date with Suárez was tonight. She called Zachary. His voice mail answered, and she waited for the tone. "Zach, it's Jasmine. I don't know what your schedule's like tomorrow, but I need to see you first thing in the morning if you don't have class."

When Jasmine arrived at the office the next morning, she found Felicidad juggling the telephone lines. By the fuzz above Felicidad's upper lip and baggy carpenter pants, Jasmine guessed that Zachary had directed Felicidad to present to the office as a male in order to avoid any more altercations like the one that had erupted between Echevarría and Watkins. She wore no makeup and had pulled her hair into a simple ponytail clasped at her neck with plain elastic. Despite Felicidad's sincere efforts, her femininity made defiant strikes through her masculine façade in occasional words and the slightest gestures.

"Reyes Bonds, would you hold, please?" Felicidad said with a courtesy that always eluded Diana. "Reyes Bonds, how may I help you this morning?" Jasmine watched Felicidad, awed by both her surprise presence in Diana's stead and her professional telephone manner. "And what is the top charge?" she asked a caller as she perused a list attached to a clipboard. "Oh, no, sir, I'm sorry, we won't be able to assist you with that, but allow me to refer you to Reliable Bonds. Would you like that number, sir?" Felicidad rattled off the number, wished the caller luck, and then hung up the phone. Then she looked at Jasmine and smiled. "Good morning, how are you?"

"Perplexed as shit."

"I came in for my appointment with Lorraine just as Diana was rushing off to her babysitter's. She called to check in on her daughter, and when the sitter said Zoë just wasn't herself today, Diana got worried and headed over there."

Jasmine glanced at her watch. At nine thirty-two a.m., two things must have occurred. One, Diana called her babysitter to check on Zoë the second she reached the office. Two, Felicidad arrived just as if not before the agency even opened. "Let me guess. She's not coming back."

Felicidad shrugged. "She said she'd call around ten. Before she left, she gave me a crash course in how to answer the telephones." She showed Jasmine the clipboard. Attached to it was the procedural manual Jasmine had written when she decided to hire staff. Felicidad had it opened to the page with a series of questions Jasmine had created for screening callers requesting bail. She doubted that anyone actually had read the damned thing besides Lorraine. "Oh, and I even have one of these for you." Felicidad handed her a bond request form.

Jasmine scanned the form. "Diana show you how to fill this out, too?" For the first month after Jasmine had hired her, Diana had handed her countless forms with lines of information skipped, transposed, or scratched out. Felicidad had completed the form in blue ink and a neat print.

"No, I just taught myself how to do it from reading the manual," said Felicidad. Then she winced. "Lots of mistakes, huh?"

"Nope, it's perfect."

Felicidad's eyes fluttered with humility. "Miss Reyes . . ."

"Jasmine."

"Jasmine, I just wanted to be helpful because I really appreciate you getting me out of that hellhole and letting me hang out here. I mean, I know my being here stirs up a bit of trouble."

That's putting it mildly. Although Jasmine appreciated Felicidad's offer to help when Diana concocted another excuse to abandon her post to play peek-a-boo with her daughter, she did not care for Felicidad's kissing up and minding Jasmine's business. She toyed with the idea of forwarding the main line to her office so she could answer it herself. Then Jasmine decided she would have to work in the reception area instead of her office in case anyone walked into the agency. She could not have Felicidad, with her razor stubble poking through her pancake foundation, receiving potential clients.

"Thanks for filling in for Diana, but I don't think . . ." The telephone rang again.

"Excuse me while I get that, Jasmine," said Felicidad as she reached for the receiver. "Good morning, Reyes Bonds, how may I help you today?" Jasmine started toward her office when Felicidad signaled for her to wait. "Just one moment, Dr. Dieudonné, let me see if she's arrived yet." She put the call on hold and asked Jasmine, "Are you available for Dr. Dieudonné?"

"No, tell her I'm in court." Diana never screened Jasmine's calls that way. She always made it obvious to the caller whether Jasmine was in the office or not, only to cop an attitude when Jasmine refused to take the call. No matter how many times Jasmine tried to retrain Diana, she always reverted back to being too forthcoming about Jasmine's availability, complaining that it created too much work for her. "And I'm scheduled to be in court all day."

Felicidad returned to the telephone call. "Dr. Dieudonné, I just checked her schedule, and Miss Reyes has court appointments for the entire day. I apologize for the confusion. Would you like to leave a message for her?" She reached for the telephone pad and began to write. "Please spell your name for me. Thank you." Felicidad repeated the spelling of the doctor's name to ensure she captured it correctly. "No, Dr. Dieudonné, I'm afraid I don't know if she'll stop by the office after court, but if she calls, I'll be sure to relay your message. Why, thank you, that's very kind of you to say. You have a good day now." Felicidad hung up the phone and handed Jasmine the perfectly scribed message.

"Thanks." Jasmine took it, then said, "Okay, you're looking for something to do while you're waiting for Lorraine, I'd appreciate it if you continued to fill in for Diana until she comes back from the babysitter's."

"God bless you, Jasmine, because I think I'd go crazy with those Neanderthals in there," she said, tilting her head toward the rec room. "Whenever I watch daytime television, I swear to God I can feel my brain cells fizzling away like Alka-Seltzer in a glass of water. I'll stay right here all day if you need me."

"Thanks, Felicidad," said Jasmine. "Thing is I can't pay you, though, even if Diana takes the entire day off. She's probably going to take this as a sick day, which means I have to pay her anyway."

"Oh, that's not a problem whatsoever. That never crossed my mind.

Like I said, I just want to help you in whatever way I can." Felicidad began to say more, when the telephone interrupted her. She answered in that congenial tone, and for once Jasmine loathed the thought of Diana making it into the office. "Hey, sweetheart, how's the baby?" It took Jasmine a second to realize that Diana had called. People called her many things, but never sweetheart. They would sooner describe Mother Teresa as a conniving bitch. "Oh, okay, I'll let Jasmine know. *Cuidate bien, m'ija.*" She hung up the telephone and shrugged at Jasmine. "That was Diana. . . ."

"Zoë's fine, but she's taking the rest of the day off because she doesn't want to take any chances."

"Exactly."

Jasmine rolled her eyes at Diana's predictability, when Lorraine walked into the agency. "Hey, you guys." Her eyes darted several times between the other two women until they rested on Felicidad. "Where's Diana?"

Jasmine said, "She had another child care emergency so Felicidad's filling in for her, and doing a kick-ass job, I might add. Anyway, I'm expecting Zachary this morning, so he can take over for her when he gets here. Mind if I speak with you before he comes?"

"Sure."

"Felicidad, as soon as Zach arrives, please send him into my office."

"Will do, Jasmine."

Jasmine led Lorraine into her office. She closed the door behind them then asked Lorraine, "So what have you been able to come up with for Felicidad?" She walked around her desk and took her seat.

"I found a couple of support groups she can attend," said Lorraine as she paced in front of Jasmine's desk. "One is for transgender people at the Hispanic AIDS Forum, and Gay Men's Health Crisis has a few groups for people with HIV. They're both free, so—"

"Great, but actually I was wondering if you came across any psychiatric services to treat her gender identity disorder."

"Look, Jasmine, you're probably going to disagree with me on this, but hear me out." Lorraine took a deep breath and continued. "I know I'm not a psychiatrist, but I am a clinical social worker. I mean, I'm not just yet, but I am—"

"Lorraine, this is one of the reasons why Zach always interrupts you. Enough with the disclaimers. Your credentials speak for themselves. Just state your point and make your case."

She expected Lorraine to become angry. Truthfully, Zachary only needed one reason to interrupt her. He constantly cut off Lorraine in mid-sentence simply because she allowed him to. But Lorraine immediately adjusted to Jasmine's feedback. "I'm of the expert opinion that while Felicidad has medical and emotional needs we should attempt to address, gender identity disorder is not one of them."

Jasmine had not expected that. "Lorraine, he's a man who wants to be a woman."

"But I'm not convinced that her desire is something that needs to be treated or cured." Lorraine stood up and began to pace. "I had several extensive conversations with Felicidad and then conducted considerable research. I even paid a visit to the Gender Identity Project at the Lesbian, Gay, Bisexual and Transgender Community Center on West Thirteenth Street, and I'm convinced that there's no such thing as gender dysphoria or gender identity disorder."

"Lorraine, please sit down. You're making me dizzy." Lorraine sat in her usual seat. "No, sit there," Jasmine said, pointing to the chair directly in front of her, where Zachary usually sat during meetings.

Lorraine complied and continued. "Nonconformity should not automatically be seen as a sign of pathology."

"I didn't go to a fancy college like you, so you need to break this down for me in simpler terms, okay?"

"What I'm saying is who are we to label someone sick simply because they're different?"

"I'm not labeling anybody. The American Psychiatric Association is. And you know what? Everyone agrees with them."

"That's not true, Jasmine. As long as there have been humans, people have engaged in varying degrees of transgender expression, and not every culture or society has frowned upon it. And I'm talking a long spectrum of behavior here, from the perfectly normal and vigilantly heterosexual man who sometimes likes to slip into his wife's lingerie to someone who goes through the time, pain, and expense of having sex reassignment surgery. In some cultures transgender people are believed to have mystical powers and play important roles in their communities. Many Native American cultures here in the U.S. call them two-spirit people."

"Meaning they have both a male and a female spirit in the same body?"

"Right. And they function in their communities as healers, artists, counselors . . . Jasmine, I was surprised to learn how many cultures across the globe accept and respect transgenders as normal and healthy people who can make a meaningful contribution to their societies."

"So basically what you're saying is it's really all about how you look at it?"

"Yes! Well, no. It's not about how you look at it. It's about how you *want* to look at it."

Lorraine had lost her, and Jasmine decided to bring the conversation back to the concrete situation before them. "C'mon, do you really buy that? We're talking about someone who contracted HIV from walking the streets. Why would anyone put themselves at that kind of risk who did not have a serious problem?"

Lorraine said, "I'm not denying that Felicidad needs help, but her case proves my point. Her issues largely stem from the fact that people have terrorized her for who she is. Felicidad wound up on the streets at fifteen because her parents would not accept her."

Jasmine did not want to hear this tragic story but accepted she had no choice. "Because they found out she was . . ." She almost said *gay* but remembered Felicidad's insistence on her heterosexuality. Jasmine shook her head as if to dust out the confusion. "They put her out."

"It's worse than that, Jasmine. Her father read her diary in which she had written love letters to a boy in her church. He tracked her down at the boy's house, dragged her out on the street, and whipped her with his belt in front of the neighbors, all the time screaming that no son of his was going to be a faggot. Do you know what Felicidad told him? As he's hitting her like some kind of overseer, she's crying to him, 'How can I be a faggot when I'm not even a boy?' Her father went from whipping her to punching her right there in the middle of the street, and no one stopped him until he knocked her unconscious. Her own father almost killed her while a crowd watched."

A familiar image flashed into Jasmine's mind. How many times had she passed by the rec room and caught her clients cheering along with the studio audience of *The Jerry Springer Show* as transvestites and cross-dressers got attacked by their lovers and relatives? Jasmine took several deep breaths and finally said, "By no stretch of the imagination am I condoning the man's behavior, but you have to imagine how difficult it was to find out his son was not . . ." She choked *normal*, feeling as if she had already betrayed Felicidad by merely thinking of the word.

"So imagine how much worse it must be for Felicidad. All she wants is for people to acknowledge her for what she is. And that's a woman."

Again, Jasmine shook her head. "I can't wrap my head around all this. I mean, if Rivera wants to go by Felicidad and wear dresses, I couldn't give a fuck." She remembered how often her own father had called Jason a faggot because he liked to draw and had no interest in sports. As easy as it would have been for her brother to go out for a team or watch a game on television, he refused to capitulate to Pedro's expectations despite his relentless name-calling. Still, Jason never questioned that his passion for arts and disinterest in sports made him any less male. "But the bottom line is, Lorraine, that not only was Felicidad born a male, but it's evident to the world. The whole world is supposed to adjust to her so-called gender identity?"

"Who does it hurt?"

"Obviously, it hurts her," Jasmine said.

"And she'll stop hurting when we let her be. If you really think about it, it really isn't all that hard for us to do. Certainly much easier than trying to shame her into changing into something she can't or won't be."

"If she can, she should," said Jasmine. "I mean, why choose to subject yourself to the constant humiliation and potential violence."

Lorraine's eyebrows knitted into a scowl. "Look, Jasmine, I don't want to get into the whole nature versus nurture debate on this. I don't give a shit whether Felicidad was born this way or she made a lifestyle choice." Her sudden vulgarity shocked and even impressed Jasmine. Lorraine had passionate opinions she vigorously defended, but she rarely cursed, priding herself on being the opposite of Zachary and maintaining a professional demeanor when she argued her position. Having never seen Lorraine this adamant about anything, Jasmine tuned in to her like she never had before. "As far as I'm concerned, it's fuckin' irrelevant."

"Irrelevant?"

"Irrelevant! Never mind whether Felicidad was born this way or chooses to be that way. What exactly do the rest of us lose by accepting and respecting the way Felicidad sees herself anyway? If you and I and Zachary and Diana . . . if everyone is comfortable with his or her own gender identity, why should we be so invested in dictating hers?"

Jasmine had no answer for her. She never gave these things that much thought. She remembered the FAQ that Felicidad gave her before her interview at Rikers Island. "Look, I'm just checking in with you to see how we can help Felicidad. Other than her living situation, I'm not too concerned about her. But I would really like to see her get into some kind of counseling for whatever, I don't know. You tell me."

Lorraine nodded and moved for the door. "I think this transgender support group would be—" A knock on the door halted her in midsentence, and she grinned at Jasmine. "How much you want to bet that's Zachary, interrupting me yet again."

"I'd bet my mortgage on that one." Lorraine opened the door to find Zachary standing there. The two women laughed.

"What's so funny?"

"Never mind. Come in and close the door behind you." Lorraine and Zachary stepped around one another. Once Lorraine closed the door, Jasmine said, "Zachary, what's up with the sloppy supervision work?"

"What the hell are you talking about?"

"I'm talking about the Booker case. There are no notes in his file about his boss paying for his school tuition. No mention of a girlfriend."

"Girlfriend?"

"Not only did Macho have a girlfriend, for a while they were members of the same crew."

"Macho wasn't in any gang!"

"Who said anything about a gang, goddamnit? He was in a crew. The Burn Masters Syndicate that you put me on to. And right until the time he was arrested. But there's no mention of the Burn Masters or a girl named Yvette in any of your supervision notes."

"Be real, Jasmine, that's not my job."

"Not your job?"

"No, that's Lorraine's job. She handles all that personal shit."

It took all Jasmine had not to fire Zachary on the spot. The "personal shit" was exactly the kind of information that proved useful when principals absconded. As a matter of fact, the "personal shit" might have even telegraphed Malcolm's disappearance. Had Zachary taken the time to learn and document these things, she could have predicted—maybe even prevented—Malcolm's running. Then again, Jasmine should have been able to do that anyway. He spent the most time with her. Zachary's weak surveillance or not, she dropped the ball on this one, too, and could only blame him so much.

That realization—and the fact that she needed another pair of eyes on the street—saved Zachary's job. Jasmine still had to save face. "You're killing me here, Zach. Why the hell do we bother to do home visits before we bail out somebody?" She waited for him to answer, but he remained silent. "That's not a rhetorical fuckin' question. Answer me."

Zachary pouted like a toddler but said, "To be sure they have verifiable community ties."

"And why does that matter to us?"

"Look, Jasmine . . ."

"I'm dead serious, Zachary. Answer the goddamn question. Prove to me that you haven't forgotten."

"Folks with ties are less likely to run."

"And?"

"And what?"

"And if they run anyway?"

"What, what, what?"

"The ties give us leads. In other words, Zachary, the personal shit matters. It is your job to know those things. Where people live, who they hang out with, who they're fucking, and any changes in all of the above, it is your job to know." Zachary began to defend himself, but Jasmine talked over him. "You want to know something, Zachary? Felicidad is sitting out there covering for Diana. A call came in from someone looking for bail, but she had no clue how to handle it. Know what she did?" Jasmine opened her desk drawer and pulled out her bound copy of the procedural manual. She waved it in the air like a manifesto and said, "She found this, and she read it."

"What the fuck's that got to do with me?"

"Two hours on somebody else's job, and she got it right. That's what the fuck it's got to do with you. Jesus, Zachary, you've been acting lately like I've never trained you." Jasmine slapped the manual on the top of her desk. "Never mind. Just get out."

Zachary unleashed a few choice words as he left her office, but Jasmine just ignored him. If he only knew how close he'd come to losing his job. For someone who lived for law enforcement, Zachary's work had become inexcusably sloppy. Jasmine hoped Calvin would fill the gaps Zachary left. At this rate, she would make as much progress in finding Malcolm if she put Felicidad on the street to look for him.

TEN

A few hours later, Jasmine emerged from her office with a stack of papers in her hand. When she entered the reception area, she found Felicidad still twisting between a stack of files on the desk and Diana's desktop computer. "I take it she's not coming in," said Jasmine as she checked her inbox for messages. "What are you doing with all those files?"

"Oh, I just thought I'd create a database for you," said Felicidad. "It's good to have both paper and electronic copies of all your important documents because anything can happen."

"Look, I appreciate what you're trying to do, but I can't let you do that."

"I don't mind. It helps pass the time. See what I've already done." Felicidad invited Jasmine to look over her shoulder at the computer screen. She had replicated the preliminary intake form in a software program that Jasmine did not even know the agency owned. "For every paper form you have, you create a corresponding electronic one. Once you input all the information, you can do things like generate reports, tabulate statistics . . ."

Although the idea of having that level of organization made Jasmine's mouth water, she had to answer to a higher principle. "Thanks, Felicidad, but you need to return all these files immediately. You're not an employee of this agency, so I can't allow you to read them. Don't get me wrong, I appreciate you're trying to put some order to this mess Diana calls a filing system, but . . ." Jasmine only knew one way to handle this situation. The blunt way. "Would you like it if some stranger walked off the street, opened that drawer, and read your file?"

"I didn't think about that." Felicidad drew away from the computer keyboard as if it suddenly emitted a foul smell. "I guess I wouldn't like that very much at all." She stood up and gathered the files on Diana's desk.

Jasmine opened the main door. "I'm headed across the street to post these bonds. Be right back."

She took three steps and bumped into Crystal Booker. "You're catching me at a bad time here," Jasmine said. "Why don't you wait for me inside?"

Crystal clutched Jasmine's arm. "No, I want to talk to you right now." Jasmine attributed this unannounced visit from Crystal to Yvette. She'd probably called Malcolm's sister to let her know that Jasmine had come to the Burn Masters' store to ask questions about him. "I understand that if you don't find my brother, you're out a lot of money. I'll give you twice the bond you posted if you leave my brother alone."

"What did you just say?"

Crystal looked around her. Because Jasmine's agency was located right across the street from the courthouse, law enforcement personnel roamed the streets at all hours of the day. She leaned in closer to Jasmine and repeated her offer. "I'll give you twenty thousand dollars if you stop searching for Macho."

"Are you trying to bribe me?"

"You don't understand. . . ."

"Look, Crystal, I bailed your brother out of jail with no collateral because he gave me his word that he would make his court appearances. He broke that word, so now all bets are off. Instead of committing another—"

Crystal's clenched fist rammed into Jasmine's face, and she went reeling against the front window of the neighboring storefront. Her face blazing from the startling punch, Jasmine threw up her left forearm to shield her face from the coming blow. Then she delivered a roundhouse punch with her right that crashed into Crystal's jaw. The two women lunged at each other as a crowd gathered around them. Jasmine and Crystal tumbled to the hot asphalt, grappling for the superior position, until two police officers dove into their brawl and hauled them apart. Her chest heaving with more anger than exertion,

Jasmine dragged her forearm across her lip, leaving a trail of blood down her arm. The cop pulled her away from Crystal and asked her, "Miss, are you okay?"

"Yeah, yeah, I'm all right." Jasmine looked over his shoulder to see his partner wrestling with Crystal, who still wanted a piece of her. Then she felt a tap on her shoulder. Jasmine turned to face a young black man in his twenties. In his hands he had the court papers she had dropped during the scuffle. "Thanks," she said, taking the papers from him.

"They're all there, miss," he said. Then the man said to the police officer, "That other woman started it. She hit her first."

Several people in the crowd began to shout, corroborating his account. The police officer asked, "Ma'am, would you like to press charges against the other woman for assaulting you?"

"No. What I really want to do is clock her one last time." Crystal had turned her into a spectacle in front of her place of business. "How 'bout you let me do that, and we'll call it a day?"

The cop grinned. "No, ma'am, you know I can't allow you to do that."

"Then this show is over."

"Are you sure?"

"Positive."

"What was that all about?"

"Family matter. I'm over it." Jasmine rifled through her papers to be sure none were missing. She stepped forward, but the officer blocked her path. "I have business at the courthouse."

"Let my partner and I clear the scene and then you can proceed about your business."

"Shit."

"You may want to clean yourself up first anyway," the police officer said. Then he turned to the crowd. "There's nothing left to see, folks," he said, waving away the crowd. "Continue wherever you were headed. Nothing left to see."

His partner had escorted Crystal across the street. She jabbered away at him, and Jasmine wondered what she was saying to him. One thing she knew for sure. It could not have been the truth. But she made the right move by not pressing charges against Crystal. That would do nothing except make things worse. Besides, Jasmine could not fault Crystal. She was fighting for her brother's life. Jasmine herself had tried to do the same for Jason and had failed.

As Jasmine pulled the cocktail dress over her head, it dawned on her that at the age of twenty-seven, she was going on her first date. As a teenager, she had too many other concerns for naïve pledges of forever at the playground or silly games like spin the bottle or seven minutes in heaven. Scrounging money for the rent and utilities and dodging social services occupied most of Jasmine's time, rendering playing with boys a luxury she could not afford. Her encounters with men consisted of motel stints with midtown businessmen wanting to score grass and ass before they crossed the George Washington Bridge to their wives and kids in Jersey and backseat trysts with truck drivers making a pit stop on the Cross Bronx Expressway as they traveled I-95 between Canada and Miami. Like most prostitutes, Jasmine euphemistically referred to these encounters as "dates" without ever kidding herself. She had no social life, only business transactions. She never even considered attempting to finagle dinner and entertainment from these men, although if they offered her a meal as they turned into the drive-through window of a fast-food restaurant, Jasmine never turned it down. She preferred this gritty honesty and worked no more or less than she needed to sustain herself and build her business. As soon as she felt financially stable enough to quit, she let go of the life without a second thought.

Jasmine fussed with her hair. This evening with Suárez would be no different from any of her past dates. She only agreed to go out with him in order to gain more information about Malcolm. Unbeknownst to Suárez, this was business, too.

For once Jasmine conceded that she needed to look the part, so she'd left the office early to stop at the drugstore for cosmetics and pantyhose. Having never purchased such items, Jasmine filled her red shopping basket with random products. When she got home, she tore two pairs of off-black stockings before writhing into her correct size without causing a run. Now the cosmetics were strewn all over the top of Jasmine's bureau as she made one clumsy attempt after another to find the right colors and then properly apply them.

Her skirmish with Crystal had left her with a bruised left eye. Jasmine asked the teenage girl pricing inventory at the drugstore how she might cover it, sneering to herself over the irony. She taught herself how to use makeup to create a fake bruise, but she had no idea how to hide a real one. Jasmine had followed the girl's instructions to the letter to no avail, and even considered calling Suárez to reschedule. But after chiding herself for the ridiculous thought, she resorted to wearing her hair loose and parted on the left side for whatever coverage it might provide. Barely more satisfied with the results, she gave up and hoped for dim lighting. Where the hell was Felicidad now that Jasmine really needed her expertise?

After he finally came and left, Jasmine washed up and left the motel. Ordinarily, she jumped into a cab and went home. But tonight had been particularly grueling because the last john could not come. He went on and on about not getting a promotion and his wife pressuring him to quit his job. Jasmine pretended to care only in the hopes that if she relaxed him enough, she'd get him off of her and out the door. Truly, she wanted to give up, hand him back his money, and send him on his miserable way, but that would have been bad for business. He would blame her for his inadequacies and go hire someone else. Jasmine could not afford to lose a regular, least of all one of her less demanding ones. This one usually rolled on and slipped off, but tonight she had to work him for almost an hour before she could go home.

She knew she should have gone straight home, but Jasmine could not imagine getting any sleep without the aid of a few strong drinks, so she ambled into the bar down the block from the motel. Jasmine had never been there before, nor had she ever heard about any drama jumping off there. She figured it'd be okay to go in, buy a shot or two, and then be on her own miserable way.

So it surprised Jasmine when the clean-shaven guy in the leather jacket with the nice build offered to buy her a drink. They talked for almost an hour—mostly about him, of course—but Jasmine expected that and did not mind. It wasn't like she was burning to talk about herself. She never did.

When she announced that it was time for her to get home, he insisted on walking her outside. As she raised her hand to hail a cab, he asked, "I wasn't going to do this, but I've got this feeling that if I don't, I'm going to regret it."

"Always follow your instincts," she said.

"You think you might want to come home with me?"

A gypsy cab pulled up a few yards in front of her. Jasmine had promised her brother that she would never pick up a man off the street. But Jason was gone now, and she rarely had the chance to sleep with someone she actually found attractive. The opportunity to make some extra cash was icing.

"Yeah, I'll go home with you, but first things first." Jasmine had never pulled an all-nighter before, so she winged the rate. "A hundred bucks an hour for whatever you want except backdoor action. I don't do that at all. Five hundred for the entire night."

He winced. "What?"

She wondered if she had gone too high. But now that Jasmine had made the offer, she had to stick by it. She was too tired and insufficiently greedy to renegotiate. "Take it or leave it." The cabbie honked as if to back her up.

"Okay." He gestured toward the cab. "Let's go."

Jasmine led the way, but just as she reached the cab, the driver veered off at the next light change. "Hey!" Then she felt the cold metal tighten around her wrist. When she turned to face her john, he shoved a badge into her face.

"You're under arrest—"

"What the fuck . . ."

"—for solicitation."

He hauled her to his unmarked car in the bar's parking lot. As she sat in the backseat during the drive to the closest precinct, Jasmine brewed in her own stupidity. She had been tricking for so long, she misinterpreted an innocent proposition for a one-night stand into a request for illicit sex. She had to beat this rap if she was ever going to leave the life at all. No surety company would contract Jasmine as a bail bond agent if she did not beat this rap.

But the closer they got to the precinct, the less worried about it Jasmine became. Somehow Jasmine just knew she would beat it. She would plead not guilty at the arraignment, and having no criminal record on paper, the judge would release her on her own recognizance. Once she told her court-appointed attorney what had happened, he would find a way to spin the tale to the embarrassment of the plainclothes cop. Maybe say that he took her down for solicitation out of drunken spite when she refused to go home with him. Witnesses at the bar would testify how chummy they were and that he had followed her out. Once her PD shook the cop's credibility, the prosecutor would drop the charge. Jasmine might still have the arrest on her record, but so long as she did not have a conviction, she had a chance to get her business off the ground.

So the only thing that still bothered Jasmine—so much more than the arrest itself and the pending hassle that lay before her—was that she had lost a rare chance to have sex for its own sake like a normal person.

She found a parking space right across the street from the clinic's entrance. Suárez had pushed to pick her up at her apartment, but not wanting to let him know where she lived, Jasmine insisted on meeting him at the clinic. He asked her to arrive at eight p.m., but she came fifteen minutes early in the hopes of gathering more intelligence.

When Jasmine entered the clinic, Suárez stood in the hallway in front of his office speaking to a young Mexican couple. At least, she assumed they were Mexican by their facial characteristics and simple clothing, until she realized that they were not speaking in Spanish. Suárez shook the man's hand and gave the woman a reassuring squeeze on the shoulder. He acknowledged Jasmine with a nod, then said something in the unusual tongue to the couple when they noticed her. Then Suárez led them past Jasmine to the clinic exit. The couple shuffled past her, avoiding her eyes even as she whispered hello in Spanish to them. Suárez ushered them out the door and locked it behind them. As he walked toward Jasmine, he removed his laboratory coat, revealing a plum silk shirt that dipped around the cuts of his muscular torso. "Hello, Jasmine."

"Hey." Her sudden nervousness annoyed her, and Jasmine reminded herself of the task before her. This was business, and she'd come to gather intelligence. "What was that language they were speaking?"

"Náhuatl."

"Oh, I thought they were Mexican."

"They are. They're from a part of Mexico where the people don't speak Spanish. Náhuatl is the tribal language of their indigenous ancestors. There are over sixty such languages spoken throughout Mexico by about seven million people—Maya, Zapotec, Otomí. . . . Some of the languages are only spoken by as few as fifty people! You have to admire that kind of resilience."

"So let me guess," said Jasmine. "They're not here legally, are they?"

Suárez smiled at her. "Are you always so blunt?"

"Is there any other way to be?"

"Yes. I mean, yes, they're in the country illegally. Not, yes, there's no other way to be other than direct." Suárez's eyes traveled from Jasmine's tousled hair to her black sling-back heels. "I like your candor. And your ensemble. You look very pretty tonight, Jasmine."

"Thanks." She felt her neck flush and hoped the color of embarrassment would not travel to her face. Jasmine motioned for the door. "Shall we?"

"Your vehicle or mine?"

Outside the clinic, Suárez hailed a cab, which drove them to the parking lot where he kept his swanky BMW. As he coasted down the FDR Drive into midtown Manhattan, he explained his philosophy to Jasmine while Juanes crooned on the stereo. "I opened the clinic precisely to serve people just like the ones you saw there tonight. Yes, they crossed the border illegally, but their status in this country makes them no less human than you or me, and as such they are entitled to health care," he said as he maneuvered the luxurious car into the fast lane.

Although she could imagine the pleasure of driving such an exquisite piece of machinery, Jasmine enjoyed being a passenger. She drove all the time, even when she had no place to go. And she considered few of the places she drove to havens. Court. Jail. Cemetery. Jasmine sunk herself deeper into the plush leather and wondered if Suárez would mind cutting off the air conditioner so she could open the window. "So you believe that health care's one of those inalienable human rights like they talk about in the Declaration of Independence?" Or was it the Constitution? Shit, she was supposed to be an elementary school principal who knew these things. She had to be more careful.

"Absolutely." He sounded a bit offended that Jasmine had asked.

"Hey, not all doctors do, you know. Some feel that you deserve exactly the amount of health care you're willing to pay for. That they didn't spend all that time and money to go to med school to give away their services."

"Well, I'm not one of those doctors. But I just don't believe that universal health care is the only moral choice. It's also sound public health policy. This country is the only industrialized nation that does not guarantee access to health care to its citizens, and you know what? It shows in our life expectancy and infant mortality rates." Suárez reached toward the stereo and turned down the volume, reducing Juanes's serenade to a murmur. "But the health care industry in the U.S. is just that, Jasmine. An industry. And industry puts profits before people under the assumption that prioritizing people is always unprofitable."

Jasmine never gave much thought to the health care system, but Suárez's analysis jibed with her experience with the criminal justice system. "So much for an ounce of prevention equals a pound of cure," she said.

"Precisely." Then Suárez gave her that smile. They had not spent an hour together and already she had grown attached to his smile.

Jasmine shifted in her seat as much to shake off the attraction as to direct a question to him. "So let me ask you something, Adriano, if you don't mind."

"Ask me anything."

"How can you afford to provide health care to those who can't pay for it?" Although Suárez might have found the question intrusive, Jasmine genuinely wanted to know.

Suárez smiled, pleased that she had asked. "When I left medical school, I chose the most lucrative practice I could find." He waited for her to guess. "Cosmetic surgery."

Jasmine howled. "No way!"

"I nipped and tucked my way to a small fortune. Then I invested my way into a larger fortune. The sad truth of the matter, Jasmine, is that cosmetic surgery is the only field left in which a doctor can make a decent living. Between the medical school tuition, malpractice insurance premiums, and the like, practicing medicine is rarely a viable career choice, let alone a fulfilling vocation."

"If you want to call giving face-lifts and breast implants practicing medicine," said Jasmine. "So what turned you around? What made you decide to go from chasing paper to changing lives?"

Suárez looked at her with a lopsided grin. "I never turned. I devoted my early career to making a great deal of money with the intention of doing exactly what I'm doing now. Those years as a plastic surgeon were always part of my plan. They were a means to an end. A much more satisfying end."

Jasmine gazed out of the front window at the smattering of red lights traveling on the highway in front of them. "You remind me of someone I know."

"A doctor?"

"No. A bail bond agent."

"How do I remind you of him?"

She's crazy. Instead Jasmine said, "She . . ."

"Oh."

". . . thinks a lot like you. For the most part, her business is like any other bondsman's. You want her to post your bail? You gotta pay the ten percent premium and come up with collateral. But every once in a while, she comes across someone who she thinks has no business in jail, and she breaks the system's rules."

"And they are?"

"The system says that a guy who sells nickel bags to support his own habit belongs in a six-by-nine cell that costs the city sixty grand every year."

Suárez whistled at the figure. "That's a down payment for a home. So where does your friend believe someone like that belongs if not in jail? Surely, the City of New York is not going to buy him a home and keep him under house arrest!"

Jasmine joined Suárez as he laughed at his own idea. "A guy like that belongs in long-term rehab. I mean, that's what she believes, and I agree with her. It costs the city half as much in the short term, and probably much less if the treatment takes."

"And does she make any attempt to see to it that he gets into drug rehab before bailing him out of jail?"

"She does everything she possibly can short of lugging him to treatment herself every day."

"Is she successful?"

Jasmine mulled over his question. Was she successful? "Most of the time."

"Enough to make it worthwhile," Suárez offered.

"Yeah, I guess so." Jasmine started to ask him if he felt successful, too, but he had already answered that question. Maybe Suárez lost a patient now and again, but he saved enough people to make his efforts worthwhile. Still, providing free medical care to illegal immigrants and poor citizens hardly compared to putting known lawbreakers back out on the street. "But let's face it," Jasmine said. "Obviously, there's a world of difference between being a crazy bail bond agent and a socially conscious physician. Only thing they have in common is that they're rare."

"I'm not so sure about that," said Suárez. "If things don't work out between us, maybe you can introduce me to this crazy bail bond agent friend." He flashed that smile and turned up Juanes.

Jasmine returned the smile. "If things don't work out between us, sure."

Over dinner at Bouley, Jasmine concocted a background that she hoped Suárez would find appealing. She claimed to have graduated from the state university and to have taught elementary school until she became the founding principal of her fictional public school. She borrowed liberally from Lorraine's background and knowledge, referring to her school as one of the city's "New Vision" schools. At first, Jasmine balked at the idea of presenting herself as some visionary educator. Then she concluded that by presenting herself as such, she gave herself the license to invent any kind of school she wanted, and that freedom made it easier for her to manage her façade. In Suárez's attentiveness, she presumed an ignorance of educational theory and policy that she hoped would work in her favor, because she barely knew any more than he did. Before she could get herself in too deep, she made the one point that would build their rapport and perhaps bring her closer to the information she sought.

"In the end, I believe that if public institutions are failing, citizens should create alternatives," she said.

"A toast to that," said Suárez as he poured more Shiraz into both their glasses. He raised his own. "To alternatives."

Jasmine tapped her glass against his and took another sip of the syrupy wine. "To alternatives."

eleven

They ended their meal with tea-flavored crème brûlée and a bottle of Madeira. Then Suárez drove Jasmine back to the clinic, where she had parked her Escalade. He parked right in front of the clinic's entrance and gestured toward Jasmine's vehicle. "That's a lot of car for one woman."

"Comes in handy though." He gave her a curious look, and Jasmine explained according to her newfound profession. "You know, for carting around school supplies, going on field trips, and things like that."

Suárez nodded, and they fell into a second of silence. "Since we're here, would you like me to look at that bruise?"

All that time Jasmine believed he had not noticed it. She did not know whether to appreciate or loathe him for the polite charade. "So much for my bad makeup job."

"Actually, I noticed it because of the makeup," said Suárez as he unlocked the car doors. "You shouldn't wear makeup at all. You don't need it."

She followed him out of the BMW and toward the clinic. Suárez lifted the metal accordion gate in front of the door, unlocked it, and stepped aside to allow her to enter. "Why don't you wash off the makeup while I relock the door? We have a bathroom right down the hallway."

Jasmine walked into the bathroom and locked the door behind her. The exposed bulb above the mirror brought out the bruise under her eye. "Shit." She turned on the faucet.

Through the closed door, Suárez said, "There should be some kind of makeup remover or facial soap in the cabinet."

She opened the cabinet and found a bottle of facial cleanser among a shelf of generic beauty products. On the highest shelf sat an expensive line of men's care products, including moisturizer, toner, and sunscreen. Jasmine pumped some of the generic cleanser into her palms and rubbed her hands. As she pressed her fingertips under her bruised eye, she felt a dull twinge of pain expand across her face. "You practically have a salon in here, Adriano."

"Lisa insisted on it, and at times, it comes in handy." As she worked the lather across her cheeks, she wondered if Suárez and his receptionist had a romantic past. She remembered how guarded Lisa seemed when she first came into the clinic, her protectiveness bordering on possessiveness. "Eventually, I thought why not keep a few things here for myself given all the late nights I keep? After all, how do you think I freshened up for my date with you?"

Jasmine smiled as she rinsed away the cleanser, now beige with foundation. She turned off the water and looked around the bathroom. Hanging from the wall were dispensers of scratchy brown paper and feminine hygiene products. "You wouldn't happen to have any towels around here, would you?"

"I have one for you right here. Open the door."

When Jasmine did, she found Suárez leaning against the doorway holding a small fluffy towel. "Thanks." She gently patted her face with it, like she always saw the models do on television commercials.

"How'd you get that nasty little thing anyway?"

"I got in the middle of a fight."

"Jesus, Jasmine! Who? Where?"

"At the school." Jasmine impressed herself. Her instincts had selected the perfect lie. "We have a summer program, and during lunch two girls got into it. I caught a good one when I tried to break it up."

Suárez shook his head. "I hate to see kids fight, especially girls. It sickens me. Let me see." He put his hand around her wrist and gently lowered the towel away from her face. While still holding her wrist with one hand, Suárez placed his other hand under Jasmine's chin and tilted back her head. "Please tell me it wasn't over something stupid like a boyfriend."

Jasmine smelled a trace of Madeira on his breath, and her mouth watered, as if she had the sweet wine at her own lips. "Actually, they were fighting over one of the girls' brother. Gal One's chasing Gal Two's little brother, and Gal Two wants Gal One to give it up."

Suárez chuckled. "Why don't they just leave it to him to decide?"

"Why make my life easy?"

Only then did Jasmine notice that he had interlaced his fingers through hers and had begun to caress her cheek with his thumb. Before she could speak again, Suárez leaned down to kiss her. The tips of their tongues touched like their wineglasses at Bouley, and he pulled away from her. "When can I see you again, Jasmine?"

"Soon."

Suárez gave Jasmine a warm compress to reduce the pain and swelling and quicken the reabsorption of the blood under her eye. Then after one more kiss that she felt deep in her belly, she climbed into her Escalade and drove away. Flushed by the sugary wine and moist kiss, Jasmine felt too restless to go home.

Instead she followed a whim that brought her past the Burn Masters storefront. To her surprise, Jasmine found the gate raised and the light on despite the late hour. She remembered how Jason would meet with other writers at the deadest night and roam the streets searching for places to paint undetected in the city's shadows. He would return home at dawn the next morning, and when Jasmine asked him where he had been all night, he would shrug and say, "Nowhere." Then Jason would sit on the edge of her bed to unlace his sneakers. "But lemme tell you where I spotted this dope piece." When Jasmine went to the location he described, she always found his tag—REY^2.

Jasmine headed home and found her unwelcome mat wedged in the door as she'd left it. She let herself in and headed to the living room to pour herself a glass of whiskey and light a cigarette. She kicked off her pumps and sat on the floor across from her coffee table, where she had strewn the materials she had stolen from the Bookers' basement apartment. Jasmine poured herself another shot as she sifted through the papers, hoping to discover something she might have missed. She replayed her conversation with Yvette and kicked herself for not having attempted to check Malcolm's e-mail. Jasmine contemplated making a second visit to his home. The last thing Crystal would expect after their fistfight would be for Jasmine to break into her place.

She picked up Malcolm's piecebook and browsed through it again. Her tailbone now aching from sitting on the floor, Jasmine crawled onto her wobbly legs and attempted to climb onto the love seat. In her woozy clumsiness, she dropped the book, and it fell open with its spine up. Jasmine fumbled for the book, grabbing hold of its back cover. After pulling herself onto the sofa, she parked the book in her lap and discovered that Malcolm had drawn several pieces on the last few pages.

Starting from the back cover and working toward the front, Jasmine came upon six drawings of subway cars. Each car featured a word in its own unique lettering and palette. She attempted to read the words of the last drawing. Was that an *E* or a *B*? An *F* or a *P*? A *Q* or a *G*? Jasmine turned the page to the next sketches and had the same difficulty deciphering the words. The only word that Malcolm had etched with legible distinction was his signature—BOUK X. "See, I ain't that fuckin' drunk," she said. Jasmine grabbed the book and flung it back onto the coffee table. "What's the point if no one can read the shit?"

She gripped the armrest and hoisted herself onto her feet. After taking a few moments to steady herself, Jasmine stumbled down the long corridor from her living room to her bedroom. She flopped herself facedown on the bed and then reached for the cordless telephone on the night table. It took her three tries to coordinate her thumb across the keypad and correctly dial Calvin's number. She rubbed her eyes while waiting for his greeting to end. "Yo, Cal, it's Jas." She cleared her throat in an effort to avoid slurring her words. "Listen, I wanna know how you're doing with the stuff I gave you. You know, the database. Did you find out anything? You are working on it, right? Call me back as soon as you're done checking it out, even if you come up empty."

Jasmine dropped her head onto the cool sheets and closed her eyes. Calvin probably would not follow through. He was pissed at her. If she failed to inspire loyalty from a blue-collar guy like Calvin, she could forget about coaxing any from Dr. Adriano Suárez. Unless she slept with him, of course. Then maybe she stood a chance.

With that last thought, Jasmine fell asleep to the buzz of her dial tone.

TWELVE

Despite a monstrous hangover, Jasmine spent the morning in court waiting for the bailiff to call Antoine Watkins's case. She glared at the slacker the court had appointed to defend Antoine—some frat boy from Peekskill with a shirttail hanging out of his wrinkled khakis and a face full of dirty blonde stubble. He looked worse than she felt. 'Toine's PD should have badgered the ADA into accepting a guilty plea in exchange for five years' probation. Jasmine resented having to appear in court to make the case for Antoine his own lawyer—who was hungover on something far more treacherous than alcohol—could not. The sap seemed almost relieved when Jasmine asked the judge if she could speak on the defendant's behalf. Although she finally convinced the judge to pressure the ADA to cut a plea, he still adjourned the case until the following month. Jesus, why were they dragging out this fuckin' thing?

Jasmine cussed under her breath as she left the courtroom. She rarely called ADAs on behalf of her clients. Very few of them appreciated the intervention of outsiders, least of all a bail bond agent who never finished high school, let alone attended law school. But the Watkins case had dragged on far too long, and with no significant reason. This was a classic 220.10, but the ADA was getting her nails dirty, as if this case could make her career. Jasmine seriously had to yank her chain.

She returned to the office to find Felicidad juggling the telephones, answering each call as if expecting her best friend to be on the other end of the line. "Where the hell is Diana now?"

Felicidad mouthed the words *Running late,* and then returned to her caller. "And what has he been charged with, ma'am?"

"It's almost lunchtime," muttered Jasmine. "She might as well not come in at all." She sifted through the telephone messages that Felicidad had left in her box. Among them she found one from Dr. Dieudonné. None were from Calvin. Then her cell phone rang. When Jasmine saw Suárez's name appear on her Caller ID, she jogged to her office, closed the door behind her, and answered the phone.

"How's the eye healing?" he asked.

She checked her face in the dim reflection of her computer monitor. "Slowly but surely." Jasmine really had no idea. That morning she had hurriedly washed up, popped two aspirins for her hangover, and ran out the door with barely a glance in the mirror. She doubted all those shots of whiskey did anything to drain the blood away from her bruised eye. "But I think you should check it out again for yourself."

"How about dinner Sunday around six?"

Jasmine marveled at the thought of having dinner before nine p.m. twice in one week. The nights she did not scarf down a fast-food burger or a meat-and-cheese calzone at that hour, she usually skipped dinner altogether. "Works for me."

"Would you like me to pick you up on my way to the restaurant?"

"No, it's much better that I just meet you there."

Suárez agreed and promised to have Lisa call her back with the location. Jasmine hung up and tried to get to work. She put in a halfhearted hour then took back to the streets.

Jasmine walked into the Burn Masters office to a completely different scene. About four guys ranging in age from fourteen to thirty-four hovered over Yvette as she showcased her latest sketch—a malt liquor ad featuring Honey Blaze, the latest female MC to break into the top ten. Wearing a bandeau dress and spiked heels, Honey held the beer bottle like a mic. The slogan Yvette had scrawled across the bottom of the sketch read *When You're Ready to Run with the Boys.* Jasmine hung back and listened as the men bombarded Yvette with their opinions.

"Too tame," a Latino in his early twenties said. "Not sexy enough."

"But I based it on this." Yvette pulled out a professional photograph of Honey onstage during a concert. "The agency themselves gave me this as an example of how they wanted her to look, so I had to use it."

"Yeah, but that moves," he said, bobbing his head as if he could hear Honey's latest track. Then he stopped and pointed to Yvette's sketch. "Right now this is too static."

Yvette reconsidered her sketch. "Okay, I can hear that."

Then a black kid in his late teens said, "And you still gotta spice it up a bit."

"Spice it up how?"

The Latino guy said, "Instead of having Honey hold the bottle like a mic, why don't you have her hold it like this?" He picked up a fat marker and held it to his lips. The men cracked up.

But Yvette did not care for his suggestion one bit. "She's an MC, not some groupie."

"She's both really," a male voice said.

"And sex sells," said another.

"Well, I don't see Snoop Dogg or Mos Def on no billboard promising to eat me out if I buy their product," snapped Yvette.

Jasmine cracked up, and all eyes turned to her. "Can we help you?" said the Latino guy in a very unhelpful tone.

Yvette eyed her but said nothing. Jasmine had not expected to happen upon a full house and instantly understood it would be unwise to approach Yvette in front of the other Burn Masters. She had enough problems convincing them to trust her vision for their next campaign without a bondswoman showing up at their office asking questions about their prodigal brother.

"I was just walking by on my way to the bodega, and I got curious about what was going on in here," Jasmine said as she backed up to the door. "Sorry, didn't mean to intrude or interrupt." Then she hauled ass out of there.

Instead of returning to the office, Jasmine went home. She lit up a cigarette, but fought the urge to pour herself a shot of whiskey. Not only did she still have a bit of a hangover, she wanted to have as much wits as she could muster to make sense of Malcolm's last drawings. Since he placed them at the end of the book and then hid it in his mattress, those pieces meant something. She popped more aspirin, sat herself at the kitchen table with Malcolm's piecebook, and studied his sketches. Even half sober she still could not read any of the six words he had drawn over the subway cars in each drawing. Every time Jasmine thought she had deciphered the lettering, she happened onto another jumble, never finding a legitimate word.

THIRTEEN

Dressed in one of the few pantsuits she owned—a brown polyester outfit she'd bought for forty bucks—Jasmine went to the office on Sunday to do the work she had abandoned the previous day. Jasmine bypassed the heavy makeup and limited herself to eyeliner, mascara, and lip gloss. Every few hours, she reapplied the compress that Suárez had given her and eventually noticed the swelling under her eye had shrunk.

At five p.m. she eased out the door and to her SUV. As she put her key in the ignition, she smiled. When did she ever have any kind of date with Calvin? He showed up at her place or called her to invite her over to his, although coincidentally she had not gone there since their first fight over Malcolm. Sometimes they ordered in food. They put on the television only to pay it no mind. They always fucked but never cuddled. Calvin usually had something to say about the force, and every once in a while she talked about the agency. If they ever dated at all, they could hardly call it that now.

Suárez took Jasmine to another TriBeCa restaurant located on the waterfront, called Filli Ponte. He requested a table in the dining room facing the Hudson River. The exposed brick and large archways made Jasmine think of damsels in distress and their knights in shining armor. Suárez requested a salad of steamed asparagus, mixed greens, and grape tomatoes topped with goat cheese and red wine vinaigrette.

Jasmine said, "I'll just have the Caesar salad." She waited for Suárez to comment on her mundane selection. But he only smiled at her and asked if she already knew what she wanted for dinner. She settled for the spaghetti with tomato sauce, ricotta cheese, and arugula, although she had no idea what that was.

"Mangeró l'aragosta all'arrabiata," said Suárez to their server. "And a glass of the chardonnay. *Esperto livio felluga."* Then he turned to Jasmine. "What will you have to drink?"

Jasmine hesitated. She really wanted a drink but feared ordering something that would make him laugh at her. Jasmine once had a "date" with the assistant to the Bronx borough president's press secretary, and he ridiculed her for ordering a glass of pinot grigio to wash down a T-bone steak. Some bullshit about drinking a white wine while eating red meat. The jerk thought too much of himself because he had graduated from one of those snooty boarding schools that occasionally lured ghetto children with full scholarships to bring color to their campuses. For all his prestigious education, he still had to pay the likes of Jasmine to have dinner with him and give him a blow job in the front seat of his five-year-old Protégé. Worst of all, he had the gall to call her again later that same week. "What do you recommend?"

Suárez told the server, "Bring the lady a glass of sangioveto, and we'll also have an order of the antipasto misto."

His graciousness made Jasmine feel comfortable enough to confess, "I never learned the rules about what wines to drink with which meats."

"It would have been a waste of your time," said Suárez, "because those so-called rules have become cliché."

"I always figured drink whatever the hell you like."

Suárez laughed. "And that really is the only rule to follow." He reached across the table and placed his hand over hers. "Jasmine, may I ask you something?"

Jasmine braced herself. All this talk about dining etiquette—or more like her lack thereof—made him curious about her background. Here came the questions about how she grew up and what family she had. She could only evade Suárez so much if she expected him to give her any insight he may have into Malcolm's disappearance. And yet Jasmine could not fathom telling him anything close to the truth. She resigned herself to continue her present strategy—playing it by ear, thinking on her feet, and revealing minimal truths via proxy and subtext.

"What do you want to know?" The server returned with their

glasses of wine and a platter of sliced meats, mixed olives, asparagus, and croquettes. Suárez motioned for Jasmine to proceed, and she slid her fork into a croquette. Still, she waited for him to take one for himself and mimed him as he took his knife and sliced it into quarters. The flaky croquette parted like a blooming flower, releasing the aroma of saffron and an orange bulb of stuffed rice. Jasmine bit into it. "Damn, almost makes me wish I could cook! What are these called?"

"*Arancine*. That means little orange. It's a favorite that can be found on the streets of Sicily."

Jasmine dove into another quarter. "So these are the Sicilian equivalents to, like, dirty-water hot dogs?"

Suárez gave a hearty laugh. "Precisely."

"So have you been to Sicily? Or Italy? Is that how or why you learned Italian? No, you know what I always wanted to know? Are Sicilians a particular kind of Italian? Or are they, like, their own distinct nation, ethnicity, or whatever? I could never figure that out."

Suárez picked up his wineglass and took a sip, eyeing her over the rim. "You're avoiding my question, Jasmine. You must know what I want to ask you, don't you?"

He was right that Jasmine was evading his question, but she had no idea what Suárez wanted to know. "Ask."

"I'm not sure what to ask specifically. I guess I just want to know if there's anything about you that I should know. You've only given me your cell phone number . . ."

"It's the only surefire way to reach me."

". . . you won't allow me to pick you up from home or work . . ."

Jasmine reached for her own glass. "We've just met." She took a large gulp and fought the urge to wipe her bottom lip. "Am I supposed to immediately trust you because you're a doctor?"

"Most people do. But, no, you're not. How do you like your sangioveto?"

"I like it enough to want another."

Suárez summoned the server. "Bring us a bottle of the sangioveto."

"Adriano, no, you don't have to do that."

He ignored Jasmine and waved the server away.

"That really wasn't necessary." She gave a nervous laugh. "It's like you're bribing me here."

"Actually, I'm saving that for the third date."

"You're sure enough of yourself to expect a third date, but you're not sure enough of yourself to come without a bribe. How am I supposed to take that?"

"I can't tell you that, Jasmine," said Suárez. "You can tell me something, though."

"What?"

"Are you married?"

Jasmine burst out laughing. Is that all he wanted to know? "I'm about as unmarried as they come."

"But you have someone, don't you?" The server returned with the bottle of sangioveto and two fresh glasses. He opened the bottle, poured a small amount for Suárez to sniff and taste, and started to pour the wine when Suárez stopped him. "I'll do that." He took the bottle from the server and filled Jasmine's glass.

As she watched the reddish black brew rise toward the rim of her glass, Jasmine said, "I don't have anyone, but there's someone around. He has a propensity to just—I don't know—materialize every once in a while." Jasmine almost added that Calvin was the reason why she had been secretive, but she decided to leave it at that.

"And how long has this person been materializing?"

"A little over two years."

Suárez speared a few slices of Italian sausage and transferred them from the platter to his plate. "If it's been that long, I guess that you don't mind him so much."

Jasmine shrugged and helped herself to some meat and asparagus. "Look, Adriano, he's not a bad guy. But that doesn't make him good for me." At once, she felt guilty as if she had betrayed Calvin, and yet she also sensed relief to name the unsaid. "I think we're at the point where we both know that we have to move on, but easier said than done, you know."

Now they were both eating directly from the platter, their forks occasionally tangling amidst the olives and asparagus. "Is there pressure from your family to make it work with him?"

"I have no family."

Suárez put down his fork to look into her eyes. "Really?"

"Yup."

"No parents?"

"Lost them both at thirteen."

"Siblings?"

"I had a brother. His name was Jason." Jasmine could not bring herself to tell Suárez that he had been her twin. "Died a little over six years ago." She moved for her wineglass, and he took that opportunity to pour her more.

They sipped wine in silence until the server arrived with Jasmine's Caesar salad and Suárez's mixed greens. "Both my parents are gone as well," he said. "And my brother . . . well, he might as well be."

"What do you mean?"

"Heriberto's a lawyer in D.C. at one of the nation's top firms. Has a fiancée who's a big K Street lobbyist. Anyway, my brother and I never saw eye to eye, and when my parents passed, so did any incentive to fake brotherhood."

"You think you'd feel that way if you were to lose him for good, too?" Jasmine asked.

"I've asked myself that a thousand times," he replied. "And every single time the answer is yes. Now if Heriberto had any kind of medical problem that I could treat, of course, I wouldn't deny him. But as you already know, I'd do that for a stranger. My feelings toward my brother are no different than they might be about a person I hear about on the evening news."

Jasmine had to ask, "Whatever happened to your parents?"

"My parents came to New York City from Oaxaca. They were among the first to come. My father took whatever jobs he could get in construction while my mother worked as a nanny for a wealthy family in Westchester County." Suárez paused to pour himself another glass of sangioveto. He took a languid sip and rested his glass on the table. "Having no documentation, my father usually worked at unregulated sites doing anything and everything they asked of him. Eventually, he ended up handling the plumbing on a site where a sewage spill occurred, and he contracted hepatitis A and died of liver failure." He pushed himself away from the table and stretched out his legs.

"Damn." Jasmine reached across the table and placed her hand over his. His hands felt smooth yet sturdy. Her comforting gesture surprised even her, and she gave his hand a gentle squeeze.

Suárez said, "The worst thing, Jasmine, is that hepatitis A is rarely fatal. Only a hundred people die from it every year. There's even a vaccine for it. A vaccine my father could not get because he was in the country illegally. And being undocumented and not having any health insurance, we could not get Papá the treatment that could have saved his life."

"How old were you when this happened?"

"Twenty-one. My father died in my last year of college."

"And your mother?"

"She passed almost a year later." Suárez exhaled, and Jasmine thought he might break down in front of her.

"Jesus, Adriano . . ."

"Mamá had become so desperate, she begged her rich employers for help. She didn't even ask them for money. She just asked if they might know of someone my father could see or someplace he could go."

"Did these people know your parents were undocumented?"

"Of course! When they were looking for someone to watch their two children, cook their meals, and launder their clothes for pennies, they couldn't have cared less about my mother's status. Not until she asked them to help us in any way their hearts could see did it matter to them. Less than a month later, they fired her. Said they thought they had risked and helped her enough by hiring her in the first place, and they no longer could take the chance of being found out."

"And how did she die?"

"She took my father to be buried in Oaxaca and decided to stay. Then one afternoon, her heart just gave out. All my relatives there swear my mother died of a broken heart." Suárez reached for his wineglass, and as he sipped, Jasmine lifted the bottle and waited for him to finish. "I believe they're right."

He set his glass down, and Jasmine poured him more wine. "That's a very romantic notion for anyone to have, especially a man of science." She herself saw no currency in romance, yet found this trait in Suárez endearing. It seemed to Jasmine that the more they showed themselves to be unfounded, the more people held fast to archaic notions of romance. That the scarcity of love at first sight, love conquers all, and all those other greeting-card sentiments somehow served to reinforce their validity, when any reasonable person should have long taken their improbable odds as evidence that such things did not happen. Now she sat across from a man of profound intelligence who believed that his widowed mother died of a broken heart. Adriano had every reason to not only be cynical but also resentful as hell at the duplicity of it all. And yet he believed simply because he wanted to. The belief gave Adriano the smallest comfort, and he allowed himself that tiny consolation. Jasmine envied him.

"It is." Then he said, "I know that there wasn't anything I could have done to save either of my parents, but I'm still haunted by their deaths. As irrational as it may seem, I still feel responsible."

Jasmine had no words for him. No one had them for her when Jason killed himself. She had no one to offer her words of any kind. But even if Jasmine knew exactly what to say to Suárez, she would have kept it to herself. Of all people, she understood that the value of such words belonged only to those who uttered them. They only brought comfort to those seeking to be healers, having little impact on those who needed to be healed. Even if she had had friends or kin around to insist that Jason's suicide was not her fault, Jasmine knew damned well that she would not have given them a second thought. So she would not pretend to have the ability to console Adriano, but she would offer him what she did have. "I know what that's like."

"Do you?"

"My brother committed suicide while in jail. I couldn't get the money fast enough to bail him out. So he hanged himself, and yes, I feel responsible."

Jasmine waited for Adriano to probe for the details that she did not want to share. But he seemed to sense this and instead grinned. "You think I'm a romantic?"

"The most legitimate one I've come across to date."

"Is that right?" Adriano seemed pleased by her perception. "I always fancied myself somewhat of a militant."

"Can't be much of a militant without holding some stock in romance," she said. "What's romance without a sense of possibility, right? And it takes a sense of possibility to champion the underdog the way you do." Jasmine finally found the opening to bring the conversation back to Malcolm and to solidify her false identity in one swoop. "And what's the point of charity—or even art for that matter—if not possibility? Tell me that the mural competition you sponsored was not as much an exercise in charity as it was a way to publicize your clinic. All along you were hoping to discover a promising young talent just full of possibilities to take under your wing, weren't you, Adriano?"

He clasped his hands and poised them over his lips, as if he wanted to hide his smile. "Malcolm was such an amazing talent, and I wanted to cultivate him in any way I could. All he needed was an opportunity to study his craft and learn to create *real* art. I was able and willing to give him that opportunity."

"But?"

"His 'homies' were jealous of his skill, and they resented his potential to make it on the legitimate art scene. They put Malcolm under tremendous pressure to 'keep it real,' as they like to say. Real to them means stealing your supplies and vandalizing other people's property."

"Okay, but you don't really think that has anything to do with why he vanished, do you?" Jasmine asked. "I mean, do you honestly believe that they would harbor enough jealousy to do him any harm?"

"I don't know anything about his associates outside of the clinic," said Adriano. "A few of them came to visit him once, and one look and I knew that their criminal behavior did not stop at vandalism. As much as I warned him about them, I couldn't control what Malcolm did on his own time. The best I could do was bar them from the premises and keep him as busy as possible."

"You banned Macho's friends from the clinic?"

"Damned right I did!"

"What if one of them was sick?"

Suárez burst into laughter that caused the patrons around them to turn and stare, and for once, Jasmine did not mind being the center of attention.

After dinner Jasmine and Adriano strolled down the waterfront, and only when they reached Ground Zero did they realize the distance they had covered. They continued along the esplanade, oblivious of the other pedestrians holding hands, riding bikes, and walking their dogs. They reached Battery Park City, and Adriano guided Jasmine through its woodland gardens and described its sculptures.

"Lower Manhattan must be your stomping grounds," she said as they took a seat on a wooden bench. "You know so much about it. Where to eat. What to see."

"Well, I live right there," Adriano answered, pointing at a thirty-story luxury building. "I own a loft apartment with an amazing view of Ellis Island." Then he took Jasmine's hand. "Would you like to see it for yourself while I fix you another drink?"

Jasmine almost never left the Bronx. All she knew about Lower Manhattan and its neighborhoods was what she heard on television, and even then she had never heard anything about TriBeCa, SoHo, and Battery Park City until 9/11. She knew her city had a Chinatown and a Little Italy, but had never seen them outside of the B movies that ran at three a.m. on a Saturday morning. Nor had Jasmine ever visited the Statue of Liberty or Ellis Island, never mind the observation decks of the Empire State Building or the now-fallen Twin Towers.

Still, Jasmine fought every temptation to accept Adriano's invitation. She knew where it would lead and that would take her charade too far. Jasmine might have been willing to risk going to that extreme if she believed that Adriano had told her all he knew about Malcolm's disappearance.

Jasmine rose to her feet and pulled her hand from his. "I have to call it an early night." Then she chuckled. "Tomorrow's a school day, you know."

Adriano stood up and pulled Jasmine to him. As he slipped his arms around her waist, he whispered in her ear, "Is that the only reason?"

Jasmine leaned into him, inhaling the tinge of coconut from his aftershave. "Look, let's be honest about what's going on here." He mur-

mured in agreement, sending vibrations down her spine. "I'm just not prepared to spend the night."

He tightened his arms around her. "Do you think you might be prepared on our next date?"

Jasmine had never been held like this before. Not by her parents, a john, or even Jason. She pressed her hands into Adriano's back and sunk herself into his chest.

"I'll take that as a yes."

And she did not argue with him.

fourteen

"If you're going to do Diana's job, I might as well pay you instead of her," Jasmine said when she entered the office the next morning to find Felicidad at Diana's desk once again. Diana had used all of her paid days off, and Jasmine had had enough of her vanishing secretary act. Diana no longer had the courtesy to call Jasmine herself to let her know that she was going to be out or late, leaving Felicidad to convey the message with her mere presence. "It's just not right for you to be doing her job and not be compensated."

"Don't worry about that," said Felicidad as she offered Jasmine several sheets of paper. "Diana just quit."

Jasmine snatched the papers from her and began to read them. Diana had typewritten a two-page resignation letter from home and faxed it from a neighborhood drugstore around the corner from her apartment. After her laundry list of parting shots, Diana wrote: *All this for a job with no medical insurance or retirement plan? I have my daughter now, Jasmine, and I have to do what's best for Zoë. That means getting a job where I can move up and have a full package of benefits.*

Jasmine crumpled up the letter and tossed it in the wastebasket. Felicidad dove into the basket to retrieve it.

"What're you doing that for?" Jasmine asked.

"You really should save this," she said as she attempted to smooth out the wrinkles in Diana's resignation. "I'll put this in her personnel file."

"Good luck finding it." Jasmine had asked Diana to create files for everyone, but she doubted she had ever bothered. Chances were she shoved all their paperwork in a drawer somewhere. Luckily, Jasmine kept most of her own records. "So do you want this job or not?"

Felicidad stopped smoothing the letter. "Seriously?"

"Deadly."

"Of course!" She jumped to her feet and applauded her unexpected achievement. "Thank you, Jasmine, thank you!"

"Slow your roll, Felicidad. We have to establish some ground rules first. You may want to hear me out before you agree to take on this responsibility."

"Okay."

"Part of your job is to open by nine and close by five. Usually I'm here to do it myself, but don't assume anything other than that it's your responsibility to open and close the office. I'm going to give you keys so you can let yourself in and out if for whatever reason I'm not here."

"No problem."

"Another thing, Felicidad. I personally don't have a problem with your . . . identifying as a woman. But if that's your thing, do it right. I can't have potential customers coming in here having any doubts about who they're talking to. So you hide what you need to hide, pad what you need to pad. Don't come in here with three-inch nails and a five o'clock shadow, because I will send you home and dock you the hours you missed."

Felicidad put a defensive hand on her hip. "Jasmine, you don't even have to worry about that. Even at my brokest, I keep my shit tight. Now that I'm employed?" She tossed her hand to punctuate her declaration.

"I don't know. You've been looking raggedy lately. Worse than I ever do."

"That's because Zachary says I shouldn't come here in *costume*, as he put it."

"Well, you don't answer to Zachary anymore. I mean, he'll still enforce your curfew and maybe occasionally give you a drug test, but you come to me if you have any questions about anything. Except for any makeup or fashion advice, because I can't help you with shit like that. And one last thing."

"Yes?"

"Under no circumstances are you to date anyone even remotely associated with this business. Staff, clients, court personnel . . ."

"Aw, c'mon, Jasmine! Staff and clients, okay. I'm not wasting my time trying to civilize any of these overgrown boys you have running around here anyway. Least of all that crusty Zachary. Jesus, just when I thought all the Cro-Magnons were petrified in a museum somewhere."

"Felicidad . . ." Jasmine struggled to maintain her professional demeanor. As much as she wanted to laugh at her accurate dig at Zachary, she could not allow Felicidad to think that they were friends.

"You mean I couldn't go out with a cute little bailiff?"

"Anyone who may have any kind of influence over this business—no matter how big or small—is off limits to you."

"Including that delicious officer Calvin?"

"Yes." Although Jasmine had no doubt that Calvin wouldn't have anything to do with Felicidad, she no longer found her quips funny. "Especially Officer Quinones."

"I was only kidding, Jasmine. Even if he were my type, it's so obvious he's your man." Felicidad reached for her telephone message pad, tore off one of the slips, and handed it to Jasmine. "He called first thing this morning and wanted you to call him as soon as you got in. Says it's related to the information you wanted him to get for you."

Jasmine took the slip from Felicidad, thanked her, and headed to her office. She dialed Calvin's number as she bustled down the corridor, and he answered after the first ring. "Calvin."

"Hold on." A few seconds later he returned. "Jasmine, I heard you and Crystal Booker held a boxing match in front of the criminal court building."

"I'm sure you did. But I'm not calling you about that. You have some info for me about the database I gave you?"

Calvin paused then said, "I haven't concluded my investigation on that matter." Whoever he initially had tried to avoid must have wandered back into earshot of their conversation. "But I think I've uncovered a pattern."

"Yeah? What? Tell me."

"It wouldn't be appropriate for us to discuss that over the telephone. If you're at your place of business now, I can meet you there. How about within the hour?"

Jasmine believed that Calvin had truly discovered something of meaning. He would not lie just to manipulate her into meeting him. "Just come by my place at the end of your tour."

"Expect me between midnight and one a.m." He hung up before Jasmine could respond. Jasmine rolled her eyes and tucked her cell phone into the hip pocket of her jeans.

At twenty to one the next morning, Calvin let himself into Jasmine's apartment, wearing a fresh haircut and new cologne. He forced himself against the door, which was caught on her unwelcome mat. Instead of helping Calvin, Jasmine just watched in amusement and waited for him to fight his way into her apartment. Once inside, Calvin kicked the mat aside and slammed the door behind him. Jasmine asked, "Can I fix you a drink?" She had already poured herself a glass of sangioveto that she had picked up on the way home. When the clerk at the liquor store asked her what kind, she just chose one at random.

"Do you have beer?"

Familiar with Calvin's preferences, Jasmine had also picked up a case of Coronas. She opened her refrigerator, grabbed a bottle and a lime, and headed to the cutting board on her kitchen counter. "So what do you have for me?" she asked as she sliced the lime. "What's this pattern you uncovered?"

Calvin took a seat at her kitchen table. "All those people in that database are dead."

Jasmine stopped slicing. "You're shitting me."

"I shit you not." He crossed his legs and clasped his hands around his knee. "I had a clerk at the precinct add another field to the database with the dates of death. Where did you get that database, anyway?"

"Found it on Macho's laptop computer at home."

"Why would he have information like that?"

"That's what I was wondering. I figured that maybe he took home some work." Jasmine wedged a slice of lime into the neck of the beer bottle and slid it across the table toward Calvin. "Maybe he was correcting or updating the database for his boss." She almost revealed that Adriano had told her that he had asked Malcolm to update their Web site and had paid for him to take a computer course to facilitate the assignment. Jasmine wasn't ready to inform Calvin that she had gone undercover and to admit to the persona she had invented in an effort to gain information from Adriano.

"I know you, Jasmine. If you truly believed that, you never would've bothered to download it." Calvin took a swig from his Corona then sneered at her. "I mean, it's not like you knew those people were dead when you copied it."

Jasmine joined him at the table with her wineglass and the bottle of sangioveto in hand. "I just had a feeling. What's an artsy kid doing with that kind of information on his home computer? I thought of possible explanations, but I didn't want to jump to any conclusions without checking it out." She poured herself some more wine. "Like maybe he was just purging the deceased patients from the clinic's system."

"Why would Suárez give him access to that information?"

"'Cause he couldn't complete the task he assigned him without it."

"Okay, then why take it home? Macho didn't strike me as a take-work-home kid. Least of all that kind of administrative, methodical, left-brain . . ."

Jasmine took another sip of wine. While not as good as the bottle she had shared with Adriano the previous night, she liked it. "Look, he was doing all kinds of computer stuff for Suárez," she admitted. "Macho was even taking a technical computer class at Baruch that I'm betting Suárez paid for. I found the registration and receipt."

"Okay." Calvin took another sip of his beer, as if to fuel himself for the next round of questions. "Why is Crystal Booker so intent on keeping you from finding her brother?"

"So you think there's a connection between that database and Crystal's determination?"

"Yes, I do, and I think you do, too. I think you're just as suspicious as I am that Macho would have that kind of data in his possession and then disappear without a trace. I think that's why you asked me to look into it." Before Jasmine could respond, Calvin blindsided her with a tangential question. "Since when do you drink wine?"

Jasmine rose from the table, bringing her bottle and glass to the sink.

Taking note of her silence but knowing better than to prod, Calvin returned to the topic at hand. "Okay, Jasmine, you've convinced me that there's more to this than I initially thought. You always suspected it, and now I believe it. I can help you with this. What other information do you have? What else do you need me to do?"

Put off by his obvious ambition, Jasmine said, "Let me get back to you on that." Not wanting to appear ungrateful for what he had done, however, she added, "It's after one in the morning, I've been working ridiculous hours. . . ."

"You always work ridiculous hours."

"And I'm still fighting this goddamned cold. I have to get some rest, Calvin, before I, like, drop dead. So just give me back the disk, and I'll call you if I need anything else." Calvin reached into his pocket and handed Jasmine the flash drive. "Thanks, Cal, for everything. Really."

She led him to the apartment door and opened it. Before he crossed the threshold, Calvin turned around to face her one last time. "Jasmine, I know how obsessive you get about these things. Don't do something crazy like go after Macho by yourself. Keep me in the loop."

"Okay, good night." Jasmine tried to close the door, but he blocked it. Then Calvin leaned forward to kiss her on the cheek before finally leaving. She locked the door behind him, adding the security chain. Then she remembered that he still had keys to her place. She hurriedly unlocked the door, threw it open, and dashed into the hallway. But Calvin had already disappeared. "Shit."

Jasmine shuffled back into the apartment and locked the door behind her. While she appreciated Calvin's help with the database, she took issue with his motivations and admonitions. She had been going after Malcolm since she heard he'd jumped bail. That was her job. If anything, she needed more information that only she could get. Jasmine had to find a way to get into Adriano's office.

fifteen

Now that she had hired Felicidad to replace Diana, Jasmine expected an end to the morning surprises, but she arrived at the office the next day to find Felicidad handing Calvin a cup of freshly brewed coffee.

"Good morning, Jasmine," sang Felicidad.

"Morning, Felicidad. Hey, Calvin."

Jasmine motioned for him to follow her to her office. "Where's Diana?" he asked.

"Gone. For good."

"Did you, like, do a background check on that Felicidad?"

"Why do you ask that?"

"Something about her . . ."

Jasmine decided to have some fun with him. "Admit it, Calvin. You think she's attractive. You were afraid that when I came in here and saw you two together, I'd get jealous." Calvin flustered, and she just laughed.

They entered her office, and she closed the door behind them. "What brings you here so early in the morning? Shouldn't you be asleep?" Jasmine seated herself at her desk and invited Calvin to take the chair across from her.

But he chose to pace in front of her desk. "Yeah, but I couldn't. Look, Jasmine, I wanted to clear up something. Yes, I want to help you find Booker, and, yes, I have a professional stake in doing so. But I also want to help because I know you care a lot about this case, and . . . well, I care a lot about you." Calvin stopped pacing. "I love you, Jasmine."

She stared at him in disbelief. No one had said that to her in years, and Jasmine never thought anyone would, least of all him. "When did this happen?"

Calvin smiled. "I don't know exactly. I mean, I know it was before our big blowout a few weeks ago. Maybe that's the reason we had it, I'm not sure. But your telling me what I feared most didn't change how I felt about you. Maybe I wanted it to, but it didn't. Let's break this stalemate we've gotten ourselves into and move forward together."

But there was nothing new about this stalemate, as he called it. In the beginning, Calvin had genuinely been interested in Jasmine, but he had tried to pull away almost immediately after his fellow boys in blue told him what they thought of her. By the time Flaherty came out and said what they all knew, things between them had already gone too far. Calvin was a coward. He did not have the guts to make a move either way—to either end it with her or stand up to his peers on the force. And Calvin was greedy. He wanted to be able to show up at her door to have his needs met, be they sexual or professional. And when Jasmine realized this, instead of cutting him loose she decided that two could play that game. After all, she, too, was a greedy coward with her own needs. They were too much alike to have a future together. Jasmine did not have futures with anyone anyway, so when, how, and why Calvin decided that he had fallen in love with her was a mystery he would have to solve on his own. The best she would ever be able to offer him was what they already and always had: a stalemate.

"Let me think about it, okay?" she finally said.

"Yeah, sure, whatever you need."

"But I still need your help with this surrender." Jasmine reached into her pocketbook for her keys and unlatched the flash drive. She handed it to Calvin. "Why don't you dig deeper into those people in that database? Maybe they have other things in common besides the obvious."

"Okay." Calvin took the drive and put it in his lapel pocket. "Anything else?"

Jasmine knew he wanted to hear something hopeful about the future of their relationship, but instead she mulled over the other bits and pieces of the Booker case. She considered asking Calvin to do a background check on the members of the Burn Masters to see if there was any truth to Adriano's speculation that they were more sinister than a harmless graffiti crew. But then Calvin would want to know how she came upon that theory, and Jasmine had neither the wits nor the heart to lie any more that morning. Besides, she owed Calvin some slack. The man had it in his head that he loved her, and that was punishment enough. Then Jasmine remembered Malcolm's piecebook.

She reached into her pocketbook and pulled out the book. Flipping to the last several pages, Jasmine asked, "Can you read this?"

Calvin walked around her desk to peer at the book over Jasmine's shoulder.

"You think it means anything?"

She could smell his drugstore aftershave and wondered what had happened to the coconut scent. Then Jasmine remembered: that was Adriano's pricey brand.

"It's just Macho drew about twenty pages' worth of stuff, starting at the front of the book like you normally would. Stuff I could read. Then for whatever reason, he jumped to the back of the book, and I can't make out what it's saying. Maybe it's nothing, but it irks me."

Calvin reached over and turned the page. "Trains." Then he snickered.

"What about them?"

"I just think it's funny that Macho drew subway trains. I mean, except to scratch your name into the windows and maybe tag the insides with a marker, they're really hard to vandalize nowadays. Between all the money the city invested in installing extra cops and cameras in the MTA yards, buying stronger graffiti-removal solvents, and immediately removing graffiti as soon as they're discovered, subway graffiti went the way of the token." Calvin peered at the centerfold before him. "I can't read this shit either. The only thing I can make out is BOUK and the number."

Jasmine sat up. "What number?"

He pointed at Malcolm's tag in the lower right-hand side of the page. "He signs it and then places a number after his name."

Jasmine turned the pages. "The number changes on each one." Was it familiarity or drunkenness that had blinded her to them? At first, she thought Malcolm merely intended to number the sketches in his series. "Eight, zero, nine, one, two, zero. They're in no obvious order, and one of the digits is repeated. They must mean something to Macho, if no one else."

"Maybe he signs them all like that."

"No, he's just BOUK X." Jasmine flipped to the front of the piecebook and began to thumb, scanning for Malcolm's tag on each page. "See, none of the other signatures has a number. I'm telling you, Calvin, they mean something."

"What?"

"Your guess is as good as mine."

Jasmine put in a late night to catch up on all the paperwork she had neglected. She paid bills, wrote correspondence, and in addition to Zachary's enforcement report and Lorraine's clinical notes, read a stack of administrative memoranda from her latest hire. In addition to a professional telephone manner and an accurate sense of time, Felicidad came with a bevy of ideas for organizing the office.

First, she wanted to update the standard operating procedure manual and write an employee handbook. Felicidad bought and read all the daily tabloids and clipped and highlighted articles about the law enforcement issues and criminal justice system that she thought would interest Jasmine. Now an employee with legitimate access, she wasted no time diving into clients' files to create two copies of a "field manual" for Jasmine to keep with her so she would not have to take files to and from the office. It included a calendar of all the clients' upcoming court dates, as well as a directory of contact information for their presiding judges, assistant district attorneys, and public defenders. She instructed Jasmine to leave one at home and keep the other with her or in her car.

To her final memo, Felicidad attached the printouts of several Internet sites selling management software specifically created for bail bond businesses. Until then, Jasmine had no idea that such a thing existed. Felicidad also recommended that Jasmine invest in a PDA so she would not have to lug so much paperwork.

Thinking about technology, Jasmine turned to her computer to continue her search for Malcolm. She logged on to the Internet and clicked to the search engine. In the window, she typed *Malcolm Booker + Suarez.* She hit RETURN and skimmed through the results. Jasmine came upon an article in the online version of a Bronx newspaper about the art competition Malcolm won sponsored by Adriano Suárez.

She clicked on the link to access the full text, and an accompanying photograph appeared on her screen. Wearing a posh suit under his pristine lab coat, Adriano had an arm around Malcolm's shoulder while he shook his hand. In his free hand, Malcolm held a can of spray paint, and on his head sat the latex mask he wore to filter out the fumes while he painted. The caption to the photograph read, *Graffiti artist Malcolm Booker receives congratulations from his benefactor and clinic founder Dr. Adriano Suárez at the mural's unveiling in Mott Haven.* Remembering her conversation with Yvette, Jasmine imagined that the article caused static among the Burn Masters, especially when she read it to find that the crew had never been mentioned. It did make a slight reference to Suárez's passionate crusade for affordable health care since losing his immigrant parents to "treatable conditions."

Jasmine backtracked to her search results page and clicked on another article published in an e-zine covering New York City's art and cultural scenes. Published before he actually painted the mural, the article announced Malcolm as the winner of Adriano's art competition. It contained no new information but offered a forum for readers to discuss articles. Jasmine clicked on the link, hoping to find useful information about Malcolm, such as the names and locations of both his fans and foes, and perhaps some interesting tidbits about Adriano Suárez, too.

> I work near the clinic and walk by that wall every day, and this sounds like a great idea. I commend Dr. Suarez for sponsoring a neighborhood beautification project like this, and I hope he'll consider doing more in other parts of the Bronx. I've never heard of Malcolm Booker, but I'm sure if he won the competition, he's going to do a fantastic job.—Vin'sGirl83, Clason's Point, Bronx

Well, I live in Brooklyn, and I agree with Vin'sGirl. I wonder if Suarez would sponsor something like that here, especially in my neighborhood, where there's graffiti all over the place. It's a fucking eyesore. I can't believe that some people have the nerve to try and call that garbage art—ElChulisimo, Red Hook, Brooknam

GRAFFITI IS VANDALISM AND VANDALISM IS A CRIME! It's as simple as that. Anyone who can't see that is either an idiot or a goddamn vandal himself—ImusForever, Rego Park, Queens

A few people on these forums are so ignorant, it surprises me that you can read and write. Some of the most respected artists in recent history, such as Jean-Michel Basquiat and Keith Haring, have their roots in graffiti. Whether you want to believe it or not, it's a legitimate form of creative expression that actually requires a great deal of skill and discipline. Stop buying everything the corporate media and the prison industrial complex feeds you and think for yourselves for a damned change—SIRE, Hollis, Queens

Well said, SIRE!—Whispers, Wyandanch, Long Island

Why even bring up graffiti, ImusForever? Malcolm Booker entered a legitimate contest and won. As a result, Suarez is hiring him to paint a mural on the wall of his clinic. In other words, Booker has—more like WON—permission from the owner of the wall HIMSELF to paint the mural. This is a LEGAL enterprise so your post is irrelevant.—1OFDOTHERS, Lost Island, HI

Well, I happen to agree with ImusForever, at least to a certain extent. You can't get away from the fact that graffiti is a crime, and I just happen to like some of it. And that's why I like what Suarez is doing. He's giving this Booker kid an opportunity to use his talent to make an honest living.—EZONDIS, Hartford, CT

The niggers and spics like writing their names on other people's property because (1) their too lazy and impulsive to work and save, and yet (2) they're jealous of people who do and eventually can afford to buy their own homes and/or start their own businesses. That's why their neighborhoods look like war zones, and if they had their way, they would have everyone else's look the same. BTW, what do you call a Hispanic with a medical degree? SPIC!—SchillingerLives, Elk Grove, USA

You're a racist asshole! But I'm sure you not only know that, you're proud of it. It's the only thing you do know, moron! You come up here and talk shit about Black and Latino graffiti writers, but how many swastikas have YOU painted on someone else's property? How many crosses have YOU burned on some family's lawn? Racist idiots like you are the biggest vandals out here, and while I'm no fan of graffiti, I'll take the kind done by minorities ANY DAY over the shit you do—MERCU1ST, Harlem World, USA

Everybody, ignore SchillingerLives. He's always coming here and posting filth. Don't dignify him with a response. To Merc: it so happens that some of the best artists during graffiti's heyday were white. From what I understand, nobody really cared about a writer's race. What mattered was having skill and being prolific. As for the art versus crime debate, I'm old enough to remember when the subways were full of graffiti, and how filthy I used to think they were. But now that it's gone, I actually miss it. Literally and figuratively, New York has lost some of its color. Still I really have mixed feelings about it because while certain walls and subway trains might be fair game, it's never cool to paint a wall or window that's part of someone's home like I see sometimes in my neighborhood. So I don't really know if graffiti should become legal or not.—2DAAM, Williamsburg, Brooklyn.

SchillingerLives, our neighborhoods are so terrible, white people are tripping over themselves to move into them. Or haven't you heard of gentrification? Why don't you come to my 'hood and talk some of that shit, you stupid MF!—DominiRock, Quisqueya Heights, NY

I hear what you're saying, 2DAAM, but you have to understand that part of the appeal of doing graffiti IS the illegality. I'm sure if given the opportunity, many writers WOULD paint for a living, but that doesn't mean heads still aren't going to throw up on a wall or train or wherever and whenever they can. Some of the ol' school legends are doing both commercial work AND illegal pieces. So it really doesn't matter if it's legal or not, if the cops crack down on it or not, or if the MTA buffs your piece hours after you get it up. Graf is as old as man and is here to stay.—FENOMINAL, Do or Die Bed-Stuy, Brooklyn.

If it's illegal, it's graffiti. If it's legal, it's art. Nuff said.—CandyLover, Camden, NJ

Don't get it twisted. Except for a few older writers who have paid their dues and gotten fame, a lot of these folks out here getting commercial work doing graffiti ain't no underground vets. They're some crunchy granola types from the 'burbs who come to the "big city" to go to art school and decide it would be "oh so cool" to do graffiti. I haven't met a single cat on the scene who's gotten into art school with a graffiti portfolio, but I've seen a lot of TOYS GRADUATE from art school with one to show their uncles and godfathers on Madison Avenue!—REKK, Shaolin, NY

Candy, are you saying that's the way it is or that's the way it should be?—ImusForever, Rego Park, Queens

I swear some of you are so insistant (sp?) on bringing race into everything. REKK, DominiRock, Mercu1st, you're not that much better than SchillingerLives if you answer him. We're talking about graffiti/art/crime. Leave race out of it.—Vin'sGirl83, Clason's Point, Bronx

Vin'sGirl, you're kidding, right? —DominiRock, Quisqueya Heights, NY

Intrigued by the fierce debate over graffiti, Jasmine spent over two hours reading each and every one of the almost three hundred posts made long after the article had been published. Toward the end, she came across the one that made the activity worthwhile.

```
To all the WRITERS on this forum. We need
to get off this board and create our listserv
to discuss some urgent issues affecting BOUK X
and the rest of US. I just created a discussion
group on Yahoo, and if you want to join, hit me
up. And don't worry. You best believe I'm going
to keep out all the toys and haters.—PRIESTS,
Burn Masters Syndicate, BX in Effect
```

And PRIESTS had posted his message a week before Malcolm disappeared.

Jasmine logged in to her e-mail service and started to compose a request to join the listserv. Just as she moved the cursor over the SEND button, she reconsidered. Her user name, REYESBONDS, revealed too much. What if PRIESTS recognized it as the name of the bail bond company that released Malcolm from jail? Jasmine had to create a new e-mail address for the purpose of infiltrating the group.

She went to the main page of her e-mail service and clicked on the button to create a new account. Jasmine pondered for a while over the new user name. Rather than choose a random name with no meaning, she had to present herself as someone knowledgeable about—or at least appreciative of—graffiti, to increase the chances that PRIESTS would accept Jasmine's request to join the listserv.

Then the perfect name revealed itself to her. Jasmine created a new, free e-mail account—REY2@yahoo.com. She addressed the e-mail to PRIESTS at the address he gave when posting to the forum. In the subject line, Jasmine wrote, "Subscribe," then hit SEND.

SIXTEEN

Jasmine had checked her new e-mail inbox three more times after sending her request to PRIESTS, only to find a welcome note from the service provider outlining the Web site's available features. She also signed into the account the next day before she left her co-op. Both times the inbox was empty.

But when Jasmine came into the office less than an hour later and logged on to her desktop, she finally saw what she had been waiting for—an e-mail from PRIESTS with her original subject line now Re: Subscribe. Jasmine clicked on the message and opened PRIESTS's response:

```
REY² IS DEAD.
```

Jasmine fired an e-mail back to PRIESTS. *Who the fuck do you think you are? If there's something you want to know, you could dead the attitude and just ask me.* Then she came to her senses and deleted her brief tirade. Jasmine took a deep breath and typed, *Never said I was Rey^2. Why would I try to front when everyone knows that there could only be one Rey^2? I'm just a big fan of his.* She paused and decided to raise the stakes. Jasmine deleted the last line and wrote, *I'm both a fan and was once a student.*

She hit SEND just as Zachary barged through the door. Jasmine jumped in her seat. "Christ, Zachary, what gives?"

"What the fuck is the drag queen doing sitting at Diana's desk?"

Jasmine rose to her feet. The possibility of this scenario had lurked in the back of her mind ever since she decided to hire Felicidad. "Her job."

"What?"

"Diana quit—before I could fire her, I might add—and I hired Felicidad to take her place."

Zachary slapped the files he had in his hand onto her desk. "You and I had an agreement, Jasmine."

"And this company had an agreement with Felicidad."

"Once I get my BS at John Jay, I'm applying to the Department of Corrections."

"I know, Zachary," yelled Jasmine. "We all know. How can we forget? We can't be in the same room for two minutes without you fuckin' reminding us that you want to be a CO."

"Let me remind you about this. I took this job because I thought it would help me get into the DOC, only to find out that they think you're a goddamn lunatic. But I stayed with you, Jasmine. You know why? Because I realized that they were just hatin' on you. That no matter what fucked-up shit they said about you, you handled your business—sometimes even their business—but they didn't want to give you props for that. That's why I could stay. But now you've gone and put that goddamn freak on the staff!"

"Which is separate from your job, Zachary, so why do you care so damned much?" Even though Calvin had agreed to help her, Jasmine suspected that it had as much to do with his feelings—or at least the feelings he believed he had—as his hopes that the Booker case might unravel into something greater than the typical bail jump. Despite all his whining about Felicidad, Jasmine needed Zachary to have her back in the likely event she pissed off Calvin and he abandoned the search for Booker. Jasmine took a swing at Zachary's competitive bone in the hopes of getting him to refocus. "Remember that database I asked you to check out? The one that you gave up on after, what was it, five names? The one you said had nothing but bullshit information and called a waste of your time? Well, I had Calvin look into it and he found something very interesting." Jasmine folded her arms across her chest and waited for Zachary to ask the obvious before she continued.

"Don't compare me to Calvin. Calvin's a fuckin' cop. He has access to people and resources that I don't." Then Zachary threw up his hands. "Fuck this shit." He spun around and threw open the door. "I quit." Before she could react, he rushed out the door.

Jasmine gave chase, catching up to him in the corridor. She never thought her tactic would backfire never mind to this extreme. Still, she maintained her game face. "Just like that, huh?"

Without breaking his stride, Zachary said, "Yeah, just like that."

Jasmine grabbed hold of his sleeve and jumped in his path, but Zachary continued to plow forward like a submarine breaking the surface. "You want to quit over Felicidad, so be it," she said. "At least stay on until we find Macho. When we do, I'll give you half the bail as severance pay." No way Zachary would refuse the possibility to make five easy gs.

"What the hell for?" He halted to face her, his large frame towering over hers. "Not like you need me anyway. You've got your drag queen and fuck buddy on the case, right?"

Jasmine hauled back and slapped Zachary across the face. Then she marched down the hallway back to her office. Zachary's derisive laughter soon followed, and she turned around to glare at him. "It's a good thing you're going into corrections, Zachary, because you suck at investigations."

"I'm the one who told you not to put Booker back out on the street," Zachary yelled. "And every time I told you that he broke curfew to go bombing, you looked the other way. Now that he's on the run, go find him your damned self."

Jasmine answered that challenge with a resounding slam of her office door.

Several hours later, Adriano called her. The second Jasmine answered, he asked, "When can I see you again?"

"I'm just great today. Thank you for asking. And how are you?"

Adriano chuckled, ignoring her sarcasm. "If you sincerely want to know, go out with me."

"When?"

"Tonight."

"Can't."

"Why not?

"I have to work late tonight." She thought of an appropriate lie. "Parent-teacher planning meeting." Recognizing the banter they had fallen into, Jasmine retreated. This was not Calvin she was talking to. And she had to get into that clinic, preferably after hours. "How 'bout I take you out to dinner tomorrow night?"

Adriano sighed. "I have to stay late at the clinic. A community group is scheduled to use our conference room for their meeting tomorrow night, and Lisa can't stay because she has class. Are you free Friday?"

"No, I'm seeing you on Friday."

"Where?"

"At your clinic. I'm way overdue for a thorough examination. Can you fit me in at the end of the day, Doc?"

"Absolutely."

The first of the few times that Jason took Jasmine bombing, he asked her to help by finding the colors and shaking the cans as he needed them. He usually called out the color he wanted next by using accurate if silly names—box-cutter orange, school-bus yellow, mailbox blue—and she found those colors with ease. But Jasmine had to listen carefully when her brother resorted to specific names, because when Jason asked for light shock blue, he meant light shock blue and not shock blue, light blue, or shock blue pastel. Jasmine would shake it for at least two minutes to ensure that she remixed the pigment that had settled in the bottom of the can. Once she skimped and Jason gave her heat, because even in the dim lighting of the streetlamp, he could see the color had sprayed unevenly.

Once Jason insisted that Jasmine cancel a "date" to accompany him to a little-used playground he had discovered in West Farms. She resisted because the novelty of creeping in the dark and painting without permission had worn off, and the rent was due at the end of the week. But Jason pleaded with her to go with him, because his writing buddy had flaked out on him. Several weeks earlier this friend had gotten a nine-to-five gig after the mother of his infant son threatened to leave him if he did not get a job. For a while he kept to their ritual. Two or three times each week, he met Jason sometime between ten and midnight depending on their itiner-

ary. Once they reached their destination, they bombed until three, sometimes four in the morning. After his boss caught Jason's friend snoozing at his desk and promised him a one-way trip to the unemployment office the next time he fell asleep on the job, he retired from graffiti.

So Jason harangued Jasmine into accompanying him to the playground, convincing her that the walk to the park would take longer than the deed itself. The park was small, with just the basic furniture and amusements—a swing set, monkey bars, and seesaws, along with grids painted on the asphalt for games of hopscotch and skully. Jason had simple ambitions. When he discovered the seesaws painted in forest green, he had the idea to tag one letter across each of the four slabs of wood. Jasmine looked out from a park bench as Jason drew with an extra-wide marker filled with permanent ink and topped with a nib he punctured with a pin to allow the ink to drip more. If anyone came to the playground at that hour, Jasmine expected it to be a couple seeking a spontaneous quickie fueled by the thrill of being in a public place, or a loner seeking to enjoy the nickel bag he just scored without having to share it with any freeloaders. When no intruders materialized, Jasmine started to doze off. The static of a police radio awakened her as a beat cop crossed the street toward the playground. "Oh, shit!" She jumped to her feet and ran toward the seesaws. "Jason, five-oh!"

Jason stopped in mid-stroke. "Where?"

Jasmine's scurrying had caught the cop's eye, and he hurried towards the park. "What are you guys doing in there?"

Jason said, "This is a public park, yo!" But then he turned to his sister and yelled, "Break!" Having thoroughly cased out the tiny park, Jason had noted all the exits. As the cop ran through the main entrance, the twins cut through the swings and dashed out the back. They ran for two blocks toward their subway station, but just as Jasmine headed for the staircase, Jason yelled, "Jasmine, no, the bus, the bus, the bus!"

The twins leaped on a random bus just as the driver started to close the door. They plopped into a bench for two, sweat beading on their foreheads and their chests heaving with both breathlessness and excitement. "Why didn't we just take the train?"

"'Cause what if there was a transit cop down there?" her brother said. "He could've radioed him, and we could've gotten caught."

"True." Jasmine glanced through the window at the dark street. "What bus is this? Where the hell we headed?"

"I don't know."

And they laughed at the narrow escape, which led them to a new section of the borough they had never seen. They waited for a half hour, until the bus route intersected with another subway line, before getting off. Then they rode that line for another hour back to the South Bronx. Jason tagged on the benches of the deserted car, and now wide awake with daring, Jasmine just basked in the exhilaration. She broke the law almost every night of her life and got away with it, never deriving a second of pleasure from it until that moment.

Almost five hours had passed since Jasmine had parked her SUV across the street from the Burn Masters storefront. Although several people had come and gone, no one triggered the instinct that had driven her there in the first place. Jasmine wanted to corner Yvette and ask her more questions about Malcolm, but she had yet to appear that night. When all the other stores on the block had closed, Jasmine wanted to go home, but her gut kept her hand off the ignition, and she stared at the office light as it beamed through the window and onto the sidewalk.

At twenty to midnight, the light disappeared. A lone figure walked out of the office with keys in hand and locked the door. He wore baggie jeans and a hooded sweatshirt that shielded his face. Slung across his shoulder was a large courier bag that bulged with weight. Jasmine recognized him from Malcolm's caricature.

PRIESTS.

Jasmine turned on the ignition. She watched PRIESTS as he reached for the bar to pull down the security gate over the storefront. When he padlocked the gate and started down the street, she revved up the car and pulled out of the parking space. PRIESTS reached the main avenue and stuck out his hand to hail a gypsy cab. Several passed by him until one finally stopped, and he hopped into the backseat.

Jasmine trailed the cab. It headed toward the Bruckner Expressway but remained on the boulevard for two and a half miles. On the corner of Lincoln Avenue and Bruckner Boulevard, PRIESTS jumped out of the backseat of the cab and continued south on foot. Jasmine kept him in sight with one eye and looked for a place to park with the other. At the first opportunity, she pulled the SUV against the curb, jumped out, and followed PRIESTS as he headed toward the Harlem River Rail Yard.

Jasmine's blood thickened as she watched PRIESTS check over both shoulders before tossing his courier bag over a chain-link fence. He latched on the fence with his hands and feet, scaled to the top, and climbed down the other side. PRIESTS grabbed his bag and disappeared down the track. "Fuck!" Fearful of losing sight of him, Jasmine ran to the fence.

She looked around for any potential witnesses and hoisted herself onto the fence. With every step closer to the top, her heartbeat quickened. Between the slight wave of nausea in her stomach and the adrenaline rush to her head, Jasmine thought she might topple to the hard earth. As she kicked her leg over the fence, she paused to catch her breath, steady her mind, and take a quick glance at her surroundings. Jasmine glimpsed a shadow just before it disappeared behind a freight train. Now with the adrenaline overpowering the nausea, she leaped down the side of the fence and took off after the shadow.

As Jasmine neared the freight train, the awareness of her surroundings hit her. The state Department of Transportation owned the ninety-six-acre site but leased it to a private developer. Still, every year some elected official, government agency, or community development corporation promised to put the site to some meaningful use. At different points, Calvin mentioned that a newspaper print plant or a paper recycling facility or family waterfront park was going to be built there. But only a waste transfer facility made good on its threat to appear.

Nevertheless, Jasmine had just trespassed on state property, and if she were discovered, she would surely be arrested. But she could not will herself to tackle the fence again. Not until she found PRIESTS. Jasmine already knew what he was doing in the rail yard, and that awareness drove her to find him and bear witness to his act. If she was lucky, she would learn his identity, too, which she could later use to befriend him online in the same way she had Adriano Suárez in person.

Jasmine walked around the freight car and spotted PRIESTS as he strolled down the gravelly path between two rows of trains. Rather than follow him, she waited. PRIESTS stopped before a particular car on the train to his right then dropped to his knees to search through his courier bag. He pulled out a small stool and perched it before the car. Jasmine doubled back and crept down the other side of the train behind PRIESTS, checking underneath the cars for his feet. When she saw them, she slipped in between two cars behind him and settled to watch.

PRIESTS pulled a respirator over his hooded face. Jason once owned a similar one made in Spain and sold on the Internet for thirty bucks. He bought it with a credit card he had stolen.

Then PRIESTS sorted through several cans of spray paint until he found the color he wanted. After replacing the tiny cap on the can with a fat one, he tossed the original cap into his bag and started shaking the can. Jasmine studied PRIESTS as he painted the freight train with the affection and care one might use to brush a toddler's hair. In one hand he held a sketch he used to guide his strokes. In the other he held the spray can, poising it with precise gestures and spraying in slow but fluid strokes.

After drawing a horizontal black line across the top of the car, PRIESTS climbed off the stool and stepped back a few paces to survey his work. Satisfied with his progress thus far, he leaped right back onto the stool and started to extend the line. But then the stool tipped to the right under his leaning weight, and Jasmine suppressed the impulse to shout a warning. The stool crashed to the ground, and PRIESTS stumbled onto his courier bag. Navigating the cans under his feet, he managed to regain his balance. But when he looked up to see how the aborted fall had impacted the piece, PRIESTS hissed a string of curses and kicked the stool so hard it rolled toward the preceding car. Jasmine peered at the painted line but could not make the error that so upset him. She just watched as PRIESTS picked up his bag, slung it over his shoulder, and moved to the next car. There he began again, setting up the stool, shaking his can, and beginning to paint.

Jasmine bided her time until PRIESTS climbed off the stool to search for another can of spray paint. As the unsuspecting writer rifled through his bag, she withdrew Shorty from the back of her waistband, aimed it, and advanced on him. "Freeze!"

Without even looking up to see who had discovered him, PRIESTS dropped the can and made a run for it. Jasmine chased after him and tackled him to the ground. She pressed her knee into his back, pinning him into the gravel as he grunted in pain. Jasmine yanked one hand behind his back as she reached for her cuffs. After cuffing him, she scampered off his back, rolled him around, and planted herself on his chest. His muffled curses filtered through the respirator that masked his face. Jasmine pulled him toward her by the lapels with one hand and tore off the respirator with the other.

"Shit!" All this time, Jasmine had assumed that PRIESTS was a man. But not only was she actually a woman, she was a woman that Jasmine had already met. PRIESTS was Yvette.

SEVENTEEN

"I know you're no cop," said Yvette from the backseat of Jasmine's SUV, "so I don't have to say shit to you." Jasmine had been driving through the South Bronx for almost twenty minutes, interrogating Yvette about Malcolm's whereabouts without success. "Where the hell are you taking me?"

"Nowhere special," said Jasmine as she pulled onto the Pelham Parkway. "We're just going to keep going around in circles until you talk to me."

"Your gas." Yvette fidgeted, leaning her cuffed hands on the seat in front of her. Before piling her into the backseat of the SUV, Jasmine had moved the handcuffs to the front so Yvette would be more comfortable. She had hoped that act of benevolence might inspire her to be more sociable. "And I am talking to you. I asked you a question. Where the hell are you taking me?"

"Asked and answered."

Yvette sucked her teeth and threw herself back against the seat.

Jasmine needed to switch tactics. As she exited off the Bruckner Expressway and headed toward Orchard Beach, she considered her options. Yvette did not want to talk about Malcolm, so Jasmine had to choose a subject that might lower her guard. She said, "You know, I was watching you for a good fifteen, twenty minutes before I stopped you. I got so caught up in what you were doing, I probably would have waited until you finished. But then you quit one car and started on another one. Why'd you do that?" Yvette remained quiet, and Jasmine glanced over her shoulder at her in the backseat. "Seriously, I want to know. Just when you were gaining momentum, you threw a fit and abandoned the job. And not being a writer, I couldn't tell what you did that was so terrible."

"When I fell off the stool, I got paint over the serial number."

Jasmine snickered. "So fuckin' what? You've already trespassed onto state property with the intention of committing vandalism. . . ."

"Whatever."

"I'm not saying that to judge, Yvette. Just putting what you just said into some context. If you're going through all that trouble to paint the damned thing, why give a shit if you get a little paint on the serial number?"

"What's the freakin' point of doing all that work just to have them buff it?"

"They're gonna remove it anyway, right?"

"Not necessarily," said Yvette, annoyed with Jasmine's ignorant assumptions. "When you do a piece on a freight, the rail inspector just might leave it alone if you don't paint over the serial number. Once I lost control of the can, I had to quit and start over on another car."

"I get it now."

"I mean, if I were just doing a throw-up, no big deal. I'd finish it and take the chance that it might run for a few days before they removed it." Yvette's zeal rushed her words. "But I wasn't going to waste my entire night on a piece they're going to buff immediately to clean the information panel."

"Sounds like you were planning something ambitious." Jasmine approached a fork in the road between City Island and Orchard Beach. She chose the beach. People might or might not be there at that hour, but City Island was a residential community as much as the Bronx's historic seaport. Better for Jasmine to take Yvette to the beach and risk being seen by a few stragglers than to drive her through City Island, where they surely would be seen.

"I was going to burn a top-to-bottom on that car until you disrupted my flow."

Jasmine guessed that a top-to-bottom was exactly what it sounded like—a piece that completely covered the car. Hearing the frustration in Yvette's voice, Jasmine decided to steer her away from their altercation in the rail yard and quit asking the obvious. To build a rapport, she had to keep Yvette's attention on her passions. "A top-to-bottom of what? Your name? PRIESTS?"

"It's PRIEST-ESS!"

Jasmine laughed at herself. So much for avoiding the obvious. "So I guess if folks realize that your tag's *Priestess*, they've also pretty much figured out that you're a woman."

Yvette shrugged. "Ain't no secret. At least not to those on the scene."

"Well, you'll be glad to know that it still is to the cops."

The backseat squeaked as Yvette straightened with attention. "How do you know that?"

"I've got a contact in the department, and he told me that you don't turn up in Graffitistat. I mean, the cops have flicks of your stuff in their database, but they don't know who you are just yet, let alone that you're not some sixteen-year-old boy."

"For real?"

Jasmine nodded and pulled into the parking lot of the beach and turned off the ignition. She switched on the light and reached for her pocketbook, which was sitting in the passenger seat. "It's Priestess," she said, laughing at herself.

Yvette nervously bounced forward in her seat. "What you doing?"

As Jasmine pulled out Malcolm's piecebook, she said, "I can't read 'em, so how am I supposed to know how to pronounce them, right?"

"Where'd you get that?"

Pleased to have caught her attention, Jasmine said, "Never mind that." She opened Malcolm's piecebook to the first two sketches of the subway series and placed it on Yvette's lap. "But tell me this. Do you still post up on subways, too?"

Yvette hissed. "I'm not fiending to go down on a terrorism charge."

"Are you serious?"

"Hell, yeah, if the po catches you in the tunnel, they automatically hit you with a terrorism charge. They figure if a writer can get down there, what's to stop one of bin Laden's boys? And that's why at almost every transit yard, the MTA has got cops, dogs, cameras, you name it."

"So you've given up on mass transit," Jasmine teased.

"I didn't say that," Yvette snapped. "I'm a writer, and a writer always does trains. I'm just saying that between the Vandal Squad and Homeland Security, you have to be more careful about getting up."

Jasmine heard the frustration in her voice, and she presumed that Yvette always had more to prove as a woman in a man's subculture. In front of her male cohorts, she had to eat her fears and never reveal hesitancy to do anything they would. If she wanted them to respect her boundaries, like when she resisted their pressures to sleaze up the Honey Blaze ad campaign, Yvette had to seize other opportunities to match and maybe even outdo their daring.

"With all that shit going on, I would say to hell with the subway," said Jasmine. Gambling that Yvette's need to prove herself might outweigh her desire to harbor secrets, she added, "And you know what? I think most writers would, too, because I don't see shit on the trains. C'mon now, when's the last time you got up on a subway car?"

"I did a motion tag just last week," Yvette bragged. "At the Eighth Avenue station on the L line, I just waited against the wall for the train. It came in, and right there while I was between the train and the wall, I posted up. Took ten seconds."

"Yeah, and they probably buffed it in as many hours."

"I lucked out. It ran for about three days. But you know what else I did to make sure heads saw it? I waited for the train at First Avenue and I took some flicks of it. Headed to the twenty-four CVS, dropped the film off at the one-hour photo, got myself something to eat at a nearby diner, picked up my flicks, and went home and posted those bad boys on the Internet."

"Im-fuckin'-pressive," said Jasmine, and she meant it.

"You know how you do subways? You work the inside. Just ride it and post up. Or you burn spots that can be seen from the elevated lines. That's how KNAVE became king of the J line. That's why we call Woodhaven K Town. And them cats out in Bushwick? YKK? They making video games with Marc Ecko and still killin' the city. Writers still do trains. Always have, always will."

"And you can always do freights, too."

Yvette sneered at the obvious. "You can still do freights. That used to be some West Coast, Midwest shit, 'cause that's all they had to bomb." Then the fleeting passion returned to her voice. "To kill in New York City, you have to bomb the streets, but I love me some freights. I mean, no disrespect to the writers who risk getting up on the subways as hard as it is now to go all-city. But you can go cross-continent if you get up on a freight train. Freights can bring you mad fame. . . ." Her voice trailed as her mind wandered into the fantasy of having her name racing across state lines.

"Nothing beats a moving canvas," said Jasmine. She thought of Jason and then of Malcolm again. They had both yearned for a moving canvas. "That's why Macho asked Suárez if he could paint the van, too. They call that a wrap, right?"

"What?"

Jasmine noticed that Yvette had made no attempt to flip through Malcolm's piecebook. Perhaps she had seen everything in it before.

"The mobile clinic Suárez uses to tour the neighborhoods, you know, to offer free tests for hypertension, TB, diabetes, and things like that." Jasmine nodded at her, appreciating both Malcolm and Adriano. "Suárez let Macho paint it."

"Don't talk to me about Suárez," Yvette said. "That fuckin' hypocrite."

"How you figure?" Jasmine caught the edge in her voice and made an effort to tone it down. "I mean, you gotta give the man his props."

"Props for what?"

"For coming out of pocket to provide health care to people who otherwise might not get it."

"Suárez gets no dap from me 'cause I've got that sucka's card, and I'm telling you he's a fuckin' hypocrite."

Jasmine had to work this opening right. If she came too direct, whether to challenge Yvette to back up her accusations or to defend Adriano, Yvette might shut down. Jasmine had to keep Yvette shooting without letting her know that she was lining up a particular target. Since baiting her had worked, Jasmine chose to try it again. "C'mon, Yvette. You can't shit on what the man does that has good bearing on other people. How would you like me to just buy into all the ill shit he claims to know about your crew, even when I've seen with my own eyes that y'all do legitimate work?"

Yvette lunged forward in her seat, knocking Malcolm's piecebook to the floor of the SUV. "What the fuck did Suárez say about Burn Masters? Just because Macho worked for him for a minute doesn't mean he knows us like that."

"I'm just saying." Jasmine threw her hands up in mock surrender. "The good doctor was giving me the business about y'all being a bunch of vandals and probably doing a whole bunch of other illicit shit."

"That shysty muthafucka!" Yvette pounded on the headrest of the passenger seat with her cuffed hands. "Suárez don't know a damned thing about us, okay. He wants to be Mr. Down for the People, but he don't know the first thing about these streets. He wants to be Mr. Art Connoisseur, but Suárez don't know his sack from his crack when it comes to graf, and he ain't trying to ask nobody 'cause nobody can tell the so-called good doctor shit. He rather stay ignorant than admit he don't know something."

As her tirade accumulated intensity, Yvette bounced over to the middle of the backseat to get closer to Jasmine. "Let me tell you how ignorant his ass is. One time he overheard Macho telling one of our boys in the crew that he wanted to kill. Fool pulled him into his office talking about, 'I hope that was just a figure of speech, because I would hate to think that you were involved in anything violent, because I cannot have anyone associated with that kind of activity working in my clinic, this, that, or whatever.' Dr. High Roller took Macho all literally and shit, and he had to break down for him what he actually meant."

"Well, break it down for me," interrupted Jasmine, "because I sure as hell don't know what it means either."

Yvette scoffed and jerked her cuffed wrists into the air. "All Macho meant was that he wanted to get up more. Just bomb everything. Have his pieces wherever you look. That's all it means to kill. Writers ain't acting the fool out here like these gangsta rappers, shooting each other up and everyone else in the vicinity on some bullshit. I'm not saying we don't have beefs and throw up our hands once in a while. We're ruthless when we gotta be, especially if some Brooklyn heads are trying to test. But for the most part, we don't get down like that. Ain't no writer out looking to kill nobody. Shit, we're too busy watching our backs 'cause we trying *not* to get killed out here, what with po fiending to crack open your skull or put a choke hold on your ass. And over what? Writing your name on a wall? Over something that used to be a fuckin' misdemeanor? When you got thugs running up on people on the street, trying to jack this one and looking to rape that one? They spent all that money to stop heads from tagging up on a train, but they still haven't found a way to stop niggas from trying to push someone in front of one!"

When Yvette paused to find her breath, Jasmine asked, "So what did Suárez say when Macho explained it to him?" She waited for Yvette to continue her rant, but she said nothing. Instead she leaned back into her seat and slid over to the window. "Yvette, what did Suárez say?" But Yvette just peered out the window into the darkness of the empty parking lot. "Talk to me, Yvette. If nothing else, tell me why. Why did Macho run?"

"I don't know."

Jasmine reached down to pick up Malcolm's fallen piecebook. Again, she opened it to the train sketches and held the book under the SUV's light so that Yvette could see. "At least tell me what these say."

"You're just like Suárez," said Yvette, shaking her head. "You're down for something, but it ain't this. If you were about it, you'd be able to read it."

The direct approach had gotten Jasmine all the information it could. She closed the book, put it back into her pocketbook, and revved up the SUV. As she drove out of the parking lot, Jasmine plotted to ingratiate herself with Yvette through other means. Now that Yvette had given her more insight into the graffiti subculture, she would exploit it to build her credibility and identity as Rey^2 and get onto that listserv.

"Where we going now?"

"Wherever you want."

"Serious?"

"You said it yourself. I ain't no cop. And even if I were, I certainly wouldn't bust your ass on this. Only thing I'm interested in right now is dropping you off wherever you want to go, and taking myself home to bed."

"Fine then," said Yvette. "Take me back to the yard. I still have time to finish that piece before the sun comes up."

Yvette sounded so much like Jason. He once borrowed the movie Style Wars *from their neighborhood library and watched it on the DVD player he had bought from a junkie for five dollars. For the first half hour of the documentary, Jason was restless with ecstasy. Jasmine wanted nothing more than to sleep, but her brother kept nudging her every few minutes and nagging her to watch along with him.*

But as the film moved into the MTA's anti-graffiti efforts, Jason's euphoria quickly devolved into depression. "Are you listening to this shit, Jas?" he said as he squeezed her shoulder. "Yo, watch this." She rolled over to watch Mayor Ed Koch brag about the anti-graffiti PSA featuring boxing greats Hector "Macho" Comacho and then-middle-weight-contender Alex Ramos. "Take it from the champs . . . Graffiti is for chumps. Make your mark in society. Not on society." "Ain't we society, too?" Jason yelled back at the screen. Then he said, "Jazzy, can you believe that shit? Niggas like that nowadays be entering the ring playing some hip-hop. Be trying to rap even, the fuckin' clowns, putting out albums and shit." Then Jasmine could not help but stay awake, taken less with Style Wars *and concerned more with her brother's darkening mood. Identifying himself as the descendant of graffiti writers, Jason's sense of betrayal ran too deep to celebrate the progress of his colleagues in rap music.*

Only now after listening to Yvette did Jasmine understand her brother's lament. Jason had grown resentful, she suspected, over the realization that he would never experience either the exhilaration or the visibility of graffiti's pioneers. In the natural order of things, the next generation was supposed to have it better. Technology elevated the MCs. CDs and MP3s crossed borders and took their creations across the globe. They seared their rhymes to their images in videos and feted their accomplishments during extravagant award shows. The youngest MC had it the best, marrying the sound of old to the technology of the day and transmitting his design to the world.

But time proved to be graffiti's worst enemy. With it came technology, and technology brought with it more tools of repression in the form of protective coatings, chemical solvents, removal processes, public campaigns, and budget allocations. Because of this, the pioneers of graffiti had it best. Unlike DONDI, ZEPHYR, or TRACY 168, Jason would never know what it would feel like to go all-city or be king of a line. Despite all his talent and discipline, he would never even have the opportunity to gain that kind of fame.

Why didn't Jason realize he could do freights?

eighteen

Jasmine awoke the next morning feeling as if she had eaten concrete. Opening her eyes became a feat that took her fifteen minutes to accomplish. She inched toward her phone on the night table and called the office. With her tongue bloated with exhaustion, Jasmine left a message for Felicidad that she would be in the office later than usual that day. She figured that she only needed a few hours of sleep to recuperate from the twenty-hour days she had been keeping since Malcolm absconded. Once she caught up on her rest, Jasmine intended to climb out of bed, drive to the agency, and put in a full day's work. No sooner had she finished her message than she fell back into a grave sleep while holding her phone.

But Jasmine awoke hours later with gravel still in her veins. She willed herself to sit up in bed and toss the sheets in search of her phone. When she recovered it, Jasmine called the office.

"Reyes Bail Bonds, this is Felicidad. How may I help you this afternoon?"

"Afternoon?" Jasmine glanced at the clock radio on her nightstand. The lunch hours had come and gone. "I guess I'm calling to say that I'll be working from home today." She climbed out of bed and headed to her computer.

"Do you have to?"

"Why? What's up? What went down?" Jasmine turned on her computer and then headed for the kitchen.

"Nothing."

"You get a call from an ADA or a defense attorney or something?" The thought of a legal drama unraveling at the office while she willed herself into a temporary coma made Jasmine antsy. "Felicidad, you know to call me if anything like that happens, right?"

"Of course, Jasmine. Calm down. Everything here's just fine."

Jasmine reached for the sack of sliced bread on her kitchen table. "So how come when I told you I was going to work from home today, you said, 'Do you have to?'" She dropped two slices of bread into her toaster, then reached for the canister of ground coffee.

"I didn't say it like that."

"Why did you say it at all?"

"Because, Jasmine—and please don't take this the wrong way—you sound like shit. When I said that, I meant do you have to work at all today. Just take the day off and chill out, *m'ija*."

Jasmine snickered at Felicidad's term of endearment. Did her own mother ever refer to her as *m'ija*? She could not remember. Probably not. And now she had a woman with male anatomy who was the same age mothering her. "Are you, like, going to make me some cure-all soup from your *abuelita*'s secret recipe?"

"If you want me to!"

"No, Felicidad, I'm just kidding. All I need you to do is promise me that you'll call if anything important comes up."

"Only if you promise me to get some rest."

"Don't blackmail me. Just do what I tell you. Call me if something comes up, you hear?"

"Yes, ma'am. And call me if you need anything. Anything at all."

"Trust me, I will."

While her coffee brewed, Jasmine went to the bathroom to retrieve some aspirin. Then she carried her dry toast, black coffee, and two pills back to her desk. Although she expected her inbox to be empty, Jasmine logged in to her Rey2 account. There sat an e-mail from Yvette as PRIESTS, and Jasmine feared that she might have figured out what she had been up to. She held her breath as she opened the message.

So send me some of your work.

Yvette's demand both heartened and intimidated Jasmine. Not only had she not blown her cover, but Yvette seemed eager to have her skepticism abated. Jasmine had a chance to maneuver herself onto the listserv that might lead to clues to Malcolm's whereabouts. But now she had the problem of proving she was something she was not. Jasmine had no artistic proclivities, let alone talents in any of the visual art. But Jason did.

To the extent her heavy limbs would allow her, she hurried to the closet to dig up her brother's work. Jasmine had saved all of Jason's piecebooks, sketches, and the like in a cardboard box and had stashed it in the back of the closet. She retrieved the box and placed it on the unmade bed. Sifting through the pages and photographs with no clue how to determine which to send to Yvette, Jasmine felt a pang of regret. She should have made a better effort to understand Jason's work. Although she had no involvement in his nocturnal lifestyle, he chose the tag REY^2 as a way to represent them both. He even took flack for it because he kept the rationale behind the tag—especially the superscripted 2—a secret between the twins. "People be asking me who's the original REY, because when you take on an older writer's name, you're paying tribute to them. You're saying, 'This is the person that inspired my styles. He's the writer I want to be like,'" Jason explained once to her. "But I keep telling 'em that my tag ain't REY Two, it's REY squared. And they be like, 'So why did you do that? What does that mean? If there's no REY before you, why not just leave it like that?' And I say never mind."

"Why don't you just tell 'em then?"

"Look, Jazzy, I know you have to do what you got to for us, and that's why you can't be out there with me. I mean, I want you out there with me, and I don't. I don't want you with them nasty dudes at those filthy motels, but what if you were to go bombing with me and some cops rolled up on us? Or some bangers? Or whatever. I could never forgive myself 'cause I'm your big brother. . . ."

"Like, by two minutes, kid."

"Still, my job is to look out for you. This is how I bring you with me without having you in harm's way. You feel me?"

"I feel you."

"I may be out there by myself, but I'm never alone."

"Me, too."

"And heads know I got a sister, but they don't realize that REY squared ain't just my name. It's your name, too. But they don't need to know all that."

"That's none of their business," said Jasmine. And she appreciated Jason for taking all the risk and doing all the work, yet sharing the glory with her. Despite the doubling hunger and the sweat of strangers she could never seem to shake, he managed to make her feel special. She should have tried to understand his art, and therefore Jason himself, better. She would have discovered how to make him feel special. If Jasmine had bothered to do that, Jason might have hung on longer when he got knocked. Had she done that, he never would have forgotten that although he was in Rikers by himself, he was never alone.

Jasmine held up two renditions of the same tag. While she noticed the subtle differences, she had no understanding of which was the superior piece. She had no ability to evaluate a piece on its merit, never mind distinguish good works from bad ones. To choose several of them and send them to Yvette for scrutiny would be a major risk, but she had no choice.

She grabbed the piecebooks and checked their dates. After identifying the oldest book, Jasmine decided to take samples from there. If she sent any of the photographs of his public works, Yvette might recognize them as Jason's, whereas the sketches in his books were less likely to have been seen by anyone else. And even if Jason did show his piecebooks to other writers, the oldest ones were most likely to be forgotten. Hopefully, the fact that they were old would not mean they were not respectable.

Logic proved of no use to Jasmine, however, when it came to selecting which pieces in the oldest book to send. She only had her own aesthetic and instinct to guide her. Eventually, Jasmine found three she liked and brought them to her desk to scan them into her computer. She spent an hour editing out REY^2 from each of the pieces. She toyed with the idea of finding a graffiti-like font on the computer to inscribe a tag of her own, but decided against it. Surely Yvette would not only spot the fraud but would take offense at it as well. Jasmine decided against placing any kind of signature on the scanned sketches at all.

But even as she started a new e-mail to PRIESTS, Jasmine knew she had to sign the e-mail with a suitable tag. After pondering the possibilities for over a half hour, she finally settled on one and kept her message simple:

```
PRIESTS,

Peep these.

Peace,
JaneDoe
```

Jasmine exhaled as she hit SEND. She scooped up Jason's three pieces and carried them back to the box. But instead of storing them away with the rest of her brother's work, Jasmine decided to tuck them into Malcolm's book. Then she crawled into bed and fell back into another comatose sleep.

The phone rang and awakened Jasmine. Assuming Felicidad was calling with some question or concern, she fumbled to answer it. "Yeah?"

"Jasmine, it's Calvin."

"Hey, Cal." She immediately sat up. "What's up?"

"I have more information on this database."

"Really? What?"

"I need to see you to discuss it."

"Sure."

"What's wrong, Jasmine?"

"What do you mean?"

"You sound really bad."

Jasmine did not want Calvin to do this. "No, Cal, I'm fine. I just woke up."

"You're sleeping at the office?"

"No, I'm home."

"But . . ."

"I didn't go in today."

"You're that bad?"

"Listen, about the database . . ."

"I'm coming over right now."

"Forget it, Calvin, I'm fine." But before Jasmine could protest, he hung up on her. "Shit."

Jasmine took a long, hot shower and changed into one of Jason's undershirts and velour sweatpants. She considered cooking something for Calvin but had no energy. Instead she brewed a fresh pot of coffee, found a box of crackers, and sliced some cheese. Only as she leaned against the sink to maintain her balance did Jasmine realize that she had no appetite, even though she'd had only dry toast and a cup of coffee over four hours earlier. How did she fall back asleep with a large mug of black coffee in her belly? Now she needed support to stand.

Calvin arrived twenty minutes later with three containers of soup, a drugstore bag of over-the-counter medications, and some rental videos. As usual, he let himself in, and rushed into the kitchen with his packages as if he lived there. Calvin pulled out the containers and lined them up across her kitchen table. "This is chicken noodle, split pea, and Yankee bean. . . ." When he turned to hand her the bottle of flu syrup, his jaw dropped. "Oh, my God, Jasmine."

"What?"

"Honey, you have to go see a doctor."

"I just needed a day off." Jasmine turned away from him. She reached into the dish rack for two spoons.

"Yeah, I know you run yourself ragged, but . . ."

"Catch up on some sleep."

"But I've never seen you look this sick before."

Jasmine almost did not want to face him, inviting him to comment on her gaunt cheeks and pale skin. "If I can get more sleep, I'll be just fine." She shoved a spoon in his hand and dropped into a chair. Jasmine opened a random container of soup and dipped her spoon. "So let's get on with this so I can get back to my Zs. I gotta tell you what I found out, too." She blew on the spoonful of Yankee bean soup.

Calvin relented and pulled up a seat for himself. "What?"

She told him about her discovery of PRIESTS's true identity, her conversation with Yvette in her SUV, and the listserv of graffiti writers that Yvette had created to discuss Malcolm a week before he disappeared.

'You know why Yvette calls Suárez a hypocrite?" said Calvin. "I think he's the one who's engaged in some kind of criminal activity and that Booker found out. Criminal activity involving the dead people in that database he copied and stored on his computer at home."

The heartiness of the soup and Calvin's intriguing hypothesis triggered Jasmine's hunger. She took another spoonful of Yankee bean and asked, "What makes you say that?" She reached for some crackers and crushed them into her soup. "They have something else in common besides the obvious?"

"I tracked most of them down, and on the surface they seem very different. Men, women, young, old. . . . Almost all of the patients were minorities, but not all, and they came from all kinds of backgrounds and lived all over the city."

"Except?"

"Well, in one way or another, they were all loners. No family ties or extensive interactions in their environments." Calvin put down his spoon and sipped his split pea soup directly from the container. "The kind of people who might have gone unnoticed when they died."

Jasmine stopped eating. "Gimme an example."

"One of the people on that list—a girl—was a runaway. She came up in the police database with multiple arrests for prostitution. She was originally from, like, the Midwest."

"Jesus."

"This other guy—one of the few white people on the list—was independently wealthy, lived alone, somewhere in his sixties. His former landlord said that he kept to himself. Called him a curmudgeon."

"Now why the hell would Zachary tell me that all the addresses in the database were wrong? I mean, that's the excuse he gave me for not following through on this when I assigned it to him. How did you find out all this information?"

"Zach was right. The addresses were wrong. But that didn't mean those people didn't exist. I just used whatever other information and technology I had at my disposal, and this is what I came up with."

They ate in silence, digesting both their warm meals and newfound knowledge. Although she put little stock in Calvin's theory about Adriano's possible criminality, Jasmine did wonder what kind of illegal activity could occur under the guise of providing free health care. "Calvin, you once said that you thought Suárez might be scamming Medicaid."

Calvin shrugged. "It's possible. But what's that have to do with our dead loners club? So he charges the state for an X-ray or test he never ran. So what?"

Jasmine stood up, abandoning her soup and starting to pace the kitchen.

"Jasmine, sit down and finish your soup."

Ignoring his order, she asked, "What about identity theft? Think about it. When you have an operation like that, you have access to all kinds of information about your patients. It's probably pretty easy to swipe their identities if you wanted to." She remembered Adriano's allegiance to undocumented immigrants, who would benefit from assuming the identities of American citizens and legal residents, but Jasmine kept this to herself. Instead she asked Calvin, "Were all these people citizens?"

"I just presumed so." He looked at her with a glint of embarrassment in his eye. "Maybe I shouldn't have."

"Well, find that out. You know what? Find out if they all died the same way, too. Natural causes, homicide, or whatever."

Calvin folded his arms across his chest. "You're forgetting something, Jasmine."

"What?"

"I don't work for you."

"I thought you said you wanted to help me." Jasmine bit her tongue on the other thing Calvin told her. The last thing she wanted was to initiate *that* conversation. "But, hey, I can just take it from here. I can probably call—"

"No, I can handle it." Calvin rose from the table. "You need to slow down, get some rest, and see a doctor about this flu."

As Jasmine walked Calvin to the front door, she thought that he should have asked the same questions she had. With such rudimentary thinking, he would continue to have problems moving up in the NYPD. Out of appreciation for the work Calvin had done for her, however, Jasmine kept her criticism to herself. Instead she said,

"Thanks, Calvin. For everything. The food, the medicine, and most of all the support."

She knew he wanted to kiss her but would not unless Jasmine made the first move. Calvin had made his feelings clear, but she had yet to respond in kind. Jasmine wanted to kiss him, too, but only because he wanted her to and he had been so helpful. That was not reason enough.

Jasmine opened the door. "Thanks again."

Calvin nodded. "Any time." He hesitated then leaned in to kiss her on the forehead.

She watched him as he made his way to the elevator. "Hey, you sure you don't want to take some of this soup with you? I think there's a whole container of chicken noodle left."

"No, you keep it." The elevator arrived. "Good night," he said before he disappeared into it.

"Night." Jasmine locked the door and headed into the kitchen. After cleaning up, she went back into her bedroom and climbed under the comforter. Like water rushing out of an overturned pitcher, Jasmine felt the wave of exhaustion drift over her. As it made its way to her head, she had several thoughts. If he had to be guilty of anything, she hoped Adriano was not involved in anything worse than identity theft. As much as she liked the man, she had to remember the reason she made his acquaintance. No matter how enjoyable they might be, their interactions were a means to an end that still remained a mystery to him.

Still, Jasmine had to recuperate enough to keep their date. She reluctantly admitted to herself that their time together would have to come to an end. Even if she found Malcolm and Adriano proved to be innocent of any wrongdoing, the false pretense under which they met guaranteed they had no future. But until that time, as hard as Jasmine worked, she deserved to enjoy some stimulating conversation, great meals, and the Manhattan skyline.

With her eyes weighted by sleep, Jasmine reached over and opened the top drawer of her nightstand. She pulled out a liter of whiskey, removed the cap, and took a deep swig. Jasmine started to recap the bottle, but then chugged one more time. As she twisted on the cap, replaced the bottle in the drawer, and buried her face into her sweaty pillowcase, Jasmine accepted one last thing before another powerful bout of sleepiness overtook her.

She was not that much different from any of those dead people in Malcolm's stolen database.

Nineteen

Jasmine first opened her eyes well after one in the afternoon the following day. "Shit." She immediately called the office.

"Reyes Bail Bonds, please hold. . . ."

"No, Felicidad, it's me." But she had disappeared before Jasmine could identify herself. She waited for several minutes before Felicidad returned to her.

"I apologize for the wait, but how may I assist you this afternoon?"

"It's me, Felicidad. Look, I'm sorry I didn't call. Can you believe I've been sleeping since about six o'clock yesterday?"

"Good, because I need you well rested."

"Why?"

"Last night the cops raided a drug ring on Creston and 183rd, so, girl, I have an inch-high stack of bail requests waiting for you."

"Okay, I'm coming in now." With Malcolm's bond on the verge of forfeiture, Jasmine had to drum up all the business she could. As much as she yearned for another day in bed, she had too much competition to stay home. "Is Lorraine in?"

"Yeah, and she's been so helpful."

"Cool. I want you two to review and rate the applications. As soon as I get in, we'll go over them and decide which ones to take. We have to move on them like lightning or the clients will find another agent." Jasmine hung up the phone and rushed to the shower. While not at her best, she felt well enough to get through the hectic afternoon and her date with Adriano that night.

After her shower, Jasmine turned on her computer and dressed herself as she waited for it to boot. When it finished, she checked her e-mail and found a message from Yvette as PRIESTS.

JaneDoe!

Are you a sister? I peeped your stuff, and you got skillz, but damn, you weren't kidding when you said you were a student of REY², LOL! Where you at? If you're in the Apple, we gotta meet up.

Peace,
PRIESTS

"Yes!" It touched Jasmine to learn that her brother's work was known and respected, and she wondered if he ever knew that. Although thrilled at the opportunity to build a rapport with PRIESTS, Jasmine had to avoid a face-to-face meeting with Yvette, but still convince her to grant her access to the writers' listserv. After some thought, Jasmine hit REPLY.

PRIESTS,

Yeah, REY² was a mentor to me before he died. His death hit me mad hard, and I stopped writing for a long time. But now I want to get back into it and develop my own style. I know hooking up with some other writers would help a lot.

Peace,
JaneDoe

Jasmine sent the e-mail and left for the office for the weekly staff meeting.

"Absolutely not," she said, vetoing Felicidad and Lorraine's vote to post bail for a twenty-three-year-old woman named Miriam Rojas. "Even if her so-called friend comes through with the collateral, she's a flight risk if I ever saw one."

"You don't believe her, do you?" said Lorraine. "You think she's lying when she says it was her boyfriend's dope."

"I totally believe her, Lorraine. And it's no wonder to me that he's not the one posting her bail." Jasmine took Miriam's screening form and put it in the pile of rejected applications. "The guy stashes three kilos of cocaine under the mattress of their son's crib, but a woman who has only known Miriam for a little over a year calls us? Besides this 'friend,' her kingpin boyfriend and her son, she has no other ties to New York City, but she has her mother, an aunt, and a bunch of cousins in Orlando? I said no." She found herself missing Zachary. If Felicidad and Lorraine had their way, the jails would be emptied on Jasmine's dime. "Any more requests?"

"No, that was the last one," said Lorraine. "But I do want to discuss something."

"My decision on Rojas is final. I don't want to discuss it anymore."

"Okay, but I do want to use this example to raise a larger issue." Jasmine relented, and Lorraine proceeded. "Remember the conversation about what it would take for us to be in a position where we could serve more women?"

"I do, and I meant it when I said that I would like—"

"Jasmine, I don't doubt that at all. But if we don't make it a priority, we never will be. It's not going to happen on its own."

"So what are you proposing we do? I mean, I don't have the money to hire more counselors or monitors or day care workers. Until I replace Zachary, I'm responsible for the curfew checks and drug tests. And with all the shit I've got going, including trying to find Malcolm Booker, I can't always do them. But I have to locate Malcolm Booker before his bail is forfeited so I can replace Zachary. As a matter of fact, the longer it takes me to find Booker, the less supervision I can do of our pro bono clients, and the less supervision they have, the more likely one of them is going to FTA. Then I have another bail forfeiture on my back. Do you see what I'm getting at here, ladies? In a matter of months, I can be out of business."

They let the stark reality settle over them like a cloud threatening to burst. Then Lorraine said, "I'm sorry."

"Me, too."

"I don't want you guys to be sorry or feel responsible. This is on me. If anything, I'm the one who feels bad to have put your jobs in jeopardy."

"Well, let's not think that way," Felicidad said. "Maybe that's a real possibility, but it's not where we are now. So let's focus on what we can do today."

Lorraine said, "With your permission, Jasmine, I want to do a few things."

"Like?"

"I thought maybe I could do some research. You know, go to Rikers and interview some women who are locked up because they can't make bail. Maybe even find and interview some who did post bail. Or I could find some women and hold a focus group here at the office. Anyway, just conduct some kind of needs assessment."

Then Felicidad said, "And I thought I could see if there's anyone who would give us money or partner with us some way to do some basic services."

"Give us money?" Jasmine laughed

"Donate some cash or food or clothes. Something! I mean, I know nonprofit organizations have government contracts and get foundation grants to do this kind of thing, and that you're a for-profit company. . . ." Felicidad snapped her fingers. "I have an idea! Maybe Lorraine can start some kind of counseling group or educational workshops for the women, right? And she could find a way to do it through her school because they can get public money that you wouldn't qualify for."

"But then you could let us have the sessions here in the rec room," Lorraine said, adding to Felicidad's train of thought. "And it wouldn't cost you anything, but my school could write you a letter saying that instead of renting space you donated it. Then you can use that as a write-off on your taxes!"

"What can I say?" said Jasmine. "You bitches are brilliant."

They all laughed. "Well, we don't have it all figured out yet," said Felicidad. "But together we'll come up with something."

Jasmine stood up and handed bonds she had completed for the

commercial principals they had approved at their last meeting to Felicidad. "Well, before you start on your quest to save the world, be sure to drop these off at the courthouse first thing Monday morning."

"Consider it done," said Felicidad, straightening the bonds by tapping the stack on her desk. She started to follow Lorraine out of Jasmine's office when she remembered something. Felicidad turned around and said, "Jasmine, since you've been battling that flu forever, I took the liberty of scheduling an appointment with that sweet Dr. Dieudonné for Monday at one. I told her that you probably would want to go during lunch, and she juggled to accommodate you, seeing you're old friends and all."

"Really?" It astounded Jasmine how oblivious Felicidad was to her seething. "She told you that?"

"Oh, yeah. When I called to make the appointment, she was so happy. She said to me, 'I am so glad that Jasmine hired you. You're so pleasant and conscientious.' She said for a moment there she thought you kept standing her up, but I told her that no, you're just really busy, and your last secretary wasn't the most reliable chick in the coop, you know what I'm saying, and we just started laughing. And Dr. Dieudonné goes, 'Well, that's good to hear because I used to babysit Jasmine and her twin brother when they were kids, and I hated to think that she would just blow me off like that.'"

As Felicidad rambled about her conversation with Nathalie, Jasmine restrained her outrage. She had to keep her cool because she could not afford to lose Felicidad now. But without a doubt, Jasmine also needed to set her straight. She asked Felicidad, "Well, we're done here for the day, so . . ."

"Oh, my God!" Felicidad burst into applause. "Closing shop at five o'clock? Could this be the signs of a new Jasmine Reyes?"

Holding back an ugly retort, Jasmine said, "Let me give you a ride home."

On the drive to Hunts Point, Jasmine informed Felicidad that she was never to take any liberties with her schedule or to discuss her with anyone again. "And if you do, Felicidad, not only will I fire you, I just might surrender you." She waited for Felicidad to protest the extreme threat, but she avoided eye contact with Jasmine, fluttering her naturally plush lashes out the passenger window. "First thing Monday morning, you call Dr. Dieudonné, cancel the appointment, and tell her that I will call her back when things are less hectic. Blame it on the raid. Once you do all that, you stay out of my personal business. Do we understand each other?"

Without looking at her, Felicidad said, "No, but I understand you."

"Whatever. Do what I tell you. Nothing more, nothing less."

Jasmine parked her car in front of Felicidad's walk-up. With her chin in the air, Felicidad swept out of the SUV with the gracefulness of a figure skater. She finally looked Jasmine in the eye, and without a hint of acrimony, she said, "Thank you for the ride home." Felicidad gently closed the door and sashayed toward her building. Jasmine almost yelled, *And find another fuckin' place to live,* but she felt she had harangued Felicidad enough for one day.

Guilt crept into Jasmine as she pulled away from the curb. She did not enjoy threatening Felicidad like that, but she had every justification. As her employer, Jasmine had to establish and defend her boundaries, yet it confounded her to feel the slightest regret over it.

As Jasmine headed toward Co-op City, she pushed Felicidad out of her mind. She never cared what people thought of her, least of all people who crossed her lines, and that was the way she had to be. Besides, Jasmine had to go home and prepare for her date with Adriano Suárez.

TWENTY

Jasmine arrived at the health clinic a half hour earlier than they had planned, hoping to catch Adriano before he shut down for the day. From the street she peeked into the window. The clinic was lighted but empty. When Jasmine tried the door, however, she found it locked. "Shit." She had no choice but to buzz the intercom and wait for Adriano to let her in.

Within seconds he rushed out of his office to unlock the door. "You're early," he said. Adriano caressed her chin and kissed her on the cheek. "I'm still consulting with a patient, so if you would just wait for me right here."

"Yeah, sure." Jasmine took a seat in the reception area and watched him as he hurried back down the corridor and into his office. She heard the click as Adriano locked the door behind him. For a fleeting moment, Jasmine imagined his patient as a young woman with endless curves from her long hair to her voluptuous frame, and even her perfect feet. Her jealousy surprised her, and she forced it down like an unsavory medicine. Then Jasmine recognized that the opportunity she had been craving had presented itself.

She got to her feet and walked behind the receptionist's counter. She found two computers. The one on Lisa's desk had been shut off, but the other one not only remained on, it seemed connected to the clinic's network. Jasmine sat before it, and with periodic glances over her shoulder, she searched for files that had the same extension as the database she discovered on Malcolm's computer. A list of files matching her search criteria scrolled onto the screen. With no time to explore each one to see if it had any value to her search, Jasmine highlighted them all, pulled out a flash drive, and downloaded every single one.

Relieved to have brought an extra drive and to have executed the theft undetected, she shut down the computer and hurried back to her seat in the reception area. When Adriano finally emerged from his office, he found her leafing nonchalantly through a dated issue of *Prevention* magazine.

A black couple in their late twenties followed him into the corridor. Although tears streamed down the woman's face, she forced a smile. The man pumped Adriano's hand as he thanked him over and over. Thinking that she recognized his accent, Jasmine guessed they were another immigrant couple. Without a word or glance at her, Adriano led the couple out of the clinic and locked the front door behind them. Then he turned to Jasmine and said, "Let me make a few calls, and then we can leave for dinner."

"No problem." Jasmine flipped to an article with the title "Lower Cholesterol in 30 Days." "Take your time, and handle your business."

Adriano disappeared into his office again, and restless, Jasmine abandoned the magazine in the seat next to her. She leaped to her feet and crept past the reception area and Adriano's door to one that read *Laboratory*. Jasmine eased the door open and peeked inside the room.

The lab was small but stocked with supplies and equipment. At a table in the center of the room, she saw a rack of labeled vials. Leaving the door open, Jasmine slipped into the room and toward the table. The thick dark liquid in the vials seemed to be blood, but fear conquered her urge to pick one up and confirm her suspicions. Jasmine turned in place as she surveyed the laboratory. The impressive array of microscopes, centrifuges, and other medical equipment gleamed with newness. She wondered if the capacity existed in that room to run and interpret tests on the blood samples. Was it normal for a neighborhood clinic to have such advanced technology on-site, especially one that served such a poor clientele?

Jasmine left the lab and proceeded down the corridor. She passed the fire exit and came upon a room with the door propped open. From the corridor, she spotted the cubbyholes and storage bins in kiwi green and lemon yellow. As she drew closer, her eyes caught the stacks of children's games and miniature furniture in primary colors. Jasmine crossed the threshold and saw that the other side of the day care center had been organized into a resource library. Lining the opposite wall stood a large shelf of health-oriented books and videos with a small television at the center. In the corner sat a display of brochures and flyers. She grabbed random sheets and skimmed them.

One flyer called for service providers to organize a coalition and campaign for the city to disburse more Ryan White AIDS grants to the outer boroughs, posing the question, *If 70 percent of the city's AIDS cases are in the Bronx, Brooklyn, Queens and Staten Island, why is most of the funding going into Manhattan?* A pro-choice group announced a bus trip to Albany to preserve Medicaid funding for abortions. A local chapter of a national push for universal health care requested signatures for its online petition. Neighborhood organizations reminded members of upcoming meetings and their agendas, and many of them listed the clinic as its meeting place. Some of the material sported Malcolm's artwork, like the fact sheets on such topics as treating burns to managing diabetes. At the bottom, each of them read, *Courtesy of the Suárez Community Health Center.*

Jasmine only noticed the mural when she turned to leave the day care center and resource library. Along the back wall of the room, Malcolm had painted a montage of the most popular children's characters, such as Dora the Explorer and Static Shock. She recognized them from the many times Diana had bought Zoë to the office and commandeered the rec room, despite the complaints of Jasmine's visiting clients. Jasmine laughed when she discovered the poetic license Malcolm had taken with the cartoons' features and clothing. Elmo had dreads and wore camouflage pants. Not only did Malcolm turn *Sesame Street*'s Ernie into an Asian, he dressed him in Yankee pinstripes and a baseball cap. In an obvious homage to Yvette, he had painted Penny Proud with the hood of her sweatshirt over her head, winking over her shoulder while holding a spray can.

She finally happened onto the examining room and found herself repressing a childish urge to play with the medical tools neatly arranged throughout the room. Jasmine reached for a stethoscope lying on a padded stool. She put it on and listened to her own heart. What did a healthy heart sound like? Although she had no idea, she suspected hers was not up to code. A tap on her shoulder made Jasmine leap. She spun around to find Adriano standing there. He said something that she could not hear.

Jasmine pulled the stethoscope out of her ears and down to her neck. "What'd you say?"

"What are you doing in here?"

She fiddled with the tubing. "I was thinking with all the props you have here, we could really play doctor."

Adriano removed the stethoscope from around Jasmine's neck. "These are not toys."

"I know. I'm sorry."

He placed the stethoscope into his own ears and pressed the chest piece against her breastbone. Adriano hummed with concern. "Turn around."

Jasmine hesitated, not knowing whether he was seriously examining her or just role-playing. But eager to dispel any suspicion Adriano might have now that he had caught her in the examining room, Jasmine complied with his order. She felt him press the stethoscope into the middle of her back.

"Take a deep breath." Again she complied. "Take another one and hold it for a few seconds." Jasmine imagined her racing heart pounding into Adriano's ears. She felt the metal disc slide down her back through her top. Without waiting for his command, Jasmine took another deep breath, held it for a few seconds, and let it go. "Very good. Now take off your blouse."

Even as Jasmine's mind rattled with confusion, her thighs grew warm and her insides moistened. She started to turn, but Adriano planted a firm hand on her shoulder. Succumbing to his silent power, Jasmine pulled the tails of her blouse from her pants and undid the buttons. As she peeled the sleeves down from her arms, the lapels grazed the cups of her filmy bra, and her nipples hardened. She felt the cool stethoscope slide across her naked back, then Adriano's free hand slither from the small of her back, around her waist, then up to her breast. His fingers teased under the band of Jasmine's bra to caress her nipples and then cup her breast. She let out a long breath, turned to face Adriano, and fell into his kiss.

* * *

Jasmine stepped into her slacks as she watched Adriano replace the tissue paper on the examining table. As much as she hated this part, she could never escape the awkward silences. The irony was that Jasmine never had them when she was tricking, yet to this day, she suffered them with Calvin, whom she had known for some time and with whom the sex was decent. She had expected Adriano to be precise and clinical in his lovemaking, compensating for his unfamiliarity with her body. But when he moved through Jasmine with a knowing that made her shudder, she thought that maybe they could avoid the awkward silence. Yet here it was.

She finished dressing and tapped him on the shoulder. "Hey, you."

He turned to face her, looping his tie around his neck.

"Don't think because you made me come you don't have to feed me."

"I would never take you for granted like that." Adriano laughed. "Besides, I thought this meal was on you?"

"That's right! So what would you like to have?"

"I already had what I wanted tonight. Since you're paying, you can choose the cuisine. But since you like Italian, we could go to Mario's on Arthur Avenue."

"Never been. Sounds great." Jasmine grasped the tails of his tie. Why did she do that when she had never learned how to knot a necktie? "So what am I doing here?" She smiled up at him and waited for him to tease her.

Instead he said, "Jasmine, before we leave, I seriously think you should let me examine you. When I listened to your lungs, they were terribly congested."

"You're kidding me, right?"

"No, I'm not. It's probably nothing I can't treat, but I'd like to take a chest X-ray and a blood sample. Please."

Calvin flashed into her mind. The man leaped to help her track down a bail jumper, but he never offered to fix a parking ticket for her. The thought made her burst into laughter. "Sure, why not?"

"What's so funny?"

Jasmine stroked his chest and shook her head. "Nothing."

* * *

She should have known that the second she became comfortable he would pull the plug. Then again, Jasmine had never been this close to comfortable. Only when Calvin asked her did she even recognize how comfortable she had become.

Jasmine leaped out of the bed and pulled on whatever she found in reach. "You should have asked me that before you fucked me."

"Jasmine . . ."

"We've been fucking for, what, two years now?"

Calvin ripped back the covers and jumped to his feet. "First of all, stop referring to it like that. If that's all that was going on here, I wouldn't be asking you this. Hell, I wouldn't have been here this long." He reached down to pick up his underwear and jeans off her floor.

"Oh, no, since we're having a truth-telling session here, you can admit it. That's exactly why you've been here this long!" she yelled. "You keep coming back because you know I'm a pro."

"Stop this."

"What I'm going to stop is pretending that I don't know that you're ashamed of me. And you're not ashamed because of what I do for a living and my unorthodox approach to it. You're ashamed about what I used to do in a past lifetime, and that all your cronies on the force know it."

"Hey, all they know is that you got arrested once for solicitation, and that the charge was eventually dropped." Calvin sat on the bed with his back to her to slip on his socks. "I mean, one arrest does not a career make."

Jasmine said, "Well, I was smarter than the average hoe."

Slowly, Calvin rose to his feet and turned around to face her with eyes propped open by shock.

"Yes, Calvin, before I became a bail bond agent, I was a prostitute. I had sex with men for money from the time I was sixteen until I was twenty-three."

"You're only twenty-six years old," Calvin said, his bare chest heaving with indignation. "And haven't you been in the bail bond business for five years?"

Jasmine let her silence answer his question. He swiped his shirt off the floor, yanked it over his head, and headed for the door.

Jasmine followed him out of the bedroom and down the corridor. Calvin did not stop until he reached the door to her apartment. He spun around and looked at her, waiting for her to speak. When Jasmine said nothing, Calvin said, "Christ, Jasmine, I'm a cop." He said it as if she had said something in an effort to make him stay.

But Jasmine refused to beg. She no longer fought for things that were not meant to be. If anything, she secretly thanked Calvin for reminding her of this now before she fell too deep. "Yeah, well, I'm a bail bond agent."

Calvin read into that some kind of plea that she had never made but he needed to hear. "I know that's who you are today, Jasmine, but I have to think about the man I want to be tomorrow."

Jasmine rolled her eyes and laughed at him. Of all the corny things to say! "Just get the fuck out, Calvin."

He gave her one last glare, threw open the door, and rushed out of the apartment.

She slammed the door behind him and locked it. Then Jasmine went into the living room, grabbed a bottle of whiskey, and walked out onto her balcony. She took a cigarette from the pack she'd left there and lit it up. Between sips and drags, Jasmine convinced herself that she was no better or worse for Calvin's departure. Just add him to the long list of cops who hated her guts.

TWENTY-ONE

After a meal of clams *oreganate* and broccoli *di rabe,* Adriano drove Jasmine to his studio loft in Battery Park City. The building had all the amenities of a luxury hotel, including a fitness center, sundeck, and driving range. They played a few games of pool in the glass lounge before heading to Adriano's loft for vintage wine and fervent sex.

The next morning Adriano took Jasmine back to the clinic to pick up her SUV, and then insisted on following her to her apartment building in Co-op City. While Adriano waited for her in his BMW, Jasmine parked the Escalade in the garage across the street. She came out and climbed back into the passenger side of Adriano's car.

"So this is where you live?" he asked, gazing up at the towering brick high-rise. "How many buildings are in the entire complex?"

"A little more than thirty, with over fifteen thousand apartments," Jasmine said. She looked at her building as if for the first time. "I read somewhere that this is the largest residential development in the entire country."

"Really?"

"There used to be an amusement park on this land. And before that a small municipal airport." Jasmine reached over and placed her hand on Adriano's knee. "You can say it."

"Say what?"

"It looks just like a housing project." She squeezed his knee and made him grin.

"Okay, I admit. I'm having a hard time believing you pay a mortgage to live here."

"Not to mention all the fees." When Jasmine seized the apartment as forfeited collateral after an alleged robbery suspect skipped to Virginia, she decided to pay the bond from her backup fund and keep the apartment for herself. "Don't let the outside fool you, though. It's nice inside. I mean, it's not your place. . . ."

They laughed and Adriano said, "Well, teachers are severely underpaid." He leaned toward Jasmine, and they shared a long kiss. She enjoyed it as best she could, considering that Adriano had just reminded her of her ruse.

Jasmine pulled away from him. "You'll see for yourself soon."

"Tonight?"

"Maybe."

Adriano smiled. "Do you know why we get along so well?"

"We're both workaholics."

"And we're both in professions where there's no such thing as a day off."

"And we respect each other's need to attend to business."

Adriano ran two fingers through the soft hair at Jasmine's temple. "So when I'm done, I'll call to check in, and we'll finalize our plans for tonight."

"Okay."

They kissed a final time, and Jasmine climbed out of his BMW and went up to her apartment. To see her unwelcome mat wedged in her door seemed like icing on the cake. All her needs had been met and none of her boundaries violated.

Jasmine went straight to her computer and inserted the flash drive after it finished booting. Once the computer recognized the disk and unfurled its contents onto the screen, she clicked on a random file. A window popped up, revealing an error message. "Fuck!" She tried another, then a third, and Jasmine finally accepted that she did not have the software needed to open the files on her home computer. She had to take the disk to the office.

Before shutting down her computer, Jasmine checked her Rey2 e-mail account. She had no response from PRIESTS amidst the unsolicited e-mails shilling penile enlargement surgery and sexual enhancement pills. Jasmine reached for Malcolm's piecebook and skimmed again through the subway sketches. On a hunch, she typed each of the numbers following his tag into the Internet search engine. She scanned through the results and found nothing of interest, but she remained determined. She began to enter all the possible combinations one at a time into the search engine, but a half hour later, she gave up. Jasmine stared hard at the first sketch in the subway series and recalled Yvette's challenge: *If you were about it, you could read it.*

Jasmine put the piecebook aside and typed *graffiti* into the search engine. From software programs that generated words into graffiti lettering to online galleries containing hundreds of photographs from graffiti across the globe to anti-graffiti resources, the results were endless. She discovered countless e-zines published from around the world, including Germany, Japan, and Mexico. An overwhelming thought dawned on Jasmine. As a member of an underground yet international subculture, Malcolm had the ability to hide anywhere in the world.

She brewed a pot of coffee and settled in front of Felicidad's computer. The database software instantly opened all the new files on Jasmine's flash disk. It took some time, but she sifted through each of them. One file was an electronic version of Adriano's address book. Jasmine noted the preponderance of female names, and the possessiveness she felt when she thought he was consulting behind locked doors with a sexy patient returned with a greater intensity. *Kimberly Mathis, MD. Deborah Guzmán, PhD. Patricia L. Shieh, MSW.* The professional appendages only added envy to her jealousy, and Jasmine scolded herself to get back on task.

Some of the names in Adriano's electronic address book were associated with art museums and galleries, and she wondered if any of those individuals might be worth investigating. When the idea failed to ignite that burn of instinct in her chest, Jasmine decided against it. Other names had no address but several phone numbers. She immediately recognized the 590 prefix as the one to offices at the Bronx courthouse. Jasmine noted other repeated yet unfamiliar prefixes and wondered if they might belong to law enforcement or criminal justice agencies. She remembered bumping into Nathalie Dieudonné at the courthouse and Calvin's remark about Adriano's friends in high places. Surely he had to have some government numbers in his address book, since he had to handle Medicaid claims, interact with health and welfare officials, and deal with a variety of regulatory agencies.

Still, Jasmine marked those entries in Adriano's address book and sent them to the printer. Then she scrawled a note to Felicidad in the margin of the first page of the printout. *Felicidad, see if you can find out where these people work and what exactly they do. Be discreet! Need this ASAP. JR*

Such little progress did nothing to abate her frustration. Jasmine spent another hour looking through the databases, hoping that something would leap out at her from the pool of data. When she started to believe that she would never find Malcolm, Jasmine shut off the computer and went home.

TWENTY-TWO

"So what would you like to do tonight?" asked Adriano when he called her later that evening.

"The truth is that I'm just not up to going out."

"Poor thing. Going to the office on Saturday—when the telephones are quiet and no one else is there demanding your attention—is supposed to make you more productive. But you sound frustrated."

Jasmine pulled Malcolm's piecebook off her lap and poured herself another shot of whiskey. "You don't know the half, Adriano."

"I think I do. I spent the day at a conference that proved to be nothing but a waste of time. Why don't I bring over dinner, and we can just have a night in."

"Fine by me."

Adriano arrived an hour later with a large shopping bag, a wicker picnic basket, and a bouquet of fuchsia roses with burgundy edges. Jasmine took the shopping bag and led him into the kitchen. "Tell me about your conference," she said.

"Supposedly, it was geared toward physicians interested in advocating for health care reform." Adriano set the basket and flowers on the table. "Do you have a vase for these?"

Jasmine ran her hand through her hair. "You know, I don't think so." Not only did she have little interest in decorating her home, until Adriano she had never had a man court her. Both embarrassed and touched by the revelation, words escaped her.

Adriano gave her a confused smile and said, "Actually, all I need is a jar of some kind."

Jasmine ambled toward the sink. "I might have something under the counter."

Adriano blocked her path. "No, you sit down. I'll handle it."

"What can I do?"

"Nothing, except give me a sympathetic ear while I vent."

"You got it."

Jasmine listened to Adriano complain about the insincerity of colleagues at the conference as she watched him maneuver around the kitchen. As he ranted, he placed and arranged the flowers in an old jar and let them sit on the kitchen counter while he set the table. Adriano covered it with a checkered tablecloth he had brought with him and then placed the flowers in the center. Pausing his tirade against pharmaceutical companies, insurance firms, and malpractice attorneys only to ask Jasmine where he might find something, he unpacked a dish of salmon rubbed with *chiles* and shrimp adorned with red onions marinated in mango sauce. Then he laid out their dishes and flatware and unpacked the basket. It contained a vast assortment of fruits, nuts, cheeses, chocolates, and candies. "These physicians claim they want to see reform, but they shit on any alternative proposed," Adriano ranted as he uncorked a bottle of Roederer Cristal champagne. "It makes me question how much change they support if it means a significant hit to their personal bottom line." He poured Jasmine a glass of champagne and fed her a strawberry. "If moving to a single-payer health care system means I have to give up my BMW and loft, so be it." Adriano finally sat down and took Jasmine's hand in both of his. He gazed into her eyes and said, "I could be just as happy living here in this housing project you call Co-op City."

Jasmine stared back at him. "But what would you drive?"

Adriano grinned, biting his bottom lip and leaning back in his seat. He reached for the salmon, carved a portion of it, and placed it on Jasmine's plate. "So school's tough on Saturdays?"

Jasmine clasped her hands under her chin. "Sometimes I wonder if I should give up what I'm doing. I came into this line of work to help people. But I honestly doubt if I'm making any real difference in their lives."

"No one stands a better chance at making a difference than you, Jasmine."

"What makes you say that?"

"Because when the government failed us, you created an alternative." Adriano took her hand and pressed his lips against it.

"One that's still dependent on the government." His lips felt warm and full against the back of Jasmine's hand. "I mean, I appreciate your saying that, Adriano, but let's be realistic. Just how effective can I be when I still have to operate within the same boundaries of the system that I want to change?"

Adriano began to venture an opinion when they heard a key slip into the lock of Jasmine's front door. She and Adriano jumped to their feet just as Calvin appeared in the doorway of her kitchen. Before Jasmine could speak, Calvin shot his hands in the air. She spun around to find Adriano standing behind her with a .380 trained on Calvin. "Adriano, what are you doing with that?"

"The correct question is what is this man doing allowing himself into your apartment."

"Put that thing away." Adriano lowered the weapon, and Jasmine turned back to Calvin. "Cal . . ."

But his eyes were roaming the romantic setup on her kitchen table. As they glazed over the champagne bottle, fuchsia roses, and chocolate truffles, Calvin reached into the front pocket of his jeans. Without a word, he clacked the keys to Jasmine's apartment against the tabletop and walked out of the kitchen. Jasmine and Adriano remained still and silent until they heard the front door slam.

Then Adriano said, "I guess that's the fellow with the penchant for materializing."

Jasmine turned to him and offered a weak smile. "And I guess he won't be materializing anymore." But before he could respond, she snapped, "And what's up with the damned gun?"

Adriano tucked the handgun into the waistband of his pants. "If you drove what I did, you'd carry one, too."

Jasmine thought about Shorty resting under her pillow. If Adriano stayed, she would have to find a moment to steal away and move her .45 to another place. And as much as she burned to know what more Calvin had learned about the database—after all, what other reason would he have had to show up announced?—Jasmine did want Adriano to stay.

TWENTY-THREE

Adriano did stay. He chided Jasmine for apologizing for not having much food in the house. They ate cereal in bed, watched the journalists' roundtables on TV, and had sex before Adriano left on Sunday afternoon.

No sooner had she locked the door behind him than Jasmine grabbed her cigarettes and cell phone and stepped out onto her balcony. She looked over the side and down the street, almost hoping to spot Calvin's silver Maxima. As Jasmine chain-smoked, she dialed his number almost a dozen times over the next hour and a half but never left a message. Knowing that her number would appear on his display, Jasmine waited for him to answer finally or return her call. But Calvin never responded. Resigned to working alone on the Booker case, she got dressed and drove to the agency.

Once in her office, Jasmine settled at her own computer with all the databases opened. They cascaded across her screen, and she pored over them. An hour passed, and she had made no progress in making sense of them. They might as well have been the drawings in the back of Malcolm's black book. She reached into her bottom desk drawer for the bottle of rum and New York Giants mug she had stashed there. Jasmine filled the mug halfway and downed most of the rum in two fast gulps. She stared at her computer screen. There had to be a more efficient way to compare all the databases, but her computer savvy only went so far even without the influence of alcohol.

Another hour passed, and Jasmine had polished off the rum and dozed off in front of the computer. She opened her eyes to bits of data displayed on the screen like a foreign language. Jasmine checked her cell phone. Calvin had not called, so she dialed again, only to hang up in the middle of his voice mail greeting. Then she called the last person she ever thought she would.

"Hello," answered a woman with a melodious voice. Behind her a group of men celebrated a play they had just witnessed on television. "Guys, keep it down, I'm on the phone. Hello?"

"Can I speak to Zachary?"

"Who is this?"

"Tell him it's his boss."

The woman hesitated but called Zachary to the phone. Despite his raucous friends in the distance, Jasmine heard her say to him, *Your boss is a woman?* Without answering her, Zachary took the phone. "Hello, who's this?"

"Zach."

"Jasmine?"

"You never told me you got yourself a girlfriend. No wonder you were slipping."

"Well, it sure wasn't some big secret. You just never asked. So what do you want, Jasmine?"

"I need your help, Zachary."

"No, you don't."

"Yeah, I do. Without you I can't find Malcolm. Help me find Macho, Zach. Pretty please with sugar on top." She giggled.

"Jasmine, what's wrong with you? Why do you sound so funny? You drunk?"

The accusation sobered her slightly. "Like I told you before. When we surrender him, I'll give you half the exonerated bail as a bonus. C'mon, Zachary. Don't you want some extra money to impress your new girlfriend?"

Another wave of cheers exploded in the background, and Zachary said, "Hold on." Jasmine overheard him asking the other guys what he had missed. An inaudible guest explained, and Zachary cussed under his breath and returned to the telephone. "Look, Jasmine, I gotta go. How're you gonna push me out and then call me begging for help? What's done is done, and we have nothing more to say to each other, so don't call me any fuckin' more."

"You're not going to help me?"

"Why don't you ask your new best friend to help you?" Zachary slammed down the phone.

Jasmine felt a wave of nausea. She took a few deep breaths until it passed. Once it did, she realized that Zachary had helped her after all. He'd made a good point.

"Hello?"

"Can I speak to Felicidad?"

"Speaking."

"It's Jasmine. Hate to bother you on a Sunday, but I really need your help with something." Jasmine snickered to herself. She could not have cared less that it was a Sunday, and Felicidad probably knew it. "You know anything—any damned thing at all—about databases."

"Sure. I studied computers for a while. You know, in my past life as a boy."

"That's cute. Listen, so do you know how to compare two databases to see if the information in one overlaps with the other? Or to see if two databases are connected in some way?"

"Oh, yeah."

"I'm at the office right now in front of the computer. You think you could walk me through it?"

"Sure, what program are you using?"

Within minutes, Felicidad had talked Jasmine though a series of commands that enabled her to compare two databases and identify which fields they had in common. She also taught her how to sort the files to order the data within them, making the information easier to understand and manipulate. Once Jasmine became comfortable with the software, she freed Felicidad to go about her weekend. After several minutes of tinkering, Jasmine discovered that the names in the database she found on Malcolm's laptop also existed in Adriano's active-patient database. Why would patients who had died remain on the list of people he continued to treat?

Jasmine re-sorted both databases on virtually every field—reorganizing them by name, address, and diagnosis—hoping for something to emerge. Taking the time to compare the entire record for each of the twenty-three names on Malcolm's database, she found it. When compared against the active-patient database, the records on Malcolm's list matched perfectly except on two fields—home address and type of insurance. When Jasmine took the name of a patient on Malcolm's list and searched for it on Adriano's active-patient database, he had the same name, sex, date of birth, and other information, but his address and type of insurance were different. Were these the same people and one of the databases had erroneous information, as Zachary had believed? Or was the Juan Diaz who lived on Kingsbridge Road and had Medicaid a different person from the Juan Diaz who had the same birth date, marital status, and allergies yet resided on Bathgate Avenue and was uninsured? As common as the name Juan Diaz might be, Jasmine doubted it.

She unlinked the two databases and independently sorted the twenty-three entries in Malcolm's list by type of insurance. The answers seemed random.

MEDICAID
MEDICARE
AETNA
HIP
AETNA
BLUE CROSS
MEDICAID

But when Jasmine searched for every one of the twenty-three deceased on Adriano's active-patient database, a pattern leaped onto the screen.

UNINSURED
UNINSURED
UNINSURED
UNINSURED
UNINSURED
UNINSURED
UNINSURED
UNINSURED

Jasmine pushed herself away from the computer screen. She talked aloud to herself to help her make sense of it. "Former patients who are now dead have insurance, but current patients who are being treated do not. But are these the same people? Maybe when they first came to Adriano for care, they didn't have insurance, and then eventually while under his care, they acquired it. Then at one point during treatment, they died. That's what it is."

But for all the self-talk, Jasmine had not convinced herself. The mismatched addresses between the two databases unsettled her. The simple and obvious explanation: these patients had moved at one point while under Adriano's care. She sorted the entire active-patient database by city and then scanned the results, learning that virtually all the clients of the community health center lived in the Bronx. In fact, when Jasmine examined the street addresses and zip codes, she concluded that a large number of Adriano's active patients lived specifically in neighborhoods like Melrose, Mott Haven, Longwood, and Hunts Point. These areas of the South Bronx comprised the poorest congressional district in the entire country, notorious for their high rates of asthma hospitalizations, HIV infections, and a vast array of health problems.

When Jasmine looked at the addresses of the people on Malcolm's list, their residences ran the gamut. Most lived in the Bronx, but one lived in Harlem, three lived in Brooklyn, and two actually lived in Westchester and Connecticut. The only thing that Jasmine had convinced herself of was that Malcolm's list was not really a subset culled from Adriano's active-patient database, as she had originally believed. This database of twenty-three patients was an independent entity.

Jasmine printed out the twenty-three records in both Malcolm's list and Adriano's active-patient database so that they would be easier to compare field by field. On a whim, she looked through the other databases on her flash drive and opened one called "Master." Even though she had not determined what this database contained and how it differed from the rest, Jasmine continued to follow her instinct and printed the twenty-three patients with the same names on that list as well. By the time she had printed out all the information available across the three databases for each patient, Jasmine had used half a ream of paper. She started to lay the sheets across her desk in three columns when she thought she heard a noise in the corridor.

Jasmine put down her papers and pulled her gun out of her purse. After cocking Shorty, she tiptoed from around her desk toward her office door. The second she stepped into the doorway, a shadow in the hall fired a shot at her.

She dove to the floor and heard the intruder running toward the exit. Jasmine scrambled to her feet and gave chase. She reached the hallway in time to see the intruder make it to the door. Jasmine planted her feet, raised her gun, and fired it. A bullet ricocheted past his head and into the window, sending glass crashing to the ground. The shooter slammed the door open and fled down the street. Desperate to continue the pursuit, Jasmine stumbled halfway down the hall but only gained several feet before collapsing to the floor.

TWENTY-FOUR

Jasmine came to consciousness to the sound of chatter over police radios and the crunch of broken glass underfoot. They had placed her on a paramedic stretcher and had wrapped a blood pressure monitor around her arm. Jasmine turned her head and came face-to-face with a young emergency medical technician. "What the hell happened?"

"Someone in the neighborhood heard shots and called the cops," she said. She pumped air into the cuff, and Jasmine felt it tighten around her bicep. "They found you here on the floor and called us. But you weren't hit."

"Yeah, I know that." Jasmine's eyes scanned the cops, and she spotted Calvin talking to another EMT. They caught eye. He nodded at her and let out a sigh. He said one last thing to the EMT and walked out of the agency.

Jasmine pulled herself up in the stretcher. "What are you doing?" asked the EMT attending to her.

"I'm fine."

The EMT summoned two plainclothes cops over to them. "Miss Reyes?"

"Yeah." She pivoted in the stretcher to place her feet on the floor and discovered that her legs had fallen asleep. "Shit." Jasmine stomped her feet to shake the pins out of her legs.

"We have to ask you a few questions."

"I figured as much." She looked down the hallway. Glass lay everywhere, and Calvin had not returned. "All I know is this. The son of a bitch is about five-eight with a slim build. He broke in here somehow and took a shot at me. Next time I see him, he better not miss again, because I sure as hell won't."

"So tell us why someone would do this to you?"

Jasmine suppressed the impulse to call him an idiot. "I'm a freakin' bond agent. I'm trying to trace a bail jumper, and he's got people who don't want him found. It's as simple as that." If they were speaking with a man, they would have cut to that scenario at the top of the interview. She inched to her full height.

"You have to let us examine you," said the EMT.

"No, I told you I'm fine. I'm . . . refusing medical assistance. However you put it, I'm doing it."

"Since you weren't hit," asked the junior officer, "why did you collapse?"

Jasmine sneered at him. "Didn't you just hear what I said? I just refused medical attention. So I don't fuckin' know why I collapsed. Your guess is as good as mine."

They tortured her through several more perfunctory questions, and just as they cleared the scene, Calvin returned. They stood across from each other, silently avoiding each other's eyes. He finally said, "You okay?"

"Yeah."

"Need me to follow you home?"

"I don't think I can go home," she said, gesturing toward the broken window of the agency's door. "I can't leave that like that."

"Look, I've got friends in the courthouse," said Calvin. "Since you're right across the street, I'll have them keep an eye on the place."

Jasmine felt badly about asking any favors of Calvin, least of all those that required him to pull his strings on the force. But she could not bear the thought of camping out at the office until Felicidad came in the next morning. Especially given that someone had broken in to kill her. "If it's not too much to ask," she said.

Calvin looked at her as if it was too much to ask, but he said, "Okay, so I'll follow you home."

"No, I'm fine. Please don't." Then Jasmine realized that it might have sounded as if she had someone—namely, Adriano Suárez—to hide at home. "I'm just going to crawl into my bed and sleep the rest of the day away."

"Suit yourself." Calvin joined his colleagues as they filed out of the agency.

Jasmine returned to her office, gathered her printouts, and walked out of the agency. She fumed at the broken door and looked across the street. In front of the courthouse stood a beat cop, who acknowledged her with a lopsided smile. Jasmine recognized him as one of the haters from Ramon's. Probably tinkled pink that someone tried to take her out and hoped it would drive her out of the business. Jasmine hesitated to leave, reconsidering whether she should camp out in the office for the night after all. But the ache in her bones forced her to finally climb into her Escalade and head home.

After a few minutes on the road, she sensed that someone was following her. Jasmine looked into her rearview mirror and saw Calvin and his partner trailing her in their squad car. She shook her head then smiled at him. If Calvin could see her, he did not smile back. The blue-and-white police car followed Jasmine all the way to Co-op City, and even waited for her to park the SUV in the garage and admit herself into the building.

Jasmine napped for several hours, and upon awakening she immediately returned to her comparison of the database printouts. She intended to push forward until she had compared each field for every one of the twenty-three patients on Malcolm's list BURN. First, she laid out the three printouts across her kitchen table in three neat stacks, noted the great difference in sizes, and made assumptions about the data contained in each. The printout of Malcolm's database consisted of only sixty-nine pages: three pages of information for each patient on the list. After scanning the field names on the first few pages, Jasmine concluded that this database contained only the most basic socioeconomic and medical data for each patient. This discovery made her even more suspicious that these particular records had been extracted from the active database for some reason other than death. She hoped that she had printed enough of both the active and master databases to compare Malcolm's patients with the others eventually to test her theory.

The unfinished printout generated from the database with the file name "Active" stood several inches taller than the complete hard copy of Malcolm's database. Jasmine glanced at the top page of this list. The first patient was named Rajata Agarwal, and Jasmine counted nineteen pages of information for her. The amount of detail did not surprise her. As one of Adriano's current patients, Rajata Agarwal's records would have to be thorough. Jasmine thumbed through the stack until she came upon the pages pertaining to Rogelio Alvarez. Pleased to have found them, Jasmine put them aside. With over seventy active clients, she could have used almost fifteen hundred pages. Jasmine only needed a sampling of patients who were not on Malcolm's list to compare their records and hopefully identify what might distinguish them—that is, other than the fact that the patients on Malcolm's list were deceased, and the active clients obviously were not.

Although she had selected the same number of clients from the master database, the printout stood only a third as tall as the one of the active-patient database. She suspected that this file represented the entire universe of Adriano Suárez's clientele, from the day he opened the clinic to the present, whether the patients were alive or deceased, past or current. If Jasmine was correct, this database contained the complete record of every patient he ever saw. Details for both the living Rajata Agarwal and the deceased Rogelio Alvarez would exist among those pages with the same level of detail that existed in the active-patient database, since that database—if correctly maintained—should contain the most up-to-date information.

Hoping that Rogelio Alvarez made it past her random cutoff point, Jasmine flipped through the printout. Relieved to find his name, she pulled out the sheets pertaining to his record. She quickly skimmed and counted the pages, and as she suspected, the master file looked exactly like the active database, except it contained several additional fields. The master file included a file closing date field as well as a field indicating the reason for the case's closing. She reminded herself that a patient could leave Adriano Suárez's practice for a variety of reasons besides death. He could have moved or switched doctors. But Jasmine could not imagine why anyone would no longer want Adriano as a physician. He was attentive, meticulous, and, if finances or insurance was an issue, free. Who would ever give up that kind of service?

Jasmine refocused on her task. She speculated that although it contained virtually all the same information as the master file, the active-patient database remained much smaller because once Suárez closed a patient's case, he probably had Lisa remove the record from the active database. Since Adriano Suárez had seen over two hundred patients since he'd opened the clinic almost seven months ago, Jasmine could have wasted as much as six reams of paper to print out the master file, and much of it would have duplicated information existing in the active-patient database.

After laying the three database records for Rogelio Alvarez across her table, Jasmine lugged the other stacks to the floor. "Start at the beginning," she said to herself, and she searched for the date on which Rogelio Alvarez of 173rd Street became Adriano Suárez's patient. In doing so she immediately discovered a difference between Malcolm's database and the other two. Unlike either the active or master files, Malcolm's database now only tracked two dates: the person's date of birth and date of death that Calvin added. As she reached for Rogelio's master file, Jasmine guided herself by speaking aloud. "Okay, so the master file should have a closing date—maybe the same date as his death, or later if it took a few days to find out ol' Rogelio didn't make it, and the reason field should say 'deceased'." She made a mental note that this should be true for all the patients in Malcolm's list. For each of those twenty-three clients, the date of death should match—or at least be a date a reasonable amount of time before—the closing date in the master file. Furthermore, not only should all these cases appear on the master list as "closed," the subsequent reason listed for the closing should read "deceased."

To test her assumptions before applying them to the case of Rogelio Alvarez, Jasmine reached for the partial yet massive printout of the master database on the floor and dropped it into her lap. She chose a name from the master printout that had closing dates but did not appear on Malcolm's list. According to the master list, Leslie Allen no longer sought care at the Suárez Community Health Center as of April 24, 2006, because she "relocated." Jasmine picked another name at random. Cesar Acuña stopped being a patient of Adriano Suárez on March 3, 2006, because of "noncompliance." Searching for an explanation of this reason, Jasmine skimmed the rest of his records. Noting the stretches of time between Cesar's visits, she concluded that he eventually ignored his appointments altogether, so Adriano wrote him off as a patient. Jasmine continued this experiment with more than a dozen random names, building confidence in her assumption as each one fit.

But then a challenging possibility entered Jasmine's mind. If the patients on Malcolm's list had nothing else in common besides the fact that they were deceased, the master file should list exactly these twenty-three patients—no more or less—whose files had been closed due to death. Therefore, the names of any and all of Adriano Suárez's deceased patients should be on both lists.

Jasmine fanned through the master printout while her eyes scanned the closing date field for the word "deceased." If the two databases were in sync, as they should be, she would come across that reason for closing the file exactly twenty-three times. But remembering that she did not have a complete printout in front of her, she made a mental note to run this test with the electronic version. Still, Jasmine continued to examine what she had in hand, for all she needed was for one patient in this listing who was described as "deceased" to not appear in Malcolm's list. She found four.

Therefore, not every patient who had died made her way onto Malcolm's list, and Jasmine finally accepted what she had suspected all along. The twenty-three names in the database of the dead had something else in common besides that. They did not find themselves in Malcolm's database simply because they were dead. Otherwise, his list would also contain the four names she found. And without going to her computer to check the electronic file, Jasmine already knew that there were many more.

She pushed away from the table to fix herself a drink, returning with a glassful of whiskey sitting on her ashtray and the half-empty bottle for refills. Jasmine took a gulp of whiskey, lit a cigarette, and returned to work. Adriano's impassioned soliloquies echoed in the back of her mind as she brooded over the printed pages, and Jasmine wanted to dismiss these contradictions as nothing more than data entry errors. But she could not ignore the haunting feeling that Malcolm ran for a meaningful reason and that Adriano knew it.

To simplify the comparison, Jasmine returned her focus on Rogelio Alvarez, the first patient on Malcolm's list. She located Alvarez on the master list, too. According to the master file, Alvarez was undergoing treatment for lung cancer and was covered by Group Health Incorporated. And then she noticed that no closing date or reason existed for Rogelio Alvarez on the master file.

Was Rogelio Alvarez alive or not?

She pounded her fist on her kitchen table in frustration. Every time Jasmine thought she understood the complex web of information before her, she stumbled onto another exception. But this could not be an exception. According to Calvin, everyone on Malcolm's list was dead, and Rogelio was on Malcolm's list. But why would the master file imply that he was an ongoing patient? Then she remembered. She had found a record for Rogelio Alvarez in the active-patient database, too, even though he was supposed to be dead. She never should have drunk that fuckin' whiskey.

Her head swimming with confusion, Jasmine reached for Rogelio's record from the active database. She flipped through the pages, filtering every date she encountered. Not only was lucky Alvarez alive if not well, he had an appointment scheduled for the following month. Unless she believed that Calvin made a mistake, Rogelio was alive despite his appearance on Malcolm's list. If a mistake existed among this mass of data, Jasmine did not believe for a second that Calvin had made it.

Listening to her instinct, Jasmine scanned Rogelio's master record for the date of his diagnosis. It indicated that on March 14, 2006, Adriano diagnosed him with lung cancer. But when she checked Rogelio's date of death in Malcolm's database, it was listed as February 3, 2006. According to Malcolm's information, Rogelio Alvarez died almost a month before he supposedly began treatment for his lung cancer under Adriano Suárez's care.

"This can't be," said Jasmine. One by one, she located the name of every patient on Malcolm's list on the master file. Although each one was dead, they were listed in the master file as if they were still alive and active patients of Adriano Suárez.

And somehow every single patient in Malcolm's database had been diagnosed *after* their date of death.

Armed with this information, Jasmine pushed aside the master file and focused on the active-patient database. For each person on Malcolm's list, she identified the diagnosis. From cancer to diabetes to heart disease, they all had serious illnesses, which certainly could result in death if left untreated. All were chronic illnesses that took long periods of time and often elaborate procedures to treat. For precisely those reasons, they were the kinds of ailments that insurance companies loathed to cover. Without a decent health plan to finance their treatments prior to their diagnoses, these patients were as good as dead. As long as the law allowed it, which it often did, the companies flatly rejected new requests for coverage from individuals who suffered from these "preexisting conditions."

Jasmine tapped the ashes of her cigarette and thought of Rogelio Alvarez. She took another puff and placed herself in his shoes. If she were to be diagnosed with lung cancer, it would only take months for her to join Jason at Woodlawn, because she herself had no health insurance. Her only chance at surviving if the disease had not progressed too far already would be to acquire insurance *prior to* her diagnosis. She could forget running around looking for a medical insurance company to cover her treatment after receiving the fateful news. If after being diagnosed Jasmine applied for medical coverage, once she took a physical and the company's doctors learned she had lung cancer, the insurer would rubber stamp a massive NO onto her request. She would have no choice but to finance her war against the disease with her meager savings. Jasmine pulled on her cigarette and scoffed at the possibility. She would consider herself lucky if the disease took her out before her bank account ran empty.

Jasmine finished her cigarette and poured herself another glass of whiskey. Although overwhelmed and exhausted, she pushed herself to check one last thing. She had to check to see if the other names on the list followed the same pattern as Rogelio Alvarez. When the next six names on Malcolm's list also had dates of death that preceded their dates of diagnosis, Jasmine believed she had uncovered a pattern. She had twenty-three people—dead on one list yet alive albeit seriously ill on another—who were fortunate enough to access the health insurance they needed to fight their chronic illnesses. This discovery struck her as bizarre as it was, but Jasmine also marveled at the irony that these patients' physician specialized in—even obsessed over—delivering quality treatment whether or not they could afford to pay. No matter how extensive or expensive their conditions might be to treat, Adriano Suárez would never turn them away because of their inability to pay. Yet it so happened that all these patients had adequate health insurance to fight their chronic illnesses.

So maybe Adriano Suárez was helping his patients secure the medical coverage they needed.

He *was* engaged in identity theft. Somehow Adriano was stealing the identities of dead people and assigning them to his uninsured patients. After assuming these stolen identities, previously uninsured people became eligible for the health coverage necessary to acquire treatment for their life-threatening conditions.

"Hot damn!" Jasmine leaped to her feet. Satisfied that she was on the right track, she called it a night. Jasmine crawled into bed, her head reeling with whiskey, nicotine, and revelation. She rolled onto her side and shifted her thoughts to Adriano. As she drifted into sleep, Jasmine found herself admiring him more than ever. True, he was breaking the law, but he was doing it to save lives. And who was he really harming? Certainly not the individuals who had already passed on and no longer needed their health insurance.

Jasmine imagined Adriano lying next to her, pressing his hard body against her back and whispering in her ear, "Did you know that Robin Hood went to medical school?" She chuckled over their secret and quickly fell asleep.

But a few hours later, Jasmine had a nightmare about chasing Malcolm Booker through a graffiti-filled subway train like the ones featured in the documentary *Style Wars*. "Macho!" she called to him as she followed him. But instead of being comforted by her presence, Malcolm raced to the door of the car and ran into the next one. Jasmine pursued him. "Macho, wait! It's me, Jasmine." Ignoring her pleas, Malcolm ran through one graffiti-covered car after another until he reached the front and could go no farther. Jasmine reached the door to this car, and through the window she saw Malcolm stop at the door. "Macho, don't!" she yelled, fearful that he would open the door, jump onto the tracks, and be crushed by the train. But as she attempted to slide open the door, Jasmine lost her footing and fell between the two cars. An almost blinding light flashed before her eyes, and at the center of the flash was the mischievous smile of the train conductor, Adriano Suárez. Then a bolt of electricity knifed through her body.

Jasmine surged forward in bed. She groped her way through the darkness to her bathroom, dropping to her knees and vomiting into the toilet. Fifteen minutes passed before Jasmine pulled herself off the cold tiles and dragged herself back to bed. Unable to shake the nagging feeling that Adriano Suárez's participation in identity theft was not a big enough reason for Malcolm Booker to jump bail, let alone disappear, Jasmine tossed and turned for the rest of the night.

TWENTY-FIVE

Consumed with the previous night's breakthroughs and the new questions they raised, Jasmine had repressed her thoughts about the attempt on her life until she saw the broken window when she arrived at the office the next morning. In front of the agency's door stood Felicidad, a fist clenched against her heart as a court officer explained the pellets of glass littering the sidewalk. When she spotted Jasmine coming toward them, Felicidad ran over and threw her arms around her. "Oh, my God, Jasmine, are you okay?"

Jasmine shook away from her. "I'm fine."

"I'm so pissed at you for not calling me."

"It slipped my mind."

"Slipped your mind?" Felicidad flayed her arms in disbelief. "Someone breaks into your office and takes a shot at you, and it slips your damned mind?"

Jasmine acknowledged the court officer and entered the agency with Felicidad on her heels. "Sounds like you didn't need me to call you after all."

"Listen, Ms. Attitude, I'm not talking about finding out the *bochinche,*" yelled Felicidad. "I'm talking about helping you."

"Felicidad, what could you have possibly done to help me?"

"First of all, you shouldn't be in here by yourself after hours. I don't care if you lock that door. It obviously didn't make a damn bit of difference to whoever the hell broke in here yesterday."

Jasmine shook her head. She had no intention of calling Felicidad into the office on weekends or making her stay late during the week. Not only did she not have the money to pay her overtime, but Jasmine liked her solitude. "And then the dude would've had two targets."

Ignoring her snide remark, Felicidad said, "And if you had called me after it happened, I would've insisted that you stay at my place. You shouldn't have gone home last night with this maniac still on the loose, Jasmine. He already knows where you work, so did you have to take the risk of leading him to your doorstep?"

Felicidad's enraged sincerity touched Jasmine. "Okay, I'm sorry. But I was fine then and I'm fine now. I just need you to call somebody to come in and replace that window ASAP."

"I took care of that already. The second I came in here and saw that window, I called around and got some companies to fax you estimates. They're in your mailbox."

"Great, and we should probably have that lock changed, too."

"Done. I checked the Rolodex Diana left behind, and there was a business card for a locksmith in there with your account number on the back of it. He'll be here to change the locks by three o'clock."

"Man, Felicidad, thanks." Jasmine stared at her with appreciation. "You're really on top of it on a Monday morning."

"I'm on top of it every morning."

Jasmine reached into her bag for the printouts. "Are you ready for a special assignment?"

Felicidad's eyes opened so wide, her eyelashes blossomed. "Hell, yeah, I'm ready."

"Have a seat and turn on your computer." Felicidad scooted to her desk and booted her computer. Standing behind her seat, Jasmine said, "Find the databases I had you upload to your computer from my flash drive. Now, last night I started to compare three of them for patterns and discrepancies, and I want you to finish. They're called Active, Master, and Burn."

Felicidad found the files on her computer and opened all of them with three swift clicks. "You want me to clean up the errors?"

"Well, let me show you what I've been doing. See this first patient, Rogelio Alvarez? According to this database, he was diagnosed in March. But on this one, he's been dead since February."

"Ay, what a mess."

"Yeah, but I don't want you to change anything just yet, Felicidad. I'm still trying to figure out which pieces of information are correct.

All I'm asking you to do is to look out for discrepancies like that and flag them for me."

Felicidad gave her a questioning look that Jasmine shot down with a hard glare. For good measure, she said, "And remember that you're not to discuss this with anyone."

Felicidad shrugged. "You don't have to tell me twice. It's not like I want strangers knowing my medical business."

Jasmine had forgotten about Felicidad's own condition. "Exactly. Discretion means everything here. No information in any form is to leave this office, and if you have to leave your desk for any reason, secure it first."

"Yes, ma'am."

"Cool." Jasmine started toward her office when Felicidad called her back. "What's up?"

Felicidad cradled her chin with her professionally manicured nails. "Since I've been the model employee, do you think we could renegotiate one of your ground rules?"

Jasmine stared at her while attempting to guess which rule Felicidad wanted her to strike. Then she remembered the court officer chatting with her when Jasmine arrived. "No, Felicidad, you cannot date anyone associated with our business."

"Not only is that unfair, Jasmine, it's sheer torture. How can you forbid me from dating any cop, lawyer, judge, bailiff . . . ? That's all I ever meet!"

"Who are you—my boy-crazy teenage daughter?" Jasmine exhaled. She could be arguing with Diana over ignoring the telephones to play peek-a-boo with her baby. "Let's compromise here. You can date any law enforcement personnel you want so long as he doesn't work in the Bronx."

"That'll really spice up my social life."

"You know what, Felicidad? You could have asked me for something else. I'd rather you hit me up for a raise."

"Can I have a raise?"

"You've just started. Ask me again in five months."

Felicidad pondered her offer. "Fair enough. And one more thing."

"What?"

"Thanks. For everything."

"No, thank you."

Jasmine settled at her desk and reached into her purse for her cigarettes. Her hand brushed against Malcolm's piecebook. She pulled it out and looked through his sketches. With every page she turned, Jasmine's pride over the progress she had made faded. Although identity theft had become the crime du jour, would Malcolm abandon all his passions because he uncovered it at Adriano Suárez's clinic? True, he could not be associated with any criminal activity, which is why he made less graffiti and attempted to pursue a legal artistic career, confining his love for the unique art form to the pages of his piecebook. But if Malcolm did not want to risk being affiliated with Adriano's identity theft operation, all he had to do was quit. According to Yvette, he intended to before he jumped bail and disappeared. Something else had to have made him run. Probably the same thing that drove someone to come after her last night.

Jasmine connected to the Internet and logged on to her e-mail. She had received no response from Yvette as PRIESTS. Could Yvette have sent someone to ambush Jasmine at the office? While not impossible, Jasmine did not believe that for a second. But she still might have raised Yvette's suspicions when she cornered her in the rail yard. Despite these worries Jasmine could not help but send her another e-mail. She simply found the last e-mail she had sent to Yvette in her folder of sent messages and sent it again.

Jasmine turned back to the piecebook, reaching for the photographs of Jason's work that she had passed off as her own. She compared the crisp letters and legible caricatures of her brother's work with the undecipherable characters in Malcolm's last six sketches, like she did with Adriano's databases. Yvette's words echoed in her mind. *If you were about it, you could read it.* Jasmine thought back to the times she had watched Jason paint, visualizing his strokes and the results they produced on the wall. Then she remembered the night in the Harlem River Rail Yard, when she studied Yvette as she painted on the train. Lifting Malcolm's piecebook off the desk and holding it open before her, Jasmine visualized Malcolm's hand as he sketched the letters of the word that appeared on the first drawing of a subway car.

Rather than study the piece as a whole, she trained her eye to see the work in its stages. None of the writers she had witnessed ever grabbed a color and slashed it across the page or wall. Each of them always began with an outline. Jasmine imagined Malcolm's hand as it whipped a black marker across the white page, outlining first the subway car and then the letters across it. Then with her eyes, she filled in the primary color. By the time Jasmine had visually drawn the second color a half hour later, she began to see possible letters in Malcolm's sketch. She grabbed a piece of paper from her printer tray and placed it over the sketch, testing her guess by attempting to trace it onto the white sheet. A few moments later, Jasmine finally saw the first letter of the word in Malcolm's first sketch.

A.

Immediately recognizing that the next two letters were the same, Jasmine honed her eye on the details of the letters while trying to recreate them on her scrap paper. With their straight back and single loop to the right, she first guessed that the next two letters were *R*s. But when she could not find their tails, Jasmine concluded they actually were two *P*s.

The word across the subway car in the first sketch was *APPLE*. As in Big Apple. New York City.

Although that made no sense to Jasmine, she trusted her instinct and leaped onto the next sketch. Now familiar with Malcolm's *A*s and *E*s, she immediately spotted them in the next word. *_ _A_ _E*. Jasmine struggled to decipher the rest, and over the course of the morning her retrained eye built a sharper focus, and she eventually read the second word.

CRADLE.

This made even less sense. The two words had no obvious relationship to one another. Jasmine fed her agitation another cigarette and coached herself to reserve judgment until she deciphered all six words. As she grew familiar with Malcolm's style and recognized letters she had already identified, Jasmine deciphered the third word.

ORANGE.

"This shit is crazy." Jasmine reached for her notepad and printed the three words down the page, then she heard a knock at the door. "Come in." Felicidad entered her office carrying a large pink insulated lunch bag with her name monogrammed across it. "What's that?"

"Lunch," she said as she cleared a corner on Jasmine's desk and set the bag on it.

Jasmine looked at the clock on her computer. It was a bit past noon. "Damn."

"I know. The morning just flew, because you weren't kidding, Jasmine. That database is a mess." Felicidad opened the bag and pulled out several food containers. "Anyway, I noticed that you almost never stop to eat, and when you do, it's usually crap, so I brought some extra with me today. I hope you like tofu, because I used it in the Greek salad instead of feta. What kind of dressing would you like? I have . . ."

Jasmine's cell phone rang, and Adriano's number at the clinic appeared on the screen. She wanted both to answer and ignore it. She worried about interacting with him, given her newfound suspicions. Then again, those suspicions made Jasmine yearn for him.

Jasmine motioned for Felicidad to wait and answered her phone. "Hey, Adriano," she said.

Felicidad stopped arranging lunch and mouthed *Adriano?* Jasmine shooed her away. Leaving behind a container and plastic utensils for Jasmine, Felicidad gathered her lunch bag, winked at Jasmine, and scuttled out the door.

"How are you?"

"Jasmine, it's urgent that I see you."

She wanted very much to see him. And she didn't. Jasmine could not see him until she confirmed her suspicions, and decided what if anything she would do about them. "I want to see you, too, but I have so much work to—"

"Meet me for lunch. Come to the clinic now."

"I wish I could, but my assistant just fixed me a whole spread." Jasmine opened the container and sniffed at the light and healthy dish. "As much as I'd prefer a huge pizza burger, I don't want to hurt her feelings."

"Jasmine, this is serious. It's about the tests I ran on you."

She resealed the salad bowl and put it back on her desk. "Well, what did they say?"

"Not over the phone."

His urgency annoyed Jasmine. "Okay, let's meet someplace near you." Even though they first had sex there, meeting Adriano at the clinic during business hours somehow felt like a violation of their relationship.

"I much prefer to see you at the clinic."

Jesus, he sounded like Calvin. "Adriano, let's get one thing straight. You're not my physician. Have you forgotten how you came about whatever it is that you have to tell me? Either you meet me at a restaurant or you just tell me over the phone, because I'm not coming into the clinic."

"Fine. There's a diner on Westchester Avenue two blocks up from the clinic. Can you meet me there in half an hour?"

"I've already left." Jasmine hung up the telephone, returned Malcolm's piecebook to her pocketbook, and walked out of the office. This was a game she did not care to play. Adriano just had to prescribe her whatever medication Jasmine needed to kick this flu once and for all.

TWENTY-SIX

As Jasmine made her way to the last booth on the aisle, Adriano rose to his feet to greet her. He kissed her on the cheek and motioned for her to sit. "How was the rest of your weekend?" he asked.

"Typical." The reverb of guns firing and glass shattering echoed in her head. "Yours?"

"Same." Adriano reached for the menus tucked between the beige wall and the napkin dispenser. "Do you have a taste for anything in particular?"

"You mean besides the truth?" Jasmine took a menu from him. "Just get me whatever you're having."

"I'm not very hungry."

"Adriano, what the hell is going on?"

The waitress appeared, and Adriano said, "I'll just have a cup of herbal tea."

"We've got chamomile, peppermint, lemon . . ."

"I don't care so long as it's decaffeinated."

"That's all?"

"The lady will have a Greek salad and the fruit plate."

"Okay." The waitress left.

Jasmine laughed at the coincidence of both Felicidad and Adriano suggesting the same lunch. But when he did not bother to ask her why she was chuckling, she quickly stopped. "Adriano, you're scaring me."

"Don't be scared." He took Jasmine's hand, placed a bottle of pills in it, and closed her fingers around them. "You have a respiratory infection. I want you to take these pills as described on the bottle."

"That's it?" Jasmine sighed with relief and opened her hand. The directions were scrawled across the bottle in longhand. Nowhere did the name of the drug or the pharmacy that dispensed the prescription exist on the label. "You didn't get these from a pharmacy, did you?"

"Why do you ask that?"

"A pharmacist would have generated this label with a computer."

"Jasmine, the particular infection you have is often a symptom of a compromised immune system. So I ran an ELISA test on your blood sample. That's an enzyme-linked immunosorbent assay test."

"You went to medical school, Adriano. I didn't. Speak in lay terms and cut to the chase."

"The ELISA screens for the presence of HIV antibodies, and you tested positive for them."

Jasmine reared back in her seat. "Are you saying I have AIDS?"

"No." Adriano lurched across the table to take her hands in his. "You may not have AIDS."

"May?"

"Not yet. But chances are you do have the virus that causes AIDS. You have HIV." Jasmine pulled her hands away from him. "Jasmine, listen to me. The ELISA test is not a test for HIV infection. It only tests for the antibodies that emerge when the infection might be present. To be sure, I have to run another test called a Western blot to confirm the positive result."

"That's why you were insisting I meet you at the clinic."

"If both the ELISA and Western blot tests are positive, we can be sure that you have the virus."

"How accurate are these tests?"

"When you combine them? Ninety-nine percent."

Jasmine climbed out of the booth and headed to the ladies room. She stumbled into a stall, dropped to her knees and vomited into the toilet. She leaned against the bowl, pressing her cheek against the cold porcelain until she recovered her breath. Hearing the bathroom door open and two young women enter gossiping about the friend they left behind, Jasmine crawled to her feet and ambled out of the stall toward the sink. She rinsed the traces of bile from her mouth and splashed water across her face, then straightened her back and walked out of the bathroom.

"Excuse me, miss."

She leaned against the door to allow a delivery man walking through the back exit to wheel a cart of cardboard boxes past her into a storage room. Then Jasmine darted out the back entrance of the diner.

She leaned against Jason's tombstone as she had the toilet bowl an hour earlier. In her drunken stupor, it took Jasmine a few seconds to recognize the moisture creeping down her thigh. She looked to find the empty glass bottle in her lap trickling the last ounce of rum down her leg. "Oops." Jasmine flung the bottle across the cemetery and then stroked the lettering on the stone like a beloved pet.

"I couldn't trick up enough money to get you outta jail," she said, "but it sure did buy you a pretty rock, didn't it." Then Jasmine patted the earth at the base of the stone. "Don't thank me. It was the least I could do." She pulled her head to the ground and stretched across his grave. "But don't think for a second I blame you for this, Jason. That's not when I caught it, you know. I mean, I would've been dead by now if I got it back then." She counted the years on her fingers. "Had to be about three years ago. 'Cause even after you left, I was still doing my thing, you know, trying to get that paper to pay them bills while getting the business off the ground. Three years ago. That's when I fucked my last john." Jasmine snorted, the forced laugh spraying rum-soaked saliva into the air. "How much you wanna bet that's the muthafucka that gave me that shit, too? That would be my luck, right, Jason? 'Cause that's how it be for Rey squared. No way I could turn my last trick and not catch a deadly-ass disease. I mean, that's somebody else's life. Not my life."

She rolled onto her stomach and rested her head on her flattened hands. "That's how come I know I got that shit, Jason. I didn't need him to tell me I got AIDS. How'm I not gonna have that shit, living the way I do? I'm a dead woman walking, bro. Been haunting this fuckin' earth for twenty-seven years, and I ain't got shit to show for it. I couldn't save you. I couldn't help Malcolm. And I probably killed Calvin.

"There's only one good thing about this whole fucked-up situation, Jason." Jasmine turned onto her back and stared at the clouds as they drifted across the darkening sky. "I'ma see you real soon." She actually would become JaneDoe.

He shoved Jasmine out of the car and tore off. Even though he was a regular, Jasmine never should have gone into the car with him. The second she realized he was high, she should have made an excuse and gotten the hell out of there.

She lay against the curb for almost twenty minutes. Every once in a while, people walked by her, pointing, staring, whispering. But no one helped her. Jasmine finally scrambled to her feet, noticing the blood she had left on the concrete in the beam of the streetlight. Her head felt like a slab of chipped marble. The crazy bastard had kneed her in the face and then pummeled his fists over and over again into her face. He wanted to make her ugly because she had refused to let him fuck her in the ass.

"I'll give you twice as much money," he said, shoving a roll of bills in her face. "You can have all that. Just turn around." He was on his back across the backseat of the car, trying to sit up.

"It wouldn't matter if you had a million dollars right there," said Jasmine. Then she made a joke of it. "A girl's gotta save something for marriage." But he didn't laugh, and she fumbled for his zipper. She had to get him excited fast. A different kind of excited. A safer kind of excited. Why didn't she follow her gut and tell him she was on the rag or had caught VD or something.

Jasmine lowered his zipper and leaned toward his crotch. But he clamped his hand on her head and tried to push it away. "I said stop it. I'm bored with that shit. I told you what I want, and I've got the money."

She grabbed his wrist and wrangled his hand from her head. "C'mon, baby," Jasmine cooed, trying another tactic. "You know you like to watch my pretty face when I go down on you." Then again she leaned in to bring her face into his crotch. He slammed his knee into her face, drawing blood from both her nose and mouth with that one shot. Then he punched her in the face, two, five, nine times before opening the car door and kicking her out onto the sidewalk.

Although Jasmine knew she could never hide what happened from Jason, she had planned to downplay it. Make it seem less than what it was. Just an occupational hazard. Had she known he had stayed home that night, Jasmine would have composed herself before entering the apartment. But because she had assumed that he was out hustling or bombing, Jasmine allowed herself to break down the second she walked though the door.

"Jasmine, what's wrong?"

"Nothing."

"Oh, my God! Jasmine, what happened? Who the fuck did that to you?"

"Forget about it."

"Hell, no, I'm not going to forget about it! A john did this to you?" She nodded, sobbing. "Which one?" She told him. Jason knew which one. He knew all her johns, although none of them even knew he existed. "Do you know where he went?"

"I don't know. Look, Jason, please let it go. He did this because he was high out of his fuckin' mind, and he wanted me to do something, I said no, and he got mad."

"I don't give a fuck what you did or didn't do." Jason bounded for the door, snatching his jacket on the way. "He had no right to do this to you. I'll teach him to beat on my sister."

"Jason!"

But he was out the door. Jason returned two hours later, this time with his hands crusty with blood rather than splattered with ink or paint. Within an hour, the police were there, too.

Jasmine awoke the next day with both a hangover and Calvin on her mind. She called Felicidad and told her she planned to spend the day "in the field." Then she said, "Felicidad, you think you might be interested in getting your bail bond license?"

Felicidad's breathing quickened. "I don't know. I mean, yes! But could I? You know, with my previous convictions and all. And I have to be honest with you, Jasmine. I have no credit to speak of."

"That won't be a problem. I mean, it won't be easy, but it's not impossible." Jasmine refrained from explaining that she knew from personal experience. "I've just been thinking. You know, one of the reasons I lost Diana—although she wasn't much of a loss by the time she quit anyway—was because she had no way to move up at the agency. But in the little time you've been working for me, you've been so helpful, Felicidad. If you were to get your own license, you'd be even more so. I wouldn't ask you to do any of the crazy stuff like the skip traces or anything like that. But just more of the court stuff. And since I don't plan on doing this forever, maybe when I hang it up, I can leave it to you and Lorraine."

"I don't know what to say, Jasmine."

Felicidad sounded as if she were crying, and Jasmine wondered if she had revealed too much without mentioning anything at all. Then she dismissed that as silly. Felicidad probably thought she would leave the bail bond business to marry Calvin or someone and have kids. Jasmine snickered at the idea. "Just tell me you'll think about it."

"I will definitely."

Lying in bed and staring at the ceiling, Jasmine tried to will herself to call Adriano and submit to that second test. She had to be sure before she called Calvin and told him to get tested himself. But she could not bring herself to listen to any of Adriano's messages, let alone return any of his incessant calls. Instead Jasmine called Felicidad again.

"Reyes Bail Bonds. This is Felicidad. How may I help you this morning?"

"It's Jasmine. One last thing. Could you give me Dr. Dieudonné's number."

"Sure!"

Jasmine called the doctor, who immediately accepted her call. They spent a few seconds on idle chitchat. Then Dr. Dieudonné asked, "So to what do I truly owe this telephone call, Jasmine?"

"I need a second opinion."

"For what diagnosis?"

She sounded skeptical, and Jasmine did not blame her. She owed her the truth. "HIV."

"Oh."

"And I need the fastest results you can get me."

"Mmm."

"I already took that, uh, ELISA test, so now I guess I need to take one of those Western ones."

"Western blot."

"Yeah, that one."

"Jasmine, if you want fast results, the Western blot is not the way to go. It takes weeks."

"Oh."

"I can give you a rapid HIV test, and I'll have your results in twenty minutes."

"Then that's the test that I want. And I'll pay out of pocket. I don't care what it costs."

"We can worry about that later. Let's schedule an appointment for you as soon as possible. Would you be able to come in tomorrow morning?"

"Yes. Give me whatever opening you have. I'll make myself available."

Dr. Dieudonné sighed. "Would you like to come in at eight a.m.? That's before my staff arrives."

"Yes, Doctor. That would be perfect." Jasmine forced back tears. After all these years Nathalie still had the ability to both sense her need for safety and provide for it. "Thank you."

TWENTY-SEVEN

The last time she had sat in the empty reception area of a doctor's office, Jasmine had come with an agenda that had nothing to do with her own health.

Dr. Dieudonné called Jasmine into her office. She took the seat at the end of the doctor's desk. "So?"

"You have been infected with HIV. I'm sorry."

"Okay." She had not expected to hear anything different.

"And your T-cell count is very low. If we don't get that count up, you will develop full-blown AIDS."

"But I don't have it yet."

"No, but you're dangerously close."

"I don't understand."

"You are HIV positive, Jasmine. That means that you're carrying the virus that we in the medical community—at least, the majority of us—believe causes AIDS. And you will be considered HIV positive until one of two things happens. Either your T-cell count falls below two hundred or you acquire one of the twenty-six diseases that the Centers for Disease Control consider AIDS-defining illnesses. If and when one of those two things happens, you will have AIDS."

"What about this respiratory infection I have?"

"Thankfully, it's not an AIDS-defining illness."

"Jesus, it's like a fuckin' Chinese menu." Jasmine stood up and started to pace. "Got HIV? Choose a disease from Column A, you got HIV and your daily special. Got HIV and choose a disease from Column B. Guess what? You have AIDS."

Dr. Dieudonné gave her a small smile. "I never thought about it that way, but, yes, that's what it's like."

"What kind of profession you guys got here? How do you determine whether to diagnose someone with a deadly goddamn disease based on some equation? HIV plus pneumonia equals AIDS. Like how do you doctors decide which sicknesses are 'in'? Do you go to your medical conferences, propose diseases, and vote on 'em?"

"I understand that this is very difficult to hear."

"Fuck, yeah, it's difficult, because I don't get how something that is in my body and is going to kill me can be based on something so arbitrary!"

"Let me start off by explaining this. The twenty-six AIDS-defining illnesses are what we call opportunistic infections. In a person with a normal immune system, these diseases are relatively harmless. But because HIV weakens your body's ability to fight these illnesses, they become deadly. They exploit the fact that HIV has compromised your immune system, and that is why the presence of the virus with these opportunistic infections is considered AIDS. Now believe it or not, Jasmine, there is some good news here."

"Well, don't hold back, Doc."

"HIV in and of itself does not kill anybody, and there are things you can do to prevent these opportunistic infections. With significant changes in your lifestyle and the right combination of drugs, we can bolster your immune system and keep those AIDS-defining illnesses at bay.

"First things first, we have to take care of that respiratory infection." Dr. Dieudonné reached for her prescription pad. "Take this."

Jasmine started to protest but caught herself. Instead she accepted the slip of paper, wanting to see if Dr. Dieudonné prescribed the same medication that Adriano had given her.

Dr. Dieudonné checked her watch. "My assistant is due any minute now, so I'll call you in a few days with some recommendations."

"Recommendations?"

"Of some physicians who specialize in HIV management. And a few psychotherapists as well. To help you adjust."

"Oh."

"I'll call you with a list, and hopefully some of them will be in your network."

"My network?"

"Of your health plan."

"Right."

"Unless you want to stay with the physician who you initially consulted. I thought since you were seeking a second opinion you were having doubts about her. But maybe that's changed now that you've confirmed that her diagnosis was correct."

"Thank you." Jasmine decided to not tell her that she did not have medical coverage, let alone a physician. She hardly thought of Adriano as her doctor.

Dr. Dieudonné said, "I understand now why you canceled all the previous appointments."

Jasmine sighed. She was right and wrong about that. Jasmine certainly did not want to reveal the soap opera her life had become since Nathalie left for college and medical school. But that proved true long before Jasmine knew she was walking around with HIV. Had she kept her initial appointment with Dr. Dieudonné, she would have learned of her condition much sooner. It remained that Jasmine had failed to avoid the very thing she dreaded: displaying the shambles that was her life. With her days numbered, she saw no reason to let the doctor think she had evaded her for any other reason. "Yeah, I want to apologize for that," said Jasmine.

"Oh, I don't take that personally." The doctor smiled. "At least, now I don't."

Jasmine offered Dr. Dieudonné her hand. "I'm sorry about blowing my stack a few minutes ago."

"That's quite understandable, too. In fact, it's a good thing. Some days this epidemic, and the way we're dealing with it—or more like not dealing with it—makes me holler, too."

She wanted to act as if nothing had changed, and just as if nothing had, Jasmine had no place to go and nothing else to do but work. Unprepared to put on a normal face at the office and uninterested in seeing anyone else, Jasmine drove around the Bronx for almost an hour. When she finally stopped, she found herself parked across the street from the Booker home. She had no reason to stake out the place, but she could not make herself leave.

Jasmine caught Crystal Booker as she walked out of the basement apartment and locked the door behind her. She watched Crystal make her way down the block toward the bus stop. Only when Jasmine saw the city bus cruise by did she give into the urge to climb out of her SUV and cross the street.

She broke into the Booker apartment and headed straight for Malcolm's room. Jasmine had no idea what she was looking for, but she could not shake the feeling that she should be searching for something. Jasmine sat at Malcolm's desk and turned on his laptop.

She connected to the Internet and scanned through Malcolm's bookmarks, trying to remember his e-mail address. Every once in a while when he lost himself in an art project and had not visited Jasmine for days, he would drop her a brief e-mail message along with an inspirational quote or dirty joke. She would read, maybe smile or laugh, and then press DELETE.

In his folder of favorite Web sites, Malcolm had bookmarked Hotmail. Jasmine clicked on it and gave a small cheer to see that he had checked the *Remember me* box on the sign-in window. Without the password being required, Jasmine easily accessed Malcolm's inbox. She wondered if Malcolm checked his messages from wherever he might be hiding, and the image of Malcolm both alive and wired gave Jasmine a hint of comfort.

To more quickly identify significant messages amidst the flurry of spam, Jasmine sorted Malcolm's e-mail by sender. Although Yvette insisted that she had had no communication with him since he disappeared, Jasmine found a string of messages with PRIESTS in the sender column. She clicked on the most recent one and read it. Rather than a personal message to Malcolm, Yvette had posted a message to the exclusive listserv she had created for graffiti writers in the aftermath of the heated forum.

Malcolm himself was a subscriber to the listserv!

Jasmine scanned the message for pertinent information, but all it contained was a link to an online interview with a writer in Sydney, Australia. She selected the next posting by Yvette, which included another link to an article titled "Erasing Urban Scrawl." Yvette introduced the posting with a brief message: *This moron even disses LEGAL walls.* Jasmine had skipped to the next message, with the title *LV Mayor on Graff Artists: "Cut Off Their Thumbs,"* when she heard the front door slam and keys jingle.

She closed Malcolm's computer and leaped to her feet. Jasmine circled in place, trying to find a place to hide as she heard Crystal's footsteps draw near. Finally, she dropped to her knees and scampered under Malcolm's bed. Seconds later Jasmine heard the door to his bedroom squeak and saw petite, caramel-colored boots step into the room. Remembering that she had left her pocketbook with Malcolm's piecebook and her handgun on the desk, Jasmine held her breath and fought the urge to peek. Just as quickly as Crystal entered the room, however, she turned and disappeared. After waiting to hear the door click against the frame, Jasmine gasped for air. She remained under the bed until she heard the front door slam.

Then Jasmine crawled out from under the bed, grabbed her pocketbook, and ran out of Malcolm's bedroom.

The faint smell of stale cigarettes and household disinfectant greeted Jasmine when she reached the fifth floor of the run-down walk-up. She found the apartment, but checked the address on the printout one last time. Satisfied that she had found the right place, Jasmine tucked the pages into her pocketbook, then knocked on the door. Behind the door, a little dog yapped and a young, feminine voice hushed him.

The door opened. With a robust baby clad in a soiled bib and blue diapers anchored to her hip, the Mexican girl gave Jasmine an apprehensive stare. Not a day over seventeen, the young woman had a round face but sharp features. A roomful of preschool-aged children climbed the walls behind her, and Jasmine guessed that she had to forgo school to watch the kids for a host of relatives who were at work.

"Consiguo a Rogelio Alvarez," said Jasmine. The young woman shook her head, but Jasmine caught the panic as it flashed in her dark eyes. *"¿Rogelio Alvarez? ¿El vive aquí, verdad?"* Of course he lived there. She found this particular address in the database of active patients.

With the look in her eye and against her own will, the Mexicana had revealed that Rogelio Alvarez resided there and that she knew Jasmine knew it.

Still, the girl shook her head. One of the boys behind her crashed his toy truck into the coffee table, and she whirled around to reprimand him in a language that Jasmine did not know yet vaguely recognized. The boy defended himself in the unusual tongue, and a little girl who resembled him jumped into the fray to instigate his demise. Their caretaker scolded them, and Jasmine pinpointed the language. They were speaking in Náhuatl. These children were related to the couple Jasmine had seen at the clinic. In fact, the man was probably Rogelio Alvarez.

Realizing that she might be giving herself away, Jasmine said, *"Perdóname."* She backed away from the door. *"Lo siento mucho."*

The relieved young woman finally smiled. "Okai," she said. Then she quickly closed and locked the apartment door.

Jasmine bounded out of the tenement building and toward her SUV. Once in her car, she pulled out the printout of the database Burn. After taking note of the different addresses listed for Rogelio Alvarez and calculating the most efficient route in her head, Jasmine tore out of the space and down the street.

The drive on the Bronx River Parkway to White Plains took almost a half hour. Jasmine parked across the street from the single-family home at the address in front of her. As she walked up the winding driveway to the two-story colonial with the beige stucco, Jasmine estimated its worth at no less than two million dollars. In a county where homes cost as much as four times more, this alleged residence of Rogelio Alvarez counted as a modest house.

Jasmine gave the door a few whacks with its solid brass knocker. A girl who looked like she could star in a WB teen drama swung open the door with a fistful of bills in her other hand. Out of eyesight but in the distance, Jasmine heard the girl's friends talking and laughing. "I'm looking for Rogelio Alvarez?"

"Ro who?" Then she gasped with recognition. "Oh, I think that's the dude who used to own this place. He died a while back from whatever."

A pizza delivery truck pulled into the driveway, and the girl walked past Jasmine, who waited for her to pay the driver. Balancing the pizza on her head, the girl seemed surprised that Jasmine was still there. She gasped again. "Oh, I'm sorry! Was he, like, a relative of yours?"

Jasmine scoffed and walked around the girl, back down the driveway, and across the street to her SUV. "Geez, I said I was sorry," she heard the girl call out to her. Ignoring her, Jasmine climbed into her SUV and drove back to the Bronx.

TWENTY-EIGHT

Before leaving for lunch, Felicidad had left Jasmine a handwritten note along with the flash drive, a fresh printout, and a neatly typed telephone list. As she walked to her office, Jasmine read, smiling at the fact that Felicidad's handwriting was more girlish than hers had ever been.

Hi, Boss Lady!

I finished the two things you asked me to do.

About the databases, I didn't make any changes, as you insisted, but these files really are such a mess, I'm just as confused as you are as to which one has the right information. If you want, I can start by contacting people to confirm addresses, numbers, etc. Just let me know.

Now I spent some time resorting the databases to see if I could find a pattern in the errors themselves. Sometimes that helps you identify which list has the most correct information, or you can at least determine how the data might have been inputted incorrectly so you can fix it. Remember how you found that the dates of diagnosis were later than the dates of "expiration"? (I mean, we don't have to be morbid, do we?) I checked to see if the discrepancy between the two dates was consistent from record to record (e.g., is the difference always the same number of days, or for one patient is the difference a week while for another it's as much as a month, etc.). At first, I didn't see any pattern from record to record, since the discrepancies between the dates went anywhere from a few months to a couple of weeks. But then

I noticed that with the last three patients (chronologically, not alphabetically), the discrepancies was just a few days. I highlighted them for you on a fresh printout so you can see. I saw that and thought hmmm, and just had to point it out. But it probably doesn't mean anything, right?

Call me on the celly if you need anything. Otherwise, I'll be back in the office at one. Unless I meet a cute public defender from QUEENS! ☺

Ciao,

Feliz

So Felicidad had instincts for this work, too. Jasmine lit herself a cigarette and parked at her desk with the telephone list Felicidad had typed. With all that had happened in the past few days, she had forgotten that she had asked her to identify the specific professions of the people in Adriano Suárez's address book. The numbers with the familiar prefixes intrigued Jasmine for a good reason. They belonged to an array of government entities that she occasionally interacted with on behalf of her clients, including the local Medicaid branch, the medical examiner, and even the Bronx borough command of the NYPD.

Reading that made Jasmine think of Calvin. Not only did she have to call him, she had to make him listen long enough to her to break the news. By burying herself in work ever since Dr. Dieudonné had confirmed Adriano's diagnosis, Jasmine did not feel as if she truly had broken the news to herself.

And as if she conjured him with just a thought, Adriano called her. True to form, Jasmine grabbed her things and took to the street. Only when she had turned the ignition of her Escalade did Jasmine remember that Adriano still did not know where she worked, let alone what she truly did for a living. Yet she had responded to his call as if he were Calvin, and might show up unexpectedly at her office. Still, Jasmine pulled out of the space and down the street. Even if Adriano had not known where she lived, she would have kept to the streets. She not only felt safer on the streets, but somehow there she felt better about her fucked-up situation. Jasmine could move in broad daylight and still hide from her demons. All she had to do was her job.

At the next stop signal, Jasmine took Felicidad's fresh printout out of her pocketbook. On the bottom of the list, she found the names of three patients highlighted in neon orange. Jasmine chose the first of two with Bronx addresses belonging to a girl named Eboni Powell.

When Jasmine turned down Eboni's street in Mott Haven, she found a block half filled with empty lots. She parked her SUV and walked down the sidewalk with the printout in hand. "Eighteen thirty-three, eighteen thirty-five, eighteen thirty-seven . . ." Only three condemned buildings remained on the street, and none of their numbers matched the one listed for Eboni on the printout. Estimating where building 1849 should have been, Jasmine stood in front of a chain-link fence that barred her from a large plot of dust. Whatever structure Eboni Powell once lived in—or maybe claimed to have lived in—was gone.

Calvin had said that one of the patients on Malcolm's list was a runaway from the Midwest who wound up as a prostitute. Was that Eboni Powell? She wanted to call Calvin and ask him but ultimately could not. Jasmine had more to confess to Calvin than she had to ask of him.

She returned to her car and called Felicidad, requesting the addresses of the three most recent patients admitted to Adriano's clientele as they appeared in the active file. According to that database, the "new" Eboni Powell lived a short drive away.

Within minutes Jasmine parked her car in front of a brownstone in Melrose. A sticker of a flag with a green, yellow, and red stripe hung in the front window. Although she could not recall which particular country, Jasmine recognized it as an African flag. Remembering the risk she took by revealing herself at Rogelio Alvarez's Bronx home, Jasmine nixed knocking on the front door. Instead she got out of the Escalade and strode toward the mailbox. When she opened it and found it empty, Jasmine went back to her SUV and decided to wait for the mail carrier.

As she waited, Jasmine broke out Malcolm's piecebook and finished decoding the words on his subway sketches. She added the new words to the list she had created in sharp print.

APPLE
CRADLE
ORANGE
BISON
FALLS
RAPTOR

On the surface, the words made no sense together. But Jasmine's instinct told her that not only were they related, their order mattered. She even had a hunch that they were already in correct order. Nor could she deny the burning impulse that access to the listserv would tell her something she needed to know to make sense of them. Jasmine kicked herself for not stealing Malcolm's laptop the last time she had broken into the Booker apartment. Casting that regret to the back of her mind, Jasmine occupied herself by playing word associations with the list in the hopes of uncovering their relationship.

Two hours later, the postal carrier turned the corner and strolled down the block, pushing his cart of envelopes and packages. Jasmine abandoned her word association and watched patiently while the mailman finished his job. Once she saw him cross the street to the next block, she crept out of her SUV and to the mailbox. Checking once over each shoulder, Jasmine sifted through the mail. All the pieces except one were for people with the surname Diakite. The sole envelope addressed to Powell came from the Claire Tow Pediatric Day Hospital of the Memorial Sloan-Kettering Cancer Center. Jasmine tucked the envelope in her pocket and jogged back to her SUV.

Once in the driver's seat, Jasmine tore open the envelope. Sloan-Kettering had sent the Powells a statement for the treatment of Eboni Powell, who supposedly lived at that address as well. From the birth date on the invoice, Jasmine calculated that she was only fourteen years old. The hospital had charged the half dozen procedures it administered on Eboni's behalf to Medicaid. Jasmine compared the statement to the active-patient listing, and it confirmed that Eboni was covered by the state's health insurance program.

Jasmine looked for the girl's diagnosis. According to the printout,

Adriano had diagnosed Eboni with a condition Jasmine had never heard of called Ewing's sarcoma. He diagnosed her approximately two weeks before Malcolm failed to appear in court. Jasmine turned to Malcolm's list. It told her that several days after the Eboni Powell who lived in a brownstone in Melrose was diagnosed with Ewing's sarcoma, the Eboni Powell who once lived in an abandoned building in Mott Haven that no longer existed was pronounced dead.

Jasmine itched to run from this discovery, but her instinct anchored her in front of the Diakite/Powell brownstone until someone returned home. She knew she could not reveal herself to them the way she had to the young Mexican woman at the Alvarez address. But Jasmine committed to keep them under surveillance until she witnessed something that either confirmed or dismissed her new and horrifying suspicion about the true nature of Adriano Suárez's charity.

So she waited for several hours until a woman with mahogany skin and wrinkled fingers trudged toward the brownstone lugging a sack of groceries. She lowered the bag to the bottom step, holding the small of her back as she straightened up and opened the mailbox. The woman looked through the envelopes, dropped them into the grocery bag, then carried the bag up the stairs. Jasmine had no proof, but she did not need it. At once she knew that this weary woman was both Mrs. Diakite and the mother of the teenage girl who was admitted to the Claire Tow Hospital under the name Eboni Powell.

Jasmine spent the next few hours driving the streets of the South Bronx, trying to come to grips with her discoveries. In order to help a young African girl fight Ewing's sarcoma, Adriano Suárez had stolen the identity of another fourteen-year-old girl named Eboni Powell who'd run away from her Midwestern home and wound up prostituting herself on the streets of the Bronx. Adriano sold or maybe even gave the parents of the Diakite girl the Medicaid card that only days earlier had belonged to Eboni Powell.

Days before the Diakite girl found salvation in a city-issued card, Eboni Powell had sold herself just like Jasmine once did—and probably died—only streets away. Unless she was an exception to the rule, Eboni was killed on one of those streets. And Jasmine could not rule out the realistic possibility that in order to give her identity to and save the Diakite girl, Adriano Suárez had had the teenage prostitute murdered.

Worst of all, Malcolm Booker, who Jasmine had put back on the street in an effort to save a brother who had long been dead and buried, might have been the one that Adriano sent to do it.

TWENTY-NINE

Sunset broke and Jasmine was finally tired enough to take the risk to go home. She had run out of booze and cigarettes, and the needle on her gauge flirted with empty. While at a red light, she called the office to leave a message for Felicidad. "I'll be out sick tomorrow, but if Officer Quinones and Dr. Dieudonné call, tell them to call me on my cell phone. To hell with everyone else." Jasmine crashed the second she landed on the mattress.

An hour later, she woke up sweating from the same train nightmare, although this time she was running through the graffiti-filled subway train with Adriano Suárez chasing her. He called her name behind her as if taunting her. Jasmine threw open the door of a car and bumped into Malcolm Booker, who gave her an evil smile. Trapped between the two men, who both reached out to grab her, Jasmine chose to dive into the subway tracks, landing on the third rail.

Resigned to staying awake until exhaustion overcame her again, Jasmine sat up in bed and lit a cigarette. She checked her phone to find a slew of messages from Adriano. Without either listening to or deleting them, Jasmine just turned off the phone and tossed it into the top drawer of her night table. She saw the bottle of whiskey, grabbed it, and took a few swigs.

Then Jasmine looked over the side of her bed, trying to remember where she had dropped her pocketbook before passing out. Spotting it at the foot of the bed, Jasmine crawled and reached for it. She took out Malcolm's piecebook along with the scraps of her word associations.

> APPLE
> Big Apple, fruit, red, green, McIntosh, keeps the doctor away

None of the relationships she discovered between several words panned out for the entire list. She saw animals in RAPTOR and BISON, but none of the other words fit. Jasmine saw fruit in APPLE and ORANGE, but could not associate any of the other words with them.

Then Jasmine discovered the names of cities. The Big APPLE, of course, was New York City. And the first thing that came to mind when she read FALLS was Niagara. Thanks to Calvin, she knew the Raptors were an NBA team in Toronto, Canada, and the ORANGE was the name of the basketball team at Syracuse University upstate. BISON was a kind of buffalo, which was also the name of a city in upstate New York. The only word she could not associate instantly with a major city was CRADLE, but at this point, Jasmine refused to believe she had taken another wrong turn.

She scrambled out of bed and hurried into the living room to her small bookcase. Jasmine grabbed the atlas and opened it to a map of North America. With a pencil she circled all the cities she had uncovered. As she dragged the pencil across the multicolored page, swiftly connecting one city to the next without any unusual turns, Jasmine knew she was right. Perhaps Malcolm was in one of these cities.

Or in all of them at different times.

If Malcolm had boarded a train like the ones on which he sketched the clues, he could have stopped in any and all of those cities. Except the New York City subway did not take riders outside of the five boroughs. Malcolm never could have taken a subway to Yonkers or Mount Vernon, which bordered the Bronx, let alone take one all the way to Syracuse or Buffalo, which respectively were five and seven hours away.

Malcolm could have taken a train to these cities, just not a subway train. Perhaps the Metro-North Railroad, which was the second largest commuter train in the United States after the Long Island Railroad. Or Malcolm could have hopped a regional train, such as Amtrak. But Jasmine had difficulty imagining Malcolm riding a commuter line back and forth for days at a time, and even if he had succeeded in stowing himself away on a regional train, he could hardly ride this long without being detected by personnel.

You can always do freights. Unless Malcolm was hiding on a *freight* train, just like the one Yvette had been painting the night Jasmine realized she was PRIESTS. Yvette was the one who told her, *You can always do freights.*

With the atlas in hand, Jasmine headed back into the bedroom and booted up her computer. She checked her Rey2 account, and still no messages from Yvette. Jasmine took her final shot.

> Yo, PRIESTS,
>
> Yeah, let's hook up. I got a dope idea for a piece I want to get up and could use your input. You down to meet me at the rail yard over there on Lincoln Avenue some night this week? If so, name the day and time.
>
> Peace,
> JaneDoe
>
> P.S. If you sent me the link to get on the list-serv, I never got it. Please send it again.

After sending off the e-mail, Jasmine went back to her map. If she was correct that both the words on Malcolm's sketches were already in the proper order and referred to cities on a possible train route, the city associated with CRADLE had to lie between New York City and Syracuse. Chances were it was a major city. Ithaca? Rochester? Poughkeepsie? Albany! Jasmine consulted the atlas, and the state capital indeed fell between the Big Apple and Salt City, or Syracuse. If she could find a plausible association between the city of Albany and the word CRADLE, Jasmine would know she had broken the code.

Turning back to her computer, Jasmine entered both words into the search engine. At the top of her results was the city's official Web site—www.thecityofalbany.com. The excerpt beneath the hyperlink described the site with the words of the search highlighted in bold. ***Albany**'s nickname, "**Cradle** of the Union," resulted from the meeting* *here in 1754 of the* ***Albany*** *Congress, which adopted Benjamin Franklin's Plan of Union . . .*

"Hot damn, that's it!" Jasmine sprung to her feet. "I broke it." Malcolm Booker was hiding out on a freight train that traveled from New York City to Toronto, making stops in Albany, Syracuse, Buffalo, and Niagara Falls. He had encoded the name of those cities into his sketches to communicate his whereabouts to his allies in the graffiti subculture. Although she had no proof, Jasmine believed more than ever that Yvette used the listserv to share information about Malcolm's arrival at these locations to an underground network of fellow writers, so that those in the vicinity of his current stop could harbor him or at least bring him food and water.

As far as Jasmine was concerned, she only had three things left to do. One, she had to uncover which freight train Malcolm was riding. Two, she needed to find Malcolm before Adriano became suspicious of her or realized she had discovered his involvement in insurance fraud through identity theft. And perhaps most important of all, Jasmine must pray that her instinct for once was wrong about one thing: Adriano Suárez's capacity for murder.

THIRTY

While waiting for the pharmacist to fill her prescription from Dr. Dieudonné, Jasmine finally listened to the litany of messages Adriano had left on her voice mail. With each one, his tone grew less compassionate and more demanding. By the tenth and final message, Adriano only said, "If you won't come to me, then I will come to you," before slamming down his receiver. Jasmine understood that she could not dodge him indefinitely, but before she could decide whether or not to agree to meet him in person, the pharmacist reappeared at the counter.

"Here you go, Miss Reyes," he said as he handed her a small white paper bag. "Is there anything else I can help you with today?"

"Actually, there is." Jasmine reached into her pocket for the vial of pills Adriano had given her at the diner. "I was refilling my weekly pill organizer when I spilled all my medications, and now I can't tell one from the other. I don't want to waste a single one because you know how expensive drugs can be. . . ."

"You're preaching to the converted."

"And I'm certainly not trying to kill myself by taking the wrong thing, so . . ." Jasmine opened the vial, took out a pill, and laid it on the counter. "Can you tell me if this is the same drug as the one you just dispensed for me?"

"Sure." The pharmacist took the pill. "I'll be back in a few minutes."

While Jasmine waited she called the agency and paced the aisle. "Felicidad, are there any messages for me?"

"You have a message here from Asad Mukherjee's defense attorney."

"Are they finally going to let him plead guilty for five years' probation, for Christ's sake?"

"No, but because of your last report, the judge agreed to exonerate his bond and release him on his own recognizance."

"Ah, that's bullshit, but I'll take the ROR. When I get back to the office, I'm going to show you how to check on the status of our bonds and follow up on exonerations. In the meantime, arrange for the Mukherjees' collateral to be returned to them. Anyone else call?"

"Dr. Dieudonné. She said she'd call you on your cell."

"Oh." Jasmine had not heard any messages from her. "Anyone else?"

"The cops who're investigating the break-in."

"Has Calvin called?"

"No, honey, I'm sorry."

Jasmine snorted. "What are you apologizing for?"

"I don't know. From the way you asked, it just seemed like the right thing to say. But when he does call, I'll be sure to tell him to call you on your cell ASAP. Or you want me to call him for you?"

"No, thanks, just have him call my cell if he calls the office. And you call me, too, just so I know that he reached out. You know, in case he gets caught up with work and can't call me again." The pharmacist returned. "Feliz, I have to go." Jasmine walked back to the counter and braced herself. "So are they the same pills? Can I just throw the ones I was able to save into the bottle you just gave me?"

"No, you definitely shouldn't mix them, because they're not the same drug."

Jasmine's stomach dipped. "They're not?"

"I mean, they both treat the same kinds of ailments, but they're different drugs."

"How are they different?"

The pharmacist eyed Jasmine, as if she should know this information. "Well, that one is a bit stronger," he said, pointing to Adriano's pill. "Has more side effects."

Jasmine clapped once. "See, that's it. I have this respiratory infection, and my doctor prescribed those pills to me first. But when I told her they were making me sick, she gave me this new prescription." She shook the white bag.

The convinced pharmacist nodded and said, "Well, you don't need to take them both. If the new ones effectively treat your infection without the side effects, you don't need the old ones anymore. I would just throw them out."

"Okay, thanks."

Relieved and even moved that Adriano had prescribed a legitimate medication to treat her infection, Jasmine dialed the clinic while walking back to her SUV. "Suárez Community Health, this is Lisa."

"Hi, Lisa, this is Jasmine Reyes calling for Dr. Suárez."

"The doctor is with a patient right now. Would you like to leave a message?"

"No, I'd like you to interrupt the doctor and tell him that I'm on the line. He's been waiting for my call."

Lisa huffed and then placed her on hold. Less than a minute later, Adriano came on the line. "Jasmine."

"Hey." They listened to each other exhale. "Adriano, look . . ."

"I miss you."

"I miss you, too."

"I just want to help you through this."

"Adriano . . ."

"I know that you must be feeling helpless right now, Jasmine, but you have to trust me. You're not. I can help you like I've helped dozens of other people if only you would let me."

"How 'bout I come to the clinic tonight after hours?"

"Please do that."

They exchanged good-byes, and Jasmine closed her eyes and allowed the hope to settle under her skin. Adriano sounded happy—and not the least bit suspicious—that she would see him. She wanted to see him, too, but for none of the reasons she used to.

Adriano locked the front door and led Jasmine into the examining room. "I have to take another blood sample so that I can measure your T-cell count and viral load."

Jasmine sat on the examining table where they first made love. "What's that going to tell you?" She already knew that hers were dangerously low and needed to increase. But Jasmine had never asked Dr. Dieudonné why that mattered.

"Your T cells are the white blood cells your immune system sends to defend your body against infections. There's one particular type of T cell that the human immunodeficiency virus—HIV—prefers to invade. They're called CD4 cells. The virus slips into the CD4 cells to replicate itself."

"Do all these cells eventually die?"

"Yes."

"Shit."

"Your viral load tells us how quickly the infection is progressing by measuring how much of the virus exists in your bloodstream."

"So I want that to be as low as possible."

"We want it to be undetectable. That will mean that the virus is not replicating itself very quickly."

"And we want that."

"We do."

"Along with a high T-cell count, because that means I still have a lot of soldiers fighting inside me."

"Yes."

Jasmine held out her forearm. "Okay, let's do this." Adriano rubbed a swatch of cotton soaked in antiseptic on the inside of her elbow. As he wrapped the elastic tube around her arm and tapped a vein, she asked, "So how long is it going to take you to find out all this stuff."

"Minutes." Adriano ripped the sanitary paper off the needle. "I have everything I need to run the tests in the next room."

"Aren't you the lucky one."

Adriano glanced up to give her a mischievous grin. "No, you are." He ran two fingers down a vein plump with blood. "You're lucky that I'm wealthy. However, I'm wealthy because I'm disciplined. Luck had nothing to do with that."

Jasmine grew nervous. She no longer wanted him to draw blood, but she could not retreat without raising his suspicions. She continued to make small talk with large meaning. "In any event, it's pretty unusual to have that kind of technology at a community health center, isn't it?"

"Yes, I can't deny that it's very unusual." Adriano slipped the needle into Jasmine's vein and watched the tube fill with blood. "Probably just as unusual as a female bounty hunter."

He knew the truth about her.

Jasmine swallowed, then said, "We prefer to be called bail enforcement agents, and we're not as rare as you think."

"Suit yourself, but I think bounty hunter sounds much more . . ." He searched for the word as he pulled the needle from Jasmine's arm. "Romantic."

"So how did you find out?" Jasmine actually preferred to know when, but the question would expose the fear that it was imperative she hide. "What'd I do to tip you off?"

"In our very first meeting in my office, you referred to him as Macho." Adriano laughed. "I never called him that, so I know you didn't learn that nickname from me." He put another swath of cotton onto the puncture wound and folded her arm so that her fingers touched her shoulder. "So starting with the information that you gave me on our first date, I tried to learn more about you. Probably in the very same way you conduct background checks for your bail bond business."

Jasmine thought of the names and numbers in his electronic address book. "With some help from your friends." She imagined that some of the people on that list also helped Adriano swipe identities as well as cover his tracks.

"Yes, I have friends in all the necessary places." Adriano placed a cap on the vial of Jasmine's blood and slipped it into the breast pocket of his lab coat. "Once I discovered what you actually did, I couldn't resist trying to learn more about who you are. I know that before becoming a bail enforcement agent, you were a prostitute, and my guess is that's how you contracted HIV. . . ."

She glared at Adriano, daring him to continue telling her about her own life.

"I know that you had a twin brother who committed suicide while locked up for almost beating to death a customer who assaulted you.

And I know that your friend with the penchant for materializing is a uniformed officer with the NYPD. You know what fascinates me the most about you, Jasmine, to this very minute? That every time you lied to me, you also told me the truth."

"Anything else you want to know about me?" Jasmine stood up and walked over to Adriano to look him straight in the eye. "Anything you care to ask me to my face?"

Adriano stared back with soft eyes and a tone to match. "After all that we've experienced together, are you still looking for Malcolm Booker?"

"If I continued to see you just because I wanted to find Malcolm Booker, it would be because I suspected that you know why he jumped bail."

"And you do." Adriano reached out and gently grasped Jasmine's wrist. He unfolded her arm and applied a bandage to the puncture. When he finished dressing her wound, he held on to her hand. "I can get you the treatment you need, Jasmine, but it requires that you secure something that I know you don't have."

"Health insurance."

"I can get you the medical coverage you need to manage this virus and keep you alive. You know now that I've done it for others, and that I can do it for you, too. And by that terrified look in your eye, I suspect that you also know how."

Jasmine pulled her arm away from Adriano and walked back to the examining table. She needed as much distance from him as possible. Her every kind of safety depended on it. "So what are my options, Dr. Suárez?"

"You can become a part of my special clientele, access the latest advances in HIV treatment available, and have a fighting chance at living a longer, normal life."

"Or . . ."

"You can refuse my offer, gamble your life by placing it into the custody of our public health care system, and likely die."

Because you'll kill me long before one of those opportunistic infections does.

Adriano peeled off his stethoscope and laid it across a tray of medical tools. "And what you have to recognize, Jasmine, is that other people's lives besides your own are at stake here. Good people. Some of them children. They, too, have chronic and even deadly conditions that they couldn't get treated if not for me. But you've come to mean a lot more to me than they do."

He stood and walked over to Jasmine. She rose from the examining table and tried to back away. Adriano advanced until he had her cornered against a counter. He reached out and caressed Jasmine's cheek. "I'm intent on helping you survive because that's the oath I took. But I want to help you live because I'm falling for you. And I won't allow you to leave this clinic until you accept my services."

"Why? You've just met me. What makes me so special?"

Without missing a beat, Adriano said, "What makes you special is the way you picked yourself up every time fate knocked you down. You could have used the things that happened to you as an excuse to continue leading an ugly and filthy life. But instead you cleaned yourself up. And not only did you help yourself, you found a way to help others. You gave them the alternatives no one ever gave you. So unlike, say, the Eboni Powells of the world, Jasmine, you deserve to live."

Because you say so? Despite Adriano's romantic words, Jasmine heard only the veiled threat behind them. He wanted her to become his patient so that her very life would depend on him. Then she could never expose his secret without putting her own life at risk. He had done so much to protect his underground operation, Jasmine no longer had any doubts about how far he would go. Perhaps Adriano did care for her, but his feelings were irrelevant. If she ever presented herself as a threat to what he was doing, Adriano was not beyond having her killed. He had the worst God complex of any doctor that ever walked the face of the earth.

"I don't know how I'm going to do this without you," Jasmine said. She meant it as a bluff, and yet the words rang devastatingly true. Before she ever suspected that murder might have been involved or had a personal stake in his underground activities, Jasmine sympathized with Adriano's crusade. She rooted for him even when she discovered that he had broken the law. And now Jasmine was dying and only Adriano could save her. And he wanted to save her, and not just because of his principles. And she wanted to be saved simply because no one since Jason ever thought of her as being worthy of saving. Despite the extremes Adriano would go to to do so, Jasmine wanted to be saved. "Tell me what to do."

Adriano pulled her face toward his and gave her a long, breathy kiss. Then he stepped back and pulled out her blood sample from his breast pocket. "We have to see what the tests say first." He walked over to another counter, picked up a stack of brochures, and handed them to her. "I collected these for you, and I want you to read them while I run these tests. They'll answer some of the questions you have, but I'm sure you'll have more when I get back. Just sit down, read this information, and trust me." Adriano kissed her on the forehead and walked out of the examining room.

Jasmine lowered herself into a chair. She looked at the first fact sheet, with the title "Now That I Have HIV, What Do I Do?" From the shape of the letters and choice of colors, Jasmine recognized Malcolm's work from the start.

Instead of reading the material, Jasmine stood up and paced around the examining room. What would be the point of all this? Her days were numbered. So what if Adriano put a hit out on her or AIDS put her down like an old dog? She should have starved or frozen to death soon after her parents left, but no, at the time, she still had Jason. The john should have killed her that night. Or AIDS should have knocked on her door years ago. Or one of these lunatics that festered in the underbelly of the South Bronx should have fired a bullet into Jasmine's head when she came looking for a bail jumper. Whoever broke into her agency the other day and busted off a cap at her should have hit her. Jasmine had been living on borrowed time for too long, and she did not feel a damned bit fortunate because of that.

She picked up her pocketbook and headed for the clinic exit. No matter all the other lives he saved—not even her own—Jasmine no longer admired or liked Adriano Suárez as she initially had. She would never feel about him the way he wanted her to, and eventually it would show. And when it did, Jasmine would be done, HIV or no HIV. After Jason, she had no capacity to feel that deeply toward anyone. Jasmine did not even have the ability to fake it even for her own damned good. Calvin could have told Adriano that.

THIRTY-ONE

On the drive home, she left Adriano a rambling message about her decision to leave before he returned with her test results. Not only could she no longer hide from him, but Jasmine had to make him believe that she had placed her life in his hands. "This whole thing's really overwhelming, Adriano, as I'm sure you understand," she said in her voice mail. "I need a few days to digest all this and then I'll be in a mind-set to hear the different treatment options you have to offer." Jasmine hoped this bought her some time.

Within minutes of leaving her message, however, Adriano called her back. She had to answer it. Dodging him was both unwise and useless. Jasmine changed lanes and connected the call. "Guess you got my message."

Adriano sighed. "I understand what you're going through, Jasmine, but there's something you need to understand. Every day is a matter of life or death for you now."

She convinced Adriano that she would call him the following day to make another appointment to see him. At that time, he would give Jasmine the results of her viral load and T-cell count tests and explain to her the treatments available. Together they would decide which strategy to pursue. "You also need to quit smoking and eat more healthily," he said. "Increase your daily intake of fresh fruits and vegetables. I'll pick you up some from the organic supermarket in my neighborhood and give them to you when we meet."

The elevator reached Jasmine's floor as they ended their call. She fished inside her purse for her keys, then noticed her unwelcome mat. Someone had straightened out the mat, which meant he had opened her door.

With a tense back, Jasmine slipped her key into the lock and entered the apartment. The creepy air that greeted her told her that whoever had broken into her apartment was still there. As she eased her way past the threshold, she imagined Adriano calling one of his thugs to tell him that she was on her way home. She had played a charade all this time, so why not have his turn?

Jasmine jiggled her keys and feigned through her usual routine to psyche out her intruder. "Calvin, are you here?" she called, hoping that the thug would fall into her ruse. "You'll never believe what happened in court today." She reached into her bag for Shorty and slid toward the living room. "Judge Castro finally RORed Asad Mukherjee. Now if I could only get Judge Iler to do the same for Bernie Epps." Jasmine spun into her living room with Shorty drawn, but found no one there. She proceeded to the kitchen.

"I mean, if you can finally release a guy charged with aggravated assault on his own recognizance after being out on bail for six months," she said as she inched toward the kitchen, "why the hell can't you do the same for a dude only charged with possession, right?" Jasmine whipped into the room to find it empty, too.

When she came back out into the hallway, however, she saw the light in her bedroom casting a beam underneath the closed door onto the corridor. Jasmine crept into the bathroom and turned on the shower. "But you know what, babe? ROR is bullshit. Just let the guy plead guilty, give him probation, and close the case. The prosecutor scores her conviction, the kid gets his freedom, the public defender lightens his load, and the judge . . . fuck! Cal, honey, I need another towel. Can you bring it to me, please?"

As Jasmine hoped, the intruder shuffled his way across her bedroom and opened the door, thinking she had invited him to ambush her. Jasmine cocked Shorty and poised herself by the door with one hand on the light switch and the other with her gun raised in the air. The second the intruder pushed open the door, Jasmine killed the lights and fired.

She heard a groan and then felt the rush of air as the body collapsed to the floor. Jasmine flicked on the light. Although he was still breathing, blood oozed from the intruder's masked head across the checkered tiles. Jasmine kicked his leg. "You're the same bastard that took a shot at me at the office, aren't you?"

He reached for her. "Jasmine."

"Oh, my God." She recognized the voice. Jasmine dropped to her knees and yanked the mask off her face.

Crystal.

Jasmine jumped to her feet and raced into the kitchen to get her cell phone from her pocketbook. As she dialed 911, she rushed back to the bathroom. After yanking every towel off its rack, Jasmine lifted Crystal's head and placed them under it. Crystal grimaced in agony, and tears coasted down the side of her face and into the pool of dark blood.

"I have a person shot in the head at one three four Einstein Loop in Co-op City. Apartment 28 D, as in David."

"Jasmine . . ."

"Crystal, hush. Save your strength. EMS is on its way, and you're going to be fine."

"I couldn't let you find him. It doesn't matter who finds him. If Macho's found, he's as good as dead."

Jasmine could see Crystal's face draining into gray. She took her hand, which had already turned cold. "Crystal, tell me where Macho is, and I swear on my life, I won't let Suárez get him. If you help me find Macho, together we can save him."

"Don't let Suárez get him, Jasmine. Promise me."

"I won't, Crystal, just tell me where he is."

"Please don't let him kill my brother. He's all I have left. Promise me."

"I promise, Crystal, but you have to—"

But before Jasmine could say anything more, Crystal died in her arms. She gently placed her head on the blood-soaked towel, then searched Crystal's body for her keys. She found them, as well as Crystal's cell phone. Grabbing the keys and both cell phones, Jasmine got to her feet and ran into the kitchen for her pocketbook. She ripped a jacket out of her hallway closet to cover her bloody top, then ran out of her apartment and down the stairwell. Jasmine sped down the steps, now in a race against Adriano that would determine whether she, Malcolm Booker, and the next Eboni Powell lived or died.

Jasmine leaped into her SUV and roared to the Booker apartment. She tore into Malcolm's room, grabbed his laptop, and raced back out. Halfway across the street to her SUV, Jasmine halted. She had to abandon it. Adriano would recognize it, and so might anyone else he had tracking her down. Jasmine ran to the corner, hailed a cab, and went to the only place she had left.

THIRTY-TWO

Jasmine rang the buzzer and prayed for an answer.

"Who is it?" Felicidad sang over the intercom

"It's Jasmine."

The door buzzed, and Jasmine dashed inside the building and up the staircase. When she reached the landing, Felicidad stood waiting for her in a satin bathrobe and fuzzy slippers. "Jasmine, what brings you here?"

Jasmine rushed by her into the apartment. "Close the door." She placed the laptop on the coffee table, then peeled off her jacket, revealing her top, now cold and stiff with blood.

"Oh, my God, he came after you again!" Felicidad rushed into the bathroom.

"She." Jasmine followed her and watched Felicidad grab towels off the rack and a first aid kit from above the sink. "I'm fine. This"—she gestured toward the blood on her clothes—"It's hers."

"Jesus, Jasmine."

"I'm close to putting this baby to bed, but I need a place to hide out until I do. I know it's a lot to ask, Felicidad, but I don't think anyone would think of looking for me here."

"Of course." Felicidad motioned for Jasmine's bloody shirt. "Let's get rid of that awful thing and get you into something warm and clean."

After fetching her a clean robe, Felicidad left Jasmine to shower. As the hot stream cleansed away the evidence of the night's drama, she calculated her next moves. She had to reenlist Calvin in case Malcolm's e-mail did not have the information that she needed.

When Jasmine emerged from the bathroom in her borrowed robe, she found two other women in the kitchen with Felicidad. The plump bottle blond with bronze skin wore a short plaid skirt, a white lace tank top with no bra, and Mary Janes. The tall black woman with micro braids that grazed the small of her back had on white go-go boots, red hot pants hiked over her full bottom, and a silver sequined halter top with a low cut and no back. The two women gave Jasmine the once-over then looked to Felicidad for an explanation.

Sweeping her hair back into a simple ponytail, Felicidad herself wore a demure turquoise pantsuit with low heels and a silk scarf dangling from her shoulder. "These are my roommates. That's Angel," she said to Jasmine, pointing to the Latina in the schoolgirl costume. "And that's Cocoa. Girls, this is . . . my cousin Justine."

Jasmine gave Felicidad a nod of approval at her discretion.

"She's going to stay with us for a few days."

Angel gave Jasmine a warm smile. "You a working girl?"

"No. Not anymore. I left the business a little while ago."

"Well, you go," cheered Angel. "Fools singing about how hard it is out here for a pimp."

"That's 'cause they ain't never walked in the hoe's stilettos," said Cocoa. She picked her beaded purse up off the counter. "Well, Justine, we can't retire just yet, so we gotta go. You make yourself at home. Any family to Feliz is family to us." Then she kissed Felicidad on the cheek. "Have fun on your date."

Angel squealed with delight. "Feliz has her first real date in, like, forever!" She threw her arms around Felicidad. "Remember, *nena*, if you want there to be a second one, don't go doing nothing that I would have to charge him for!" The three roommates laughed, and even Jasmine had to smile.

When Angel and Cocoa left, Felicidad rushed to Jasmine holding two mugs filled with tea. "I know I'm not supposed to be living here." She offered one of the mugs to Jasmine. "It's just until I save enough money to get my own place, and that's going to take a little time."

"Felicidad, I really don't care about that right now." Jasmine accepted the tea and eased onto the couch. "If anything, I have to thank you for letting me crash here. And being discreet."

Felicidad sat down next to her. "Do you want to tell me what happened?"

"Yeah, I do." It even surprised Jasmine to say that. "But for your own good, I can't just yet. I'll explain it all when it's over, which my gut's telling me will be soon."

"Fair enough."

"But can I ask you something?"

"Sure."

"What's it like . . ."

"The life of a tranny?"

"To live . . . to live with HIV."

"It's hard, but it's still living." Felicidad kicked off her pumps and curled into the sofa. "When I first found out, I wanted to slit my wrists. And I came close to doing it, too. I bolted the door and unplugged the phone. I got the razor. I filled up the bathtub. And as I was lying there reflecting on my life, thinking that all those painful memories would drive me to go through with it, it hit me. I might not have gotten infected if I wasn't already trying to kill myself in the first place." She took a long sip of tea. "Funny thing is, walking the stroll was probably the only thing I did do that was about survival. Hoeing was about keeping a roof over my head and food in my belly, no more, no less. I tried to do straight work, Jasmine. Believe me, I did, but I don't have to tell you the marketplace is a jungle for a girl like me. Tricking was about doing what I had to do. But the smoking, the drinking, the snorting, the unsafe sex with all the squares who promised to free me from the life and all that? Just suicide in slow motion, honey. But now? I do all the things I should have been doing when I was out there putting myself at risk." Felicidad pointed to a fitness ball and yoga mat tucked into the corner. "I exercise. I eat right. I quit smoking and drinking. I mean, I have a glass of wine now and then instead of getting shit-faced. I don't take any drugs that aren't prescribed as part of my therapy. Now that's hard, I admit. Adhering to my treatment can be a bitch. It's, like, so many pills, so little time. But my girls keep me on track." Felicidad giggled. "Oh, my girls. I love my girls. Every chance I get, I hang out with my girls, I play with boys, and I laugh and laugh and laugh. Believe it or not, I've never been happier than I am right now." Felicidad sat up and placed her mug onto the coffee table. "Can I ask you something now, Jasmine?"

"Only fair."

"Why did you tell Angel and Cocoa you used to walk the strip?"

Jasmine stood up and looked out the window onto the dark street. "Because I did." She saw a man in a sharp coat crossing the street toward the building.

"Really?"

"Really."

"You don't have to answer this, but . . ."

"Yes, I'm HIV positive, too. I just found out. You're the first person I've told."

The intercom buzzed, and Felicidad cursed under her breath. "I can cancel that if you want me to stay home . . . so we can talk."

Jasmine turned away from the window. "I could use some time alone. Plus, I have work to do. You go and have fun." She walked to the coffee table and picked up Malcolm's laptop.

Felicidad slipped back into her pumps and headed to the intercom. "You have my number if you need anything. And if you have any more questions, I have some books in my room that might answer them. It's the door right across from the bathroom." The intercom sounded again, and Felicidad buzzed her date into the building.

Jasmine started toward Felicidad's bedroom. "Feliz?" She stopped and turned. "This is none of my business, so feel free to send me to hell for asking . . ."

"Sure."

"Does he know?"

Felicidad scoffed. "Of course. Honey, I don't play those games anymore. Every day women get killed out here."

"Tell me about it."

"Besides, I don't need to lie. Finding a man who'll wine, dine, and divine me is actually easy. Getting him to take me home to his mother is another story."

Jasmine waved good-bye to Felicidad, who grabbed her keys and purse and went to meet her date on the landing. Jasmine went into

Felicidad's bedroom, plugged in Malcolm's laptop, and settled on the bed. After signing into his e-mail account, Jasmine resorted his messages by subject, then looked for the earliest posting among the group of messages posted to the graffiti listserv. As she hoped, it was the introductory message for new members, ending with a link that would take her to the actual server on the Internet. She clicked on it.

Through Malcolm's user name, Jasmine was able to search through all the postings as well as see the other members' profiles of the listserv. Since Yvette had created the forum, it had attracted over a hundred members all over North America, including Puerto Rico and Canada. Jasmine found a dozen members from Madrid, London, and Sydney. They had posted over five hundred messages.

In the search box, Jasmine typed in *Malcolm* and hit RETURN. It found no messages with his name. Then Jasmine remembered that he was most likely to be referred to by his tag. She entered *BOUK X* and yielded almost two hundred results. Either he posted relentlessly to the listserv or he had become a major subject of discussion. Jasmine scanned the subject lines and clicked on the one that started with the word *Urgent*, posted by Yvette as PRIESTS. Seconds after she opened it, she knew she had found the thread she needed.

As she had suspected, the writers formed an underground network with cells in major cities from New York to Toronto to harbor Malcolm as he hid on the freight trains. Yvette encouraged members in each city to bring him food, water, clothing, and even art supplies when Malcolm's train to arrived in each station. A member named FREEZ in Syracuse posted a question: *How will we know exactly where to find him when he comes to town?* PRIESTS replied, *Refer to the maps.*

Jasmine looked to the electronic folder where listserv members could upload files they wanted to share. In a column beside the forum, she found a list. She clicked on the link *Files*. There she found several PDF files, including one called "maps." But when Jasmine opened it, she saw it contained something she already had: Malcolm's sketches. He or perhaps Yvette had scanned his sketches and uploaded them to the listserv. They had to contain another clue to his whereabouts besides the words scrawled across the trains.

Jasmine went into the living room to retrieve her pocketbook. She consulted the pieces at the back of Malcolm's book, attempting to look at them with fresh eyes. The words on the trains were now clear to her, but she could not "see" anything else. The only other text on each sketch was Malcolm's tag, BOUK.

Actually, his tag was BOUK X. On each of the pieces, however, he had replaced the *X* with a number. Just as she always suspected, the numbers mattered. She found a pen and wrote the numbers across her palm: 8 0 9 1 2 0. Jasmine remembered Yvette telling her that if she had not painted over the serial number on the train car, the rail inspector might leave her piece alone.

Jasmine believed the time had come to call Calvin. She sent him a text message—*911*. She imagined the police were swarming her apartment that second and putting an APB out for her. No matter how upset he might be with her, Calvin would not ignore her calls now.

THIRTY-THREE

By the following morning, he still had not called. Jasmine had spent the night reading every single message on the listserv in search of a theory, but the writers spoke in vague terms, allowing Yvette's upload to communicate all the necessary information. She monitored both Malcolm's and her Rey2 accounts, but nothing of value materialized in either of them.

Jasmine wondered if Suárez had anyone infiltrate the underground network to find Malcolm's trail. When he put his mind to it, Suárez had found out everything about Jasmine. How easy would it have been for Suárez to bribe a disgruntled writer—perhaps another artist who was jealous of Malcolm—to befriend him, only to betray him?

As the hours passed with no pivotal word, Jasmine began to consider Adriano's offer. Now that she had killed Malcolm's sister, Malcolm really had no one, and despite what Jasmine had promised Crystal, she could not keep him out of jail. She never had the power to do that for him or anyone. From the start, Crystal saw through Jasmine's hubris. Among the system's many players, she was a mere pawn. The best thing Jasmine could do for Malcolm was to let him be.

And if she let him be, she could focus on herself. She had to. It had become a matter of life or death. Adriano wanted to help her live, and of the three people who knew Jasmine's status, he was the only one who truly could. Nathalie Dieudonné might have given her an early appointment and run a free test, but she had referred Jasmine to other doctors. At least she was bound by her professional oath to keep Jasmine's confidentiality. Felicidad relied on Jasmine for a job, so she had an incentive to toe the line. And given her own HIV status, if Felicidad ever needed an incentive to stay quiet, Jasmine would introduce her to Adriano so that he could care for her, too.

But then someone else would have to die.

Jasmine paced Felicidad's bedroom, trying to make a decision. She visualized Adriano Suárez's father dying of hepatitis in his mother's arms, only to relive Crystal Booker turning cold in her own. She wondered about the original Rogelio Alvarez, who had amassed the wealth to buy a two-million-dollar colonial in White Plains, and then considered the "new" Rogelio Alvarez, who lived in a dilapidated apartment with a dozen other people. Jasmine imagined the Diakite girl lying in a hospital bed at Sloan-Kettering battling Ewing's sarcoma, until she saw Eboni Powell lying in the street with a bullet in her head.

She paced by Felicidad's bookshelf, and a book with *HIV* boldly printed on the spine caught her eye. Jasmine reached for the book. *After the Diagnosis: HIV.* She scanned the other titles stacked across Felicidad's shelf. *Alive and Well: A Guide to Living with HIV. Positively Delicious: Eating Well for People with HIV/AIDS. Built to Last: The HIV+ Woman's Bible.*

Jasmine pulled the last book off the shelf and sat down on Felicidad's bed. She opened it and read the first few lines. *You've just found that you have HIV. Now you're probably thinking that you are no longer the woman you used to be. But HIV isn't the disease it used to be either.* Jasmine propped the pillows against the headboard and continued to read.

Jasmine awoke with the book splayed across her chest and her cell phone ringing. She grabbed at the phone, answering it without reading the display. "Hello?"

"Jasmine!"

"Calvin, thank God you finally called!"

"It took me this long to get back to you because they've been grilling me about you. What the hell happened? Where are you?"

Jasmine wondered if calling him had been a mistake. Calvin had an agenda, and they were on the outs. He did not sound like a man who presumed that she had killed Crystal Booker in self-defense. Then again, Jasmine ran like a guilty murderer. She had to stay alive long enough to find Malcolm. "Calvin, I desperately need your help, man."

"Jasmine, I don't know . . ."

"I know how to find Macho. I just need some information that only you can get me. If I gave you the serial number to a car on a freight train, would you be able to pinpoint its location?"

"Yeah, I can track it just like a package."

Jasmine's heart raced with hope. "Really?"

"I might even be able to do it online. And if that doesn't work, there are some people I can call."

"And I can make it easier. I can give you a list of cities where this train is supposed to stop. This train runs between New York City and Toronto, and I think Macho's hiding out in the car with the serial number eight zero nine one two zero."

"How did you find this out? Did Crystal tell you?"

She had to appeal to Calvin's ambition. "Do this for me, and I can give you some information to bring down Adriano Suárez. He's definitely involved in identity theft and insurance fraud. Maybe even murder."

"What? Jasmine, where are you? We have to do this face-to-face."

"Tell me when and where a freight train that has a car with the serial number eight zero nine one two zero comes into New York City, and I'll meet you then and there."

Jasmine disconnected. Whether or not Calvin could track down the information she needed, she knew he would call her back. She wondered, if she had reached out to him with only a plea for emotional support—to express her regret over Malcolm, mourn again for Jason, or even to reveal her HIV status—without the promise of a reward, would he have been as eager to see her? For once she admitted that she cared. She cared for Calvin more than she thought. More than she thought she ever could.

THIRTY-FOUR

"The train is coming in tonight!" Calvin breathed into the phone several hours later. "It's pulling into that rail yard on the east side of the New York Harbor at about eleven."

Jasmine had not expected it to happen this suddenly. She pulled off her robe. "Where should I meet you?"

"On the northeast corner of Sixty-fifth and York. I spoke to someone at one of the rail companies that operates out of there. She's going to make sure that we have access to the yard without any assistance from the security detail."

Felicidad had discarded Jasmine's bloody clothes, so she resorted to borrowing hers. She almost turned over the room looking for a simple pair of loose-fitting jeans and a T-shirt. Jasmine would have been content with a sweat suit, but Felicidad seemed to harbor something against casual wear. She finally settled on a pair of khaki cargo pants and a white button-down shirt.

Before this went down, she had to call Adriano. Jasmine found it hard to believe that he had not learned about Crystal Booker's death, and it said something to her that he had not contacted her. Perhaps he feared being associated with her now that she had blood on her hands, especially because he did not. Jasmine had no doubts that she could clear her name in the shooting death of Crystal Booker. In time, the police would be able to ascertain that Crystal had broken into the agency and attempted to kill her. Surely, they already could tell that she had broken into Jasmine's apartment. And with Malcolm still on the run, Crystal's motive for wanting Jasmine dead was clear and plausible.

Jasmine dialed Adriano's cell phone number, and he immediately answered. "Jasmine."

"Hey."

"Are you safe?"

"That depends. Who's looking for me?"

He laughed. "I'm always looking for you. I don't know what Crystal told you, if anything. But I had nothing to do with her coming after you. I don't think she knows what's going on here."

As close as Malcolm and Crystal were, Jasmine preferred to gamble that she did. Why else go to such extremes to keep Jasmine from finding her brother? If she gunned down a doctor—a neighborhood hero, no less—without a doubt, Crystal would pay. But who would care if a female bail enforcement agent was found slumped over her desk with a bullet in her head? Only those who wanted their collateral returned. "But if she had known, would you have gone after her?"

"Why are you asking me that?"

"It's not really what I want to ask you at all. What I want to know is did you have something to do with Malcolm's disappearance? Did you give him a reason to run?"

"Did Malcolm ever tell you that his sister was sick?"

"What?"

"She suffered from sickle-cell anemia."

"And she had no health insurance," Jasmine guessed.

"She did, but hardly enough. Malcolm not only discovered the work I do here, he supported it. Eventually, he wanted to avail himself of it. To have his sister benefit from it."

"That might explain why Crystal came after me, but it doesn't tell me shit about why Macho took off."

Adriano gave a long pause. "Never mind the Bookers, Jasmine. I want to talk about you. Have you made a decision?"

"Yeah, I have. I got this, Adriano. No one deserves to die because I have this infection. Least of all me."

Then Jasmine hung up.

"Don't use that," she whispered to him. "It'll give us away."

Calvin turned off the flashlight and returned it to his utility belt. They stepped gingerly between the tracks, pausing at every car to check the serial number.

"They're not in any sequence," Calvin said of the serial numbers. "We can be here all night looking for that particular car."

"So long as we find them."

"Them?"

"Don't expect Macho to be alone."

"Shit! Why didn't you tell me, Jasmine? I could have called for backup."

"Hush!" Jasmine listened. "Hear that?"

"Hear what?"

She thought she heard chatter coming from the train on the track deepest into the rail yard. Jasmine motioned for Calvin to follow her. She crept in the direction of the sound and caught a soft hush. He nodded at her, acknowledging that he heard it, too. Although she could not see the serial number in the dark distance, Jasmine knew the car on sight from the BOUK X and PRIESTS tags all over its panels. Jasmine drew Shorty, and Calvin reached for his revolver.

A young man—the same one that gave Jasmine a hard time on her first visit to Burn Masters—was standing guard in front of the car and spotted them. "Five-oh!" he yelled before bolting down the track. Calvin took off after him while Jasmine ran for the car. Several young men leaped from the car, scattering in all directions. She reached the car in time to leap onto it and corner five writers, including Yvette and Malcolm.

"Jasmine!"

She looked around the car. The underground network had brought him everything he needed. Food, clothes, toiletries, batteries, CDs, and, of course, markers. "Nice setup you got here. No wonder you didn't want to come home."

Malcolm rose to his feet, his breath heavy with both anxiety and relief. "It's really good to see you, Jasmine."

Jasmine felt tears burning their way through her eyes, and she blinked hard to fight them back. "It's good to see you, too."

Calvin jumped onto the car with his gun drawn. With one hand he reached for his police radio. "I'm calling for backup."

"Wait!" Jasmine clamped her hand on his wrist. Then she turned back to Malcolm. "I know why you ran. I know about Crystal. And I know about Suárez."

"No." Malcolm shook his head. "You don't know about Suárez. And I wanted to help my sister, but I wasn't trying to hurt nobody, I swear to God, Jasmine."

"I do, Malcolm. I know how he helps people and how far he goes to do it. With what we both know, we can stop him."

"I'm already looking at five to seven, remember. Plus, whatever they throw at me for jumping bail. I come and cooperate, and the next thing I know, I'm doing life while he's still out there doing his dirt."

"Right now you might be safer in jail," said Calvin.

Although he spoke the truth, Jasmine glared at Calvin for interfering. "Macho, if you don't come in and tell us what you know, everybody who's helped you might get implicated."

"What?" said Yvette.

"I didn't tell none of 'em nothing. They know I had to break, and they watched my back, but that's it. I didn't say nothing, precisely to not get them involved."

"I believe you, Macho, but I'm not the one you have to convince."

"I'll go, and I'll talk. But only if you let my people go."

Jasmine looked at Calvin. "Fine," he said. He lowered his gun, and all the other writers except Yvette ran to the entrance of the car, leaped onto the ground, and disappeared into the night.

"Yvette, go," Malcolm said.

Instead she clung to him. "No, I'm not going. I leave you here alone and the next thing homeboy does you like Michael Stewart."

"Then you can come along for the ride," said Calvin, reaching for his handcuffs.

"Fine then." Yvette offered her wrists to him.

Malcolm looked at Jasmine and did the same. "You do the honors."

"C'mon, Macho."

"For real."

Jasmine sighed and pulled her cuffs from her back pocket. "Lean up against the wall." Calvin motioned for Yvette to do the same, and she complied. Jasmine frisked Malcolm. "I'm sorry."

"Don't worry about it." He readily pulled his arms backward, and Jasmine cuffed him. "Do what you gotta do."

"You have the right to remain silent," Calvin said. "If you give up that right, anything you say can and will be used against you in a court of law." While he continued to Mirandize them, he walked Yvette to the door of the freight car, and Jasmine and Malcolm followed.

When they reached the exit of the rail yard, they encountered a half dozen writers who'd chosen to wait rather than flee. Jasmine recognized some of them as members of the Burn Masters Syndicate. The second they spotted Jasmine and Calvin escorting Malcolm and Yvette off the premises in handcuffs, the writers booed and hissed them. More writers awaited them outside the yard, and they, too, began to jeer. "Chill, chill, chill," Malcolm soothed them. "It's all good." They walked across the street to where Calvin had parked his car. As they drove to the nearest precinct, Calvin radioed to announce their arrival.

Then Malcolm said, "I was kinda hoping you'd come find me, Jasmine, 'cause if you hadn't, it would've meant that you'd given up on me." He leaned forward in his seat. "You gotta believe me. Suárez didn't start killing people until after he helped Crystal. Once he hooked up my sister with those meds, he thought I owed him. Said with his connections in the system, and mine on the street, we could be 'proactive.'"

"Shut up, Macho!" warned Yvette.

"Nah, I want Jasmine to understand," he barked. Then Malcolm turned back to Jasmine. "I kept telling Suárez *I ain't no thug. My peoples don't get down like that.* But he refused to believe me, talking about *After all I've done for you.*"

"You a fool," said Yvette. "Talking to her in front of this cop with no lawyer."

"Chill, Yvette, it's all good. She's got my back." Jasmine looked at Malcolm's reflection in the rearview mirror, his eyes gleaming with a sense of safety. "Jasmine knows me. That's why she came for me and found out the truth."

Calvin asked, "Did Suárez threaten you?"

"Damn straight. Suárez said if I didn't get down with his program, he was gonna set me up for what he had done to the little Eboni girl and those other two people. Said it would be my word against his. Then I got to thinking what was to stop Suárez for having me iced, too?"

Jasmine could no longer bear to listen "Okay, Macho, that's enough. Just sit back and relax." Between his revelations and her exhaustion, her head was pounding and her heart breaking.

"Jasmine, I need you to do me one favor, though."

She turned in her seat to look at him. "What?"

"Call Crystal and let her know that I'm all right."

Jasmine hesitated, and Calvin intervened. "One thing at a time, Booker."

At the precinct, Jasmine maintained her cool as she remanded Malcolm into the custody of the NYPD. Calvin decided to release Yvette, but she stayed behind to ensure Malcolm's safety. Jasmine and Calvin passed her as she spoke on her cell phone in the precinct lobby as they left the building. "Crystal, it's Yvette," she said into the voice-mail system. "They found us. As soon as you get this, come down to the Nineteenth precinct on Sixty-seventh and Third."

Once outside, Jasmine paused and pulled out her cigarettes. Calvin reached for his lighter. As she dipped her cigarette into the flame, he asked, "Are you okay?"

"No, I'm not okay." Jasmine took a single deep drag, only to flick the cigarette onto the sidewalk and crush it under her boot. "I'm all fucked up."

"So I guess you don't want a ride home."

"Actually, I do."

"I'm over here." They reached his car, and Calvin walked around to the driver's side while Jasmine waited for him to unlock the door. Then he stopped. "Jasmine, you can't go back home. Not until they pick up Suárez."

"I hadn't thought about that."

Calvin shrugged. "You can come home with me."

"If that's okay."

"Yeah, sure."

They drove in silence until Calvin made it to the highway. "Well, it's over."

Jasmine shook her head. "No, it's just starting."

Calvin conceded, "You're right." They drove a few more minutes without saying a word. "Before it really gets hectic, we should talk."

"I guess now is as good a time as any." And she meant it. With the Suárez affair about to start, the time had come to bring theirs to an end.

"I know that with all that's been going on, you probably haven't given too much thought to what I told you. You know. About how I feel about you, and what I hope we can have."

"Actually, Calvin, it's because of all this, I have. Because there's a lot more to this than what you know. There's something I found out during all this that I have to tell you."

The leather on the seat creaked as Calvin straightened his back. "I already know about you and Suárez, unless . . ."

"This is not about Suárez. Not really. I mean, if I had not gotten involved with him, I might not have ever learned things about myself that I needed to know. Please know that I don't say this to hurt you, Calvin, but I'm not sorry I met him."

Calvin locked his eyes on the highway in front of them. "Okay."

"There are going to be some major changes in my life, Calvin. And I know now that I'd like you to be a part of them. But when I tell you why, you may no longer want to be with me, and that's totally okay."

"Jesus . . ." Calvin's eyes now shifted back and forth between the road and Jasmine. "You're pregnant with Suárez's kid."

Jasmine snickered. With that wild guess on the table, why not just come out with it? "I have HIV."

"You what?"

"At one point, I let Suárez examine me, and he diagnosed me with HIV. You have to get yourself tested, Calvin. I can refer you to a great doctor who will give you a test that will let you know immediately."

They were almost at his place when Calvin finally spoke again twenty minutes later. "Changes."

"What's that?"

"You said that you had to make changes. And you said that you wanted me to be a part of them. What exactly were you talking about?"

"Lifestyle changes. I have to quit smoking and drinking, exercise regularly, eat right. Take my medication like clockwork. I gotta clean up my life at every level."

"Okay. So what does that have to do with me?"

"If I'm going to keep AIDS at bay—and I can, Calvin, I believe that now—I need support. Friends. I know that's a lot to ask, especially if I . . ." She could not bring herself to say *infected you*. "You said that you wanted us to move forward together, and I know this is a far cry from what you had in mind, and that now that I've revealed this, you want to take it all back. But just like learning that I used to be a prostitute didn't change the fact that you loved me, Calvin, discovering that I have HIV and knowing that I might have given it to you doesn't change the fact that I still need you. Now more than ever in a way I never have before. If I'm going to survive this fuckin' disease, despite everything that has and might happen, I need you to be my friend."

Without another word to her, Calvin preoccupied himself with the search for parking near his building in Parkchester. He finally found a space a block away from his building on East Avenue. As they crossed the street and passed a small twenty-four-hour market, Calvin asked, "Do you need anything? Maybe we should stop and get some food before we go up."

"That's okay." His mundane question sapped Jasmine's taste for everything. "I'm sure whatever you already have will do."

They entered his building and rode the elevator. Jasmine remembered the last time she had been to Calvin's place, and the memory caused her to snicker. "What?" he asked.

"Last time I was here, we had another fuck-'n'-fight. . . ."

Calvin shook his head. "That's what we always . . . did."

"Yeah, but do you remember what it was about that particular time?"

"No. I never remember. It's never about anything important."

The elevator reached Calvin's floor and opened its doors, but they both hesitated to step off. "It was another fight about my bailing out Malcolm Booker."

"Can't be." Calvin rushed off into the corridor and searched for his apartment key on his ring. "We've seen each other plenty of times since then."

"But not here." Jasmine followed him to his door and leaned against the wall while he unlocked it. "You stole my spare key and kept showing up at my place unannounced."

"Well, I'm really sorry about that, trust me." Calvin pushed open his door and gestured for Jasmine to precede him. "You take the bed, and I'll crash on the couch." She started to protest, but he cut her off. "Just go and . . . you know where everything is."

"Thanks." On her way to the bedroom, Jasmine stopped at the linen closet for a towel. She crossed the hallway to the bedroom and closed the door behind her. On a chair by the window, she saw a basket of clean laundry. Jasmine found a Police Athletic League T-shirt, stripped off Felicidad's clothes, and put on the T-shirt. As she folded Felicidad's clothes, she remembered what she said about adhering to her treatment. Neither Suárez nor Nathalie had prescribed any medications to manage the virus, but Jasmine still had the pills to treat her respiratory infection. She had yet to take a single one.

Jasmine found both vials in her pocketbook—the neatly typed prescription she received from Nathalie Dieudonné and the handwritten contraband given to her by Adriano Suárez. She took them both into the kitchen and placed them on the counter as she ran herself a glass of tap water. Jasmine took one pill from Dr. Dieudonné's bottle, tossed it into her mouth, and washed it down with the tap water. Then she picked up the bottle Adriano had given her and dumped the pills down the kitchen drain.

When Jasmine turned around, she found Calvin standing there holding a bottle of spring water. "I was going to tell you," he said as he offered her the bottle. "I've got plenty of bottled water in the fridge." He looked over her shoulder and saw the medication on the counter. "Glad to see you finally did something about that flu."

Jasmine laughed until she broke down, and for once, she let Calvin comfort her.

THIRTY-FIVE

"Tell me something good, Doc," said Jasmine as she watched Nathalie cross the room and sit at her desk.

"Very good news." Nathalie opened up Jasmine's medical file. "Your T cells are up, and your viral load is down. You've been very good, haven't you?" She sounded to Jasmine just like the teenager who once babysat her.

"With Calvin around, I couldn't be bad if I wanted to. The man watches me like a hawk. 'What did you eat today?' 'Did you take your medication?' 'How much sleep did you get last night?' If not for the Suárez trial, my life would be a real bore."

"About that, Jasmine," said Nathalie. "It's really important that no matter what happens, you don't let that trial consume you. Are you still seeing that therapist I recommended?"

"Oh, yeah, she's great," said Jasmine. Although she'd immediately begun to make changes in her lifestyle, she'd put off going into psychotherapy for almost a year and a half. Then the trial began and pushed Jasmine over the edge. Regardless of their stands on AIDS, immigration, and health care reform, people all over the political spectrum had vilified her. After fifteen months of living clean, Jasmine had fallen off the wagon, smoking a whole carton of cigarettes in one sitting. Just as she had reached for a bottle of whiskey, she'd called the psychotherapist. "And Felicidad's been wonderful, too. What does she call herself? Oh, yeah, she says she's my peer counselor. It's because of her I'm, like, a public speaker." Jasmine laughed at the thought.

"How'd you do that?"

"It all started when she invited me to come speak to her HIV support group. They were discussing the Suárez trial and got into this huge debate. I guess someone said something nasty about me, and Felicidad stuck up for me, and the next thing you know, I'm standing before this group telling my side of the story. The doctor who runs the group invites me to speak to her coworkers, and they invite me to talk at their university, and before you know it, I'm on the lecture circuit." Between her speaker's fees and the bail bond company, which now had offices in Queens and Manhattan, Jasmine made enough money to pay her medical bills.

"I think telling your own story can be the most powerful medicine you can have," said Nathalie. She reached over and placed her hand over Jasmine's. "I'm very proud of you, Jasmine."

"Thanks."

Nathalie reached for her prescription pad. "Now, are you okay with medication? Do you need any refills?"

"Not until next month," said Jasmine. She saw her opportunity to ask her question. "Nathalie, can you tell me what these are for?" Jasmine reached into her purse and handed her the two vials of medication she had found in the medicine cabinet of the Booker apartment almost two years ago.

Nathalie read the labels. "Meperidine, hydroxyurea. These are prescribed to treat sickle-cell anemia." She squinted at Jasmine over her eyeglasses. "What are you doing with these?"

"They belonged to Crystal Booker. She had sickle-cell anemia, although I didn't know it until . . ." Jasmine still could not say it. Just another issue to address in therapy, she guessed. "The meperidine prescription was written long before Malcolm went to work for the clinic, but I think he got her the hydro whatever from Suárez. I was just curious as to what the difference, if any, is."

"A very big difference. Meperidine is used to manage sickle-cell crises. Basically, it's a painkiller. During a crisis a person may have to be hospitalized for five to seven days, and they'll be given meperidine every two hours."

"Damn, that's often."

"And quite risky. It can be chemically altered by the body and reach toxic levels. And that can lead to seizures."

"And the other drug?"

"Hydroxyurea is a much superior treatment option than meperidine. While it doesn't cure the disease, it can drastically reduce the occurrence of sickle-cell crises. The medical community still has a lot to learn about it, but so far it's shaping up to be the most effective therapy for managing this disease."

"In other words, Suárez gave Crystal the best you guys had to offer."

Nathalie nodded her head. "Short of a bone marrow transplant, I'm afraid that's correct."

For a moment, Jasmine felt heavy with regret. If not for her, Crystal would not only be alive, she might literally have been well. But then Jasmine remembered to ask herself: at whose expense?

Jasmine promised everyone she would stay away from the courthouse until her turn came to testify, but she watched the trial on television. It always played in the background as she worked at the office and from home. Because of her schedule, Jasmine missed Mrs. Diakite's testimony, but she taped it and curled up in front of the television to watch it on Friday night.

Just when Suárez's defense attorney opened his cross-examination by asking Mrs. Diakite if the prosecutor had granted her immunity in exchange for her testimony, Jasmine's intercom buzzed. She paused and rushed to respond to it. "Who is it?"

"Calvin."

She buzzed him into the building and went to open her apartment door and greet him. He stepped off the elevator with a bag of groceries. "What you got there, detective?"

"Some fruits, some vegetables . . ."

"Yum."

"Don't be a smart-ass." He gave her a kiss on the cheek and carried the bags into the kitchen.

"I may be a smart-ass, but I'm not ungrateful." Jasmine went back into the living room and resumed Mrs. Diakite's testimony. Calvin entered, handed her an apple, and sat next to her on the couch. Jasmine explained, "She's the first of the patients that turned state's evidence to testify."

"There was a poll in the paper yesterday, and the city's practically split down the middle," said Calvin. "Half of the people surveyed said the patients who are citizens should be prosecuted and the ones who are immigrants should be deported. Even if they're in the country legally."

"Damn."

"Meanwhile, there's some citywide campaign demanding amnesty for the patients, citizens and immigrants alike," said Calvin, in a tone slightly tinged with disapproval. "This case has this city in an uproar over everything. AIDS treatment, immigration reform, health care, and even illegal graffiti. Every week there's a rally about this or a march about that."

"I think it's great," said Jasmine. "Hopefully, it'll spread across the country like hot lava."

Calvin sneered at her. "Well, I don't feel like arguing with you tonight."

"Don't."

They both turned their attention to the television in time to hear Suárez's attorney ask Mrs. Diakite if she ever suspected that the young girl whose identity her daughter had assumed had been murdered. Mrs. Diakite emphatically said no, that while Dr. Suárez had informed her that the real Eboni Powell was dead, he never told her how she had died.

"That's smart," Calvin said with begrudging respect. "When Suárez finally takes the stand, he's going to say that he did not know either. He knows he couldn't convince a jury that he didn't know they were dead, but he's going to gamble that they won't believe that two-time loser when he testifies that Suárez paid him to hunt and kill those three people."

Jasmine agreed. "He'll say that he just wanted to buy their identities so their patients could assume their medical coverage, not knowing that this guy was killing people to get them."

"Exactly." Calvin reached for the remote and said, "Do you mind if we pause this for a few minutes. I want to ask you something."

"Okay."

Calvin paused the tape and turned in the love seat to face Jasmine.

"What I wanted to know is . . . well, I think I know the answer to this, I just don't know how it's done. I mean, I have an idea, but . . ."

"Just ask, Calvin!"

"I want to talk about sex."

"Why do you want to talk about sex with me? I ain't having any!"

"That's exactly why I want to talk to you. Don't you want to have sex again?" When Jasmine stared at him, Calvin became more specific. "With me?"

"You want to sleep with me?"

"It's the only thing missing from a great relationship."

"We're not even, like, dating."

"I'm saying I want to with all that entails."

"You're crazy!"

"I'm serious."

"Okay, you're seriously crazy. Calvin, aren't you worried about my infecting you?"

"Of course I am. But I've been reading a lot about this, and there are precautions we can take. I'm not saying I'm totally comfortable with it, but I'm trying to come around, and I wanted to see where you were with it. I mean, not just about sex in general, but about being in a relationship with me."

"I don't know about this," said Jasmine. "I mean, yes, I want you, but I just don't know if I can or even should give you all that you want and need." She knew people with HIV had normal lives that included relationships and children, but she always assumed they either had those things before they were diagnosed or found them with other HIV-positive people. Did positive and negative mix? Even if Jasmine could ever see herself dating again, never mind having sex, she had difficulty imagining doing so with Calvin. Even if he was the man she loved. Precisely because he was the man she loved.

And as if he read her mind, Calvin said, "I'm not going to tell you how to feel, and of course I'll respect whatever you ultimately decide. But I just want the record to show that if there is an issue, it's yours. Don't put your shit on me."

Jasmine jabbed him in the shoulder. "Gee, that's real supportive."

Calvin smiled at her. "I think it is."

"I'll take it up with my doctors."

"That's all I ask. That and a kiss."

"I can swing that." And she did.

Jasmine drove to court to submit the paperwork to have her last bond exonerated. She really did not want to leave the business, but she could no longer maintain a twenty-four-hour schedule. She thought about establishing a nonprofit organization to run an alterative-to-incarceration program, and Lorraine and Felicidad tried to help her. But they quickly learned that no one would fund it. No government agency or charitable foundation had the political will to support it. Her efforts ruffled a few feathers at the existing programs, but Jasmine never meant to suggest that they were inadequate or attempt to compete with them. If anything, she felt there were not enough of them, and she wanted to use her experience in the bail bond industry to complement their work. Jasmine felt terrible that her intentions were misunderstood, but what the hell could she do? She had been through worse. And now Jasmine was considering going to law school.

She was halfway to the courthouse when her cell phone rang. Jasmine ignored it until she pulled into the garage. Yvette had called her and left a message.

Jasmine, you gotta come to the clinic now. No, not now. Right now! For real. Drop everything and come over here.

Jasmine dropped the phone in her passenger seat and tore out of the garage. She arrived at the clinic, parking her car in front of the entrance. The gate had been bombarded with graffiti. Some were ordinary tags and throw-ups from burgeoning writers just wanting to get up. But most of the writings were passionate words about the Suárez case. *Adriano Suárez = Hero. The ends justify the means. BOUK X lives. Kill Suárez. Any eye for an eye. Eboni Powell R.I.P. Dr. Hood. Murderer. Send them all back.* The people had turned the entrance of the now-extinct clinic into their public message board.

Jasmine checked up and down the street, looking for Yvette, and found her nowhere. She called her. "PRIESTS, where the hell are you?"

"Where are you?"

"I'm here in front of the clinic."

"At the gate?"

"Yeah."

"No, turn the corner. Go to the wall."

Without hanging up the phone, Jasmine walked around the corner and saw the new mural. Over the mural Malcolm had painted for Suárez, BMS had painted the SUPERJAS sketch that he had drawn in his piecebook.

"You see it?"

Overwhelmed, Jasmine could barely speak. "I see it." As much as she appreciated the public display of love from the writers, she also saw hope in it. "Is Macho ready to see me?" In exchange for his testimony, Malcolm received immunity in the Suárez case, but he still faced five to seven for his robbery in the second and evasion of prosecution. Jasmine had advocated hard for him, as well as for all the other writers who had harbored him. While she managed to convince the prosecutor to either drop the charges or offer five years' probation in exchange for guilty pleas for PRIESTS and the others, the best she could get for Malcolm was two to three years.

But her inability to get him a lighter sentence had nothing to do with why he refused to communicate with her. His prison sentence paled in comparison to life without Crystal. Everyone told Jasmine that he eventually would understand that she had had no choice, having killed Crystal in self-defense without even knowing that it was her until it was too late. That when he did he would take responsibility for his role in his sister's death and stop projecting his anger at himself onto Jasmine. It all sounded so psychologically correct, if there were such a thing, but it gave her no consolation.

Yvette sighed. "I'm sorry, girl. But when I told him what we were planning to do, he gave me the sketch. I didn't even ask him for it, I swear. I had forgotten all about it. So maybe in time, you know."

Jasmine had to accept this. She also had to accept that Malcolm might not ever come around, and she had to let him go. After all that she had been through in her life, she deserved to find some peace and security. All she had to do was let go.

Jasmine reached over and ran her hand along the fresh mural. Then something occurred to her. Although the city shut down his clinic, Adriano Suárez probably still owned the building. Maybe not for long as his high powered attorney racked up billable hours and solicited expert testimony, but until then any alterations to the property required his permission.

"Yo, Yvette, is this burn illegal?"

"You bet your ass it is!"

Photo by Leonardo de Vega

Black Artemis is a hip-hop activist, writer, and speaker in New York City. She holds a master's degree from Columbia University and has worked with many social justice organizations throughout the country. Artemis is also a screenwriter who has won recognition for her work. She lives in the Bronx, where she was born and raised, and enjoys working with youths to find their voice through art and politics.

READERS GUIDE

Black Artemis

READERS GUIDE

A CONVERSATION WITH BLACK ARTEMIS

Q. Burn *is your third hip-hop novel. How is it different from* Explicit Content *and* Picture Me Rollin'?

A. The truth is that although it is my latest novel, *Burn* is my "oldest" story. It's been incubating in my head for almost ten years. *Burn* is the one most informed by the work experiences I actually had before I became a novelist. I never worked in the music industry although I researched and explored it for *Explicit Content*. The main character of *Picture Me Rollin'* had a variety of experiences I never did—from being in an abusive relationship to having spent time in prison. But at one time in my life, I was the deputy director of two alternative-to-incarceration programs pioneered by the Vera Institute of Justice. One was a nonprofit bail bond agency in the Bronx, and the other was a substance abuse treatment program for nonviolent offenders. When I worked at Vera, I came to appreciate how difficult—yet important and necessary—it was to experiment with daring approaches to persistent issues. Several years later, I was the director of advocacy and policy at the Hispanic AIDS Forum. While doing AIDS work, I once organized a focus group of transgender Latinas in order to challenge and expand my beliefs and opinions about gender and sexual orientation. These experiences were about the benefits and risks of thinking outside the box when responding to complicated social issues, often starting with being willing to part with your attitudes toward the people who are involved.

Q. So in what ways does Burn *"qualify" as a Black Artemis novel? In other words, what constitutes a Black Artemis novel?*

A. There are elements you will always see in a Black Artemis novel. The first is a central female character. So far all my protagonists have been relatively young women of color from working-class backgrounds from the Bronx, like yours truly! The second thing you'll always see in a Black Artemis novel is some aspect of hip-hop. Even though my works obviously share some characteristics with street lit, the hip-hop element is what distinguishes my novels from the majority of works in that genre. The third element—and this is the one that it has in common with street lit—is that of crime. I've always been fascinated by issues of crime and criminal justice. Just for the record, this is certainly not because I equate hip-hop with criminality. Clearly, as a hip-hop activist, I don't ascribe to that belief at all. Rather what interests me about crime as a phenomenon is the philosophical questions it raises about human nature and social contracts.

Q. Describe the research you conducted on graffiti subculture for Burn?

A. Even though what I have learned about graffiti could inspire two more Black Artemis novels with it as a central element, I still don't feel I know enough about it. The bulk of my research was based on books and films that are either dated or based outside of New York City, where *Burn* takes place. The way writers ply their craft today is quite different from when I was growing up. What I would've done to have gone bombing! However, writers are protective of their cipher for obvious reasons that I understand and respect. One particular writer, however, gave me valuable insight into the current scene, and I want to give him a shout-out for it, but I don't know if he'd want me to!

Q. Did you have any concerns about how readers might react to characters who are transgender or have HIV/AIDS?

A. Well, I had no doubts that doing so was risky, but I felt pretty confident that my readers would ride with me. The reality is that women like Jasmine account for almost eighty percent of reported AIDS cases. That means, eight out of ten people with AIDS are either African-American or Latina women, so imagine how many are HIV positive! What was important to me was to strike the balance between acknowledging how deadly this epidemic remains yet depicting people with HIV/AIDS who lead happy lives. Until she's diagnosed with HIV, Jasmine is slowly killing herself. Ironically, it's the diagnosis that compels Jasmine to choose life. And what enables her to do this is having a person like Felicidad model the determination to be happy and healthy regardless of what life dishes out. As for Feliz, I think the biggest risk I took with her character was not so much making her transgender but depicting her as normal. Our society makes it so much easier to either ridicule or pity transgender people than it is to recognize that they are human beings with the same capacity, need and right to live lives full of love and free of harm as the rest of us. There would have been no risk in presenting her as a tragic freak or the comic relief because that's the way we usually see transgender people in the popular media. Those *Jerry Springer*–like depictions are safe. Presenting Felicidad as the most self-actualized character in the novel? Now *that* was risky. And after having many wonderful experiences meeting my readers, I think they're quite up to the challenge. Maybe they won't agree with me on this issue—I'm with Lorraine the social worker on this one—but they're certainly intelligent and open-minded enough to at least give some consideration to an alternative viewpoint.

Q. Of all your novels to date, Burn *has the most open and ambivalent ending. Is there any chance that we'll see a sequel?*

A. People always ask that about all my novels, and it's such a tremendous compliment because it means that I have succeeded in creating characters readers have come to care about. In fact, sometimes they give me a little hell for bringing a character they like to a tragic end, and that's a compliment, too! This kind of feedback makes the prospect of writing a sequel tempting, but I haven't been compelled to just yet. I put so much of myself into creating my novels that when I finish one, I'm more than ready to let go and move on to the next one. That's because the final product usually raises so many issues and themes you can only imagine the things I actually leave out due to space and time and even for the sake of good craft! The stuff that's left out is often what I'm itching to deal with in the next book through a new set of characters who can do it justice. So while I'll never say never, I'm just not inclined toward sequels. If I were to write one for any of my novels, it'll mostly likely be because my readers have talked me into it.

Until then you can visit www.blackartemis.com and participate in the fan fiction forum. I post writing exercises based on my characters, and let *you* tell me what happens. It may not be a full-fledged sequel, but at least whatever you want to happen to your favorite (or maybe not-so-favorite) character will! My Web site also has a blog, a calendar, and more, and I publish an e-letter to let subscribers know about contests, hip-hop happenings, commentaries by other hip-hop activists, and opportunities for aspiring artists especially other writers. I can also be found on MySpace and on AmazonConnects.

QUESTIONS FOR DISCUSSION

1. Some would describe Jasmine as an antiheroine. What other female antiheroes have you encountered in books and films? What exactly makes a woman an antihero? Is it different from what makes a man an antihero? Do those differences, if any, make it more difficult or easier to root for them? Why or why not?

2. In the novel, many characters at different points not only break the law, but they feel justified in doing so. How did you feel about the criminal actions of particular characters and their rationale for their behavior? In your opinion, what makes an act criminal?

3. In chapter seven, Suárez says, "And isn't illegality par for the course in the hip-hop scene? Violence. Beefs. Isn't that what hip-hip is all about?" Do you agree with him? Why or why not?

4. What did you think of the online debate about graffiti in chapter fifteen? Has reading the novel changed your opinion of graffiti? Why or why not?

5. Prior to reading the novel, what was your attitude toward transgender people, such as the character Felicidad? Was your opinion shaped by actual experiences with transgender people? Has your attitude or opinion changed since you read the novel?

6. A recurring theme of the story is the relationship between siblings, especially that between brothers and sisters. How is this bond depicted? In what ways is the sibling relationship as explored in *Burn* similar from other novels you have read? How is it different?

7. Before the novel begins, Jasmine has transformed herself from a prostitute who once broke the law to survive to a businesswoman who generally lives by society's expectations. Despite these accomplishments, she is rather self-destructive. To what do you attribute her initial self-destructiveness?

8. By the end of the novel, Jasmine has transformed herself again. How has she changed? To what do you attribute her new outlook on life?

9. Another recurring theme of *Burn* is that of alternatives: leading alternative lifestyles; finding alternative means of earning money; building alternative institutions to government structure; and using alternative means of creative expression. Which alternatives presented in *Burn* do you feel warrant consideration? Why? What makes an alternative a legitimate response to existing beliefs, institutions, or practices?

10. In chapter twenty-two, Jasmine asks, "Just how effective can I be when I still have to operate within the same boundaries of the system that I want to change?" What would be your response to her?

11. Imagine you are writing the sequel to *Burn*. What is the verdict in the Suárez trial? What becomes of Jasmine? What does the future hold for other characters in the novel?